Wings of Time
Breaking Darkness

Ruth— I hope you enjoy the adventure of my story as much as I enjoyed writing it.

Suzanne Barron 3-2-19

SD Barron

SD BARON

SDC Publishing, LLC was established to promote and encourage aspiring writers and artists. It is a family oriented vehicle through which they can publish their work.

Contact SDC Publishing, LLC at allenfmahon@gmail.com

Or on the web at SDCPublishingLLC.com

Wings of Time: Breaking Darkness

SDC Publishing, LLC

ISBN: 1723183725
ISBN-13: 978-1723183720

DEDICATION

I dedicate this book to my father, Harry William Weiss. You are loved and missed by all who knew you pop. Xo.

ACKNOWLEDGMENTS

I give my thanks to my supportive crew: Kenneth Barron, Jr; Kenneth Barron, III; and Abby Barron. They are my everything. I love you all with every bit of my fiber.

I hold unfailing gratitude to Dee Davis. Her beautiful Wings of Time jewelry inspired the title of my story and gave me direction. Her unfailing energy draws me to seek her out at any craft event she is at. Hugs to you Dee.

I thank my beta readers for reviewing this book in its many stages:
Dana Abney
Alden Baker
Abby Barron
Kenneth Barron, Jr
Kenneth Barron, III
Joan Miles
Jennifer Mulligan
Debbie Weiss
Lana Whited

I thank my first editor and biggest cheerleader, inspiration, friend.
Elizabeth Rutrough
Elizabeth, you cannot imagine how much your time and dedication, your love and unfailing support, and your incredible energy mean to me. I love you for who you are and for the light from within you that shines so bright.

And thanks to my final editor, Chuck Sambuchino.
Chuck, I feel like you opened so many doors of understanding for me. You are superb, and I am very grateful to have had the opportunity to work with you. Thank you.

Thanks also to Franklin County Historical Society. One visit to your library inspired my 1950's era Ferrum. Your preservation of the county's traditions and history is so appreciated.

Author's Note

Readers, this is a complete work of fiction. Any character in this novel that you feel resembles someone (living or deceased) is entirely coincidental. It is set in real places in Virginia. While I have done research to make the history and setting as realistic as possible, I have also taken creative liberty in nearly every detail. Some events in the story are loosely based on things that occurred, but most details are from my imagination. I am privileged that you have selected my story to read, and I hope that you enjoy it.

Prologue—1720, Darkness.

Resmelda's magic will no longer be gray. It will be as black as her cruel jailer's blood which now flows from his neck onto the dingy cell's floor. As she finishes tearing the blade through his flesh, the line is drawn where she crosses into darkness leaving her humanity behind. She releases his greasy locks and his head slumps forward while his last gurgling breath struggles to escape. A shiver crawls along her skin, and she remembers pacing this border throughout her life—wanting the power of the dark—afraid to leave the light—finding compromise in the gray. She neared the edge of darkness so many times while curiously searching for her shadow cast by the illumined perch from where she stood. Now, she suddenly understands that her shadow has always been there mingling with the dark.

She draws in a long breath of stale air. It is done. She needs this blood sacrifice in order to barter with the demon, and she needs the demon in order to attain her revenge against the man who put her in this pit of a place. It had to be done now. Publick times are upon them, and court will soon be called to session. Despite the injustice of her capture and imprisonment, she knows that she has no argument to offer for her innocence. Until now, she has never practiced the dark arts, but magic of any kind is illegal. She knows her fate is the gallows, and over the weeks of imprisonment one thing has dominated her thoughts. Revenge.

"Revenge," she hisses the mantra that has spurred all her preparations since her imprisonment. She had to bribe the now dead jailer, Smyth, to smuggle in what was needed. Every bit of it paltry and low-quality, but not much could be expected from a dull-witted man even with the impious enticement she had to offer him. She tosses aside her shiv, and stands allowing a brief flash of satisfaction to curl to life in a smile as she thinks about Smyth being the means to his own bloody end.

She walks around him whispering her binding chant to form a summoning circle for the demon. A muscle twitches at her neck, and she ignores it forcing concentration. The circle must be strong enough to contain him, and she beckons to the sacrificial blood coaxing a bit of it to snake obediently behind her until the boundary is drawn and closed. Stepping aside, she casts a protective circle around herself and scratches a makeshift altar into the floor's grit with her ingredients for the spell close by. She ignites shards of wood with the stub of a candle that only moments earlier lit the pathway to Smyth's demise. As she rubs the herbs between her hands over the meager flame, a cloud of smoke lifts into the air.

Her eyes flicker over to the summoning circle assuring herself that its boundaries are secure and starts to call forth her ally, the Demon King. A stricture in her throat grabs hold of her words. She blows out a breath and focuses on the altar before her, but flashes of the Demon King's blood lust during their previous encounters dance in the smoky wisps of the fire. Her eyes divert to the lump of a man that used to be Smyth where the candle's flame flickers its wavering light in his pool of blood. With a quiver she swallows back her qualms convincing herself that what she has done today will not make her a victim of the Demon King, but one-in-the-same with him.

She clears her throat and takes a deep breath ignoring the beads of sweat forming on her neck. "Paimon of Tartarus you are called, and I demand you show yourself!" She has this one chance to summon him, and commands him again to appear calling out more loudly and clearly. Nothing. Again, louder and clearer. The fire flares and silt wafts down as the ceiling and walls tremor.

In the next moment, he is there snarling like a caged animal while perversities of all manner flow from his mouth. She hasn't heard Enochian uttered in a long time. Outside the demonic and angelic worlds, the language is not known. It had taken her years to learn it, but now she only needs seconds to adjust. She understands him perfectly, and he is not happy to have been summoned. He challenges the boundaries of her summoning circle, and her hands become fists as she focuses, willing him to stay in place.

She tilts her head back taking him in. It has been awhile since she summoned him. She admires the hint of muscle on his frame knowing his desire to maintain a slender build does not allow for a more obvious display of demon testosterone. His clothing, an opulent dark plum-colored long coat over a white dress shirt with cravat and tan breeches, is fashionable and impeccable as always. The ever-present shaded spectacles, today with moss-green lenses, sit perched on his straight and narrow nose.

He careens into the side of Smyth's body slamming it into the barrier. She flinches, but her magic holds firm. The demon's perfectly shined boots are immersed in the thick pool of blood from the now pale and nearly drained Smyth. The Demon King looks down as he lifts his foot and watches the blood slowly drip from the sole of his boot. He raises his eyes looking towards Resmelda with a thin and restrained smile. His lip twitches with anticipation as he gestures a wave with his hand vanishing Smyth and his puddle of blood. The blood line at the boundary remains. Resmelda's grip relaxes, and her palms throb from where her nails have dug into her flesh.

"A blood sacrifice?" Paimon speaks calmly in English. "This changes things. This changes you."

"Yes, well things are changed."

He nods, walking the perimeter of the summoning circle and puts on a cordial grin. "What matter of strife have you gotten yourself into?"

"Never mind, Paimon, my lot is set. I..."

"Tsk," he interrupts her offhandedly. "Call me...Joe."

She glares. Her back snaps straight as though her corset strings have been pulled tight. His glib manner and donning of his sheep's clothing so smoothly seem to mock her. "Enough. Your earthly titles are no consequence to me any longer. I have been unjustly imprisoned by a man who I thought was a friend...maybe more. A connection not by any spell conjured by me but through mutual volition." Resmelda rubs her hands together to rid herself of their prickly sweat and Smyth's blood.

"This man came on a scouting mission of sorts looking for new routes of trade within the Virginia Colony for his Williamsburg business, and he was waylaid at Watt's Island with illness. I thought he was a good man, but I should have known better when his business partner proved to be in league with that scheming privateer, Marcus Butler."

She holds onto her arms and shifts to the side as a bead of sweat skims down between her shoulder blades. "I thought he was…genuine, yet I was betrayed by him." Her hands slide from her shoulders down, and she speaks more to herself than Paimon. "Love cannot be trusted and kindness is not a trait I admire unless there is a profitable end to its means. I should not have lost sight of this tenet. I will not again."

Paimon gives a stiff nod with what looks like an attempt at sympathy.

She lifts her chin high straightening her shoulders, and ignores his untrustworthy gesture as she pushes on. "Paimon, I want you to complete a works for me. Once I got word of this man's treachery, I began conjuring a spell for revenge. The works of it were nearly complete when I was torn from Watt's Island. The spell still lingers within a ley line that I have not been able to access without my grimoire. I want you to retrieve it, and see it conveyed as I intended. I have had a vision, and I am not sure I will be leaving this place in time to take care of it myself. It is unfortunate, but I believe Hester unintentionally made it so."

She strategically throws the fallen angel's name into the parley knowing Hester and her stolen keys can sway the demon to help her. The slightest twitch of his lip betrays a glint of desire on his face, and Resmelda knows she will have leverage for bargaining with him.

"In addition to the blood sacrifice I have already made to you, I am willing to make a pact with you as payment for your services—a bridge between our realms, and…other connections."

Paimon's eyes flicker behind his shaded spectacles with cautious interest. "Please, tell me what it is you need, and perhaps we can come to an accord. I think, however, for such a task we should stand on neutral ground. To assure good faith in what is discussed." His eyebrows raise, and he glances at the summoning circle boundary.

Bile rises to the back of Resmelda's throat as her stomach lurches. A gritty sound escapes her as she clears the bitterness, and she bites down on the inside of her cheek. There is no such thing as neutral ground with the Demon King.

Revenge. The word reverberates inside her, and she knows she has no choice. She must see this through, so she squats to pick up a smoldering remnant of birch wood from the makeshift altar. Forcing a steady hand, she blows the smoke towards the summoning circle. The smoke courses around the periphery. She stands and stiffly claps her hands once causing the smoke to suddenly stop and dissipate into the dirt floor taking the last of Smyth's blood and breaking the boundary. Paimon smiles broadly and strolls around the cell.

He turns to Resmelda. "And your protective circle?"

"First, we are to be clear that my soul is not part of the pact. You are to leave it be. I will not break the circle until this is agreed upon." She manages to muster a haughty air.

He snarls. "You cannot be clinging to hopes of stepping back into the light, can you?"

"Do not concern yourself with what hopes I have or have not. I know my destiny."

He twists his head and pops his jaw studying her intently and then removes his spectacles. Resmelda's muscles seize. The fire behind her dims, almost as if he has penetrated her protective barrier. For a moment she worries that he may have found a way to her, maybe not to harm her, but to see into her soul. The blood sacrifice and her newly won dark power maintain the shield. His eyes remain dark, and the fire's light flickers higher again. He exhales as he briefly closes his eyes, and she knows he has failed.

She is statue-like watching and waiting.

Eventually, he steps to the outer edge of her circle and breaks the silence. "Very well, but I will not extend this offer to any future beckoning."

Resmelda resolutely steps to the inner edge of her circle directly in front of Paimon. "There will be no future meetings between you and me. Today will be the last."

He hesitates, and she swears she sees a hint of regret, maybe even sadness, swim across his eyes. It is brief, but she is certain. She has bartered with him since she was a girl, and those eyes have never reflected anything but evil. She uses his almost human moment to steal her nerves when he takes a step back, and she steps forward into his previous position outside the circle breaking the protective barrier. The color of his eyes, now able to fully penetrate to her core, seeps from black to a brilliant crimson in the presence of such a formidable soul. His face flushes with strong desire, however, he maintains his composure and honors his word.

Together they work through the terms of their pact, and then it is done.

Chapter 1—Present Day, Embers

A sleek black sports car glides by Hallie. The passenger window is down, and a woman is sitting with her arm draped over the door frame. Her silky black hair flutters in the wind, and she casually turns her head catching Hallie's eye in a glimpse. Hallie's curiosity is tugged, but she shrugs it off and eagerly steps into the Gull Island's grill and gift shop on the Chesapeake Bay Bridge-Tunnel. She looks around stopping short, and a lasso of disappointment corrals her good mood. Nothing appears to be the same. It's the first stop on her trip from her home in Burton's Shore to Virginia's Blue Ridge, and already a glitch intrudes on her plan. She wonders if the penny pressing machine is still around and starts to walk through the aisles in search of it when a sunny woman with a lop-sided walk comes up to her.

"Hallie O'Meara, is that you?"

"Mina." Hallie turns and embraces her warmly.

"It's been a while, but I knew it was you. Taller, but you. Even without the Facebook updates, those beautiful ginger locks are a giveaway."

Hallie smiles and self-consciously twirls a bit of hair.

"So." Mina puts a hand on her hip. "Where are the aunts? Six years and no trips through."

"I know, but Beattie and Dot's business took off, and we just haven't been able to get away so much. Most of our trips have been camping on the beach near home."

"Well, I am glad things are going well for them, but I miss seeing y'all. Used to be I'd see you several times a year."

"Yeah, I know what you mean."

"So, they're home tending business, huh?"

"Yep, and I am heading out to the Blue Ridge to work for the summer. My first trip alone."

"Well, how about that? A solo adventure. How exciting for you." Mina beams.

Hallie nods and looks around the shop again. "I wanted to make a few stops at some of my favorite places along the way like I did with Beattie and Dot on our trips when I was a kid." She gives a shy shrug of the shoulder. "Kinda silly I guess."

"Silly? Not at all." Mina gives Hallie a motherly smile. "Rekindling the past often makes us happy, and I dunno— revitalized maybe. 'Course that last part may just be for geezers like me." Mina laughs and then shifts her weight and flips her hand back. "Course this place may not be doing any of that for you. New management came in a couple years ago and did a complete make over."

Hallie nods thinking Mina must have read her thoughts. "It's nice though."

"Yeah, more keeping with the times I guess."

"Mina, is the penny pressing machine still here?"

"Almost hidden, but still here. They put it in the back that way." She tilts her head to the side. "It's still makes the same 'ole picture."

"Oh, that's okay. I get one every trip and then etch my initials and the date on the back. I have a jar back home with the pennies for a keepsake."

"Gotcha. Come on then." Mina leads her to the old contraption. "Here you go darlin'." Mina pulls a handful of coins from her tip pouch. "My treat."

"Thanks, Mina." Hallie takes two quarters and a penny.

"Well, best I get back to the café. How 'bout I put a breakfast order in for you? Still a hot dog and fries?"

Hallie cuts a chuckle short, "You remember that?"

"Sure do. Weirdest breakfast appetite in any kid I ever met. 'Course this new café is a far cry from the short-order grill that used to be here, but I think you'll still like it."

"Sounds great. Thanks, Mina."

Mina gives a wink and heads off. Hallie glances over at the café's modern design as a memory flashes of her standing on her tippy-toes to give her order to Mina over the short-order grill's tall counter while Beattie and Dot stood back and watched from a short distance away.

Hallie flashes a nostalgic smile and then turns to the penny pressing machine setting her coins in its time-worn slots. She

Thank you so much for your purchase.

I hope that you are kept awake trying to finish the next chapter!

If you have an Amazon account, please search my book, click reviews, and write a review. Five-star reviews move it up the ratings list. Thank you for your support!
SDB

pushes the lever in with a bit of effort setting a whirl of wheels and cogs into motion. It grinds to a halt, and the refashioned coin drops with a clink into the chrome dish. Retrieving the now oval penny, she rubs her finger over its embossed surface while a crooked smile lights her face.

She can't explain the swell within her—it is like her first bike ride without training wheels maybe. A token of her newly started independence sitting in her hand. Her true independence. She tucks the penny into her pocket brushing her hand against the amber heart her aunts gave her for her birthday this year. It is a family heirloom with an upward curve to its apex. She grasps ahold and a familiar warmth radiates from her hand up. It is like having the comfort of home inside her pocket.

Hallie is always amazed by this effect the amber has on her, and she can hear Beattie saying, "There's magic in everything. You just need to know how to find it." And, maybe Beattie is right. Accomplishing the first goal of her trip certainly has a magical feel to it. She makes her way to the café and takes a seat at a table to wait for Mina. A vase with delicate white flowers on wispy stems sits in the center. Across from her are two talkative little girls and a subdued woman who looks to be their grandmother. The girls watch seagulls through the window giving a full play-by-play of the birds' antics.

Hallie turns sideways in her chair and sees the woman from the parking lot walk around the end of an aisle. She is petite with almond-shaped eyes, porcelain skin, and her black silky hair falls long against her back. She is angelic, and Hallie almost cannot pull her eyes away, but then a slender well-dressed man steps in front of her to look at some wood carvings. He has a pair of wire-framed sun glasses on—inside. *What's up with that?* He says something to the woman without looking at her, and she closes her eyes and makes a slight bow of her head. Like a servant, or something. *This is so weird.* Hallie slides closer to the edge of her seat.

The man slides his sunglasses down his narrow nose to get a better look at one of the wood carvings on display. He slides them back up, but not before an unnatural red glint seems to flash. Hallie's skin prickles with gooseflesh as though ice has slithered down her back. She turns abruptly in her chair as the menacing chill frosts over her curiosity. She starts to reach into her pocket seeking the amber heart's warmth and comfort just as the two talkative little girls rambunctiously run by bumping into her table. Hallie jerks her hand forward to rescue the vase with its delicate arrangement before it topples over.

She looks after the girls to see them run abruptly into the slender man. He stiffens with the intrusion, but does not move. He turns his head looking down at them, and the girls too are now perfectly still looking up at him. The feel of spiders crawling up her arms makes Hallie recoil. She looks over to the girl's grandmother. She is busy talking on her cell while pushing the leftover food on her plate around with a fork. Hallie looks back to the girls, they have not moved, and the man is reaching up to lower his sunglasses again. Without thinking she is out of her seat and at the girls' side taking them each by the hand. They mechanically turn their heads to look at her blinking as though they have just woke up.

"Hi." Hallie says to the girls, and then shoots a quick look at the petite woman whose face she cannot read. "Uh, your grandmother was looking for you. How about we go back over to the café?"

Each girl gives a stiff nod.

Hallie smiles and gives them a gentle tug to pull them away from their almost magnetized stance. *No way am I looking at him.* She keeps her eyes down as she walks away with each girl in hand, she feels a pounding like drum sticks beating against her chest. Half expecting to see her shirt start quivering to the beat she takes a deep breath willing her heart to slow. *Oh my God, calm down.*

She stops at her table to take candy from her bag and hands a piece to each girl before walking them back to their table. Their grandmother glances at her to flash a smile but continues with her phone conversation. The girls sit down quietly in their chairs holding onto the candy. Hallie watches the girls for a moment worried, but then they suddenly open their candy taking a bite before starting their chatter back up between themselves.

Hallie looks back over her shoulder to see that the couple is gone. She wipes away beads of sweat from her upper lip and walks back over to her table trying to sort through what just happened while studying the delicate white flowers with yellow centers in front of her.

"Here you go kiddo. I put it all in a bag for you thinking you may want to go out on the pier to eat like in the old days."

Hallie flinches. Mina seems to appear from nowhere. *It's just a creepy guy and his...gosh, what was she doing with him? Calm down. Focus.* "Oh Mina, thank you." She stands pulling her wallet from her bag. "I think I am going to just get back on the road." She glances at Mina hoping to look casual while she takes a bill from her wallet flustered by her shaking hand. She forces it to steady, so Mina will not notice. "I'll be sure to tell Beattie and Dot that I saw you, and I promise to stop back by on my way home at the end of summer. I'll save my walk on the pier until then." She flashes a reluctant smile handing the money to Mina and accepts her breakfast in return.

"Well, that sounds mighty fine darlin'. I'll look forward to hearing all about your summer."

Hallie gives Mina a hug and turns to leave. As she walks outside, an imagined sensation of the fine silky weave from a spider's web wrapping itself around her face and neck strikes her quite suddenly. She stops and steals a look down the row of cars seeing her baby blue Mustang, but no sign of the sleek black sports car. The eerie sensation passes, and a wisp of a wish for Beattie and Dot's presence floats by, but she dashes it away with a puff between pursed lips that flips a stray strand of hair away from her face. She walks up warily looking at the Mustang feeling an urge to check for sabotage for some reason, but then she sees her back pack in the front passenger seat and reminds herself of the adventure that lays ahead. She gives a quick squeeze of her amber heart inside her pocket, gets into her car, clicks down the lock with her elbow, and brings the engine to life with a turn of the key. Her radio bursts with sound while she rolls down her window and puts the car in gear. Road trip tunes spill from the window as she drives away willing the sound to carry all that creepy-feeling stuff out the window to be left behind.

Chapter 2, Vestige

> *Beattie & Dot—*
>
> *I got packed and the Mustang loaded more quickly than I thought, so I decided to head to Joan's early. Sorry that I didn't wait for you to get back, but you know I love you (lots).*
>
> *Hallie*

"Hallie left a note." Dot holds it up, as Beattie comes into the kitchen with sacks of groceries.

"Figured she got on the road when her car wasn't in the yard. Good for her." Beattie glances Dot's way to catch a reaction. Hallie's big summer excursion to go live with a friend of theirs and work at a state park this summer has been especially hard for Dot. She tends to be a mother hen assuming a protective role.

"Sure. Sure." Dot is deflated like yesterday's party balloon.

Beattie walks over and gives her a hug and pat on the back. "It *is* good, sister." She stretches her arms out holding onto Dot's shoulders while imposing eye contact.

"But what if this is the beginning of what we have wondered about for so long?"

Beattie turns to go through the sacks. "Well, might be, but truth is we don't know for sure. Only time will tell."

"Could we be wrong?"

"Dot," Beattie puts a hand on her hip working to conceal any frustration. "Who knows? We've had time to sort most of it out. The rest is up to Hallie. Consider this trip…a test."

Dot gives a shrug. "Maybe we should have taught her the craft."

"She doesn't even know that we know the craft. No, that is who we are. Not her. Her gift, if it is even there, lays elsewhere."

"Yes, sister, you are right, but our attempts to prepare her like it was a story. I just am not sure it was the way it ought to have been done. No matter how many times she heard it."

Beattie's frustration finds the surface and breaks through with a gasp, "Why all this tribulation? The girl is eighteen years old. We agreed long ago she should have insight, but only vaguely. We planned to allow her to draw her own conclusions. If you thought differently, could you have not brought it up sooner?"

Dot shakes her head but not her tribulations away, "I'm sorry. I'm just all a flutter now that we are here. Now that Hallie is not here. She is just so young."

"And, how young were we when we took off for our first adventure?"

Dot gives up a short laugh. "Ach, you bring that up now?" She rubs her arms, and her shoulders release the tension that was holding her muscles hostage. "Alright, alright. I suppose that turned out okay."

"Indeed," Beattie stocks shelves. "Besides, Dot, she truly is so innately gifted and doesn't even know it. If we happened to miss something vital, I have faith that her instincts will serve her well." She turns to Dot, "And, she has the amber heart with her."

Dot flicks a smile.

"Now, there you go. A spark of something positive to hold onto." Beattie lifts a bunch of asparagus up in a mock toast, "To Hallie's grand adventure."

"May she travel well." Dot taps the asparagus and chips in to help with putting away the groceries.

Chapter 3, Vapor

The pebbled finish on Colonial Parkway gives a different hum to the drive, and there is a change in the acoustics when Hallie turns onto the asphalt road heading into Williamsburg. She turns her radio up a bit to make up for the emptiness the smooth roadway fills the Mustang with. There are too many streets in the city for Hallie to remember how she and the aunts used to drive into the colonial section. However, in a place visited by so many tourists, directive road signs are plentiful. She finds a place to park and gets out of the car to walk around. This stop is the most important to her because her mother had been here long ago.

Strolling leisurely she looks at houses, restaurants, store windows, and gardens wondering about her deceased mother. Hallie's questions about her were always vaguely answered by Beattie and Dot, and the pain in their eyes when they did speak of her made Hallie sorry that she had asked. She eventually stopped asking because she could not bear to cause her aunts any despair. What little information she did have, she clung to. One bit is that her mother was a historical interpreter for the city during her college years at William and Mary. Hallie has an old photograph of her mom during that time and, from this, she knows she has her mom's hazel eyes and freckles across her cheeks. She walks along wondering if she is retracing steps her mother had taken long ago.

Eventually, Hallie's meandering takes her down Duke of Gloucester Street and to Bruton's Parish. She remembers the quaint brick church from previous trips with Beattie and Dot and feels drawn to walk around the grounds. Some of the ancient gravestones are aged and difficult to read, but a few are newer, or at least revitalized stones that are more legible showing a chiseled epitaph about the person buried below giving a connection to the person's life. Shade from trees offers relief from the mid-day sun, and Hallie walks towards an old live oak in the back corner of the graveyard. She sits on a bench under the tree near a large black stone.

A network of thorny branches with roses burgeon the ground twisting their way over the church yard wall as though working to escape. The nearby tree's lower branches are canopied with the deep red roses as well, and their fragrance makes her think of the soft drape of a velvet sash as the scent encircles her. She looks about seeing make believe fairies within the sunlight prancing along the ground as it filters through the tree. Hallie is distracted from the imaginary dance when she notices a strange light pattern with thin electric-looking waves and explosive bursts coming and going in swirls about the black stone. The light wavers and fades only to return to the beginning once again. She looks up through the leaves of the tree searching for the source of the unusual light pattern but cannot find one.

The lights flash more frantically, and Hallie finds herself reaching towards the sparks. A tangle of lights erupts, and it lashes onto her hand pulling her toward the stone. She gasps, and she tries to resist, but without success. Suddenly she is standing in an office with dark wood trim and a large Georgian-style desk before her. She clutches the desk while her leg muscles quiver like the buzz of her cell phone. She looks at her hand, the wiry lights are gone without a trace, and then she looks around forcing herself to slow her breathing. Tall windows about the room are open and a breeze carries the smell of roses into the space, but she is no longer anywhere near the graveyard. She spins around unsure of what just happened before noticing she is no longer alone.

A man is sitting at the desk all of a sudden. *Was he there before?* She did not think so. He is wearing a white shirt with laced sleeves and loosened cravat under a deep blue coat with elaborate buttons and decorative trim. He looks up towards Hallie. She struggles to speak. He ignores her. Stacks of currency and coins sit in front of him, and a glass of drink is in his hand. A tall sandy-haired woman walks past Hallie brushing against her shoulder but seemingly unaware of Hallie's presence. The woman's emerald eyes are piercing and unrevealing. She is dressed plainly with a shapely figure that is not muted by her long grey dress. Hallie tries to speak to her, yet again she is not acknowledged.

Hallie inhales sharply realizing she is invisible to these people. She holds back onto the desk's edge. Looking around the room she finds its colonial design matches the era of dress of its other two inhabitants. Blue damask print covers the walls that are framed by elaborate crown and chair molding. Hallie's skin prickles with heat due to an obvious lack of air-conditioning in the confined space and the aftermath of her initial panic. The woman speaks, and Hallie startles.

"Jake, the house slave, asked me to come."

The man takes a drink from his glass looking at the woman from over its rim. "And, you are?"

"Resmelda Bigelow."

An electric-like shock sparks Hallie's heart to race. She knows that name from Dot's story that Hallie must have heard a hundred times during their trips and excursions. It was a tradition with her and the aunts. Hallie gives the woman a more intense look curious to know, if it can be so. She is so much more beautiful than could be imagined from the story, but she stands tall and proud exactly as Hallie had imagined.

"I was told that your business partner is ill and needs attention. I have already seen him, and I can provide healing care for him at the cost of a full sovereign."

The man snorts and sets his glass down. "The apothecary, McKemmie, would not approve of a guest in his home being gouged in such a manner."

"McKemmie is not here, and he would not approve of your familiarity with his household and goods in his absence either."

Bold. Exactly like Dot described her. *My God, what am I doing here? How can this even be?* Hallie ignores her twitching nerves unable to pull her attention away.

The man chuckles and strokes his chin eyeing Resmelda. He tells her he will pay a half sovereign and no more. She quickly informs him that the price is for her services not the value of his partner's life. The price for her services is not negotiable nor will a guarantee of success be part of the bargain. She repeats the cost.

He leans back in his chair biting his lower lip as a spark lights his eye, and he attempts to remark on services she could

29

provide for him that may bring the value of what she has to offer to a full sovereign but, before he can finish, she cuts him to the quick, and Hallie remains amazed. Resmelda is as daunting as Dot described her.

"I advise you to take caution sir. Keep your filth out of my way lest dire consequences will befall you, and that I will provide at no charge at all. If, however, it is healing that is needed, the cost, a full sovereign, is due now."

Hallie takes advantage of her invisibility and walks to the other side of the desk looking closely at the man. He has to be Robert Holt, The surly business partner of Harry White in Dot's story. Hallie struggles wondering how this beloved childhood story told to her over and over again throughout the years could be coming to life before her. What is happening? She pinches her arm thinking she may have laid down on the bench in the graveyard for a nap, but there is no change in scenery. It seems Dot's words are finding a life of their own right before her eyes, and she shakes her head with amazement.

Resmelda holds his eyes in her stare, and he picks up a sovereign piece from the desk thinly smiling as he extends his arm towards her—his hand just out of her reach. She takes him by surprise when she reaches out and fully grasps his hand in hers holding it tightly. Hallie jumps even though she knew it was coming. And, even though Holt's face betrays nothing, she knows he is feeling a constricting discomfort crawling up his arm while his heart pounds against his ribs, and his breath is drawn with increasing difficulty.

If Hallie didn't know his character, and that Resmelda had no intention of truly harming him, she would have tried to break them apart. Hallie stands perfectly still unaware that she is holding her breath until he withdraws his hand with some effort bringing it to his side of the desk. Hallie's breath escapes its confines in a rush, and she brings a shaky hand to her chest.

The thin smile now comes to Resmelda's face as she places the coin in a hidden pocket at her dress waist. She advises Holt that she requires a full night for the remedy and six more for the man's recuperation. He opens his mouth to speak, she maintains her eye contact, and he closes his mouth acquiescing while casually waving her away. She remains just long enough to show her departure is of her own accord and not in compliance to his flippant command.

Hallie watches her walk towards the door and leave still wondering what force landed her in the company of Resmelda Bigelow and Robert Holt. She has never experienced anything like this in her life. *Did that wiry light on the black stone carry an electrical charge knocking me unconscious and into this imaginary world?*

A strong breeze surges through the windows slamming the heavy door shut startling Hallie from her reverie, and suddenly she finds herself sitting in a different room. It is a small chamber with painted walls, a trunk and tall chest of drawers are off to the side, and a long window across from her has heavy drapes pulled closed with faint bits of dim light filtering through where they do not quite come together. Light flickers off the walls and ceiling coming from many candles sitting throughout the room. There are a variety of drawings and entomological displays along the walls as well.

The smell of fever is in the air along with the staccato cadence of labored respirations. She sees a sweat-soaked man lying on a small bed that has been pulled away allowing a passageway between its headboard and the wall. The man has a thick shock of dark hair, and a handsome face that needs a shave. His shirt is off, and he has a pair of dark pants on but no shoes. *This has to be Harry White, Holt's ill business partner*. Resmelda stands at the foot of the bed.

"Hester, he is prepared sufficiently. Let us move on to the ritual. Have you arranged all that is needed?"

Hallie realizes that Resmelda is looking directly at her. She wants to turn her head to see if this person, Hester, is behind her, but her muscles do not respond to the command. She suddenly is aware that her peripheral vision has a kaleidoscope look to it like peering through a pair of goggles in a virtual reality game, and she wonders if she is even seeing through her own eyes.

"Hester, come now," Resmelda beckons impatiently. "This all must be completed and the circle closed in order to begin the final portion of the ceremony at the proper hour. Be quick."

There. *She is definitely seeing me, but it is not me. It is someone named Hester. Could I be seeing things through this Hester's eyes? What rabbit hole have I tumbled into?* Her mouth feels like a desert all of a sudden. Before extreme panic can set in any deeper, Hallie is distracted as she feels herself moving forward towards a table with a thick slate top that sits near the man. It is the strangest sensation to ride along inside what she decides must be Hester's body.

Set upon the slate table top are candles, containers of oil, water, salt, some sort of bark, and a variety of herbs. Hallie recognizes St John's wort, tansy, woodruff, and there is another herb that is not familiar. There is a piece of rock just barely visible from underneath a piece of fabric. The rock is a translucent deep golden brown with darker speckles and a bubbled texture. She feels her hand move forward, but it does not look like her own hand. It is delicate, a saffron-brown, and it reaches down smoothly sliding the rock out of view. There is a small cauldron with a steady flame burning beneath. Hallie tries again to make her muscles obey her, but all the preparations continue not of her own accord. A nervous spasm harasses her stomach, but Hallie is now so enthralled, she wouldn't have pulled herself away even if she suddenly could. The view shifts away from the bedside as she almost floats back to the corner of the room sitting down on the floor again.

"Very well," Resmelda speaks again towards Hallie. "It is time. Hester be sure to remain away from the circle once it has been closed. You must remain quiet, no song, remember?" Hallie feels herself nodding in agreement, and watches as Resmelda picks up a beautiful knife that comes to a very sharp point with a black handle. The handle is embellished with a silver symbol showing a circle and two crests on either side. Hallie is entranced by it for a moment. *It looks so familiar.*

Resmelda points the knife downward and circles the bed as she begins speaking slowly and deliberately, but Hallie cannot make out her words. The candle light glints off the blade of the knife, and a jolt of recognition slams against Hallie's chest—*it is an athame.* It looks just like the one that sits in a black wooden box in the desk in the den back home. Hallie ran across the knife once when looking for a letter opener. She was about eleven or twelve and, even then, she recognized the fine craftsmanship and splendor of it. With it being tucked away inside the desk, she realized it was being hidden. She knew her discovery had to have been a transgression, so instead of asking her aunts about it, she Googled it to learn more.

At the time, she saw the knife as a relic her aunts must have picked up in some antique shop. Although the internet showed her its use as a ceremonial knife, the thought of her middle-aged aunts ever using it like Resmelda is now, never crossed her mind. She feels the jagged edge of anxiety melt and reform into a smooth yet restless cusp of curiosity. Every action before her is fascinating and new. Her mind races trying to find some other connection in her memories with this ceremony aside from the athame, but there is none.

Resmelda finishes her third circle around the bed and stands at the table with the cauldron and other ingredients.

"These candles are dedicated to the healing of Harry William White in the names of the lady and the lord." The candles are then set to each side of the cauldron while two yellow candles remain unlit and are placed in the center. She picks up a small stick lighting it from the flame below the cauldron and lays it inside a small bowl. Smoke begins to wisp into the air, and the faint fragrance of sandalwood catches Hallie's attention. It is one of Beattie's favorite scents.

She sprinkles salt over the yellow candles reciting, "I consecrate these through the power of elemental earth." She lifts the yellow candles and passes them through the incense smoke. "And through the power of elemental fire." She sets the yellow candles on the table once again sprinkling them with water. "And through the power of elemental water." She takes the athame and etches symbols on the candles before elegantly moving to light each from the tall white candles, and then she returns both back to the center in front of the cauldron. Picking up each of the herbs on the table, she crushes them in her hands and lets the pieces fall over the flames of the yellow candles.

Hallie thinks about walking through her aunts vast herb gardens back home that supply the ingredients for their botanical products, and she wonders if she has found another connection.

"Ash bark for health and protection." Resmelda calls out each ingredient's purpose. "Saint John's wort for health, protection, and strength. Tansy for health and the love of the goddess. Woodruff for victory and the love of the god. And, devil's nettle for the healing of Harry William White." She finishes, and rests both of her hands on the table. A hand lands on the cloth that has been covering the rock. Resmelda slides the rock from beneath the cloth, and stares down at it blinking several times before her face hardens. She glares towards Hallie's corner of the room holding up the rock in her hand shaking it.

"Hester! What have you done? Why is this piece of 'tree sap' sitting on my altar?"

Nothing. A jack hammer comes to life inside Hallie's chest. *Tree sap?*

"Answer me. Why? I cannot break the circle until it has been incorporated into the ceremony. What were you thinking?" Resmelda's arm quivers against her fury. "Answer me now!"

A chiming voice delicately reverberates from inside where Hallie is—the first time Hester has spoken. "It was Sophia."

"What? What are you talking about?"

Hallie wants to know too. *How much more could there be?*

"Sophia had a vision that this man was intended for you during your time on Earth." Hester's voice quivers with fear, and Hallie is feeling it too. Hearing about Resmelda's fierceness in Dot's story is one thing, and witnessing it another, but having its full force directed at you is unnerving. Hallie is glad to be shrouded by Hester.

Hester pushes on. "He has lost true love, his wife Sarah, to the spirit world. You are in need of true love to be complete and assure happiness before your final departure. She said the tree's blood will tell you it is so, if his life is spared by it tonight. She encouraged me to sacrifice this gift in order to help you find happiness and remain within the ways of the light. I am giving it to you willingly and hopefully."

Hallie feels the long-ago excitement of sitting next to the campfire on a trip with her aunts while Dot brought to life some new detail to the well-told story, but none of what she is currently witnessing had ever been revealed by Dot.

Resmelda stands without moving. Her eyes glisten until she inhales deeply commanding control of her emotions. "Sophia is with child and cannot trust what images are brought to her during her confinement. Neither she nor you, Hester, have any right to interfere with what is already destined. And this," she holds the yellow-brown rock up higher, "may have been in your possession for a long time now, but it is not yours to give. How dare the two of you scheme against me?"

"There is no conspiracy of ill will. Sophia is convinced by what she saw. She says that your path is not how you think it is laid out, and this man can show you a different way. I feel the harmony in her vision."

"Damn her. And damn you too Hester. I should have never brought Sophia here. Her union with Halbrook has brought into this world two souls that should not have been, and now a third is on the way. My sentiment momentarily stole away my good judgment all those years ago, and I am paying for it now. Despite my youth at the time, my foolishness was reprehensible. I angered the Fates, and now they are punishing me."

The room falls silent, and Hallie wonders if the pulsing in her ears is from her heart or Hester's.

Resmelda turns to face the man on the bed. His skin is now dry, and his respirations are taken with greater ease, but he still has not aroused. She stands there surveying him for a long moment and hesitates before laying the yellow-brown rock on his chest. A gentle glow of light begins to spread outward. It brightens overcasting the candle light and obscures the man while showing Resmelda only as a silhouette now leaning over him with her face inches from his. Her body briefly shadows a portion of the light allowing Hallie to see his face as well as hers, but only for a moment before both are engulfed by its brilliance. It remains this way for a while, and Hallie's eyes strain against the light. She wants to shield them but, still being concealed within Hester, her hands will not move. Suddenly, the intensity begins to wane, and Hallie sees that Resmelda has moved her hand to where the rock rests on the man's chest. Resmelda encloses her fingers around it lifting it from his skin. The light disappears, and the room looks as it had before. Resmelda remains momentarily gazing into his face before standing upright and turning towards Hallie stretching her arm outward with open hand. The rock is now a heart-shape that is smooth with a more brilliant deep tawny-gold color, and the heart's tip has dripped down only to curve back upwards.

It is not a rock at all. Hallie's breath catches in her throat while the prickle of sweat beads up above her lip and brow. A high-pitched buzz fills her ears. It is her heart-shaped amber amulet that her aunts had given her. There is a sudden sharp tug within her chest stealing her breath away, and she pulls away from the quickly fading scene at a dizzying speed. She stops abruptly with a solid seat beneath her.

Chapter 4, Cimmerian

Hallie sits with her eyes closed almost afraid to open them. There is a faint scent of sandalwood in the air, but it quickly becomes lost in the fragrance of roses. She wills her hands to move, and is both shocked and relieved when they obey wiping the sweat from her brow and lip. She squints an eye open. No wiry lights dancing on the black stone in front of her. Back in the graveyard. She exhales with relief and then rifles through her bag grabbing her cell phone. She dials home. Her shaking finger pauses. If she slides the screen to connect, and storms into what just happened, the aunts may get worried and pull the plug on her trip. She commands control of her breathing as her mind races. *Maybe I fell asleep, sitting up, on this very firm bench, and it was a dream. An incredibly real dream. Way more detailed than Dot ever offered in her story.* She sighs and lets go of her phone.

She looks at the black stone warily just as a person's shadow casts across it. A hand reaches past her and drops a stem with multiple pink bell-shaped flowers onto the ground in front of the stone. Hallie looks behind her. Her throat seizes and refuses any air passage for a moment and then she gasps. *Oh-my-God—creepy guy from the bridge-tunnel.* And, he is standing close enough to touch her. She instinctively shifts on the bench to put some distance between them. Her face must have a quizzical look despite the dread she knows should be there because he speaks to her.

"Foxglove," he states it as though she has asked a question. "A little can heal. A lot can kill." He flicks a smile.

She is transfixed by him seeing her bewildered reflection in the dark purple lenses of his spectacles. His eyes are hidden, and an image of the flash of red she saw in them at the gift shop on Gull Island demands caution. She starts to reach back into her bag for the cell phone. *Who cares what the aunts will do about the trip? Maybe they will just have an explanation to make sense of all this.*

"It is a tradition for my companion, Hester, and I." He tips his head.

Hallie pauses to take a look over her shoulder in the direction he indicates. *Did he say Hester?* His companion is standing not too far behind her. She holds a lovely bouquet of deep purple irises tied together with a simple but elegant bow. Hallie looks into her dark eyes feeling the quiet sadness within them realizing that her discomfort with the couple is really with the man—not this delicate-appearing woman. Hallie takes a quick survey of the grounds. They are alone, and she represses a shudder. *Can that excursion into the past truly be a dream, and this second encounter with this strange man and...Hester be just a coincidence? That wasn't a dream—no way, and I have no idea what this is.* Her phone is just inside her bag, and she is wondering if the number for home is still up. All she has to do is brush the lower screen to get it to connect.

Her common sense is screaming at her to do it, but she thinks about the pressed penny and amber heart in her pocket. She thinks about the newly real independence she has claimed, and takes a breath then clears her throat to ask, "I'm sorry, a tradition?" *Seriously, how about, "Are you stalking me or what?"* Politeness before panic, maybe it's placation before panic, but either way, one or the other will have to do. *He could probably grab me before I could put any serious distance between me and them.* She calculates her chances and decides to wait for a better opportunity to leave.

The man seems to be studying her intently from behind the dark lenses. "Are you on a trip?"

Although accurate, his question is like a poke in Hallie's ribs. She breathes in sharply and lets her reply escape on her exhalation. "Uh...Yes."

"Yes, I see. We did see you at that gift shop and café on the bridge-tunnel, but I thought maybe you were employed there or something of that nature."

"No, I'm on a trip."

"Yes, so we have established." He looks about them. "And, what brings you here? It is a bit of a curious stop for a young person like yourself. I assume you are traveling alone."

Hallie's internal alarm has hit the set and is firing off obnoxiously. Time to leave, but no, the conversation continues.

"Uh, well I knew someone who worked here."

"Worked, but not currently working?"

"She died some time ago."

"Ah." He takes another look around focusing on the graves. "Surely, not 'resting' here though. This part of the graveyard is from a different era."

"No, no…she was a historical interpreter for the city."

He grins and nods his head. "I see. So, she must have told you about this gravesite then." He gestures towards the black stone, and walks around to lean against the live oak and rest a foot on the black stone. He studies his well-manicured but cloudy nails.

"No. I didn't even realize it was a grave. There's no engraving on the stone." Hallie's curiosity is piqued, yet she internally admonishes herself. *Why am I talking to him?* Worse, she finds herself tilting her head a bit trying to see behind those purple lenses. Trying to see if there truly is that unnatural red blaze behind them. Stupid curiosity is winning the melee within her.

He toys with her. "It is Hester's wish that we come to visit, and I acquiesce because this 'Colonial' Williamsburg fascinates me." His words are mocking.

A gentle breeze dries the persisting beads of sweat from Hallie's brow while her nerves continue nagging her. She looks again to see that Hester has not moved and turns back to face the man raising an eyebrow.

"The story of this grave is quite fascinating. Hester and I are…well, we are 'history buffs' so to say. Perhaps, like your friend was. Hester, although she wants to come every year, is actually so disarmed by this gravesite that she will not move any closer to it than from where she is now standing. And so, although she takes great effort to bring her bouquet of flowers each year, it is only my 'gift' that is actually delivered. I often ponder on this. Wouldn't you?" He is still evaluating his hands not looking in the direction of either young woman, and he doesn't wait for a response before continuing.

"Did you know that back in colonial days most people buried their dead near their homes where they could care for the graves and keep the departed close by?"

Hallie shakes her head.

"Well, they did. Bruton's Parish, however, was deeded this small parcel of land as a gift, and it became a graveyard for those wishing an internment somewhere else besides home." His words ring with careless disregard.

"There are some famous people buried here." He now looks in Hallie's direction as he spouts off a list including a governor, the original rector for the parish, and two of Martha Curtis Washington's children—noting that they were from her first marriage when she was just Martha Curtis, and before George had come along.

"Back then, you know, there were no regulations about how a grave was to be dug—depth, spacing, that sort of thing—it led to some folks being buried on top of other folks and such. Quite funny actually when you think how particular people can be about that sort of thing. Anyway, this grave," he points downward at his perfectly shined shoe resting on the black stone, "is rumored to be the grave of a dark witch, Resmelda Bigelow."

Hallie flinches at the mention of the name hoping he did not notice. Somehow, without knowing why, she does not feel it is good for him to see a weakness in someone. *What could he know of Resmelda? She is part of Dot's story not the real world. Right?* Then, she thinks of what she has just experienced, or dreamed, or something. *Could Resmelda Bigelow have truly existed?* She shifts a bit in her seat thinking about her amber heart.

"Perhaps, if you have time, you will indulge me, and allow me to share a bit of history with you."

Hallie shrugs a shoulder. She does want to know, yet staying here and talking with him feels like every horror story foray she has ever watched with indignant disbelief towards the heroine's stupidity. Still, she hears herself say, "Okay." *Stupid girl.*

"Very well then. You see, the witch was a beautiful woman, and she had enchanted a prominent business man into falling in love with her..." The man pauses for effect.

Not all is true here. Beware of his trickery. The whimsical chiming voice, or whatever that was in the sickroom of Harry

White, softly whispers to Hallie. She wants to turn and look at Hester, but the man does not seem to hear the voice, and he goes on with his account. Hallie catches her breath at the sound of the voice, but remains still.

"…It was later speculated that she was after his fortune and power. She had deceived him during the time they knew one another." He pauses and annotates, "I know, beauty and the thought of an evil witch does not seem congruent, but Resmelda was beautiful…and evil indeed…so the legend has it."

Legend. Not story. That could explain a real-life Resmelda. Hallie listens on.

"The man remained in his state of bliss for quite some time intending to bring his new-found love back here to Williamsburg. He wanted her to become his bride and meet his son. Before any of these plans could be put forth her deception was brought to light by the man's business partner. The time of their affair was nearly thirty years since the Salem Witch Trials, but people of the time, even in the Virginia Colony, were still very wary of witchcraft and fallen women who made bargains with the devil." He pauses and chuckles a bit to himself before continuing.

"The businessman's superstitious mind was easy to persuade and, in his anger over her trickery, he took hast in having her arrested and sent here to Williamsburg for trial. She was left to sit for weeks in horrible conditions. I believe a restoration of the jail can be found here. Although, spelled g-o-a-l like it was back then. It was quite a piddling place really." He strokes his smooth chin and interjects, "Although, it housed some of Black Beard's men before they were hung in 1719—just a year before the time we are speaking of. Despite the place's small size, Resmelda was kept isolated from the other prisoners. Her presence in Williamsburg was a well-kept secret lest hysteria may occur within the city, if people knew a witch was among them. There ended up being no public hearing, and many pockets were lined in gold to keep the entire affair quiet.

"You see, they were in a quandary in deciding exactly how she was to be dealt with until the problem was resolved when it seemed she had been murdered by a guard that was found missing that very same night. A knife had been savagely plunged into her abdomen. There was no formal investigation, but objects known to be tied to black magic were found in her cell. The meaning of this discovery was not understood until the businessman's beloved son died most tragically just before his twentieth birthday. The death had the markings of dark magic from a curse that could have only be cast by a very powerful and dangerous witch. It was said that the businessman eventually went mad succumbing to a pact with one of the devil's finest and lives to this day in the underworld enslaved and miserable." The man touches a gold ring with a green stone on his finger turning it back and forth for a moment before looking at Hallie intently.

Hallie wants to respond to his inquisitive look. She wants to question him. Ask about things she knows from Dot's version of this story, but the chimed voice's warning still resonates within her mind. *Beware.* Despite the tingle tapping along her spine spreading its chill down her arms, she remains straight-faced sensing he is looking for some sort of reaction. She holds her cards close, and he gives up seeming somewhat disappointed.

"Well, it just so happened that the businessman's partner was at the jail seeking retribution from debtors when he became aware that she had been murdered. To spare his partner any disgrace, he generously offered a burial spot he had recently acquired at Bruton's Parish." The man makes a theatrical sweeping of his arm towards the ground below him. "This burial spot to be exact."

He sighs. "She was taken to this site that very night and buried before the next day's light. The grave was marked with this plain black rock as was common practice for the burial of slaves and criminals of the time. Shortly after, this rose bush began to sprout of its own accord taking over this corner of the graveyard over the years, never dying, making steady growth. I suppose people have wondered about this remote corner, but I have not come across any written accounts about it. There is only the legend that I have just shared with you. I wonder how many people even know about it. I doubt very many, or it would have been made an attraction."

"There's nothing written about it?" Hallie looks from the man back to Hester who looks at Hallie but says nothing. Hallie looks back to the man wondering what mutual acquaintance Beattie and Dot, who know this story so well, could possibly have with this unnerving man. *How else could they too have knowledge of the legend?*

"No nothing is written that I am aware of, although in the early 1900's a local clergyman, named Goodwin, who began restoring and recreating Colonial Williamsburg, did some excavation and restoration of this graveyard early in the project. But, he never wrote a single line about this grave site. You would think a man like him would be able to sense something more here than just an unruly rose bush and investigate." He taps his chin and frowns. "Perhaps, he did though, and there was something…maybe a supernatural warning, that kept him from seeking, or writing about, any mysteries that lurk below this tangle of roses. This grave was never excavated, and it remains untouched to this day."

"Well," Hallie offers. "I can see a clergyman being wary of something evil, if the legend is true."

"Can you?"

"Yes."

"No, I mean can you see it? Or, is it more a feeling? What drew you here to begin with? Was it just the thought of your dead friend, or something else drawing you close?"

Hallie stammers not sure how to answer, as she is barraged with thoughts of her trip to the past. *Why exactly did I come here? Was it just about my mother?*

"What is your name?" He doesn't wait for answers to his other questions.

What? Why? Yet, she gives him an answer. "Hallie. And, you are?"

"You can call me…Joe."

Hallie looks at him having difficulty getting the name to fit with the man who stands before her. "Well, Joe I came to Colonial Williamsburg because of the person who worked here. I just happened to walk by the graveyard and decided to check it out."

"Check-it-out. Your own curiosity then. What if, however, this place was curious about you, and drew you to it?"

Okay, this guy's creepiness is crawling too close for comfort. Time to go. Hallie pulls her cell phone from her bag. "Oh, the time is so late." She looks back to Joe. "I'm not sure what forces brought me here. I was thinking just along the lines of the 'tourist bit' thing, but who knows. I do know though that I am running behind. I have a friend to meet." *A lie.* "And, I have to get going."

His lips purse slightly, and he nods his head a few times in thought. "Yes, time is precious." Still he disregards her urgency. "Hester, do you recall some years back during our traditional visit here coming across another young woman, not too different from Hallie? She even had a similar aura…uh, appearance with a soft curl to her hair and similar…fair complexion as this one. Very curious." He is toying not only with Hallie but with Hester as well. "She too was sitting in this same spot, and I recall that she had said she felt drawn to visit it nearly every day. She, like us, was some sort of amateur historian. I would suggest perhaps Hallie's dead friend may be her, but this was much before Hallie's time. I do wonder what ever became of her. Do you remember who I am speaking of, Hester?" He removes his foot from the black stone and steps closer to the bench.

Hallie stands and skirts around the bench closer to Hester. She slings her bag over her shoulder. Hester glances Hallie's way, but then returns her focus towards Joe. She has not said a word during this entire time, and Hallie gets the feeling that Hester always awaits instruction, a command, something from Joe. The creepiness threshold has been reached, and no amount of curiosity could hold Hallie here any longer.

"Well, thanks for the story, and it was nice to meet you…both." She looks from Hester to Joe. "Like I said, I gotta go." Hallie takes a few steps backward then turns and goes. She braces for a grab of the shoulder, of the arm, maybe a choke-hold, but nothing comes, and she inhales deeply as she quickens her pace to reach the front of the graveyard where she is immersed in other tourists. She glances back over a shoulder, and sighs relief that there is no sign of Hester or Joe.

Oh, my God! What was that all about? All of it? Hallie is back in her car and driving out of the city in no time. She takes the ferry across the James River into Surry. The ride on the water calms her, but she foregoes her planned stop at the Surry House for a late lunch thinking she will simply pull into a drive-through of a fast food place.

She wants to put miles between her and the couple. No more stops. Not even to any of the beautiful plantations along the way like she planned. She fights the urge to call Beattie and Dot not wanting to worry them, and really not wanting them to ask her to return home. She has about four hours left to figure this out and get rid of the butterflies in her stomach so Joan will not pick up on anything amiss.

Chapter 5, Incandescence

The blue Mustang eventually comes to a stop sitting in the right hand lane of the interstate bumper-to-bumper with an eighteen wheeler in front and a minivan in back. "Well, this is going nowhere real fast." Hallie shuts the engine off and grabs her phone from her bag to call Joan.

"Listen, no worries about your delay. You just be careful. We have had a veterinary emergency here this afternoon, and I'm in a bit of a rush to get back to the park. I'll fill you in later, but just in case I haven't gotten back home before you arrive, I am going to leave the back door unlocked and a light on the porch for you."

"Okay, Joan. I hope everything is alright." Hallie offers, but isn't sure Joan heard since she has already hung up. "Huh, wonder what that was about?" Hallie thinks out loud as she turns the dial of her radio trying to get a station to come in. *Barton Hollow* by the Civil Wars comes in tune, and she settles on that while contemplating the incredible events of the day. Her thoughts ricochet between the jaunt back in time and the unnerving encounters with Joe and Hester. She can rationalize chance as the cause for meeting the unsettling couple twice, but there is no rationalization for what happened to her in the graveyard before their appearance.

Even as the traffic begins to move, and she finds herself closer to her destination, her mind will not quiet. It is not until she catches her first glimpse of the gentle sloping peaks of the Blue Ridge that any sense of calm washes over her. A spring shower has left a light mist over the mountains painting shades of gray over their deep name-sake hue. The sun has already dropped behind their crest with its warm red glow lingering along the tops, and she remembers Joan saying that she loves living in the Blue Ridge Mountains because they surround you with a cozy contentment. At this point in her day, with all that has happened, she is in great need of the mountains' magical feel.

She releases a tension-filled breath and trades it for a calming inhalation of mountain air. The mustang carries her off the highway and along the back roads towards Joan's house. Alongside Fayerdale Drive, Joan's familiar red barn mailbox at the end of her lane comes into view, and Hallie smiles hearing the pops and crackles as she makes her way down the graveled drive below a canopy of trees. She pulls her car up and around to the back of the house where she sees a dented, well-worn, green pickup parked alongside Joan's back outbuilding.

The outbuilding had always been a favorite place for Hallie to hang out during her visits here with her aunts when she was younger. It is the original homestead for the property, and Joan said that after she and her husband built the new house she wanted to keep the quaint building intact. There is a small pottery studio inside and a space with comfortable chairs and a rug off to the side where Hallie created tent dwellings, and played with the latest litter of kittens or puppies that Joan seemed to have an endless supply of.

Hallie gets out of her car slinging her back pack over her shoulder and grabs her duffle bags from the trunk. She makes her way up the steps to the house's screened porch juggling her bags while the porch door hinges squeak their greeting when she pulls on the handle. She tosses one of the duffle bags onto the floor of the porch, and it slides near the back door. Turning she squeezes herself and the back pack and other duffle bag she has through the narrow opening. Joan left a small table lamp on as promised, and Hallie takes a look around the porch. It is still decorated with the woodland-style furniture that was here during her other visits long ago. The lamp gives the earthy colors a warm glow. She turns towards the kitchen door to collect her duffle bag from the floor. Hallie bends over reaching to grab up the bag while also trying to keep her book bag balanced. As she stretches up to turn the knob on the kitchen door, she is startled when the door swings open seemingly of its own accord.

She finds herself standing in front of a well-muscled torso of tanned skin with the fresh scent of soap in the air. She looks up finding a square chin and full lips and then a pair of deep brown eyes. A shock of thick black hair, wet and tousled, hangs down just above the pair of beautiful eyes. All these attributes belong to a striking young man. Hallie takes an awkward step backwards bumping into the duffle bag still on the floor nearly tripping. He reaches out to catch her by the arm. She notices a white towel draped across his shoulders and a pair of slightly loose-fitting faded jeans with a waist band that sits nicely over slender hips. At that moment, a smooth masculine voice with a slight accent brings her attention back up to his face. *Was it British? Not quite.*

"Sorry, I did not mean to startle you." He is polite, almost formal. Hallie notes that once he feels she is out of danger, he removes his hand from her arm taking a step away to put more space between them. Her arm has a flush of warmth and gentle tingle where his hand has been, and she notices that he flexes his hand ever so slightly, as he pulls it back to rest it against the door frame.

"Oh…no…uh…I just wasn't expecting anyone to be here." Hallie stammers. A sensation of shyness hits her stomach like a vice grip with a mission. *What is this?* He seems to stir something deep inside her with no conscious effort. Hallie feels put off balance once again today, but it is with a very different effect this time.

"I'm Hallie, Joan is expecting me." Hallie finds her voice pulling herself together—sort of. *Just grab the duffle bag. Be cool about it, Hallie.* Her other bags shift as she starts to bend over to rescue the bag on the floor.

He moves forward brushing against her stirring the air and bringing the fresh clean scent of soap back to her nose again threatening to disorient her once more. He reaches passed her lifting the duffle bag from the floor before she can grasp it, and he holds it above their heads stepping aside against the open door to allow her passage.

Now that was cool. Hallie makes her way past him shifting her back pack to get through as she moves into Joan's welcoming kitchen. It is not much different from what she remembers. Deep coppery brown color on the walls with oak cabinetry and glass doors revealing beautiful pottery, stained glass pieces in the windows, and a refrigerator covered with pictures and clippings of poetry and quotes of wisdom. The floor is a light tan tile that Hallie remembers was always so cool on her feet even on the hottest summer days. It is the only place away from Burton's Shore that feels just like home.

Hallie opens her sweaty hands to unload her burden onto the floor. He sets her duffle bag down as well. She notices on his right arm a horrible scar starting just above the wrist as he moves past her. It has a sunburst pattern looking as though an explosion occurred ripping through his flesh with tendrils snaking upwards toward his inner elbow where it turns into wiry strands. She only looks at it for a moment, but her glance is not missed, and he brings his arms up to grasp the ends of the towel around his neck in a way that turns the mark away from her view. He pauses hesitantly for a moment and turns to go.

Hallie quickly speaks up, "Thank you. Thanks for your help."

He turns back only nodding to acknowledge her gratitude.

"So, are you staying here with Joan?" She asks delaying his departure.

He flashes a reticent smile. "I have been here for a while now. I have a small space in the back of her outbuilding where she has her studio. I sleep and keep my things there, but I usually come into the house for meals and showers."

"Oh." Hallie is not sure what else to say. She wonders why Joan did not mention having a boarder, and wonders if the aunts would have allowed her to come if they were aware, or maybe they knew. She has no recollection of them discussing any particulars about her living arrangements for the summer. *What did any of this matter anyway? Focus Hallie—don't look stupid.*

"Well, I'm Hallie, as I said. Hallie O'Meara. It is nice to meet you…" She tilts her head towards him in anticipation of a reply, and he obliges.

"Liam."

"Liam," she says. *I like that name.* "So, Liam, do you know when Joan will be back?"

"She should be here shortly. We both headed back from the park at about the same time, but she wanted to stop and pick up a few things for breakfast tomorrow I believe."

He holds eye contact with her maintaining a decorum that does not seem to match that they are standing in a kitchen—she in shorts and a tank top and he, *well, he in a very nice pair of faded jeans—uh, stop! What is wrong with you?* She blushes self-consciously and forces herself to speak. "Right, she said there was some sort of veterinary emergency this afternoon. She sounded really rattled when I spoke to her."

"Yes, pretty tragic actually, but I think we have things under control. Time will tell. Well, I should go. Can you manage from here?"

It didn't seem like he was going to give much more details on the events of the afternoon. Hallie isn't worried with this though. She knows Joan will tell her everything that went on. Besides, a shower before bed seems to be beckoning, so she smiles at him and says, "Yes, I'm good. Thank you again. I guess I will be seeing you around?"

"Yes, I am sure." He says, eyes fixed on hers, before he turns smoothly and steps out the door.

Hallie watches him go with a smile on her face. She grabs her cell from her bag because she wants to let Beattie and Dot know she arrived safely. She hesitates not trusting herself with a phone call. They know her too well and something may come up about the drive that triggers a catch in her voice or a hesitation in a response, so she opts for a text message. They have become quite accomplished with texting, and she knows they won't mind. She fires off a message, and then gathers up her bags and makes her way through the kitchen to the hallway that leads to the stairs and her room. Her phone pings with the aunts' response as she is laying her bags down in the quaint room that has always been hers during prior visits.

Hallie stands at the window and sees Liam standing by the green truck. He glances back at the house and up towards her window, but she steps back hoping he can't see her looking at him. He stands there for quite a while before grabbing a t-shirt from inside the truck and pulling it on. He gets in and pulls away. Joan's Jeep comes around the corner and Hallie sees them exchange a wave outside their windows.

.

Chapter 6, Glow

The soft edges of Hallie's PJ's brush her leg as she heads down the steps to the kitchen. "Joan, it's so good to see you! Let me help you."

"Hal, it is so good to see you too!" She grabs a hold of Hallie and embraces her warmly.

The smell of patchouli and the outdoors bring back many happy memories for Hallie. Joan's graying hair is clipped up on her head with wisps of curls hanging softly along the sides of her face and over her neck. Joan pushes Hallie back at arm's length to take appraisal.

"Beautiful. See you got through those tween years quite well young lady."

Hallie blushes a bit and laughs. She is a little taken back to see that Joan has aged more than she expected. Maybe it's that she hadn't seen her in so long, and her aunts, who are about the same age as Joan, just seem to remain so young and vibrant.

"I brought some goodies from the aunts' shop just for your pampering pleasure."

"Excellent! I need some of their lavender bath product to soak in tonight and relax. Whew, what a day." Joan starts putting up the groceries. Hallie chips in, and they chat as they go about the task.

"Yeah, you sounded a little frazzled when I spoke to you earlier today. What happened?"

Joan stops and puts a hand on her hip looking over towards Hallie. "A horse." She shakes her head in disbelief raising her hands up emphatically as she continues. "This gorgeous horse somehow got loose in the park and fell down one of the steep ridges."

Hallie's stomach twists with concern for the poor creature. "A-a-and? How?"

"Well, we have no idea. No owners have come forward. It's like she came out of nowhere." Joan goes back to the groceries and, as she talks, lifts a bag of cheese puffs in the air. "You still like these things?"

"Oh, yeah. No changes there." Hallie says as she lifts a gallon of milk into the fridge.

"So, this poor horse is down in a ravine and squealing out in a most horrible way. She was in so much pain, and it took a while to get to her. Liam…did you get a chance to meet him when you got here?" She interjects while putting some cans into an upper cabinet not bothering to look back at Hallie.

"Uh, yes. He helped me get my bags in." Hallie stings with heat just at the thought of him.

"I saw him leaving as I was pulling in." Joan finishes with the groceries and leans against the countertop folding her shopping sacks to put back in a drawer. "I'm sure he is heading back over to the park to check on that poor horse."

"So the horse is still alive?" Hallie sees a flicker of sunshine for the situation.

"Yes, by some miracle. Liam got down to the horse and kept her calm and called me on the radio. He stayed with the pitiful creature until we could get a vet there. The horse was impaled on an old metal post or something that was left over from when the area was being timbered and mined for iron. She had a horrible wound on her chest after they cut away the flesh to get the post free and several other nasty cuts."

"Oh, my gosh! So what did the vet say?"

"Believe it or not, she thinks the horse is going to be okay. She really is a beautiful mare and has had such an effect on Liam. I don't know how much Liam said to you, but he isn't much of a talker. I'm not sure he is much of a people person—kind of a loner really. He has been staying with me for a year or so now, and I really know very little about his past. He is a good guy though. There is just something about him I like."

Hallie smiles and nods. "He seems really nice." *Really nice.* The tingling heat intensifies. Then she refocuses the conversation back to the mare in an effort to control the foreign sensation cascading over her. "I hope the horse gets better. Where is she being kept?"

"Don't get me started with that whole story, Hal. To make a long story short, I'll just say that right now she is being kept in the old stable at the park. What an act of congress that was to get approved. Lordy! But then we liked to have never got her up and out of the woods. She was in rough shape, so we really could not have transported her anywhere right then. What a mess with it being a state park and all. They have long since taken horses out of the park due to insurance and a whole bunch of other stuff."

"Wow, maybe I can go over and help with her some tomorrow since I have time before we start working this weekend." Hallie's eyelids suddenly falter with the weight of a long day, and her muscles feel wilted like weary blooms all of a sudden.

"Hey, you're looking exhausted. Get yourself off to bed. I am heading to a nice hot bath with lavender magic from my buddies at B & D Botanicals, and then I will be off to bed too. You are more than welcome to ride into the park with me tomorrow, if you want to visit with the horse. I don't have to be there until ten-thirty, so you can sleep in a little."

"Okay Joan, that sounds good to me." She walks over and gives her a hug before turning to make her way upstairs to her room.

"Oh wait! I almost forgot. I didn't send your birthday gift to you this year because I knew you were planning to come here for the summer. Let me get it real quick." Joan hurries out of the kitchen into her den to grab a small box from the desk. It is a simple brown box that she stamped with a flower pattern and tied with a lace bow.

Hallie unties the bow and opens the lid. She lifts out a soft leather pouch imprinted with a cross surrounded by a heart inside a circle. It is very finely crafted. Hallie's face lights up. "Thank you so much. It is really beautiful."

"I hope you like it. It was a gift to me many years ago from a friend. It was originally a small medicine bag, but I used it to hold precious mementos that I wanted to keep close. It can be worn as a necklace or pulled through a belt loop, so it doesn't get lost."

"It's perfect! Beattie and Dot gave me their amber heart for my birthday, and I have kept it in my pocket, but I am always afraid that I will lose it." Hallie runs her hand over the soft pouch. "This will be just right for keeping their gift safe. Thanks!"

"You're welcome. Now you better head off to bed. You look tired kiddo."

"On my way. I'll see you in the morning." Hallie gives Joan another hug and heads up the steps.

Against the wall in the center of her room, is an old iron bed with crackled white paint. It is covered with a plush chenille comforter topped with an antique doll sitting amongst a collection of pillows at the head of the bed. There is a night stand with a lamp and picture on it beside the bed. Hallie picks up the picture of a young girl with a cheerful smile. She is sitting under a tree and has a small American flag in her hand. Hallie remembers this is a picture of Joan's older sister, Priscilla, and that she had tragically died shortly after the picture was taken.

Hallie sets the picture back down and gently moves the doll placing it on the rocking chair nearby and pulls back the comforter. She puts her amber heart, pressed penny and leather pouch on the night stand before turning the light out and climbs into bed. The curtains are sheer and the shade has not been drawn, so the light from the moon filters into the room gently illuminating the furniture and decorations. A slight twinkling of light plays against the wall opposite from her that seems to be reflecting from something outside her room, but she is too exhausted to give it much thought. Despite the light taking on a dance with explosive bursts coming and going in swirls just like the light on the black stone in the Bruton's Parish, it quickly fades from her vision as her eyes gratefully close, and she drifts off into a haunted and restless sleep. She does not see the tangle of flashing light erupting from the wall out towards her.

Chapter 7, Combustion

Hallie tosses in her sleep as voices drift through her mind. The small tear in time she slipped through in the graveyard seems to have expanded pulling her back once again disguised as a dream.

§

"Hester, quickly cover the grimoire with this bit of weaving." Resmelda works to conceal a few other items she uses for her dark magic and rituals. "He has come up over the dune and is nearing the cottage." She speaks in low tones because the windows are opened to allow the sea breeze in. Mister White steps onto the porch just as she slides the last container behind a less incriminating basket of freshly gathered shells. She smoothes her apron and glances at Hester who is sitting, tatting a piece of lace averting her eyes from any reproachful look that Resmelda might send her way. A knock comes, and Resmelda opens the door, catching Harry a bit off-guard by her quick response.

"Ah, hello, Miss Bigelow. I am hoping I have not been too forward in coming by without invitation, but I am wondering if you will take a moment to walk with me. I would like to talk, if you have some time."

Resmelda considers him for a moment sensing he is ill-at-ease, but unsure if it is due to discomfort with the impromptu visit or something else. She senses a whisper for caution blow by and opts to delay answering his question. "Mister White." Her expression softens as she smiles at him. "I see that you have fully regained your strength. It will serve you well when dealing with your partner, Mister Holt." She cares enough about Harry to attempt to open his eyes to the true nature of his business partner.

He merely smiles and asks again very politely, "Is this a good time for you? I can always return later in the day, if you desire."

"No, I can come with you. Hester and I were merely doing some handwork, and it will be nice to have a break." She steps out onto the porch of the small cottage. Its clapboard siding is worn by the sea air, and the porch boards creak beneath their feet. There are seashells that Hester has strung by the dozens to create wind chimes hanging all along the eaves, and there is a small table holding a vase tied with a delicate bow containing purple irises sitting between two rocking chairs that are swaying in the breeze. A brazen seagull perches on the arm of one of the chairs intently watching the couple.

Resmelda takes Harry in. "Yes, you have most definitely regained your strength. I can see from your effortless walk across these sandy dunes. A truly robust constitution has bloomed, but I detect an ailment in your nature today none-the-less. Tell me what is on your mind Mister White."

"Miss Bigelow, I have a true appreciation for your straight forward nature," he says with regard. "I have come to tell you that I am leaving. It has come to my attention that Mister Holt has traveled to Tangier making a chance liaison with a former colleague, Mister Marcus Butler, who has made an offer to work some of our future expeditions for exchange of goods as well as acquirement of contracts with merchants along the eastern shore of the Virginia Colony. I no longer seem to have the temperament for traveling very great distances by water, and I am considering this offer. However, I would like to consult with some of my business colleagues back home before I come to an agreement with Mister Holt and Mister Butler over this matter. I am departing for Williamsburg for this purpose, and to seek investors as well as other resources for the endeavor should an agreement be reached. I am going to head out taking our crew and ship, and I will be leaving early on the morrow with the high tide. Mister Holt will travel a few days after aboard Mister Butler's schooner. He has stated that he has a separate business arrangement concerning one of his other holdings that needs to be taken care of before returning to Williamsburg."

They walk a short distance before Resmelda responds. "Mister White, I am happy that you will be able to make this trip home a healthy man. I know the son you have spoken of so many times will be glad to have you back home." They walk a little further along the beach and Resmelda considers her next words carefully. Despite their friendship, she remains wary of stepping out of boundaries that she uncharacteristically is unsure exist.

"We have not known each other long, but I recognize you are a good man, and I would like to give you a word of caution in regards to your potential business partners. You are not a fool, and I hope that you are not offended by my comment, but I wish for you to take care if you form a partnership with Mister Butler and Mister Holt. Each lack moral fiber, and I fear that an alliance between you and the two of them has potential to lead to your demise."

Harry feigns surprise. "I should say, 'such harsh words,' were it anyone but you speaking Miss Bigelow. Because it *is* you I will simply say, thank you." Harry stops to pick up a piece of worn shell from the sand tossing it into the rolling water. "It is not my desire to discuss my business partners. I only bring them up to explain to you my departure."

"Of course, Mister White."

He rubs the back of his head and goes on, "I would like to invite you to join me in Williamsburg. I would appreciate an opportunity to get to know you better, let you get to know me better, and for you and my son to get acquainted. I would very much like you to give this consideration. Hester would be welcomed to come with you."

Resmelda stops walking, and so Harry stops as well. It is a moment before she responds. "Mister White….I am…unsure of what to say to you. You may believe that you have clearer thinking, and that you feel you have come to know me somewhat well during the time we have spent together the past few weeks; however, I must be honest with you. Like your business partners, I am not sure an alliance with me is in your best interest. You do not know me as you think."

"Hence the invitation," Harry quickly adds before she can say more. "I understand your hesitancy. I know more about you than you are aware, and I am willing for you to decide on this matter at your discretion. I am asking for an opportunity for us to get to know each other better. I only wish for you to know the invitation is there. I will send a servant to you from Mister McKemmie's with my contact information. If you do not want to travel with me now, you can choose to come at a future time, or you can decline. I only ask you consider my offer and then make me aware of your decision when you are ready. I am a patient man. What say you to this invitation?"

Resmelda takes a long and disbelieving look into his gentle eyes and kind face. *Could Sophia have been right about him?* Resmelda has never had good experiences with men. Her younger years were plagued with a variety of abuses. She struggles to allow consideration of a life within the light and no follies into the darkness in order to feed her revenge. She hesitantly speaks up, "Let us give this some time. We have had time together, and now let us take time apart to see what becomes of the decision. I will either find way to your home, or I will send written word to you. I cannot tell you when this will happen.

"My Sophia's girls are due on the island this day, or the next, as it is our usual summer routine. They spend some time here with me each summer, and I take them home at the end of the season spending the colder months in Onancock. I keep a permanent residence there. Sophia is a friend…she is like a little sister…and she lives there with her family. I have an obligation to see her girls returned home and soon winter will follow, so it will be at least until the spring before I will make a decision. Can you live with this?"

Harry's face brightens. "Yes, I am sure that I can. Thank you." With this he takes her hand in his, a gold ring with a green stone on his finger glints in the sun light as he bends to tenderly kiss her hand. He holds onto her hand gazing into her face.

Is he contemplating a kiss? Resmelda regards his dark brown eyes, a small scar to the side of his left eye, the way the sea breeze causes the slightest flutter in his hair, and how the streaks of silver in his hair catch the late afternoon light. It seems that only a thin line of etiquette prevents him from yielding to an apparent great desire to place the same gentle kiss he gave her hand upon her lips. She has to restrain herself from leaning any closer to him. Her blood runs hot, and a soft flutter comes to life within her.

The moment is brief. He straightens his back, but does not release her hand when he turns and leads her back to the dune crossing.

Once it is reached, Harry stops. He releases her hand and the sea breeze cools her palm making it feel naked and empty. He takes his wallet out removing a small blue feather with black stripes and a white tip from inside the wallet, and holds it up between himself and Resmelda.

"A blue jay feather?" Resmelda's eyes light with amusement.

"Yes, my son found it some years ago just before I left for a business trip. We are not often apart from one another, but occasionally business requires a separation. He gave me the feather saying it would remind me of home when I was gone. When I came back home I returned the feather to him. Each time a departure occurred we repeated the exchange, and it became a ritual of sorts. Even at nearly twenty years of age, he made sure that I had the feather before leaving on this voyage. It has brought me comfort during the more challenging times of the trip. I would like for you to take it until you are able to come to us, my son and me."

Resmelda reaches up and encloses her hand over the feather and Harry's hand. She bites her lower lip and smiles at him taking the feather. The touch of his skin against her hand re-ignites the feeling of warmth that now rises up her arm towards her heart.

"Thank you, Mister White." She brushes the feather against her lips giving him a parting smile as she turns off the beach towards her cottage. She feels an unfamiliar ache in her heart as she walks away from him and turns back. He is still standing there, watching her, he waves, and she raises her hand up in farewell as she backs away until he is out of her view.

Just off in the distance, both Harry and Resmelda are unaware of Holt's presence as he sits in the sea grass and reed with a bottle of drink in hand and a temper brewing within. His eyes set dark as though scorched by an evil fire.

§

Breathing somewhat irregularly, Hallie turns restlessly in her bed. There are tiny beads of sweat on her forehead, and her eyes move rapidly underneath their closed lids. The electric dance of light continues to spark along her bedroom wall. Trapped in her dream, she is now in the kitchen at the McKemmie house. She flinches in her sleep when she hears Holt's angry voice bellowing to the kitchen maid.

§

He bursts into the room and barks that he will be taking his evening meal in his quarters. Despite the fact that the master of the house has returned, Holt maintains an entitled attitude towards the household slaves whenever McKemmie isn't around. The kitchen maid is stirring a pot of clam chowder on the stove. The creamy soup fills the kitchen with a hint of the ocean and the savory smell of onions, potatoes, and fresh herbs. Her young son is clinging to her skirt terrified by the brash man, and her husband is sitting at a small table eating a bowl of the chowder. He gives her a cautionary look, and he waits for Holt to be well-clear of the kitchen before speaking.

"That man is some bad news, Melba. You keep Samuel out of his path. Mista McKemmie ain't the only one 'round here gonna be glad when he's gone."

Melba bends to comfort Samuel, and then ladles him a bowl of chowder sitting it down on the table by his father. He climbs up into his father's lap to eat his meal. "I'm thinking that advice would be good for you too Jake."

"Best I can, Melba. I try. Mista White is much better now and is gonna be leaving in the mornin'. I know things gonna be tough 'til them other two git on their way." He suddenly stops with a spoonful of his chowder half-way to his mouth. "Oh, Lordy I done forgot! Mista White wanted me to bring this here note over to Miss Resmelda." He taps a piece of parchment folded inside his shirt pocket. "I needs to get on over there before it gets too dark. I know we are beholding to her for saving young Samuel here when he was born, and probably you too Melba, but she gits my nerves all in a twist."

"Yes, Jake, I know she do. She is a right powerful creature, but I'm thinkin' only those up to no good are the ones needin' to fear her."

"Maybe, but how she judges who is doin' no good and who ain't just ain't all that clear to me. I just assume keep my distance when I can." He lifts the bowl to his mouth drinking down the last bit. He wipes his mouth on his sleeve and lifts his son as he stands turning to put the boy back on the chair. Samuel adjusts to sit on his knees so the table won't be too high for him to finish his meal. Jake gives him a pat on his head before turning to give his wife an affectionate peck on the cheek. Then he heads out of the kitchen towards the yard where he left his walking stick.

He makes his way along the back side of the house towards the beach when he hears Holt talking to Butler through an open window near the end of the house.

"When I think of what I have spent in time and energy to get this partnership going with Harry White it boils my blood. The idiot has become smitten with that supercilious wench and is going to ruin all my effort. By my plan, he is to marry my step-daughter and secure my grip on both business and personal holdings for White Plantation."

The smooth conniving voice of Butler answers, "From what you said, your girl Melinda has laid out a bed of affection for him. Once he returns to Williamsburg, and is away from here, she can again compel him deeper into her charms. He will soon forget about Resmelda."

"I am not so sure. He was not as deeply attached to my Melinda as I would have liked. How do you know the name of this woman? Tell me what you know of her that may be of assistance in thwarting White's affections."

Jake ducks behind a bush near the window. He fears discovery, yet he wants to hear more of what is being said.

"How important is this information to you Holt?" Butler's voice becomes enticing.

"If it results in the end I want, I will cut you in at twenty percent on the haul from my last trip to Charleston."

"Ah, now. That would be a tempting bargain, but I think that a service such as I can offer you is worth at least thirty percent of that booty."

There is a pause in the conversation before Holt breaks the silence. "Very well then, tell me what you have."

Butler gives a crooked smile and leans forward in his chair. "I have known Resmelda Bigelow since she was a young girl. She and her brother were quite a pair—unattached to any sort of family just living wild in the woods. Him concocting all sorts of odd works, and her unnatural abilities putting everyone near her on edge. It was dodgy. I later learned she stowed away on one of my vessels traveling down from Salem way. Of course I never knew it at the time, and I don't know what happened to her brother. There is much speculation about her, and her dealings with the devil." He takes a deep draw from his pipe and exhales a thick plume of pungent smoke. It snakes its way out the window towards Jake's hiding place. Jake's eyes burn, but what he is hearing gives him a greater discomfort. His chest squeezes tight like a snake has him in its coils.

"Are you saying she is a witch?" Jake hears the sneer in Holt's voice and his heart races with anxiety. Holt continues, "This is good information, if you can provide convincing proof. I will take this to White and persuade him not only of severing his ties to this woman, but also seeking prosecution and punishment for any magic we can associate her with." Holt stands up and walks towards the open window.

Jake fidgets and holds his breath looking up to see it is starting to get dark. He moves out of his hiding spot and rushes to warn Resmelda. In his hurry to get away, he doesn't notice the piece of parchment when it falls from his pocket onto the ground beneath the shrubbery nor that he has left his walking stick behind.

Back in the room, the conversation continues. Butler interjects, "I am not sure drawing White's attention to the fact that she is a witch is a good idea."

Holt listens intently.

"Perhaps, you should let him go on his voyage in the morning no wiser. Once he is on his way, you confront the witch, and have her arrested and brought to justice in a manner that silences her for good."

"Yes, this is quite wise my friend, but I am not willing to wait until he is gone. The fool may make a second attempt to convince her to leave with him before he departs. It needs to be done tonight." Holt's eyes show a glint of cruelty. "How can we be sure there will be no retribution by the witch?"

Butler puffs on his pipe and his brow furrows until an idea lights on his face. "She must be separated from her home and companions."

Holt paces the floor. "For God's sake man, how will that get accomplished? I am expected back at Williamsburg not too long after White."

"You take her with you. She can be disposed of along the way back to Williamsburg."

"Do you know how much money is going to be needed to insure silence over this matter?" Holt jerks his head, and an incredulous scowl contorts his face.

"Do you have the resources?"

"Yes, of course I do." Holt spits the words out.

"Then, this is what needs to be done. The potential return on your money is great, if what you have told me of White's holdings is true."

Holt regroups as he continues to pace the room stirring Butler's pipe smoke into frantic circles. "Yes, yes I can see this working out. Let us put together our heads and whittle the details."

Outside, in the moonlight, Jake runs nearly the entire way crossing over the dunes by Resmelda's cottage out of breath, his lungs burning. He stops for a moment leaning over with his hands on his knees to catch his breath. Lights from the cottage windows and torches near the porch, as well as the laughter of children and Hester's singing, let him know he is close. His heart stalls and panic steals what breath he has left when he realizes that Miss Sophia's girls are here already. Collecting himself he runs down toward the house.

"Jake," Resmelda speaks to him from her rocking chair. The girls are in the front yard playing games in the torchlight. Their shadows dance along behind them on the sandy ground. "What brings you here in such a state of agitation?"

Jake gives her a breathy explanation. "Miss Resmelda, beggin' your pardon, but I have come to warn you." He hesitates glancing nervously towards the girls, but Resmelda gives a nod encouraging him to go on. "The travelin' men have accused you of black magic and are comin' to take you away."

"Who are you speaking of? Mister Holt and Mister Butler?"

"Yes, ma'am. And they's bringing Mista White too!"

"Are you sure Mister White is involved?"

"Yes, ma'am. I heard Mista Holt saying they's all coming over here to have you taken in."

Resmelda stands resolutely. "Thank you, Jake. You need to get back to Mister McKemmie's. I know you do not like to be about in the dark. I will take care of this." She looks at him from the end of her nose.

Jake hesitates briefly and turns patting each of the towhead girls on the shoulder before leaving. The girls watch him go before turning expectantly towards Resmelda.

Resmelda looks towards Hester. "You need to gather the girls' things. I want you all to stay with Jake and Melba. You will be safe there. I am going to prepare for a protective charm…and other works." She removes the blue jay feather from the book she has been reading, holding it up, and twirling it between her fingers. "That will assure payment for such treachery."

"No! You cannot do this. I know he is innocent of this, and that feather is a shared possession. You will send ill will to the son who has nothing to do with this." Hester's plea is desperate and louder than she intends. She cowers back a step.

"All the better," she hisses towards Hester. "No one suffers more than one who has lost a child."

The two girls are now standing hand-in-hand and fidgeting.

Resmelda feels their eyes on her, and she turns planting gentle smile on her face, "Beatrice and Dominica, do not worry. We are going to play a wonderful game, but we need Samuel to be a part of the fun. I want you to go with Hester to find him, and when you do Hester will help you play the game. Once you have had all the fun you can you will lay your heads to rest. When you wake in the morning Miss Melba will have the most wonderful breakfast for you." She walks over to grasp each of their hands forming a circle and leans over slightly to meet them at eye level. The moon and torchlight dance in their eyes and she realizes that, although they favor their father, they have Sophia's eyes—hazel eyes.

The taller of the two speaks up, "That sounds like it might be fun. Will you come and meet us in the morning to share in the breakfast?"

"Yes, I will. So, you are up for the adventure then?"

The girl turns to her younger sister asking, "What do you think Beattie? Do you want to go see Samuel with Hester tonight?"

"Sure, Dot. I have missed playing with Samuel *and* Miss Melba's good cooking."

§

Hallie struggles to wake feeling that every limb is glued to the bed. Her eyes refuse to open. Her airway refuses to cooperate as she struggles to breath. Then instantly, sleep's hold is broken, and she shoots bolt upright clinging to a pillow as she gasps working to slow her breathing. The dancing lights crumble to the floor with a final sparkle before they sizzle out. She releases the pillow and wipes the sweat from her forehead running her hand down the side of her face holding it over her mouth trying to make sense of the dream.

Were Beattie and Dot on my mind so much today that my subconscious worked them into this dream-version of Dot's story? The vivid details of the dream dance in her mind. It revealed so much more of the tragic love story than Dot ever did. *Where did the two girls come from?* The story is taking on a life of its own just like in the graveyard earlier today—no yesterday, as she looks at the clock seeing two-fifteen in blue digital format. The room is dark except for the moonlight filtering in and the glow from the clock.

Hallie collects herself and gets up to get a drink of water from the bathroom. She comes back and stands by the back window of the room. The cool night breeze is soothing against her skin, and she looks out towards the outbuilding seeing a stream of light from its side window. The green pickup truck is parked in the yard. She ponders where Liam is from, and how he ended up here living with Joan. He definitely has a handsome face and those dark brown eyes are like magnets. Her heart flutters. She rubs her chest.

She turns away from the window, and sits on the bed looking at the amber heart and the pressed coin from the bridge-tunnel. It seems like a lifetime since yesterday morning and crossing the bay. Picking up the beautiful pouch that Joan gave her, she loosens the opening slipping both inside. She pulls the strings closing the bag and grasps it in her hand as she climbs back into bed laying her head on the pillow where she finds a more restful sleep.

Chapter 8, Luculent

Wiccan Rede

Bide the Wiccan Laws we must In Perfect Love and Perfect Trust.
Live and let live. Fairly take and fairly give.
Cast the Circle thrice about to keep the evil spirits out.
To bind the spell every time let the spell be spake in rhyme.
Soft of eye and light of touch, speak little, listen much.

Hallie awakens in the morning with the same cool breeze from the night gently blowing into her room. She sees that the brilliant moon remains visible in the morning sky as well. The sun has not risen above the mountain ridge, but its brightness promises a beautiful day.

She glances at the clock. *Huh, only seven o'clock.* The haunting dream from the night before is still very vivid in her mind while she sets into motion preparations for the day.

Hallie makes her bed finding the leather pouch with its contents under her pillow. She sets the pouch on her night stand and pulls some clothes from her bag. *I have to get unpacked, but not right now.* She bites down on a smile anticipating going to the park with Joan to take a look around and maybe see the horse.

The shear curtains billow in, and she goes to the window. The green truck is gone, and a twinge of disappointment catches her off guard. *That is going to have to stop.* She sees someone in the yard. *Is that Joan heading to the woods for a walk? What a great way to start the day.* Hallie pulls her toiletry kit from her bag and makes her way down the hall to freshen up before heading to the kitchen.

She comes downstairs wearing a pair of shorts, t-shirt, and old tennis shoes tattered and worn-in to perfection. She grabs a glass of orange juice and steps out onto the back porch. Joan did not go for a walk in the woods but remains at the edge of the yard near an old stone that is flat on top. *I love that stone.* Memories of the smooth texture and its warmth when she lounged on it enjoying summer afternoons playing or reading during previous visits surface. There is a weeping willow near the stone, and its branches sway low creating a fluid yet sheltered space.

She closes her eyes remembering the gentle rustle of tree branches, feeling the soft breeze, and smelling the tangy sweetness of the bordering woods. Hallie smiles and opens her eyes to watch Joan with casual interest. She is walking in a circle with a small bundle that wafts tufts of smoke into the air. Joan is waving a hand coaxing the smoke outward as she completes her circle and repeats the motion two more times. Hallie notices there are several items set up on the stone. The hairs on her arms stand straight. Her interest percolates, and she feels a strong desire to walk closer but is afraid of interrupting the ritual.

Joan sits before the stone, meditating for quite a while. Hallie is startled when Joan stands and collects her items up placing them carefully into a bag before turning back towards the house. *Should I stay on the porch? Should I go into the house, so it doesn't look like I'm spying?* She opts for staying on the porch and sits on the loveseat, sipping her juice.

Joan climbs the steps opening the screen door and steps onto the porch. "Hallie, you're up so early! Come on in the house and let me fix you some breakfast." Joan is already walking into the kitchen and stands by the door coaxing Hallie inside.

"You gonna make some of those great pancakes you used to make for me when I was little?" Hallie asks, heading towards the door.

"You know I am. I even have some nice blueberries for them."

"What can I do to help with breakfast?"

"Not a thing now. You sit down there and chat with me while I get things going. You think you could do with some eggs and bacon, too?"

"You know me. I can definitely eat when it comes to meal time."

"Alright then, a full breakfast it is." Joan gets busy with preparations, and Hallie watches from the kitchen table. It is a beautiful handmade table that Joan's husband crafted. He died before Hallie and her aunts started making their trips to Southwest Virginia, and, although Hallie never met him, remnants of his skillful handwork adorn the cozy farmhouse.

Hallie, studies the grain of the wood, sipping her juice as she hesitates to ask her next question. "Joan?"

"Yes, Hallie?" Joan doesn't turn to look at her. The bacon is beginning to crackle in the skillet filling the room with its aroma.

"I was wondering if you would tell me about what you were doing out in the yard by the big flat rock."

"Well, of course. It's not something I get to do every morning, but I try to. It is a morning ritual of thanks, and verbalization of requests or goals for the day that I wish to accomplish."

"What about the smoke and items on the rock?"

"The 'smoke' is actually burning sage. I like to use it to define a circle of purity. There's lots of ways to set a circle, but I like to use sage."

"I see. Is it like smudging? I have seen that done with Native American rituals and healing ceremonies before."

"Yes, in a sense it is. My ritual has a Wiccan foundation though." Joan continues casually.

"You mean, like witchcraft?" Hallie's jaw nearly drops.

"Hallie, are you okay?"

Am I? She takes a breath in. *Yes, I'm good, but oh my God. Resmelda, yes definitely witch stuff there. But, Joan?*

"Hallie?" Joan starts to walk towards her

Hallie clears her throat. "So… are you a witch?" Hallie furrows her brow. "I mean, I remember going to church with you on Sundays. I don't *ever* remember any witchcraft, spells, or other stuff like that."

"Yes, that's right. I'm Christian, but I come from a long line of witches. I prefer Wiccan for myself though. It is more a religious experience for me than the practice of witchcraft. I choose to honor the pagan rituals and incorporate them into my Christian beliefs as well."

Hallie nods her head and then looks down to study the grain of the wood table again.

Joan stops her preparations to look at her. "Hallie you look very confused. Is this information new to you? I would have thought you had some exposure to it all with Beattie and Dot."

It is as if someone gave her head a firm pluck and she looks up. "Umm… no. Not with Beattie and Dot." *At least I don't think so.* She had to admit though that her recent visions had hinted in this direction. *Joan will think I am crazy, if I go off about my 'Resmelda' visions. How can Joan and Resmelda be one-in-the-same? How can Beattie and Dot be? Or, is there more to all this?* She clears her throat. "I guess I don't see how Christianity is compatible with witchcraft or Wicca or…whatever. Don't witches have a connection to the devil or something like that?"

Joan puts her hand on her hip. "Black magic—a different type of witchcraft. Yes. But, that's not what I am doing. I practice Wicca, and I could cast within the light, but I don't. It's complicated I suppose for someone standing on the outside." Her brow furrows. "So, you are saying you have never…"

"No, not at all."

"Okay, well for me, and your aunts by the way, it is a spiritual connection to the Creator and the Earth with all of the gifts that come from them. I look for a balance in my life with nature. I do not actively perform magic, but some Wiccan's do. For me, 'magic' is everywhere, if you know how to look for it. It is not something I choose to conjure, although I could. I prefer to find my connection with God, our Creator, and nature through rituals that help me center. And, with meditation to open my mind in order to achieve goals. Interpretation of the faith is widely varied." Joan goes back to finishing up the bacon.

Hallie fidgets with her hands. *What about Resmelda? There is no way I can ask Joan about her.* She shakes her head slightly and frowns.

Joan turns her head to look at Hallie and raises her eye brows. "You know, I had no idea that Beattie and Dot never shared this with you. I hope I have not crossed a line. Maybe I should call them."

No! Hallie flinches, but catches the word before it surfaces. "Uh, no. Please don't. I think I would like to ask them myself. You know." She shrugs her shoulder.

"Well, okay, but talk to them soon."

"Yes, soon. I will." Hallie bites her lower lip. "Joan, I need to ask you about dark magic, demons and devils, and stuff like that."

Joan finishes the bacon setting it aside and starts mixing up the pancakes. "Need to?"

"Yes. Uh, want to."

"Is there a reason?"

"Curiosity." *Don't lie.* "Mostly." *Okay, a white lie.*

Joan nods and purses her lips. "There is light and dark in all aspects of mankind, Hallie. Practitioners of the dark arts have different approaches to conjure a desired result. Some use summoning spells to bring forth different demons or deities that can serve a variety of requests. There is usually some sort of bargain entailed with the process. Such practices often carry a high price. You know the expression 'be careful what you ask for' right?"

Hallie nods.

"Well, most practitioners of the dark arts are invoking requests that are not for the greater good. In Wicca, there is a credo to do no harm."

"Do you think someone could do both white and black magic, Joan?"

"Sure. There is something called gray magic similar to what you ask. I think though that eventually a person has to choose." She flips a pancake. "It's all about balance."

Hallie thinks about Resmelda. "Choose, or be pushed." *Did I just say that out loud?* She grimaces and shakes her head.

Joan folds her arms and leans against the counter. "Halle, what's really on your mind this morning?"

"Oh, it's just this vis…uh, weird dream I had last night. Then, I saw you this morning, and it kind of put me off balance I guess."

"Huh." She tilts her head to the side. Hallie feels like Joan is about to say more but changes her mind.

The sound of the green truck pulling around the back corner of the house catches Hallie's attention. She unwittingly blushes taking a quick survey of herself.

It is not missed by Joan who looks towards the window and back to Hallie smiling with a sparkle in her eye. "Yes, there is all kinds of magic afoot, if you know what I mean."

Hallie looks at Joan giving her a reluctant smile. The back door opens and Liam walks in. He steals a look Hallie's way and then to Joan as she is finishing up a batch of scrambled eggs. She pulls an extra plate from the cabinet.

"Good morning," Liam says. He stops short looking back from Joan to Hallie. "Have I interrupted something? If so, I apologize."

"Well, good morning Liam," Joan says. "No, not at all. Hallie and I were just discussing the many colors of witchcraft."

Liam's shoulder spasms and he stretches out his chin as if releasing a kink in his neck. His face reddens, and he darts a look Hallie's way and then down at the floor.

What was that all about? She sends Joan a questioning look. Her leg starts to bounce and she drops her hand onto her knee to force it to still.

Joan flashes her back a quick shrug and crooked grimace. "Just silly talk really." She clears her throat and swats her hand. "I see you got an early start. Did you get over to Mister Hairston's for the hay already?"

A change in subject. Thank you. Hallie takes a deep breath.

Liam looks over to Joan and his face softens. "Yes, ma'am, the bales are in the truck. I thought I would stop back by here before heading over to the park. I was there late last night, and the mare is doing pretty well."

"I am really glad to hear that." Hallie looks up.

Liam gives her a thin smile.

"That's fine," Joan says as she sets a plate on the table for Liam and has him sit down. She reaches across the table and sets a plate down for Hallie giving her a quick wink. "That horse is in good hands, so she is bound to get better. Hal made mention of maybe helping out with her a little today. Perhaps she can ride over with you to the park after breakfast. I have a few things I want to get finished up here before I head in."

"That may not work out."

Hallie's leg has to be stopped once more. *Really?* She is unsure if it is Joan or Liam that pushes her heart rate into overdrive.

Joan looks at Liam and raises an eyebrow.

"Well, I am working today, and Mister Perkins may have other things for me to do."

"Well, you can just bring Hallie up to activity building, if he does. She has paper work to get done today, and you both need to see the safety videos. A few others are coming in as well."

Hallie feels that she has slipped back into the sick room of Harry White. Invisible. She focuses on her breakfast.

"Yes, ma'am, I suppose that would work," Liam forfeits the objection and hesitates before looking over to Hallie. "That is, if you want to do that."

Hallie is in the middle of drinking some orange juice. She gets the juice swallowed with effort dribbling a bit on her chin, and wipes it with her hand while nodding. "Sure, that's fine with me." She tries to keep her words cool and quickly re-focuses on her breakfast.

Liam gives a single nod of his head.

"Good then, that's settled." Joan smiles broadly. "Liam, keep your two-way radio with you—no cell service at the park, Hal. I will call you, if I need you to head on up."

"Yes, ma'am." Liam carries his plate to the sink. "I will wait outside."

"Okay, then. I'll be right out." Hallie says as he is walking out the door. She clears her plate.

"I'm so sorry, Hal. Who knew he would have a reaction like that."

"It's okay. I guess he doesn't see how the 'colors of witchcraft' fit into breakfast conversation. I'm not sure I understand it either, but I appreciate you explaining some to me. I guess there is just so much I don't know. Never really thought of I guess." She smooths her shirt.

"Yes, so I gathered. I'm glad you asked though. Just let me know, if you have more questions. And, have that chat with Beattie and Dot soon."

"I will. I better be going though."

"Right.

Hallie rushes upstairs. She pauses in front of the mirror of her dresser shrugging, no make-up, hair piled up on her head with some loose strands hanging down, old t-shirt. "Ugh," she gasps in frustration over her appearance, but quickly pulls back her shoulders and replaces it with, "Good enough." She grabs her back pack, and heads out of her room to get on with the rest of her day. She stops abruptly, remembering her pouch and its contents, and goes back scooping it up off the night stand fixing the leather lacing through a belt loop on her shorts. She pulls the back pack over one shoulder and heads down the stairs.

Chapter 9, Warmth

The heart speaks a language the mind cannot even hear, let alone understand.
Anonymous

The sweet smell of the hay catches Hallie's attention as she approaches the truck. There are a couple bags of grain and several square bales of fresh hay stacked in the back. Liam is leaning against the passenger side door and opens it when she walks up. Hallie stops short and looks at him.

"That's not necessary."

"Yes, I am aware." Yet, he doesn't move.

She shakes her head and steps up into the truck, and he shuts the door just as she moves her leg inside. Hallie startles and looks his way, but he is already walking around the truck.

Silence leads off the drive to the park until Liam breaks it. "So, is it Hallie or Hal?"

"Excuse me?"

"Your name. Last night you said Hallie, but this morning Joan referred to you as Hal."

"Hallie." *Really? What difference does it make?* She sighs. *Be nice, Hallie.* "It's a nick name my Aunt Beattie has for me. Joan uses it sometimes."

He nods, but stays focused on the road.

She looks his way seeing his tan arm with a ripple of muscle disappearing beneath the sleeve of his t-shirt. Only a bit of the scar she saw last night is visible, its tentacles snaking up his forearm. His dark hair is shiny and thick and, although mostly straight, there is a slight curl just above the collar of his shirt behind his right ear.

He glances over at her, and Hallie blushes realizing she has probably been staring longer than she should. "So, how long have you been living at Joan's place?" She opts to initiate conversation hoping to cover her embarrassment.

"It has been about a year now. She did not really know me well before then, but I had been to the park a couple times, and she always made a point to talk to me. She told me one day that she liked me, thought I needed an opportunity to do something different for myself, and invited me to work at the park for the rest of the summer. She said they had an employee who broke his arm, and they needed to fill the position. I was not living close enough for it to be feasible, and so she made arrangements for me to stay with her." He speaks keeping his eyes on the road, and barely shakes his head adding, "I still cannot believe all the trouble she went through for me. It has meant a lot."

"I'm sure. My aunts and I have always thought a lot of Joan. She has a kind soul."

Liam looks over at Hallie. "Yes, it is something how a person's soul can shine through when you really look. Or, I guess, know how to look." He turns his attention back to the road as they pull into the park entrance.

Hallie isn't quite sure what Liam means about looking at a soul, he didn't elaborate, and she didn't ask, but the esoteric feeling it inspired stays in the cab until they reach the stable. Liam pulls the truck into a parking area and crosses over a grassy field next to the stable. Although, horses officially are no longer kept on the premises, the buildings are still well cared for. He backs the truck up to a set of sliding doors before shutting off the engine.

"Would you like to see the mare before I start unloading the hay and grain?" He asks.

Her eyes light up. "I would love that!" She reaches for the truck door handle and is out of the truck before Liam can walk around to open the door. He smiles at her excitement.

"Have you been around horses much?" Liam asks.

"A bit. I have a friend back home who has horses. He and I used to ride on the beach whenever we could. There's a horse rescue near where I live too, and I have volunteered there doing mostly grooming and stall cleaning."

"Ah, yes—stall cleaning—always the best part of having a horse around."

They both laugh and Liam opens the stable door for Hallie. They step into the center aisle which is flanked by stalls. Most serving as storage areas. They walk through the cool stable, and she can hear movement. The horse must sense that they are in the barn because she becomes still, and Hallie can only hear breathing now. They approach the stall and Liam calls out gently to the mare.

"Hey, girl, how are you doing?"

She brings her head over the stall door and nickers quietly towards Liam. She is a deep chestnut color with a long red mane and tail. Hallie can see that she is breathing slightly labored, but she is alert and responsive to Liam's voice.

"That a girl." Liam talks soothingly to the horse as he unlatches the stall door and makes his way in. Hallie stays back not wanting to startle her. The wound on her chest looks severe. The stitches are holding with some dried blood on them, but no other drainage. Liam looks into the water bucket. "Good, she drank most of the water. Looks like she has nibbled a bit at the grass I brought in for her last night, hopefully, she will take to the hay. Mister Hairston sent a couple bags of grain for her too, so I will have to see how she does with that."

"Liam, she looks good for having been through so much."

"Yes, but time will tell. Infection can set in quickly. I will need to wash her wound off this morning to keep it clean and keep proud flesh from developing. She also has an antibiotic shot that I need to give daily for the next few days." He strokes the side of her neck firmly but gently. The mare turns her head towards him nuzzling the side of his face. Then she turns towards Hallie with her velvety nose and takes a sniff stretching closer to where Hallie stands.

"Here, come in and meet each other." He makes room for Hallie. His demeanor is so much more relaxed.

Hallie steps into the stall and holds her hand up to the mare's nose. She runs her hand over the mare's face up near her ears rubbing them. The horse presses her head towards Hallie's hand, her eyes relax, and her lower lip hangs a bit looser. Hallie laughs.

"I think you found her 'chocolate' spot." Liam laughs. "She likes you."

"Well, I like her too. She seems like a very sweet horse. How could she have gotten herself into so much trouble?"

"No telling, and I am not sure we will find out any time soon. Will we Acacia?" Liam rubs the mare's back.

"Acacia? So, have you given her a name already?"

"Oh, I guess I have. I, um, actually had a horse very much like her a long time ago named Acacia. I suppose the familiarity just brought the name up for me."

Hallie looks from the mare to Liam. There is a slight flush to his face and the muscle of his jaw tightens, but he relaxes quickly as he focuses on the horse. The scar on his arm is evident as he strokes the mare's back, but he does not hide it from Hallie's view as he had done last night. She feels the distance between them shrink a bit.

"That is a pretty name, but it's unusual. Isn't Acacia a tree? I think I remember reading something about its wood and King Solomon and the Free Masons too."

"Yes. Actually, my uncle had named my horse, and he was a Free Mason. It's remarkable that you know about them."

"Why?"

"Well, they are a bit of a secret society."

"Oh, well not so much with Google. I had a school project on legends and lore."

"Yes, I see."

"But, you were telling me about your uncle and the horse you had when you were younger. Go on."

"Well, he gave her to me when she was just a filly. I was having a bit of a rough time back then, and she had a rough beginning. Her mother was killed by coyotes, and she was injured pretty badly herself. Much like this horse has been. They look very similar, so the name just seems natural I guess. Hopefully, this Acacia will have the same vigor as the one from my past and heal just as well. She looks good now, but that can change quickly. Do you have much experience with sick or injured horses from your rescue work?"

"Yes, a bit." She answers him. Sunlight is filtering in through the stable windows giving her hair and hazel eyes a deep glow.

Liam looks at her for a moment, and she thinks he may have forgotten that he asked her a question, but he suddenly turns back to the mare to rub her back. He clears his throat. "Well, good then. Perhaps you can be of some help with her over the next several days."

"Yes, I'd like that."

"Excellent. I will get her hay and grain into the barn, and you can groom her, if you would like." He unlatches the water bucket from its holder and moves towards the stall door.

"I would love to, but do you need help?" Hallie starts to step out of the stall.

"No, that is okay." He reaches for a brush that is on the ledge outside the stall, and moves it towards Hallie, and walks away.

Hallie watches him go and then reaches for the brush turning to Acacia. "He is a hard person to read. Don't you think?" The mare stands swishing her tail, but offers no opinion.

The barn is quiet and peaceful. She starts grooming Acacia who stands relaxed as Hallie brushes her neck and back. The horse's respirations and gentle swish of her tail add to the soothing environment, and Hallie works to bring the reddish coat to a shine. A patch of twinkling light plays off the side stall wall, and Hallie's hair on the back of her neck rises. Twinkling light has taken on a new meaning to Hallie, and she looks around exhaling a sigh of relief when she sees a piece of dangling aluminum roofing outside the window causing the light display.

Hallie thinks about the tragic love story that had always been a favorite part of campfire lore shared by her Aunt Dot during their many camping trips during Hallie's childhood. The story grew in detail revealing more information as Hallie grew older, but it was always her tell-it-again request whenever the aunts asked, "what shall we do next?"

Both the vision in the graveyard, and the dream last night follow the story she knows plus some. She can't avoid thinking about Joe's version of the story and, again, the hair on the back of her neck stands on end as she wonders how he even knows about the story. Is it coincidence that Hester—and now Beattie and Dot—have become part of the story? Her imagination has to be taking hold of it all somehow.

She tries to think about the last time Dot talked about the story. She remembers that it was a few years ago because once the aunts' business began to grow their camping trips dwindled in frequency. Now, with Hallie's new insights, she realizes that it really wasn't so much a "telling" of the story that last time as much as it was Dot's grieving farewell to it. It was at a time that Hallie's life too was changing and becoming busier. She does not recall the story being recounted again after this.

§

She and Dot are sitting outside on the Adirondack chairs behind their house enjoying the view of the gardens. Beattie is in town running errands, and Dot has come out with some iced tea taking a seat in the chair next to Hallie.

"I love the rainbow colors." Hallie muses as she lazily sips on the tea with her leg hanging over one arm of her chair.

"What's that dear?" Dot too is deeply relaxed, and lost in the pleasure of having nothing to do.

"The irises, there are so many different colors of them," Hallie says looking at the extensive patch of flowers along the back of the yard displaying a multitude of colors.

"Ah, yes the fleur-de-lis." Dot takes a long drink from her glass. The ice cubes clink as she empties it.

"Huh?" Hallie asks as she sits up in her chair and turns to look over at her aunt.

"Well, the iris was the inspiration for the fleur-de-lis symbol that you see in coat of arms and symbols of royalty. It also is part mythology that dates back to Ancient Greece when the goddess Iris, who personified the rainbow (the Greek word for rainbow is iris), acted as the link between heaven and earth. She was said to be the messenger between humans and the goddess and god, Hera and Zeus. It is told that she traveled from the heavens to earth on a rainbow to transport souls to the afterlife. Even today, the iris is planted at graves by some people." Dot leans back in her chair and gets a melancholy look in her eye.

"Dot, are you okay?" Hallie leans forward in her chair with concern

"Oh yes, dear. It just makes me think about Resmelda from our story."

"Really? Why?"

82

"Well, she was someone to be reckoned with, so it was told. She had to grow up quick, and she had a hard life for many years until she settled into her own. Yet, she always kept purple irises in a vase during their blooming season. I wonder if she knew about the legend of the goddess Iris, and if she held onto the hope of passing into an afterlife of light instead of the darkness which seduced her most of her life."

"Dot?"

"Yes, dear."

"How about you tell me the story one more time? It has been awhile, and who knows when we will be able to again."

Dot chuckles. "It always has been a favorite of yours now hasn't it?"

Hallie nods.

"I feel like you could tell it better than me nowadays, but there are some details near the end that I always left a bit vague not wanting to scare you."

"Really?"

Dot puckers out her lower lip tilting her head to the side with a guilty-as-charged look. "Well, you know most of the pleasant parts on the island, and the later parts about her time in prison, and her unusual disappearance, but not so much about what led up to her imprisonment."

"Yes, she had believed that Harry had turned against her."

"It's what put her over the edge of darkness. I often wonder, if she knew differently, if there would be a different ending for our story."

Hallie draws her knees up to her chin and wraps her arms around her legs knowing Dot was leading into the story.

"But, alas that was not the case. That last night on the island, after Jake brought her the warning about Mister Holt, Mister Butler, and mistakenly Mister White, Resmelda prepared one of her darkest conjurings ever. A casting for revenge."

§

Even without the dancing lights pulling her back in time, Hallie is able to envision this part of Dot's story, and she gets lost in the tale while she continues to groom Acacia.

§

Torchlight dances against tree branches in the scruffy pines forming a sparse patch of woods on the island. Holt and Butler lead a group of their wary crew from the McKemmie home to Resmelda's cottage near the dunes.

"Come now, you lot. We haven't got all night." Holt sneers over his shoulder as they make their way through the woods.

Butler holds up his hand as they approach the clearing. Beyond is the cottage, and Resmelda stands within a circle of torches casting eerie shadows that stretch across the sand and beach grass.

Holt's command is barely above a whisper. "Move in, but be quiet."

The men's torches betray their sweating brows and wavering arms. None take a step.

"I said," Holt shouts. Stops himself and looks back towards Resmelda. She takes no notice. He recaptures his whisper through gritted teeth. "Get moving, or your pain will be severe and your regrets deep."

The men hesitantly trudge forward. The closer they get the more evident it is that she is engaged in some sort of ritual. Holt circles around the back of the group and physically pushes men forward.

They are only several feet away, and still she remains unaware of their presence. She stands in the center of a circle of mist that snakes and swirls in a continuous circular motion. Her lips move to form words they cannot hear. Her hands reach for strange items that are tossed into a cauldron with a fire heating its bottom perimeter to a red glow. Each object causes an upheaval in the mixture. Her robe and hair ripple back as though she is standing in the middle of a storm, yet not even the slightest breeze is coming in off the shoreline. In fact, it is silent all about them.

One of the men approaches the swirling mist and steps into it intending to grab her. He instantly shrieks in pain and dissolves from flesh—to muscle—to bone—to dust. The others would run, but their legs fail them. Holt and Butler hold strong. Resmelda makes no indication she is aware of anything outside her protective circle.

Butler tugs at a thin leather strap around his neck. Pulling it from underneath his shirt, he reveals a piece of triangular silver inscribed with symbols. He raises it out in front of him and turns to Holt. "I got it from a might powerful voodoo practitioner in the Caribbean. It's a protective talisman made with strong magic."

Holt scoffs, but raises no objections.

Small beads of sweat form on Butler's brow, and his hand shakes as he steps towards the circle passing the piece over the bordering edge of the mist. Immediately, a green flash erupts and a rift in the circle occurs. The vapor swirls angrily at the border of the ripped opening making hissing sounds like hundreds of snakes.

Holt pushes the closest two men through the rift and they grab Resmelda restraining her arms behind her.

"Unhand me you pigs, or I will see to it you have no hands to serve you." She twists and swears. The air around them swirls and blows in violent howls. Holt walks into the circle fighting the squall and punches her full force in the face. She slumps forward. The wind stops. The vapors vanish. The fire under the caldron sucks below it with a high-pitched sizzle and extinguishes.

The men stand wide-eyed with labored breathing. Holt straightens his back breathless and points to the two men with Resmelda. He clears his throat. "You two take her back to Butler's schooner. The rest of you lot take those torches and burn this despicable place." They hesitate looking to one another, and Holt back-hands the man closest to him sending him to the ground. "I said burn it." His voice is full of venom.

"What of the firelight in the sky?" Butler questions almost child-like.

"All at the McKemmies have long gone to bed. This tinder shack will be nothing but smoking ash within a couple hours." He turns back to the men. "Burn it!"

§

Hallie flinches recalling his brash voice from her dream. She continues to work through the knots in Acacia's main and tail remembering Dot's final words from this newly enhanced portion of the tragic love story Hallie always thought she had known so well.

85

§

Dot gives one of her wistful sighs. "The voyage home for Holt only fed his rage. It seemed that none of the crew would allow her disposal off the side of the ship as had been planned. Every man suffered Holt's wrath, but not one gave into any demands that he brought down upon them concerning her. They feared her much more than him. Even Marcus Butler began to second guess his involvement in the destruction of Resmelda Bigelow and would not assist Holt.

"It was left to Holt to bring her a plate of food and cup of ale each day. He made a point each time to discuss Harry falsely advising her of his displeasure when presented with information regarding her dealings with witchcraft and the devil. He spoke as though Harry were on the vessel, but so disgusted by her that he refused to seek company with her. Resmelda never answered or spoke to Holt, but she always held eye contact with him causing him great discomfort that required extraordinary effort on his part to keep concealed."

It is then that a few drops of rain begin to fall on them. She and Hallie get up from their chairs and walk back to the house.

"Dot, that is so awful. I'm glad you sugar-coated it for me when I was younger."

"Yes, me too." Dot puts her arm around Hallie's shoulders as they make their way back to the house.

"Dot, do you really think Resmelda's irises that she grew had anything to do with a wish to be escorted to heaven some day?"

"I don't know for sure Hallie. I think that she was deeply troubled and wanted to move into the light, but she just didn't know how or didn't take the opportunity to make it so."

"It's so sad."

"Yes, yes it is." Dot opens the door for Hallie, and they step into the house just as a summer shower comes down in full force.

§

The stall door opens with a creak and Hallie startles a bit with the sound.

"I am sorry," Liam says as he latches the full water bucket onto the hanger on the front stall wall. "I did not mean to startle you."

"Oh, no I'm fine. You just caught me day dreaming while I was working the tangles out of Acacia's mane and tail."

"Her coat is shining. You really do know a bit about horse care." There is a sarcastic intonation with his declaration.

Hallie purses her lips and postures her head back with a jerk. "Thanks." She shakes her head and steps outside to place the brush and a comb she found back on the ledge.

Liam clears his throat. "Look, I am sorry. That did not come out as I intended."

Hallie folds her arms and looks at him. "Let's just get this out. You got in a huff earlier at breakfast. I thought that we had gotten past that, but now it is back."

He presses his lips and looks down at his shoes, but does not offer an explanation.

Hallie rolls her eyes and flings her hands out. "Okay, so if we are done here, can you take me up to where Joan is?"

"Are you always this quarrelsome?"

She coughs. "Do not make my reaction to your behavior out to be the cause of any friction between us. Your actions are the source."

"Perhaps." His reply is garbled as he rubs the side of his face along his shirt sleeve.

"Sorry, I didn't catch that. Perhaps, the huff you're in has your words jumbled."

He shakes his head and laughs. "What is this 'huff' you keep throwing at me?"

"You know. Anger. Discontent. General contempt. Mostly, I feel like towards me."

"Ah, yes. But, not towards you."

"But, you admit it's there?"

"Perhaps."

The eyes roll again.

"It was the mention of witchcraft." He rubs the back of his neck. "I have a distaste for the subject."

Her face softens, and she starts to reply.

He holds his hand up. "It is not something I wish to elaborate upon." He shifts his weight and Hallie bites down on her lower lip. She is fine with that. She doesn't want him thinking she is crazy anymore than she wants Joan thinking it.

He looks at her straight on. "However, may I extend a more sincere apology? For my behavior towards you. It has been…ungrounded."

She tucks her chin a bit and raises her eyebrows.

"Truly. A sincere apology. Please, we will step onto the grounds of friendship should you accept it. This morning has been…a pleasure."

Really? Hallie's heart skips a beat. She wills herself to calm and manages to coolly shrug a shoulder and extends her hand. "I'm good with that."

He hesitates and then takes her hand and they shake. The release is reluctant, and they both flash a smile.

There is a moment of awkward silence, and then Hallie speaks up. "So, grooming Acacia was really nice. She is a very sweet horse."

"So far, she has been. But I am holding judgment until she is feeling better and healed up. Then we will see what she is capable of." Liam scratches the horse's neck up below her chin and she stretches her nose out with pleasure. It brings out a belly laugh for Liam and Hallie.

"Well, we need to head up to the office. Joan called on my radio while I was finishing up with the hay. I just need to give Acacia the antibiotic injection that the vet left, and then I will come back later this morning to clean her wound."

"Okay," Hallie says. Liam had set a few flakes of hay outside the stall, and she picks them up to put them inside the stall for the mare. Acacia sniffs at the hay and immediately begins to eat.

"That a girl. You eat and get strong," Hallie encourages.

Liam gives the shot and secures the stall door. The two make their way out of the barn and back to the truck. Looking out the truck window she sees flowers growing near one of the trees, and an image of Hester's beautiful bouquet of purple irises with the delicate bow flashes before her eyes momentarily.

Liam turns the key and the truck comes to life interrupting Hallie's thoughts. He moves the truck away from the stable and towards the beach area of the park where Joan waits for them.

Chapter 10, Burnished

"Liam, this is Perkins. Are you in the park yet?" The two-way sitting on the truck's dash squawks to life with a cranky voice.

Liam grabs for the radio as he continues driving. "Yes sir, I am heading towards the beach area right now."

"Well, I need you over at cabin eight. Randy ran across a rhumba of rattlers when he was clearing away some brush, and you know how he is about snakes. I need you over here right now to help me get them cleared out. I've got the sacks for 'em so you head on over here A.S.A.P. Got it?"

"Yes, sir I am on my way." Liam sets the radio back on the dash. "Sorry. I am going to drive you down by the beach area, and let you head over to where Joan is. Just walk past concessions and turn right at the end of the building. You will see the meeting room right beside it."

"That's no problem. I'll find her. Snakes, huh?"

"Yes, they are starting to come out more now that the weather has warmed up. It is pretty normal to see them around, but most of the visitors do not do too well with them, and the poisonous ones need to get cleared out. We will get them up, and relocate them somewhere else in the park away from where people tend to go. It protects the people, but it also protects the snakes."

"Did he say a rhumba?"

"Yes, kind of like a group of musical instruments. I guess because of the sound their tails make. Of course, it could also be a reference to the dance I am sure Randy did when he ran across them. He really hates snakes."

Hallie grimaces and shudders. "I'm not a huge fan myself."

Liam laughs and turns the truck onto the roadway towards the beach area. "Here you are."

"Thanks, Liam. I really appreciated getting to meet Acacia and spending some time with her."

"No problem. I think she likes you. If I survive the snakes, I will see you later. I have to watch those safety videos too."

"Okay, see you later then—hopefully." Hallie smiles and pops the truck door open gathering her backpack from the seat before hopping out of the truck. Liam waves at her as he pulls back out onto the roadway.

It is turning out to be a beautiful day. There are tall trees all around the park, and a flying squirrel takes a daring leap from a pine tree landing safely onto the branch of a huge oak scurrying away. Hallie makes her way towards the neatly painted buildings sitting at the bottom of the hill. She can see a grassy area and walkway leading to a beach with brightly colored play equipment on the sand and in the water as well. It makes Hallie think about the Easter Baskets her aunts would make for her with all the colorful treats waiting to surprise her.

"Don't tell me that Liam White had you in his truck." A haughty voice pulls Hallie's attention away from the scenery.

Two girls are walking towards the buildings on a path leading from a parking lot off to the left. The one speaking to her has thick blonde hair and is dressed in a pair of white shorts and a turquoise camisole. Her diamond stud earrings sparkle in the sun and can be seen easily even from where Hallie is walking. The girl next to her is a brunette with cropped hair who is dressed similarly. Both look out-of-place in a woodland setting. Just beyond them, parked at the edge of the walkway, is a shiny red Camaro.

"Excuse me?" Hallie's muscles stiffen. She also realizes that until now, she didn't know Liam's last name.

"Liam. Mister Aloof himself. You actually were in that truck of his?"

Hallie stands within several feet of the girls. She notices an old beige SUV pull up near the Camaro, and a slender boy in a pair of cargo shorts and a t-shirt climbs out. She looks back to the girl addressing her. "Um, yes, I was. I'm sorry, but who are you?"

"Ivy Parkhurst and this is Roxanne Bishop. And you are?"

"Hallie O'Meara."

"So, where are you from? And what is the deal with you and Liam?"

"Well, I'm not from here, but I came here to work for the summer. Liam, as you just witnessed, gave me a ride in today. Do you have a problem with that?"

Ivy smiles shrewdly. "No problem here, but how nice for you. He is definitely a hunk of eye candy, but good luck with anything more than the view."

Hallie's upper lip curls up and she clears her throat. "What…"

"Ivy, Roxy! Over here!" A third girl also dressed similarly steps around the corner of the building from the beach side letting out a loud shriek.

"Tessa!" Ivy and Roxanne call out in unison, and immediately run to her. All three embrace and giggle. It is as if Hallie were invisible all of a sudden.

"Don't mind them." It's the guy who parked next to the red Camaro. He saunters towards Hallie with a smile that dimples his cheeks. He reminds Hallie of the laid-back surfers back home. "I'm David."

"Hi, David, it's nice to meet you. I'm Hallie." She looks back over her shoulder catching a view of the girls as they turn the corner of the building and shakes her head. "Oh, my God. That was unreal."

"Yea, well they are part of Patrick County's 'finest'. We all graduated from the same high school this year. If you have met Liam, then you know he is a nice guy. He's just private and, unless someone is oozing complements on Ivy, she figures they must be flawed in some way."

"Hm." Hallie nods. "So, Liam went to high school here? I thought he wasn't from here."

"Well, just senior year. He came to work here last summer, and I guess decided to stay on."

"So, what's the deal with Ivy then?"

"Ivy is just a rich girl who gets whatever she wants but couldn't get Liam, so now she is sour about him."

"I see. And if she is so rich, why the summer job here?"

"Not sure, but I hear her dad thinks it's important for her to get work experience. Of course, he got her the job last year, and

SD BARRON

she takes more days off than she works. I'm surprised to see her back this year, but whatever."

"So, the park has a lot of summer employees then?"

"Um, there's about twelve or fifteen of us I guess. Most of us live nearby, so where are you from?"

"I live on the Eastern Shore. Joan Shively is a friend of our family, so I came to stay with her and work here for the summer."

"Rad. Welcome. I think you'll like it."

"Me too." Hallie smiles and nods her head. David's easy-going nature is genuine, and she likes him immediately. They walk into the meeting room. It reminds Hallie of the summer camp hall at the 4-H center back home. There are tables with a mix-match of chairs around them throughout the room. An ancient-looking television on an audio-visual stand is against the wall. Ivy and her two cohorts are already seated at a table near the windows with their heads together talking and giggling. Tessa looks up at David and Hallie when they walk in, but only takes brief notice before returning to her conversation with Ivy and Roxanne. Joan is at the front of the room talking with a park ranger. She smiles at Hallie and David, and Hallie gives her a wave.

They walk over to a table where a girl is sitting whose dark eyes light up when she sees David. Her brown skin is flawless, and her smile contagious. She scoots her chair a bit to the side to make room for Hallie to get by.

"Hey, Becky, this is Hallie. She is going to be working here this summer. Hallie this is Becky."

"Hi, Becky."

"Hi! Do you know what part of the park you are going to be working?"

"You know, I don't. What do you do?"

"I'm usually at concessions. It can get crazy some days, but we have a lot of fun."

"So does the park get a lot of visitors for the beach then?"

"I'll say," Becky waves her hand, "and on a hot day they can get pretty grouchy when things don't move quickly. Most people though are really nice."

"Okay!" Joan calls them all to attention before Hallie can respond to Becky. "It looks like everyone we are expecting today is here."

Hallie looks around the room. Several more people have come in. They all look to be students from high school or college.

"We're glad you all could come today. Those of you who worked here last year remember me. For those of you who are new I am Joan Shively, and I am in charge of the summer employment program. This is Rick Martin, and he is lead ranger. We are going to go through your employment paperwork with you, and have you watch the safety video. Any questions before we get started?"

Joan pauses for a moment, but no one speaks up. She and Rick hand out the packets and the next forty-five minutes or so are spent filling out forms. Rick and Joan walk around giving assistance as needed. The room begins to fill with chatter as people finish up.

Liam and a tall boy with teal blue eyes and red hair walk into the room taking seats at the table with Hallie, David, and Becky. Liam and the boy nod greetings to Becky and David.

"Hallie, this is Randy. Randy—Hallie." Liam introduces them and Randy nods towards Hallie. Liam looks over at Hallie for a moment and smiles before turning his attention to Joan as she speaks up again.

Hallie feels a flush rise up her neck. *Ugh, that has got to stop.* She feels the stab of eyes on her, and rubs her chin against her shoulder cutting her eyes towards Ivy who is glaring at her. Tessa leans over and says something to her, and Ivy turns away.

Hallie rolls her eyes. She flashes a look Liam's way to see his attention is on Joan. She sighs and shifts in her seat while propping her head with her hand trying to focus when Rick pushes the controls on the prehistoric VCR player. The television comes on with a logo for the state of Virginia before transitioning to the narrator's voice and a scene with two workers in an industrial setting. Hallie's mind is anywhere but in-focus with the video. Thankfully the video is short.

Ivy makes a point to bump into Liam as they walk up to Joan to turn in their paperwork. "Liam, it's so good to see you!" Her tone is almost syrupy as it strains with forced sweetness. "I didn't think you would be working here again this year. How nice it was of Missus Shively to get you back in."

"Ivy." Liam gives a slight bow, and glances towards Joan who jumps in to bring Ivy's attention to an omission on her paperwork pulling her off to the side to finish it. Liam glances back at their table raising his hand with a quick nod and smile.

Is that for me? Hallie glances around and sees Becky and David talking. Randy is taking a last look at his paper work. She smiles and holds a hand up bending her fingers good bye. Liam turns and heads out the door.

Becky rolls her eyes at Ivy's interaction with Liam, and shakes her head at David who just shrugs back at her in agreement. "Seriously, David. What was that all about?"

"Can't say for sure Bec." He stands up. "Come on let's go get something to eat."

"Okay." Becky picks up her paperwork and turns to Hallie. "Well, I hope we get to work together in the concessions area, Hallie. We'll have a good time."

"Me too, Becky. See you soon."

"See you Hallie." David turns back to give her a quick wave

"See you later," Hallie says and turns to Randy. "Did everything go okay with the snakes over at cabin eight?"

Randy shudders and nods. "You knew about that, huh. Yeah, it did. Thank God Liam was in the park, or Old Man Perkins would have made me help him with them."

Hallie laughs. "Well, I'm glad it worked out okay for you. What do you do for the park?"

"I am usually at the boat house since all the summer help is mostly for the beach area, but Liam and I help out the groundskeepers occasionally too. We both come during the rest of the year when they need extra hands. It pays pretty well, and it's not bad…except when there are snakes to deal with."

"Is that very often?" Hallie silently hopes not.

"Considering where we are, not really."

"So, if I remember right from when I came here with my aunts, people can rent cabins or camp, right?"

"Right. It's a pretty decent set up." He rubs the back of his neck. "Plenty to keep us all busy during the summer that's for sure."

Randy's two-way blasts with Mister Perkins' voice. "Randy, you about done up there? Cause I need you back at cabin ten, and fetch a plunger before you head out this way."

"Yes sir, Mister Perkins. I'm leaving right now." He holds his radio up for Hallie to see, and shrugs. "Gotta go."

"Okay, maybe I'll see you this weekend when the park opens."

"Yea, come down to the boat house on a break, and I'll show you around." He turns and gives Joan his paperwork before stepping out the door.

Joan puts everyone's papers into a folder. "How's it going Hal? Looks like you've had a chance to meet a few of the kids working this summer."

"Yes. Becky was asking where I was going to be working for the summer."

"Oh, guess I didn't tell you that." Joan grabs a box. "Are you good with concessions?"

"That would be great. Becky said that she works there, and she can show me the ropes."

"Well, concessions it is then. Hey, grab that other box for me. We'll get this stuff to the ranger's station and grab some lunch. Sound good?"

Hallie's stomach growls on cue and she grabs it. "Sounds good. I guess I am pretty hungry. Is Bru's place still around?"

"Yes, it is. Great idea." Joan props the door with her foot for Hallie to pass through.

They load the back of the Jeep and climb in. The vehicle is hot from the sun, and they both roll down their windows to let some air flow as Joan drives back through the park entrance towards the ranger's office.

"So, have you had a chance to call Beattie and Dot?"

Hallie grimaces wrinkling her nose. "No. I haven't, but I will."

Joan nods thoughtfully. "You had absolutely no idea about anything to do with wicca?"

Hallie shakes her head with her eyebrows raised.

"All those trips here when we Turned the Wheel, and nothing?"

"Turned the what?"

"The Sabbats, Hallie. Celebrating each Sabbat is like turning a wheel throughout the year. I know you didn't come for the winter ones, but the spring, summer and fall equinoxes, Beltane, Lammas, and Samhain. We always had a gathering of friends and ceremonial events."

"Well, I do remember the gatherings, but not really the purpose of them. The last time we came I was eleven or twelve, and I was more interested in your newest litter of puppies or kittens back then. Beattie and Dot did not explain it to me that way. You know, as a Wiccan-witchy kind of thing, and I usually was asleep before most of the festivities ended."

"Yes, I do remember that now that you bring it up. It just seems odd that they would not have shared more with you." Her brow furrows.

Hallie bites her lip. "You don't think they were hiding anything from me do you?"

Joan blows out through her lips and looks at Hallie. "I don't think so. But, I guess I don't know for sure. Why would they not include you, or tell you? Just call them sometime. Okay?"

"Sure. I will."

Joan adjusts the radio and then changes the topic. "How did your morning go?"

"It was good. I got to spend time with the horse. She's really beautiful."

"Yes, she is. The veterinarian worked with her quite a while, and Liam is very knowledgeable too. I was a bit surprised."

"Why?"

"Well, he had been at Hope Springs, a residential place for abandoned youth. You know, they don't really say orphanage today. The kids from there come to the park, and I got to know him the couple summers he was with them, and before he came to work here last year. He was quiet, but I could tell he was a really good kid. When I set things up for him to live with me his file was pretty sparse, and I guessed that he had been very underprivileged."

"Hm, Maybe."

"You don't think so?"

"I don't know, but his speech is very refined, and he has this certain formality about him." Hallie shrugs. "Kind of like an English school boy, or something. I like it."

Joan smiles. "I never really put it together that way. Did he say anything about what had him irritated this morning?"

"Yes. And, no. He said the mention of witchcraft puts him on edge. And then he said, he didn't want to talk about it. He said it in a very final way too. I didn't push it."

"Really?"

"Yep, but he also apologized and asked for a fresh start. A friendship."

"Really?" Joan's voice dropped an octave, and she raises her eyebrows. She pulls the Jeep into Bru's parking area.

"Yep." Hallie smacks her lips. "I guess we'll see how it goes."

Chapter 11, Bright

On the way home from lunch, Hallie and Joan decide to stop at the Haynes 57 gas station and mini market to get popsicles There is a sign in the parking lot "Haynes 57 Home of the Fairy Stones".

"Why 'home of the fairy stones?" Hallie asks as they walk from the Jeep.

"Oh, well behind the store you can find fairy stones. You can find the fairy stones all around these parts, but there seems to be a lot of them in this little patch of earth."

"Really? Do we have time to look for them?"

"Sounds good to me." Joan opens the door for Hallie.

"Well, hey there Joan!" The woman behind the counter greets them warmly.

"Hi, Mary, this is Hallie O'Meara. She is Beattie and Dot's niece—not sure if you remember my good friends from over on the Eastern Shore."

"Sure, I do! Nice to meet you Hallie."

"Nice to meet you too."

"Y'all gonna walk the trail a bit?"

"Yes, we thought we'd get some dessert and take a short walk before we have to head back over to the park." Joan reaches into a cooler for two popsicles.

"Well, it is a beautiful day for it. Course I heard some storms are moving this way later. Supposed to be pretty bad from what I hear." Mary hands Joan her change.

"I hadn't heard the forecast. Thanks for the heads up. You take care now, and be sure to tell Ronnie I said, 'Hi!'"

"I will. Come back by and see us soon!"

Hallie waves goodbye to Mary and follows Joan out the door towards the back of the store. As they step into the woods, they do not need to go very far before the sounds of the highway fade, and the pungent woody smell of the forest surrounds them.

"It is just so beautiful everywhere you turn around here. I mean the lake, the trails, the mountains, and all the wildlife that lives here. And, even here with a gas station and mini market just beyond the trail head." Hallie comments as she walks alongside Joan looking up into the canopy of the trees.

"That it is," Joan bends down to pick up a stone. She holds it in her open palm for Hallie to see. It is a tan rock that, at first glance, just looks like an irregularly shaped rock, but then a cross shape can be seen within its form.

"A fairy stone! They are really so unusual. They're in the stores all over the place here, but I don't remember Dot and Beattie taking me here to look for these when I was younger. It just seems like something they would have done."

"No? I guess we never did do this on any of your visits," Joan hands Hallie the stone. "They are staurolite, and right here in Southwest Virginia is the most abundant source of them in the entire world. There's a belief that they are lucky—made from fairy tears after the Christ was crucified. That one is a Roman Cross shape. There is also a Saint Andrews that is kind of like an X, and the Maltese which has equally sized and shaped arms, and is the rarest type of fairy stone. Some even have small pieces of garnet in them."

"I've seen them before, but I guess they were cut to better show the cross shape. This is really cool to see one natural. How does the shape get into the stone?"

"Lots of heat and pressure. You keep that one." Joan takes a quick look at her watch. "I probably need to head back to the park. How about I take you back to the house and let you get unpacked and settle in?"

"Okay, thanks for the stone and for lunch. How about I make spaghetti for dinner tonight?"

"Dinner, ready when I get home? That sounds really good!" Joan puts her arm around Hallie's shoulders, and gives her a squeeze as they step out of the woods.

Ivy's convertible is parked at the gas pumps with Roxanne in the passenger seat and Tessa sitting in the back seat. Ivy walks from the store and gets into the car. The engine starts, and she pulls out of the gas station onto the highway with a squeal. An approaching car has to slam on the brakes to avoid hitting her. The three girls in the Camaro laugh carelessly.

Joan gives Hallie a look and shakes her head as they get into the Jeep.

"That girl is trouble," Joan comments as she pulls out of the lot. "I have to work especially hard to remain professional with that one. If it weren't for whatever connection her daddy has with the state park service—or whatever government official it is he is thick with—she would not have been back to work this year. Fortunately, she takes more time off than she works, but when she is there...well, I'm sure you will get a chance to find out."

Hallie smiles and nods her head knowingly. "I've already gotten a sample. Say no more."

"Well alrighty then! How about some tunes?" Joan says cranking up the radio.

Chapter 12, Flash

A Thunderstorm
The wind begun to rock the grass
With threatening tunes and low,
He flung a menace at the Earth,
A menace at the sky.
By Emily Dickinson

The green pickup truck pulls around the back of the house just as Hallie is walking up from the garden with a basket of fresh lettuce and greens for the salad she is making along with the spaghetti. Liam climbs out of the truck, and he is covered in filth and reeking of sewage.

"Oh, ewww!" Hallie stops short and brings the back of her hand up to her nose squinting at the odor.

"I know, I know." Liam holds up a hand to warn of the need for a safe distance. "Randy and I got slightly immersed in a little septic line problem at one of the cabins when we were working with Mister Perkins."

"Slightly?" Hallie crinkles her nose and takes another step back.

"Yes, well even a little is a lot when you're talking about sewage. Mister Pruitt sent us home early to clean up."

"I'm sure that had nothing to do with him not being able to tolerate the smell." Hallie furrows her brow and gives a crooked smile offering sympathy.

Liam laughs and shakes his head. "Well, I am going to use the shower behind the outbuilding before I come in for dinner; otherwise, I think Joan's house may need to be fumigated."

"Okay, sounds *very* good. I'll finish up with dinner. Joan should be home any time now. See you in a bit." Hallie renews her sympathetic smile, and he shrugs shaking his head before turning to walk away. He pulls his grimy shirt off as he goes. She watches him noticing the cut of his muscles in his back. He flips his shirt over his shoulder and runs his hands through his hair. *What more could a girl ask for?* A breathy sigh escapes her, and she heads into the house.

Hallie is tossing the lettuce with other vegetables she has cut up for the salad when Liam comes through the back door in a clean shirt and pair of shorts. She gives him a sideways look, and he grins as he walks in.

"Anything I can do to help?" He asks.

"Sure, can you grab some glasses out of the cabinet?"

Their rhythm syncs as they work side-by-side. Joan comes in just as they finish setting the table.

"Hey, Joan." Hallie greets her cheerfully.

"Hey, you two. Liam, looks like you survived that fiasco at the cabins this afternoon." Joan snitches a bit of carrot from the salad, and sits in a chair as she pops it into her mouth.

"Yes, ma'am. Safe and sound and starving. Liam says, and he pulls a chair out to sit. "Dinner smells good."

"Yes it does," agrees Joan as she gives Hallie a wink.

"I hope you like it. You had the ingredients for Dot's sauce recipe, so that's what I made to go with it." Hallie sits next to Joan and across from Liam.

"Well of course I do. Where do you think she got the recipe from?"

They laugh together enjoying the meal as they listen to Joan talk about her day, and Hallie tells Liam about the short hike she and Joan took at lunch. They are just finishing up when the phone rings. Joan picks it up.

"Hello! Well, hey there Henry! Oh. Let me come over, and see if I can help her out some. You think she would be okay with that? Good then, I'll be right over." Joan hangs up and turns to Hallie and Liam.

"That was Henry Cox. You know Henry, Liam." She says to Liam and turns to Hallie. "Henry's grandmother is Ida Cox. She is a good friend of mine and knows Beattie and Dot as well. She fell some time back and broke her leg. She has been giving that poor boy and his mother a fit insisting on being independent and not having any help. Looks like this evening is a more challenging one. I'm going to head over there for a bit and see if I can help. Do you all mind cleaning up?"

"No, not at all," Hallie starts to clear the dishes.

"No, ma'am," answers Liam as he stands helping clear dishes.

"Alright, I'll be back as soon as I can. It looks like that nasty weather they predicted is starting to head this way, so I am going to try to get back before it hits, but if not I will call." She picks up her purse and heads out the door.

Liam turns to Hallie. "You cooked, and so let me wash up."

"That sounds great, thanks. I can dry." She puts things away as he stacks dishes and gets the dish water ready.

Hallie hops up to sit on the counter by the sink as Liam puts dishes into the water. He smiles almost shyly as he loads dishes into the sink.

"What?" Hallie asks.

"Nothing really, I just remember a time when I would not be caught dead doing women's work."

Hallie guffaws. "Seriously, Liam? You sound like an old guy sitting on a bench complaining about the 'whipper snappers' running amuck in the park."

He clears his throat and pinches his lips together before laughing. "Yes, I guess I do, but you did not let me finish. I was going to add that Joan has cured me of that though."

"Well, good then. I never really understood all that stereotyping anyway, but then again most of my life has been spent primarily around women being raised by my two aunts. I've not given much thought to what makes something women's or men's work. My aunts tend to do it all."

"I remember a time when there was a very clear distinction between the two. There was a sort of symmetry to it really when people worked together but separately. It also created a feeling of mystery about a woman's world. It was intriguing. I was always fascinated by it." He looks out the kitchen window, but it feels like he sees something much farther away, and Hallie hears a yearning in his tone.

"I can see a certain romance in that," she quips.

He stops washing and looks at her incredulously. "Romance? Now, that is definitely a female's vision on the whole thing." He flicks a puff of bubbles at her, and she giggles as she swats it back towards him.

They work in silence for few minutes. The storm can be heard rumbling in the distance. The lights flicker, and they pause until they come back on again.

"Have you ever been on the beach during a thunder storm?" Hallie asks.

"No. you?"

"Oh, yes." She closes her eyes and smiles. "Seeing those thunderheads roll in is scary and beautiful all at the same time. Sometimes great water spouts will erupt from the water like tornados in the sky do, and it makes my heart want to jump out of my chest."

"No fear of a lightning strike?"

Hallie shrugs a shoulder. "Maybe a little, but nature's dance is so awesome. It's just a rush, you know?"

"You are a thrill seeker then?"

"Um, no. I just appreciate the beauty. The rest is…the price of the ticket I guess."

He looks at her thoughtfully, and Hallie almost gets lost in his eyes until a lightning flash and loud crack of thunder makes her flinch a bit.

He smiles and brushes the back of his fingers under his chin. "You have an interesting way of expressing yourself Hallie, sometimes Hal, O'Meara."

"What do you mean?"

"Colors of witchcraft, nature dancing, the risk of danger as a ticket to something more beautiful."

"Hey, you said discussing witchcraft was off the table, and Joan said that not me." She straightens her back and squares her shoulders."

He holds his hands up. "Just an illustration. I probably should apologize. Again."

"Don't bother. And, since you brought it up. I have nothing to do with witchcraft." *I don't, right?* "And, Joan was discussing the Wiccan religion not something evil. I did ask her a few questions about magic, but only because…some weird things have been happening since I left home."

"Weird? In what way?"

Hallie blows a stray tuft of hair out of her eyes and walks over to the window. She looks back at him over her shoulder. "Off the table for discussion. Remember?"

He flicks a crooked smile at her and starts to say something when a bright flash and almost immediate crack of thunder erupts. A heavy down pour ensues. Hallie looks up at the sky through the window and then across the yard.

"Oh, Liam, the windows of your truck are still down!"

"I doubt it will hurt anything in that old truck, but I better go shut the windows." He grabs a rain jacket from a hook by the door and heads out. The phone rings just as he leaves, and Hallie answers it expecting to hear Joan's voice. It is a man.

"Hi, this is Rick Martin over at the park, is Joan there?"

"Hi, Mister Martin, this is Hallie O'Meara. No sir, she went over to help a friend out for a while, but I'm expecting her home later this evening."

"Oh, I see." There is a pause. "Is Liam there?" His voice pitches a bit like a ship in distress.

"Yes sir, he has just run outside to secure his truck from the rain."

"Well listen Hallie, can you have him come over to the park right away? I was making my evening rounds, and that mare he has been caring for must have spooked with the storm. It looks like she broke out of the stall and may be injured again or sick. She is down in the field by the stable. I have gotten a hold of the vet, and she is on the way, but I think Liam would want to be here."

"Yes sir, I will let him know right away. Thank you for calling."

"No problem."

Hallie grabs one of the rain jackets and heads out into the rain. Liam is already running back to the house, and she nearly runs into him.

"Liam! It's Acacia, Mister Martin called, and she's down. He thinks she may be sick or injured again. He needs help right away. Can you go?"

"Yes, of course." He turns to head back to the truck, and she reaches out, hesitates, but then grasps his arm. He turns looking first at her hand and then to her face.

"Can I go with you?"

He bites down on the inside of his lower lip and gives a curt nod.

Chapter 13, Kindle

Liam pulls into the lot near the stables. The rain starts to ease up, but lightening still brightens the sky at intervals. A sick lurch grabs Hallie's stomach when a flash illuminates the field, and she sees Acacia lying on her side with Rick Martin pacing back and forth. She and Liam run to the mare. Liam drops to his knees stroking Acacia's neck. She lifts her head a bit letting out a guttural sound.

Liam looks up at Hallie. "Can you go into the stable and get her halter and lead rope? I left them outside her stall earlier today."

Rick hands her a flash light. "There's a light switch just to the right of the door when you go in. If the power is up, you will have plenty of light to see."

Hallie heads towards the stable. She makes her way to the door and finds the latch and feels along the inside wall. *Please have electricity. Please have electricity.* The lights come to life with a crackle when she finds the switch. The roof echoes with the pattering rain filling the deserted space with its rattle as she makes her way to the stall. The latch on the stall door is broken, and a side door to the barn is ajar with rain blowing in and puddling the dirt floor. She finds what is needed, and runs back out to the mare's side handing the halter and lead rope to Liam. Her breath forms puffs of mist in the cold air.

"Okay, I am not sure what is going on with her, but I have checked her legs and it does not seem like any bones are broken. We need to try to get her up and back into the stable. When the vet gets here it will be easier to evaluate what is going on if the mare is in a dry, well-lit area. Hallie, I am going to get her halter on, and I think it will be safer for you to hold the lead rope. Keep steady pressure on it over here to the side. Mister Martin and I are going to try to get her to roll over and up onto her feet. Mister Martin, if the mare kicks or slips, clear out of the way so you are not hurt."

Hallie finds Liam's steadfast control reins in her nervous energy allowing her to focus on the task. The lead rope is wet all ready, and she grasps it tightly to keep if from slipping through her hands. She pulls back with steady pressure at Liam's cue wrapping the rope around her hand for better control. Her hand numbs as the rope squeezes tight, but she keeps the pressure firm.

Their feet slide into the spongy and slick ground, and Liam slips onto his knees once. "I am okay, keep putting pressure on her. She is almost there."

Acacia rolls straining to gain traction. Liam and Mister Martin lean into her side with their shoulders. "Come on girl get on up now." Liam commands Acacia with a grunt putting more pressure against her, and with a throaty huff she gets her footing and stands. Her chest heaves with each breath. Liam walks around her checking her legs and then gives Hallie a nod to lead her into the stable. Acacia's head is hanging low, and she is shivering by the time they get her back into the stall.

Rick brings a basket out from one of the storage areas with a bunch of towels. "Can you all take it from here?" He grabs a towel and dries off a bit. "I need to go and check to see if the cabins and camp ground are okay."

"Yes sir, thank you for everything Mister Martin."

"Here, take this two-way and give me a holler, if you need anything."

"I will. Thanks again." Liam sets the radio on the stall ledge and grabs a couple towels handing one to Hallie, and they start drying off Acacia.

"Hallie," Liam looks at her from across Acacia's back. "Are you doing okay?"

Hallie doesn't realize it, but her face is red, and her eyes suddenly start spilling over with tears. "She just looks so bad. How could she go from doing so well to this?"

"Things can change quickly for a sick or injured horse."

Hallie bites down on her lip, and Liam reaches over laying his hand on Hallie's. "We will get her back. Healing can happen quickly too."

She sets her jaw and gives him a curt nod. He slides his hand off hers and returns to his task. Hallie's hand is warm and her fingers stretch of their own accord beckoning the return of his touch. She curls them up and takes a breath to clear her head then wipes her eyes.

Together they dry Acacia as best as they can and then themselves. Headlights pierce through the darkness towards the barn and, in no time, Doctor Cox is making her way towards the stall with a tackle box in her hand.

"Liam, sorry to see you are having trouble again. What do we have here?"

Liam jiggles the stall door's broken latch. "She must have gotten spooked with the storm and broke through the stall door. She opened that chest wound up again, and I noticed a red swollen area at her flank over here on the near side when I was drying her off. It seems pretty tender."

The vet lifts the mare's upper lip. She listens to her heart and belly and then takes a closer look at the chest wound and swollen area near the back leg.

"I must have missed something in her stifle yesterday when I came to see her. It's definitely swollen and fluctuant, so it's likely an abscess that needs to be drained. There's probably too much infection in the area for the antibiotic to have a big impact. I'm going to give her a local anesthetic and open it up to see what I can get out. There's just a small area at the chest that needs repair." The vet gets everything prepared. Liam helps her. Hallie stands by Acacia's head with quiet soothing words and reassuring strokes. The horse leans her head towards Hallie blowing warm breath onto her skin. She watches as Doctor Cox and Liam work quickly to get the abscess opened. An ooze of green cottage cheese-looking stuff flows from the wound. Hallie watches intently as she croons quietly to Acacia. Doctor Cox explores the wound with her gloved finger removing something.

"Huh."

"What is it?" Liam asks.

"Looks like a broken tip of a canine tooth. It's a bit pointed for a dog—maybe a coyote. We do have some in this area, but it is rare for them to venture where people are constantly coming and going. It's really odd though because I don't recall any of her wounds looking like an animal attacked her. There's no way an abscess would have formed so quickly from a fresh attack today. Maybe it's from an old wound, and it just incidentally started to fester with her weakened immune system....Well, it's out now." She shrugs handing the piece of tooth to Liam. He looks at it, and hands it to Hallie.

She runs her finger tip over the sharp point and hands it back to Liam. He puts it in his shirt pocket and helps Doctor Cox finish up.

"Hopefully, she will start feeling better here in the next hour or so and drink some water. She's a bit dehydrated, but I don't think we need to run an IV or anything else at this point. You'll need to stay the night with her. I'll give you my cell number. Don't hesitate to call me, if you need me back out here."

"Yes ma'am, I appreciate you coming out here on a night like this." Liam carries her tackle box back out to the truck. The storm is over with only distant thunder rumbling from the other side of the mountain. On his way back towards the stall he picks up a soft blanket that is lying folded on a barrel and opens it up draping it around Hallie's shoulders.

"Thank you for your help."

"Oh, I was glad to." She grabs ahold of the blanket feeling warmth from both it and his gesture.

Liam stands by Hallie and reaches up to the mare's ears to give them a rub. "I need to get you back to Joan's so you can get some dry clothes and rest a bit. Then I'll come back here and stay with Acacia."

"I don't think you should leave her—even for a short time." Hallie objects. "We can contact Mister Martin on the two-way, and ask him to call Joan from the ranger's station to let her know where we are. She will understand."

Liam pulls his upper lip with his teeth and furrows his brow looking from Hallie to Acacia. He nods. "I will radio him and then go fill her water bucket."

"And, I'll get her some fresh hay."

Liam takes the bucket outside to the hose, and Hallie carries a few flakes of hay into the stall. She brushes off her shirt and then swallows hard. *What was I thinking? Here. All night. With Liam.* She looks over at Acacia who is breathing with less effort, but still stands with her head low. "Gotta be sure you get better. It'll be okay, right?" She rubs Acacia's neck and looks around. "Well, nothing helps keep the butterflies in my stomach occupied better than staying busy." She goes and finds stall cleaning supplies and gets to work.

Liam comes back and hangs the full bucket. Acacia turns dipping her head near the water sniffing and snorts before drinking.

Hallie's face lights with a smile. "Look at that."

"See? Things can change quickly given the right circumstances." He looks at Hallie and reaches up gently pulling a piece of hay from her hair.

Hallie flushes immediately and knows that her traitorous pale skin is lighting up pink. She sighs and nods her head before refocusing on raking out the stall. Liam takes a shovel and muck bucket to clear things out.

He shovels the last bit in and moves the bucket into the aisle. He jiggles the broken stall door latch. "We need to fix this too. I have a tool box in the truck—be right back."

"Hey, Liam?"

He turns towards her.

"There are some bags of bedding in one of the stalls. You think we can use them?"

"I do not see why not. Let me carry them for you."

"Oh, I can get them."

"Together?"

She smiles and nods. They carry the bags of bedding to the stall.

While Liam fetches the tool box she works on opening the bags. The stall quickly fills with the scent of pine as she spreads the soft wood shavings throughout the space. She closes her eyes and inhales. Acacia nudges her a bit as she moves to nibble at the hay.

"Aw, there you go." Hallie strokes her neck and feels her heart skip a beat. She catches movement from the corner of her eye and startles. She grasps her chest when she turns to see Liam leaning on the stall door watching her.

"I didn't hear you come back."

"Sorry, I did not mean to startle you."

She purses her lips and breaks into a smile. "No more apologies, remember?"

He glances down at his feet. "Yes, of course." And, holds her emotions hostage while he looks into her eyes again.

God. It's like he can see my soul. How is he doing that? She reaches up and wipes the back of her hand across her forehead and moves a stray hair behind her ear.

"You have the stall set real nice." He runs his hand through his hair and clears his throat. "How about we get this door fixed?"

"Right. Did you find the tools you need?"

"Enough to fix the latch temporarily. I may have to get a replacement for it later."

She hands him things and holds the door steady as he gets the latch reset.

"It looks good as new, Liam." She raises her eyebrows impressed by his handiwork.

Hallie notices a small knot hole in the wood just above the repaired latch and pulls the stone Joan gave her from her pocket wedging it into place. It's a perfect fit.

"A fairy stone?" Liam looks at her quizzically.

"Um-hum, they say they provide protection and healing *and* luck."

Liam folds his arms. "Like a talisman?"

Hallie hesitates unable to read his face and returns her focus to the fairy stone. "No. Like a stone made from fairy tears according to legend."

Liam smiles and reaches past her to adjust the stone. "Well then, it is here to stay I believe."

Hallie flashes him a smile and folds her arms over the stall door propping her chin on them watching Acacia eat the hay. She tries to suppress a yawn.

"Here, we can sit inside the stall."

"Okay." Hallie pulls the blanket Liam had given her earlier close around her neck grateful for its warmth. She sits leaning her back against the stall wall. Liam settles in next to her.

"Liam, what do you think about that tooth Doctor Cox found?"

He shrugs his shoulders taking the tooth from the pocket of his t-shirt holding it up for both to see.

"It's kind of strange isn't it that the horse you had when you were younger and this horse would have both been attacked by coyote?"

"One would think so, but coyote can be a problem in most rural places and even for an animal as large as a horse." He returns the tooth back to his pocket and leans back against the stall wall.

Hallie nods leaning against him. *What a nice comfortable fit.* It is a dreamy thought that quickly starts to swim through her fatigue.

"Hallie?"

"Hm?"

"Tell me about yourself."

"Well, I grew up an orphan. Kinda like you."

"Me?"

"Yes. Joan told me that you used to live at Hope Springs." She nestles her head next to him, and he raises his arm to put it around her shoulders. *Oh. My. God. How awesome is this?*

"Oh, yes I see. But, you had your aunts. Did you always live with them?"

"Um, hm." Hallie clears her throat. "My whole life, but I'm not sure I really knew them like I thought I did."

"How is that?"

She draws in a breath and sighs it out. *Don't ruin this moment Hallie.* "It's a forbidden topic. Between you and me I mean. I think they were more 'colorful' than I was aware of."

She feels him stiffen a bit, but he does not withdraw.

"I see."

"Do you?"

There is a long pause and Hallie wonders if he is going to answer her.

"Yes, I do. You are…forthright and kind, although you have a stubborn nature. I think you have been steeped in love, and that is a reflection of your aunts. No matter what sort of news about them has been heralded recently."

"Huh."

"Huh?"

Hallie's fatigue temporally abates. "Well, firstly, wow. And, thank you. I have never been described that way in my entire life. Never. I mean not so…I don't know. You said before that I have a different way of saying things, but I think you do too. Very…I dunno." She crinkles up her nose not wanting to offend him. "Old fashioned maybe?"

He shifts a bit and puffs a breath through his nose. "Yes, sorry about that."

"No. you misunderstand. I like it. We say things differently, but seem to understand one another."

His muscles relax, and he draws her closer to his side.

Hallie's butterflies have slowly settled, and she turns her face up to look at Liam. "So, tell me about you."

"There is not much to tell. I lived at Hope Springs for some time."

"Until you came here to live with Joan."

"Yes, she is an old friend with a kind nature, nearly like yours."

"An *old* friend?"

He clears his throat. "Like an old friend. Sorry, I think fatigue is grabbing hold."

Hallie stifles another yawn.

Liam reaches over and adjusts her blanket. He gently grasps hold of a curl of her hair and runs it through his fingers.

A warmth from within wraps around Hallie overshadowing any comfort the blanket has to offer. She closes her eyes and drifts off into sleep feeling very safe and content.

Chapter 14, Flickering

The next morning, the air is crisp and clear. A bird sings somewhere just outside the barn, and Hallie opens her eyes to see Acacia eating hay looking content. Hallie finds that she is lying with her head on Liam's folded jacket snuggled up warmly beneath the blanket. Bits of dust float through the air sparkling in the streaming light from the window. She sits up stretching her neck to each side trying to work out a kink, and she brushes wood shavings from her still damp clothing. There is a chill in the air. She rubs her arms to spark some warmth.

Hallie stands and gives Acacia's neck a nice rub. The mare's eyes are clear and bright this morning. "Hey, girl. The night started out pretty rough for you, but look at you now." *Look at you and look at me.* Hallie tugs at her short legs and pulls a hair band from her wrist to put her hair up into a messy bun. She looks out of the stall for Liam. "I guess we're alone Acacia. Where did Liam go?" The mare provides no clues—just a swish of her tail and a sparkle in her dark brown eyes. Hallie smiles and then shakes out the blanket and Liam's jacket folding them both.

Peeking in the water bucket she sees that it is full of fresh water, and fresh flakes of hay are in the corner. *Man, I must have been dead asleep not to hear Liam get all this set. I hope I didn't make any weird noises. Good thing I don't snore.* She draws in a quick breath. *I do talk in my sleep according to Beattie. God, I hope I didn't say anything stupid...or too revealing. He's just starting to like me, and I am sure that Resmelda, Joe, and Hester talk won't go over well.*

She bites a nail and then feels her testy bladder letting her know it's full. She leaves the mare in search of a bathroom eventually finding one inside the stable office. It's dusty, but has most of the essentials, and she quickly sits to relieve herself of her bladder's nagging ping. Then she grabs a towel and wipes the mirror off.

"Oh, so glad Liam left." She puffs air into her cupped hand grimacing. "Yea, real glad."

There's a grungy bar of soap on the sink and she rinses it off and then pulls her shirt off and washes up. There's a crinkled tube of tooth paste in a plastic cup, and she kneads its remnants out onto her finger, smells it, and decides its safe. With her finger as a toothbrush she gets the job done. A shiver glides over her arms, so she grabs her shirt to put it back on. It's still damp but better than nothing.

"Hallie!"

She pokes her head out the door and pats her hair self-consciously. "In here, Liam. I just…wanted to freshen up a bit."

"Well, this will help." He holds out a bag, and she reaches through the partially opened door.

"My clothes." She looks back at Liam with a furrowed brow. "But how…"

"I needed to get the two-way back to Mister Martin, and Joan was there with him. She brought us both a change of clothes. And," he holds up a paper bag. "She told me you like hot dogs for breakfast. They were getting the snack bar set up, so I made us a couple."

"Oh, my God. Yes. I can smell them, and I am starving all of a sudden." She leaves a small crack in the door and quickly changes into warm, dry clothing. She sighs and hugs her arms around herself feeling immediately better. She takes her leather pouch with her amber heart and pressed penny from her shorts and ties it to a belt loop on the ones she changed into.

Liam has turned his back to the door despite there only being the narrowest of cracks in its opening. "So, hotdogs for breakfast?"

"Well, yeah." Hallie steps through the door fully changed and with a broad smile lighting her face. "I have to admit that cold pizza is my all-time favorite, but a hotdog on a warm bun keeps a close second."

"Ah, yes. Cold pizza is a very good way to break one's fast."

Hallie cuts a giggle short by putting her fingers lightly over her mouth.

He looks at her with his eyebrows knitted together, and then his mouth drops open. "The weird talk again. I really do not normally do that with other people around."

"Right. Word is you're pretty quiet around people. A bit of a loner."

"Yes, well perhaps that too." He jerks a quick shoulder shrug and twists his lips to the side. "I suppose. I suppose I feel."

The word just won't come out, and Hallie can't take another second. "Comfortable?"

"Yes, comfortable. With you that is."

Her heart skips a beat and she gives him a smile. "Same here. I mean. Comfortable with you. Maybe it was because everything was so intense last night. I dunno, but I like it."

"Yes, me too." He holds up the bag of food as though looking for a quick change of topic. "How about we bring Acacia into the paddock and eat our breakfast outside?"

"Excellent idea."

"Oh, and Joan asked us to come by and see her on the way out. I think she was worried."

Hallie's face falls. "Mister Martin called her last night didn't he?"

"Yes. But still. A summer storm, a sick horse, you, me, all night in the stable."

Hallie tilts her head back. "Ah, right. Gotcha." Hallie fidgets with her bag of clothes not wanting any of this to end too soon, but guilt pangs inside her chest. "Maybe we should head up now. I feel bad that Joan has been worried."

Liam starts to say something and then presses his lips together.

Is that disappointment I see in his eyes? Could he really be thinking the same things as me? Hallie twirls a renegade curl of hair by her ear.

He finally breaks the silence. "Yes, we could head up now, but she seemed to be very reassured when I spoke to her earlier, and I do think Acacia would do well with some time outside."

"Hm, okay, then. I'm good with that."

The stable is surrounded by a field with lush grass and wild flowers bordered by tall trees. It's noisy with waking wild life yet peaceful at the same time. Hallie releases Acacia, and then climbs on the fence to sit and eat. Liam leans on the fence close by.

"Mister Perkins decided to hire a plumber after yesterday's series of unfortunate events, so I have the day off." Liam watches the mare for a while. "Would you be up for a hike, and maybe a canoe ride with a tour of the lake area today?"

Hallie smiles at the uncertainty she hears in his voice. It is such a contrast to his demeanor last night where he readily took charge helping everyone pull together and focus.

"Yes," Hallie replies. "I would very much like to do that today."

He flashes a brilliant smile and nods his head.

They finish their breakfast and sit longer to give Acacia time to enjoy the grass and fresh air before putting her back into the stall. They stop by the beach area to find Joan. She is with Rick in the meeting room.

"Well, hey there kiddo!" Joan looks up when Hallie and Liam come in. "Liam and Rick told me that you all had quite the adventure last night. I am so glad that the mare is doing better this morning."

"Yes, it was a bit scary there at first, but Doctor Cox and Liam were a great team. Acacia truly is doing so much better today."

"Acacia?"

"Oh, yes ma'am. I thought it would just be easier for the mare to have a name while we took care of her—until we can find her another home." Liam puts his hands in his pockets.

Joan smiles and nods approval. "Glad you got changed into some dry clothes Hallie. I was so worried about y'all last night. Thanks for having Rick give me a call. It helped."

"Thanks so much for thinking to bring the clothes. I am sorry about not coming home last night, but I thought leaving Acacia alone, even for a little while, wouldn't be a good idea."

Joan nodded. "Yep, I agree. It was the right decision."

She and Rick have a calendar and papers laid out in front of them, and Hallie just notices. "I'm sorry we interrupted you, but we want to explore the park a bit today. Is that okay?"

"Of course it is. There is so much history and beauty to discover here. Liam, be sure to take her along some of the Stuart's Knob Trails. She would enjoy hearing about Fayerdale and the area's history."

"Yes, ma'am I will."

Hallie and Liam start to leave.

"Before you two go give us your opinion about something." Rick speaks up. "We are making plans for the summer activities for the employees this year, and thought that we would do something new."

Hallie looks quizzically at them, and Joan interjects, "The park has always organized events throughout the summer for its employees to get together and build camaraderie. At one time the summer employees all lived here while they worked, and it was a social gathering place for locals as well. Even though the summer employees no longer live here, we still like to have a few activities organized for everyone to take part in."

"Right," says Rick. "This year we are thinking about bringing back a tradition from the 50's and 60's when they used to have dances at the restaurant that was on site. It's the community center now, and a great place for a party. We thought about having a dance with a 50's theme to commemorate that era."

"A 50's dance sounds like fun." Hallie is enthusiastic.

Rick smiles. "The style clothing, the music, the food, everything like it was. We are going to also try to contact the folks who worked here in the past, or their family members. The park originally opened in 1936, so many folks are no longer with us, but we could honor them through their children and grandchildren."

"Kind of like a reunion, but with a twist bringing together the current and previous employees," Joan interjects.

"I think it's a great idea. Don't you think a dance would be fun, Liam?"

"Sure."

Hallie senses a return of his withdrawn demeanor starting to resurface.

"Well, maybe we should get going." Hallie starts edging towards the door.

"Okay, see you all later then," Joan calls after them as Liam follows Hallie out of the meeting room.

They make their way back to the truck. The acrobatic squirrel Hallie saw on her first visit to the beach buildings takes a daring leap in the tree limbs above them. "Amazing, isn't it?" Hallie asks as they walk along the pathway.

Liam laughs. "Yes, it is. There used to be many more of them in this area a long time ago, but not so much now."

"What a shame. It's fun to watch. I guess this place has seen a lot of changes over the years."

"Yes, it has." Liam reaches for the passenger door handle to open it for Hallie. She climbs up, and he shuts the door and then makes his way around to the driver's side. Hallie feels like Liam's comment is almost reminiscent but can't tell for sure. He is so hard to read, but she truly enjoys being with him. Her cheeks flush and she can't help but smile.

Chapter 15, Auroral

All truths are easy to understand once they are discovered; the point is to discover them.
Galileo

Hallie showers quickly and gets dressed. She pulls her hair back into a loose pony tail, and grabs her leather pouch securing it to a belt loop before making her way to the kitchen where she put some fresh fruit and granola bars into her back pack and heads outside. Liam told her he was going to use the outside shower, so she goes into the outbuilding.

"Liam?" Hallie walks towards Joan's pottery studio, and where Liam said he was staying. In an adjacent room there are shelves with pottery drying, a pottery wheel, and a kiln off to the side. She sees bundles of spring herbs hanging to dry on a wood rack, clay pots and planting supplies on a shelf, and various gardening tools stored against a wall. She thinks of Beattie and Dot and takes a minute to send them a text. *I really should call them like Joan told me to, but I just can't. Not yet. I have no idea what to say, and I don't want to bring up the Resmelda visions.* She just can't shake a growing feeling that her aunts may have hid their wiccan-witchy lives while, at the same time, they were trying to convey a message to her with the tragic love story. *I have to figure more of it out before I try to talk to them about it.*

She keeps her feet planted in the storage space and cranes her neck to look towards Liam's space. There is the rug and over-stuffed couch that Hallie remembers from her previous visits, but now a bed, dresser, desk with a laptop computer on it, and shelves on the wall share the space as well.

"Liam?" Hallie calls out again. She walks over towards the couch where an orange tabby is sleeping contently on the soft cushioned seat. Hallie gently rubs behind his head and ears, and he looks up at her sleepily with a bravado purr gearing up. She scoops him up and walks over to the shelves by the desk seeing some framed vintage pictures and other items. There is a photo of a moonshine still with three men standing casually beside it, another of a teenaged girl holding a puppy sitting on a porch in front of a store, and a third of a white farm house with several people in the yard. It looks like a picnic gathering was going on. There's an old railroad tie, a Mason jar filled with fairy stones, a pocket knife, a clay pipe, a small basket with a collection of feathers in it—each with a delicate thread-like ribbon tied at the quill—and a few other antique items arranged on the bottom shelf. Above, is another shelf full of books.

Hallie turns to look at the rest of the space. Liam's canvas back pack is lying at the end of the bed next to a plain brown leather journal tied with a single cord. A guitar is leaned against an oak wardrobe which stands opposite the bed. There is a narrow window above the bed, and Hallie sees the top of Liam's head walk by. She steps over to the couch sitting on its arm and waits trying to adjust her seat to look more casual. She hopes her presence isn't an intrusion.

Liam shows no surprise to see Hallie sitting on the couch holding the orange cat. "Hey." He tosses a towel onto the desk chair. "I see you have met Oscar. He has laid claim to that couch. If he was not so fat, I would think he never left that spot, but I know he is not missing any meals." He reaches over to give the cat a scratch on the back of the neck brushing his hand ever so slightly against Hallie's.

A stomach flutter starts to percolate. She laughs shyly, and sets the cat on his cushion. He arches his back and curls back up to resume his previous position.

"I like your space." She grasps at conversation for a distraction.

"Thanks. Joan wanted me to take a room in the house, but I really like being out here." He shrugs a shoulder. "So, are you ready to head out?"

"Yep, all set." Hallie picks her back pack up from the floor, and follows Liam. "How about we take my car this time?" Hallie asks.

"Sounds good." Liam turns opening the driver's door for Hallie. "This is a great car! You do not see too many in top condition like this one."

"I know, it really is fun to drive. My aunts completely surprised me when they gave it to me for my birthday." Hallie climbs into the car, and Liam shuts the door making his way around to the passenger side. Hallie turns the key and Liam closes his eyes for a moment listening to the gentle rumble of the engine.

"Very nice. Your aunts have excellent taste."

"Yes, Beattie and Dot are a bit eccentric, but both have an excellent eye and are very talented business women. It amazes me considering their age, and the era they grew up in."

Liam hesitates for a moment. "Did you say...Beattie...and...Dot?"

"I know, unusual names right? But Beatrice and Dominica, their given names, just don't suit them for some reason. Everyone calls them Beattie and Dot."

Liam nods in acknowledgement and studies Hallie for a moment before looking ahead with a distant stare. He suddenly shifts a bit closer to his door.

Hallie feels as though some unseen force just passed between them, and she has no explanation for the prickle triggering the hair on her arms to rise. She focuses on the drive, but eventually has to ask. "You okay?"

Liam breaks from his reverie turning to look and orient himself to where they are. "Um, yes. Quite."

Hallie shrugs. "Okay, but it seems like something just happened between us. I mean when I was talking about my aunts." She turns onto Union Bridge Road heading towards Fairy Stone.

He adjusts his seat to face her a bit more. "No, it is nothing. They just have unusual names as you said. Unforgettable names even."

"Yes, I suppose they do." She clears her throat and glances at him. "Do you think you have met them?"

"Two elderly yet spry women perhaps?"

"Yes, and very young at heart."

He nods with a crooked smile. "No, I don't believe I have met your elderly aunts, but I do like their names."

Hallie raises her eye brows and sighs. *Okay*. She changes the topic. "So which trails are we going to hike?"

"The Stuart Knob Trails across the lake from the beach area. I thought you might like to do the Iron Mine Trail and maybe pick up the Lower Stuart Knob Trail loop. They are not too long. That way we will have time to eat and get a canoe from the park, so I can show you the lake this afternoon. The trail head is just down the road on the right."

"That sounds good to me. I remember walking some of the trails near the beach area when I was younger, but I don't remember hiking any of the trails on this side of the lake."

"They are very nice actually." Liam points towards the side of the road in front of them. "See that area just ahead? You can pull in there." They get their backpacks and lock the car.

"This land was originally owned by the Hairston family." Liam tells her as they start towards the woods. "They ran a plantation and started mining iron ore from the mountains. We can see one of the mines on this trail." Sunshine filters through the tree tops and the crunch of leaves and pine needles below their feet give a cadence to their progression.

"What happened that the mining stopped?"

"Well, a whole series of events. The Hairston family owned thousands of acres of land, but eventually they sold the iron works portion of their holdings to a couple of men who were not as savvy in business matters. It began to falter and fail. The land laid pretty much abandoned for thirty-five years or so. It was eventually sold, and the new owners worked to clear the land of the dilapidated buildings and rebuild the area. Eventually they got the mines as well as the furnace and forge back up and working. They formed the Virginia Ore and Lumber Company, and soon they started smelting iron again as well as timbering. With the business came people, and a town started to form."

Hallie listens intently as they make their way along the trail.

"The town was named by one of the company owner's wives. She took the first letter of her husband's name, 'F' for Frank, his middle name 'Ayer,' and the middle name of another partner, 'Dale', creating the name, Fayerdale. Up until then the area had just been called Iron Works at Union Furnace. There were houses for the people, mercantile stores, a school, doctor's office, a stable and blacksmith, and even a railway that ran from Fayerdale to Philpott where you could catch a train to Bassett or even Martinsville." He points out across the mountain and back towards the lake showing her where different parts of the town were located. He describes in detail about where buildings were located, as well as where the main road ran, and where Gobbletown Creek flowed through the area before the lake was created. The images light up in Hallie's imagination as shadows of the past rise to greet her. It is a magical feeling for her, and she wonders about the people who once lived here.

At the mine heavy bars cover the entrance. Hallie grasps ahold looking deep into the mine trying to get her eyes to adjust to the darkness and shudders. "I can't imagine going down into that long narrow passageway."

"In the early years, it was the labor of slaves that dug the mines and worked them. Later, it was a paid job, but the men who worked the mines did not make very much money." Liam steps up next to Hallie to peer into the mine, their hands meet as he grasps ahold of the bars. The motion of her heart revs up, and a new heat flares. She looks over at Liam. Their eyes hold locked for a moment, and she wonders if he feels it too, but then he turns from the mine to sit on the ground and offers Hallie a drink from his canteen. She sits down beside him and takes a drink of water, feeling its coldness cool down her parched throat. She reaches into her bag and pulls out two granola bars handing one to Liam. A twinge of disappointment blows cool over her heart.

"How do you know about all this?" She focuses on opening her snack hoping to hide her emotional swing.

"Uh well, I guess talking to some of the old timers and reading old newspaper articles. There is a pretty good book at the gift shop that talks about the history of the land too." He slides his foot a bit brushing aside gravel. "Knowing about it makes being here more meaningful, and I feel more connected to the place somehow." Liam takes a long pull from the canteen, and leans his head back against the bars.

Hallie senses there is more, but he doesn't volunteer it. She finally gets the granola bar free from its stubborn wrapping and takes a bite. She sits quiet for a moment before asking, "Well, what happened to Fayerdale then? There obviously isn't a town here anymore."

"It boomed for a while until the Germans started importing iron ore cheaper, and the timber began to run out. Moonshining became the primary business and, with it, corruption and violence."

"Serious violence?"

"Lots of bickering, some destruction of property—mostly competitor's stills, and a few murders."

"Really?"

"Yes, it got bad. People began to move away. Eventually it was a ghost town."

"Wow. All that here in these peaceful foot hills."

"Peaceful now, but not always. Eventually, one of the owners of the Virginia Ore and Timber Company bought out all the land—nearly five thousand acres all together. The state was taking part in a national movement to establish a state and national park system that was to be built by the Civilian Conservation Corps."

"Right, I remember reading about them in school. The triple C. Wasn't it a program started by President Roosevelt to get the country out of the depression?"

"Yes, exactly. The state set up a planning commission for the project, and they sent engineers into the area to investigate the feasibility of a plan for a dam and the creation of a lake in the early 1930's. Up until then there were some creeks and an area of water that had been dammed to create a holding pond for timber, but nothing like it is now. The man who bought the land ended up donating it all to Virginia for a state park under one condition. He wanted the park to be named Fairy Stone."

"That's amazing! Who would imagine so much happening here."

"Yes, I guess in a way it has returned to the times of the Native Americans' inhabitance of the area—except for the lake of course. This area was home to Native Americans for hundreds of years before white settlers began to arrive in 1776. I imagine that those were the years when it was really a place to be seen."

"Hmm, you're right. I'm sure the beauty of it all back then could never be matched again which is so hard to believe given how beautiful it is now." Hallie finishes her granola bar and bunches up the wrapping working it into a side pocket of her back pack.

Liam watches her. She looks at him feeling that annoying flush hit her neck again, and she flashes a smile that he returns.

Both sit in silence for a while taking in their surroundings. Hallie is distracted by rustling in the distance, but she isn't able to see the source. The quick movements and pauses along the ground sound like a squirrel. She looks in the direction of the sound, and she sees twinkling lights swirling and sparking in the same pattern she saw in the graveyard at Bruton's Parish in Williamsburg. Her skin crawls, she glances over at Liam.

She has that kaleidoscope rainbow view like she had in her vision in the graveyard. Liam seems to be resting his eyes, but she worries he may be in a trance or something. She reaches to touch his arm, but only feels a silky barrier between them. Her throat tightens, and she hesitantly turns back to the bursting light pattern that dances joyfully at the base of a tree in an otherwise shaded spot of the woods. Hallie feels like she is in a vacuum and all the air around her has been sucked out. *Are my ears ringing?* She forces herself to still. The distant sound of a twinkling wind chime and a sing-song voice echo incoherently in the distance.

She catches her breath looking back through that kaleidoscope at Liam. He appears unaware of any change in the woods' voice as he continues breathing regularly, his muscles relaxed, his eyes closed. *Am I the only one able to see these lights?* Hallie steals a look back, almost afraid to acknowledge it. The twinkling light intensifies repeating its pattern more quickly almost inducing dizziness. A drop of sweat makes its way from Hallie's hairline in front of her ear and towards her jaw line.

She becomes transfixed as a wispy chiming voice makes its way towards her.

*The threat draws near. Beware! Cleave its
course by clinging to the hope that whispers near
the edge of darkness—at the border of new
lovers' hearts. Allow hope to gently stir
memories from forgotten lives. Hold onto lost
keys while unlocking the path meant to entwine
two lives forever setting free more than the pair.
It is a course not to be interrupted by a fate
endured beyond unimaginable time.*

Then the light vanishes, and the sound of the woods
returns. Hallie startles, and she is shaking all over. Beads of sweat
have moistened her hair creating small ringlets. She gasps drawing
in a huge breath as the vacuum enclosing her seems to burst open.
She scrambles against the loose gravel beneath her trying to stand
up.

Liam opens his eyes and quickly stands grasping her
shoulders. "Whoa. What happened? Hallie, are you alright?"

She is not able to answer him. A fierce trembling continues
to course through her. He stands and helps her up brushing her hair
back from her face, and he takes her chin gently in his hand.

"Hallie, what is wrong?" He searches her eyes.

His hand on her face brings back the deep smoldering heat
she tried to dampen, and she finds it pushes away the feeling of
dread and fear that had grasped her with the sing-song voice's
message. She blinks, still unable to say anything. She looks up into
his eyes seeing the concern that flares within them and something
else…

Liam leans down. She can feel the warmth of his breath on
her mouth, her lungs refuse to exhale, and he hesitates fixing his
eyes on hers starting to pull back. Hallie leans up closing the
distance between them. Before he can react she kisses him
tenderly. *Is that my heart racing or his?* The pace quickens, and
the heat intensifies.

This kiss is…more than a first kiss. He pulls her against
him kissing her deeply. This kiss has been *missed*. It has been
ardently yearned for and, now found again, it rekindles an
awareness that is more familiar to her than the novelty of the first

kiss it presents itself to be. *How can this be?* It ignites a simmering fire heating not just body but soul and, just at the very moment she prays it will not end, he draws back from her.

Hallie's lip tremors and she gasps quietly. She sees wonder and a hint of fear in his eyes. Her head feels light as she struggles to control her emotions.

He falters for a moment. "Hallie, I am so sorry...I should not..."

Hallie reaches up and slowly puts her fingers over his mouth. "Shhhh." She is breathless kissing him again before she speaks. "I have had no idea what it is I have been feeling since I first met you, Liam. But...just now...*that* was a powerful connection. It was something bigger than the moment. It was..."

"Familiar. Missed." He swallows and presses his lips together. He takes a step back from her. "This cannot be. It is not right. I should have known better coming here. Being alone with you. You just..." He puts a hand through his hair and grasps ahold momentarily, but doesn't finish the sentence.

"Please do not apologize for it." The confusion she sees in his eyes is a contrast to the calm she now feels despite her bewilderment. The chiming words from the dancing light are still clear in her mind, but only curiosity is triggered. The fear has stalled.

Liam's stance becomes more resolute, but he reaches back out to her taking her hand. "Hallie, you do not understand. People who...people who care about me end up getting hurt."

"What do you mean? How?"

He wets his lips and sighs. "It is not something I can explain." He releases her hand, but his eyes hold her captive. "It is too fantastical. It is beyond comprehension. I cannot let you...I will not let you get hurt."

She looks at him sizing him up. "Liam, I'm not understanding. You're right. I don't know how we got here. How we got here so quickly. I'm pretty sure there is a lot about this that I don't understand, but I know that *not* caring about you would hurt. I can't go back to before this moment. Please don't ask me to do that." *Please.*

Liam closes his eyes for a moment. He takes a deep breath and shakes his head.

She reaches out taking his hands. They raise them up interlocking fingers.

He opens his eyes. They are misty, and then he nods reluctantly—it is an admission of defeat. A swirl of elation cautiously stirs within her.

He draws Hallie near hugging her close to his chest stroking her hair. "Okay then, no turning back."

"Together then?"

"Yes, together."

Chapter 16, Golden

Loud music and laughter greet them just beyond the trail head. Hallie glances over at Liam. *Is that a twitch at his lip? Best keep focused on the trail ahead.* She is still worried about him and the sudden change in their relationship. Elated. But worried.

They step away from the woods' magic and back into reality. Ivy's red sports car and a customized black truck with shiny chrome trim and air-brushed detailing sit parked near Hallie's mustang. Ivy is sitting on the truck's tailgate with her legs dangling back and forth. A tall blonde, muscled guy wearing a Virginia Tech football jersey leans against the truck laughing and talking to her. Tessa is draped around another boy oblivious to Liam and Hallie's approach. Roxanne and a boy are casually talking near the trailhead.

"Liam, how's it going?" The boy with Roxanne greets Liam.

"Hi, Rodney." Liam pauses a moment, and Hallie stops at his side. She looks over at Roxanne who gives her head a slight nod to acknowledge Hallie's presence. Hallie returns a quick smile.

"Tell your dad that the mare has done well with the hay he gave me. I appreciate it very much."

"Sure. I'll let him know. He'll be glad to hear that she's doing well."

Liam nods and there is a brief moment of awkward silence. Rodney smiles at Hallie.

"Oh, I apologize." Liam starts, "Rodney this is Hallie O'Meara. Hallie—Rodney Hairston. And this is Roxanne Bishop."

"Hi, nice to meet you." Hallie greets both not bothering to mention that she has already met Roxanne.

"You too," Rodney replies. "That's got to be your Mustang. Looks like a sweet ride. Very nice."

"Thanks." Again, a short awkward pause before Liam starts to step away.

"Well, see you Rodney."

"Sure, sure man." Rodney turns his attention to Roxanne, and they walk onto the trail.

Hallie feels Liam bristle as Ivy giggles and calls out in a slurred, drawn out, wet-sounding voice. "Li-am White...well..., how you doin'?" She leans forward on the tailgate as she waves dramatically almost falling face first off the truck. Football Guy prevents the tumble smirking a cocky grin towards Liam.

Liam continues without a word making his way towards Hallie's car not bothering to acknowledge either of them.

"Well, fi-ne then jus' you keep walkin'." Ivy's companion does his best to keep her on the tailgate. She waves a rubbery arm in disgust towards Liam, and leans back on her hands extending her head back laughing. She reaches into the cooler sitting next to her, and pulls out a bottle of beer.

Hallie walks towards the driver side of her car following Liam's cue while Liam skirts around Tessa and her friend. They are so entwined with each other that they are oblivious to his presence. Hallie is rummaging through her back pack looking for her keys.

"Got 'em." She looks over to Liam. He has a strange look on his face. *Oh, God he is having second thoughts about the kiss.* He hesitantly reaches under the wiper blade on Hallie's car. "Is that a feather?" A bit of relief frees her muscles.

The blue plume has a sparkle of gold at the quill, and Liam's color pales ever so slightly. He gives it a twirl between his fingers and then slides it into the pocket of his shirt. He glances over at Hallie, and clears his throat. "Yes, a blue jay feather with a bit of twine or something tangled with it." He looks up. "Must have fallen from a nest or branch."

Hallie flashes a smile, but then her brow furrows. "A blue jay feather?" The car door clicks as she turns the key in the lock.

"Yes."

Hallie twitches and reaches up fidgeting with her amulet bag. She can feel the amber heart inside with the pressed penny. *Resmelda's curse.* She looks up at the trees too and then where the feather was on her car. *No dancing lights.* She shakes the thought off willing the extraordinary to return to her dreams and out of her reality. She relaxes a bit. *How much longer will brushing these images aside work?* She gets in the car leaning over to unlock Liam's door. He sits staring off through the windshield.

A sparkle from the golden thread catches Hallie's eye, and a flash of the basket of blue jay feathers in his room distracts her for a moment. Each of those feathers had a thin thread tied about them as well, but they were simple threads of various colors. "You have a collection of blue jay feathers in your room." Her voice sounds far away to her.

No answer.

Is it the appearance of the feather, or is he truly upset about what happened on the trail? He doesn't know anything about Resmelda. This is something else. She grips the steering wheel. "Liam, are you okay about everything?" *Please say yes.*

He pushes the feather further into his pocket and suddenly turns to her, and she startles a bit finding her focus back on his face and his liquid brown eyes. He leans over placing a tender kiss on Hallie's lips. "Yes, I am very well."

"Ok, then." She nods her head and gives a relieved laugh. Her fingers tingle on the wheel, but she manages to pull the car onto the road heading towards the park.

"How about we grab a couple burgers before we go into the park?" he asks.

She looks over at him and gives a short laugh. *Here we are back to the ordinary.* She successfully pushes the thought of Resmelda and blue jay feathers behind the joy revving up her heart. "Sounds good to me. I'm starving. Joan and I went to a place yesterday just off the highway. Is that good for you?"

"Bru's Place?"

"Yes, that's it."

"Excellent choice." Liam reaches to turn on the radio and pauses. "You mind?"

"No, go ahead."

He turns it on tuning it to a local station, and begins tapping his leg to the beat. Hallie muffles a laugh and shakes her head.

"What?" Liam looks over at her.

"Heavy metal?"

"You are not a fan?"

"It's not that."

"What then?"

She shrugs a shoulder. "It's just not what I thought you would be into."

He nods his head pressing his lips together. "What would you expect?"

She clears her throat. "Well, I guess I don't know." She laughs. "What do you like? I mean which music genres."

"Actually, I like it all. Music is inspiring. It can take me somewhere new, and it can take me back to somewhere familiar."

"And, where does this music take you?"

"It feeds my energy. This music pulses like the electricity in my nerves. The words demand I think of things in a different way. It moves me forward."

Hallie smiles. *Yes, forward. Together.*

Chapter17, Phosphorescent

The late afternoon sun sparkles on the water as the canoe skims through the water towards the Triple C Beach which was abandoned years ago by the men who built the park. It is an "off limits" area of the park for the public so, naturally, it is a favorite spot for park summer employees after hours. There is always a traditional bonfire and party before Memorial Day weekend to start off the summer. Liam and Hallie spent the afternoon exploring the alcoves of the lake and are now making their way around a bend towards the beach. They can hear laughter and there is a smoky smell from a bonfire in the air.

"Aye-eee!" Randy lets out a loud whoop while jumping from a make shift diving dock flipping in the air and splashing into the water with reckless abandon as they approach.

Becky and David are on the beach. Becky catches site of Hallie and Liam and waves them over. Liam steers the canoe in their direction, and beaches the canoe off-loading a cooler and gear with David's help.

"Hallie, I'm so glad that you could come!" Becky helps Hallie with her bag as they make their way past football tossing, stereo setting up, and others spreading out blankets. "And I'm really glad to see Liam. He is such a good guy, but I hardly ever see him just having fun."

"I'm not sure he planned on coming. He was just planning a canoe tour around the lake for us, but we ran into Joan at the boat house, and she had this cooler and bag put together for us."

"She's so cool."

"I know. She's pretty awesome."

"How is the horse doing?"

"Great! Last night I thought for sure she wasn't going to make it, but Doctor Cox and Liam helped her through it all. Today she is back on the mend."

David and Liam come over, and Liam takes a seat close to Hallie comfortably settling in next to her. Becky gives a knowing glance over at David smiling broadly.

"How about a swim?" David asks taking off his shirt.

Once in the water, they all swim out to the diving dock. Hallie loves being in the water. Although she has not been gone long, she misses the ocean and summer afternoons swimming in it. Once they reach the dock they climb up and take turns diving in. Cutting into the water with a smooth dive is almost as exhilarating for Hallie as riding a wave on the ocean. She watches Liam admiring the power of his swimming strokes and his speed.

A few of the other employees are on the dock as well. "Hey, let's burst the bole!" One of them shouts back towards the beach. There are whoops and yells. Hallie glances at Liam with her head tilted and eyebrows raised. He just smiles.

She looks over at Becky. "Bursting the bole?"

Becky leans in to explain. "The bole is an old tree trunk that has been here inside the lake from when this part of the water was a holding pond for logs back in the day of the timbering mill. It's just over there." Becky points over towards the side opposite of the platform.

Hallie can see the end of what looks like a huge log just below the water's surface. "And?"

"It's hollow, and these idiots dive down to swim up through it for 'fun'."

"Really? You swim up it?" Hallie looks over towards the tree trunk straining to see it better.

"Not me. Them." Becky purses her lips and jerks her head back. "You aren't going to see the bottom. It's down pretty deep—about twelve feet." Becky rolls her eyes as one of the rowdier boys dives in to make his way towards the bottom of the trunk. "It is so unsafe." She folds her arms and moves next to Hallie

Hallie bites a nail and glances over at Liam. He watches calmly. Anxiety creeps up the back of her neck like a spider's spindly legs waiting for the rowdy guy that just dived in to surface. He bursts up through the water standing on the end of the tree trunk beating his chest and whooping. Hallie lets out her breath not even realizing she was holding it.

Someone else dives in, and it continues until David dives in eventually surfacing coaxing Liam to follow suit. Liam dives smoothly into the water disappearing.

"So, this is a tradition, huh?" She asks Becky who is now sitting on the side of the deck looking somewhat bored.

"Yeah, pretty stupid though. A couple years ago someone almost drowned bursting the bole." Becky shakes her head. "If he had really been hurt, it would have messed it up for all of us. Yet every year they keep on doing it."

Liam surfaces and swims over towards the dock by Hallie and Becky. "Come in and swim."

Hallie slides off the dock slipping under the water surfacing several feet away. Liam makes his way towards her. She treads water watching a raspberry hue settle over the horizon as the sun drops below the mountain range. The air becomes crisp, and she shivers.

"Ready to get out?" Liam asks.

She nods. Everyone eventually follows suit to sit around the bonfire. Hallie and Becky sit nearby on the blanket listening to David and few others pick guitars and sing. Liam is sitting at the edge of the blanket with Hallie. She listens to the music and runs her hands along her upper arms appreciating the warmth of the fire. David coaxes Liam over to take one of the guitars.

He is an excellent guitarist, and a wave of goosebumps pop up along Hallie's arms. She sits mesmerized until Becky leans back looking up at the sky. "What a beautiful night. The stars are gorgeous!" Becky exclaims pulling Hallie's attention away. "It's hard to believe that tomorrow we will be immersed in selling beach passes, ice-cream, hot dogs, and nachos."

Hallie leans back on her hands taking in the twinkling display above them. It's brighter than any starry night she remembers along the shore back home. "You think we'll be busy tomorrow?" She muses while trying to pick out different constellations.

"Oh yeah, Memorial Day is always a busy weekend."

"Well, what better way to get inducted than a crazy busy weekend, huh?" Hallie smiles and turns back to watch Liam. He looks up from the guitar and holds her gaze for a moment. She feels her face flush, and glances away only to look back up at him to see his steadfast regard. He gives her a smile. She dips her chin down and returns a smile. He warms her heart even from across the beach.

Chapter 18, Radiant

Feet aching, Hallie leans against the counter as the day comes to an end. A record number of people came through for beach passes, and the snack bar nearly sold out of hot dogs. The day was challenging, but she and Becky managed to make it a good one. David and Liam came by at lunch to eat with them. Hallie had a run in with Ivy when she came up from the beach for a break, but David ran interference, and Ivy was thwarted.

"Don't mind her," Becky comments when Hallie brings the incident up. "She's like that with everyone."

"I'm afraid that I may have made an enemy of her though." Hallie cleans the counter while Becky sweeps the floor. "We ran into her, Tessa, and Roxanne yesterday by the Stuart's Knob Trail. She was with a boy, but she seemed upset when she saw I was with Liam."

"I've never seen Liam give her a second look Hallie. Who knows where Ivy's possessiveness over him comes from? It's totally weird, but don't pay her any mind."

"Well I can try, but with us both working here it's going to be kind of hard."

"Yeah, well Ivy and work are like oil and water. She won't be here all that often, so no worries."

Two last minute customers interrupt the conversation. Becky rolls her eyes as the two interlopers walk over to the ice-cream freezer tracking sand across the floor she just swept. The taller of the two turns and leans casually against the freezer nodding at his friend towards Becky.

The other takes an immediate interest in her. "Well, hey there brown sugar you are looking mighty fine...um mm! You are one hella hella sexy young thing!"

Hallie has not known Becky for very long, but she puts her elbows on the counter resting her chin on her hands knowing that this is going to be an amusing exchange to watch.

Becky puts a hand on her hip and points at him. "Are you for real? Coming in here last minute tracking sand across the floor with those nasty boats you got at the end of those skinny legs, and then creeping on me? If I was you, I would go over there to the register, pay for that ice cream, and move on out the door." She postures waiting for a response.

Yep, I knew it. Hallie chuckles and straightens with her hand on her hip.

"Whoa, just trying to lay out a complement on a sister, and you are crashing down on me." A smirk crosses his face as he reaches into his pocket pulling out a wrinkled five dollar bill handing it to Hallie while keeping his eyes on Becky.

Hallie makes change. He holds out his hand and she moves her hand a bit to the side dropping his change on the counter with a few coins falling onto the floor. "Oh, sorry." She shrugs at him as his mouth drops and he shakes his head. He bends down to pick up the coins.

Becky folds her arms and watches him steadily.

The two interlopers push through the door, and she walks over to lock it.

Hallie looks at her and laughs. "You slammed down on him pretty hard."

Becky laughs and starts to re-sweep the floor. "Yeah, well you got him pretty good too. You know, it's not the flirting that bugs me. It's the total disregard for walking in here all uppity and making a mess when we are trying to close up. And besides he wasn't that cute."

Both bust out laughing and go back to cleaning the snack bar. David swings by just as they are leaving.

"Hey, you two finished up for the day?"

"Yep," Becky answers. "What's up?"

"Nothing much, just thought I'd check to see if you needed a ride home."

"That would be great David. Thanks!" Becky smiles broadly. "Hallie, did you drive in today?"

"Yes, I'm good thanks"

"Hey, Becky and I are going over to Ferrum next week on our day off. Do you want to come?"

"What's there?"

"Well, The Blue Ridge Institute is a museum in Ferrum, and they are doing a display that my dad helped put together. It's called *Ghosts and Haunting Tragedies of the Blue Ridge*—kind of a historical ghost storytelling about some of the losses and unsavory events around this area of the Blue Ridge. Some of it is true and some is just folklore. Dad said it's a good exhibit. I think the college is having an arts festival going on at the same time. Maybe you could see if Liam would like to go."

"Sure, sounds like fun. I'll ask him tonight. See you two tomorrow." Hallie cuts over towards the lot to her car and climbs in. She sits for a moment twisting her neck to the side and giving her shoulder a rub feeling some of the hectic day's tension melt away. Driving home with the windows down and wind blowing through her hair, the rest of the day's tension disappears as she concentrates on the twisting turns of the road until she arrives at Joan's. When she pulls around towards the back of the house she can smell barbeque. Joan is standing by the grill basting ribs. Hallie parks her car and heads towards the house.

"Hey Hallie." Joan looks up with a welcoming smile. "How was your day?"

"Hi, Joan. Well, it was busy, but not that bad. I had a lot of fun." She tilts her head back inhaling with her eyes closed. "Dinner smells so good."

"Thanks, it won't be too much longer. I've got corn on the cob on the stove inside boiling and some potato wedges in the oven. Can you check on those for me? I'm thinking about another thirty minutes for the ribs, so if you want to wash up and relax before dinner you have a little time."

"Okay, sure. I'll be back out in a bit." Hallie goes in stopping at the kitchen to check on the veggies before going upstairs to take a shower and change. Her muscles relax in gratitude as the hot water showers over them. She gets dressed and looks out the back window of her room to see Liam standing by the grill talking with Joan. She stands for a moment watching him marveling that they just met a few days ago. It feels as though they have always known each other. He must sense her presence and looks up seeing her at the window. She holds her hand upward. He returns the gesture as though their palms are touching and smiles making her knees quiver. She turns to head downstairs just as the timer for the potatoes goes off.

Hallie carries the vegetables outside to the picnic table where Joan has set out the dinnerware and a bowl of fresh fruit. Liam carries the ribs over.

"Hey," Hallie says to him.

"Hey," he returns a warm smile.

Joan looks at them both and coaxes them to sit and eat. The three of them enjoy the delicious food and talk away most of the evening. Liam lights yard torches when the sunlight starts to fade. Eventually, Joan stands saying she has an early day tomorrow and is going to get things cleaned up and head on to bed. Hallie and Liam insist on doing the cleanup and Joan happily accepts the offer.

Once finished they go back outside to sit for a while on an old metal glider. The Tiki flames give a soft glow of light. Hallie snuggles next to Liam. His arm is over the back of the glider, but he lowers it onto her shoulders drawing her close. Liam's scar on his arm is visible, and Hallie timidly runs her finger tips up from the bottom of the scar towards the inner part of his elbow where its tendrils end.

"I do not actually remember how I got it. It was before…uh, quite some time ago." Liam answers her unasked question. "There was an…altercation of sorts with a…man, a vile man. I thought I was dead at first, but the overwhelming pain told me differently, and I made my way to a neighbor's house for help. I blacked out—for a while I am guessing because when I did arouse the blood was gone. I had this wound on my arm. It was more a deep purple but already healing. Eventually it became this scar that you see now."

"How awful. Do you think you have just blocked out the memory then?"

"Occasionally, I will have flashes of memories from that night but not enough to piece it all together." He pauses for a moment and pulls back from the memory turning to look at Hallie. "It no longer has any physical pain."

Hallie watches his face as he speaks seeing a deep sadness. She raises his arm to her lips placing a gentle kiss on the scar near his wrist where it starts and then a little higher and higher until she reaches the area where the longest tendril ends at the crook of his arm. His breathing quickens and a tremble briefly crosses his chest as she turns to kiss his mouth. Her hair gently falls against his arm. Hallie is shaken by the intensity of the kiss as their lips touch feeling a burn deep inside her and a rush of warmth spreading as her heart pounds within her chest.

They sit together for a long time both feeling comfort and a quiet joy in finding one another. The feeling remains with Hallie after Liam walks her up to the back door kissing her good night, and when she climbs into her bed she finds sleep—a deeply peaceful sleep, uninterrupted by dreams, or what she has decided is angel song.

Chapter 19, Cresting

Discovery consists of seeing what everybody has seen and thinking what nobody has thought.
Albert Szent-Gyorgyi

The following week at Fairy Stone goes well. The crowds decline in number some after the holiday weekend. A long hard summer storm ensues on Tuesday afternoon, and the beach and snack bar close early. Hallie spends the rest of the afternoon with Acacia. The horse's wounds are healing well and Acacia is growing stronger. Soon Liam will need to find a home for her outside the park, and the thought makes Hallie a little sad. She and the mare have become quick friends.

Thursday morning David and Becky meet Hallie and Liam at Joan's. Hallie is running a little behind, so when she steps outside Liam, Becky, and David are standing by David's SUV talking and kidding. Liam is laughing at something David said, and Becky has her hands over face shaking her head.

"Hey! Sorry I kept you waiting." Hallie walks over to the car fixing the strap on her back pack as she goes. "I have been running behind since I woke up for some reason."

"Ah, it's no big deal." David's easy manner is always so comfortable. "It's not like we are on any schedule anyway."

"Cute top, Hallie," Becky comments.

"Thanks, got it at a craft show back home from a woman my aunts know that does amazing things with tie dye. Do you all want me to drive?"

"No, I'll drive," David says taking keys from his pocket.

The drive gives Hallie a chance to see more views of the Blue Ridge. Something different waits around every bend with the mountain landscape's rolls and breathtaking views.

A sign outside the Blue Ridge Institute announces the exhibit *Ghosts and Haunting Tragedies of the Blue Ridge.* There

149

are several cars in the parking lot, and a few people are standing near the door chatting. David's dad greets them as they walk up to the entrance.

"Hey, so glad you all could come over." He pats David on the shoulder, and gives Liam a warm hand shake and Becky a hug. "And, who's this young lady?"

"Dad, this is Hallie O'Meara. She is staying with Joan Shively this summer and working over at the park."

"Glad to meet you Hallie. You happen to be Beattie and Dot's niece?"

"Yes sir, do you know them?"

"Sure, sure. My late wife was a good friend of theirs. They are quite a pair. How are they doing? I haven't seen them in several years."

"They're doing great, thanks. I'll be sure to let them know that I met you."

"Yes, please tell them I said hello. Now, you all go on in and take a look around. I hope you enjoy it."

"Thanks Dad, we will."

Inside people mill around colorful exhibits and antiques.

"Wow, David this is really pretty awesome!" Hallie says as she takes in the space and displays.

"Yeah, it looks good. My dad was honored to be asked to help out with the exhibit. The museum has been around since the 70's and has grown over the years sponsoring events and exhibits both here and across the state. For a history teacher, like my dad, being a part of interpreting our local history, and bringing it to life is a lot of fun. Although he doesn't consider the folklore historical, he said it was enjoyable sorting through all the stories."

There is an exhibit dedicated to the history of Fayerdale. There are photographs of some of the buildings and houses in the town, the iron works, and general store. One of the photos is of a picnic gathering, and another of a group of teenage boys standing in front of a stable. There is a map showing the general layout of the town and a more recent map of Fairy Stone showing an overlay of the two. *It is just like Liam described.*

"The house in that picture looks familiar," Hallie says pointing to the photograph of the picnic.

Liam glances over at the photo. David leans in to get a close look. "I don't recognize it." David says. "But a couple of the houses from back then are still standing. You may have passed by it or something."

"Hmm, maybe." Hallie studies it a bit more until Liam moves over to look at some of the artifacts set up including a replica of a still.

"Looks like moonshine definitely became the primary business for the town once the iron works closed and timbering died out." Hallie looks over Liam's shoulder as he checks out items set up near the still. Pictures are accented with mason jars, remnants of a sugar sack, some personal items including a dented pocket knife with a story about how it saved a boy's life in a shooting, a pair of wire-framed glasses, and a copy of an old book. Hallie leans down trying to read the faded title. It looks like it says *Cane* by Jean Toomer.

"A moonshiner who was into literature?" Hallie muses aloud.

"It would look that way from the display." Liam answers still focused on the exhibit.

"You don't think so?" Hallie notices a strange look on Liam's face.

"Oh, I would not know. It was obviously recovered from a still site. Someone brought it there. It could have been a moonshiner, or revenuer, or some unlucky soul who ran into a still site. I have heard that could be a lethal blunder."

Hallie skews her lip to the side before strolling over to another display showing multiple newspaper clippings concerning a variety of murders and shootings that occurred during the final years of Fayerdale providing both a ghost story and haunting tragedy for the exhibit. There is one article about the local doctor and a beautifully carved walking stick.

Liam and Hallie move over to look at another display about folklore and tales from local areas. It's a collection of stories from the residents. One is about the Ferrum Witch. The title catches Hallie's eye. *Hm, another witch. It seems my visions and dreams of*

Resmelda have opened up new gateways, and now they are everywhere I turn. What is becoming of my world?

She leans in to read more details. There are numerous accounts from locals in the 1940's and 50's about the witch and her abilities to cast a hex. One account told about her jinxing a cow—threatening to dry up its milk when the owner had crossed her in some way. It seems, however, that her brother would always have the appropriate counter curse for the price of a dozen eggs or a ration of smoked pork belly often preventing the whims of his sister from causing too much damage. There is a photograph of them. *Well, maybe this one not so much a real witch.* She smiles and blows a puff of breath from her nose.

"Quite a character, huh?" Liam asks her.

"She sounds quite the con-artist." Hallie smiles at him, and he shakes his head laughing. "No, really." She pushes his arm. "She and her brother had quite a scam going there don't you think?"

Liam looks back at her anticipating her theory, arms crossed over his chest, smirk on his face.

"Well you know, she threatens a curse, and her brother rushes in to save the cursed fellow for a 'price'. Just saying…it must have been a good way to make a living."

Liam laughs. "Oh so cynical! I am *sure* that she was an eccentric who thought..."

"What?" Hallie folds her arms too. "Do not tell me you are going to defend a supposed wit…uh, person with a colorful life."

He furrows his brow at first, and then the "ah-ha" hits him. "Right, the taboo topic. Yes, well as I was going to say she was probably an eccentric who thought of a way to push people off guard who may have angered her. And, I am equally sure that her brother was a kind-hearted soul just trying to keep the peace."

Hallie laughs. "Um, hm." She takes a closer look at the picture of the Ferrum Witch. "She does look a bit whimsical and gypsy-like. Unusual for the time and place she lived in, huh?"

Liam looks at the picture, putting his arm over Hallie's shoulders. "Um, yes. She is whimsically evil without a doubt." He makes his way to the next display taking Hallie with him. As they turn they bump into David and Becky.

Becky gives David a squeeze. "Well, hey y'all. Having fun?" She smiles approvingly, but David gives her a gentle nudge.

Liam looks from Becky to David. "Yes. A very nice time, thank you. You?"

Becky shrugs. "Yes, even though it's all this old stuff. It's been pretty interesting and kind of weird. You know, seeing things about places where we've been, but seeing them from a different time and perspective."

Liam looks at Becky a moment and crooks his smile to the side. "Yes, weird."

They walk over to another display high-lighting a series of unsolved murders that happened in Patrick and Franklin Counties in the 1950's. Young women were the victims. One young girl, the last victim, survived the ordeal. She had been rescued by a local man. Her sister, however, was not so fortunate. It is a sad story highlighting the sheriff's investigation and obvious frustrations. There was a suspect, but he had a strong alibi putting him out of town at the time of the last attack. There are quotes from people who were there the day of the last attack. There are multiple pictures and newspaper clippings. It looks like a carnival or some sort of celebration was going on that day. Hallie moves to look at some of the newspaper clippings, but Liam tugs her hand.

"You hungry?"

"Hmmm?" Hallie has to pull her focus from the photos. She looks up at him seeing his tight-set jaw.

"You okay?"

"Yes, fine. Sorry. I am a bit hungry though. I think David and Becky just walked outside."

"Oh." Hallie takes a look around. "Let's go on out then. Lunch would be great." She glances back at the display about the serial murders wondering what about it triggered the change in Liam's mood. *If anything, I would have thought the story about the Ferrum witch would have done it, but he almost seemed amused by it. He is definitely hard to figure out sometimes.*

Chapter 20, Kindling

"So, this place is all about home cooking." David explains as they walk up to the restaurant. He opens the door for them.

"The '77 Restaurant?" Hallie asks.

"Yea, it's named after the Ferrum Flash's race car from back in the 50's. He was a local stock car driver. He doesn't own it anymore, but things haven't changed much over the years."

Hallie steps in and looks around. The original signs for the menu are nostalgically up on the wall in the front section of the restaurant behind the counter—now just faded decorative reminders of times long gone. A shelf near the kitchen has pictures and old books sitting on it. A counter with stools occupies the front while a dining room area with a mix-match of chairs and tables is in the back. Shelves also run along a wall in the dining room with the same sort of collections. They sit at a table and Hallie takes interest in some of the books on the shelf.

"Aw, honey, be careful something doesn't jump out at you from them books." A cheery waitress walks up. "Those things have been up there since the beginning of time. They get an occasional dusting off, but I bet not a one has been opened in ages. Folks around here are more interested in the food."

"Oh, I'm sorry!"

"Oh heavens honey, you go right ahead. I just wanted to warn ya so you'd know what you might be getting into." She laughs laying some menus out for them. "What can I get y'all to drink?"

They give her their drink orders, and she leaves them to look through the menus. Hallie is busy eyeing the book she took off the shelf. "Wow, this has got to be a first print of *The Martian Chronicles*. Its publication date is 1950."

David wrinkles his brow and smiles. "I wouldn't have taken you for a sci-fi geek, Hallie."

She distractedly looks up from the book. "Oh, no I'm not. My Aunt Beattie is really into old books, and she has this fantastic collection. I just love to read the books in her collection, but I couldn't help learning a little from her about how books are put together too. This is a pretty well-preserved book." A thin card falls onto the floor from the book and Hallie leans over to pick it up.

"What is it?" Liam asks

Hallie looks at it. "An old unused train ticket from Ferrum to Danville. Huh, I don't remember seeing a train station anywhere. Do you know where it is?"

Becky shrugs, but David speaks up. "Well, it used to be just across the street from here over where the post office is now, but it has been gone for years. Is there a date on the ticket?"

Hallie looks at it. "Yep, July 3rd, 1958. Huh." Hallie looks at the ticket more closely.

"What?" Asks Becky.

"Oh, nothing…it's just that the serial number for the ticket is the same as my birthday, 04042000, too weird." Hallie shrugs and sticks the ticket back into the book and replaces *The Martian Chronicles* back to its original spot.

After lunch they walk onto the Ferrum College grassy campus mall area towards the sound of a Celtic-tribal and raw beating music. The music is being made with a collection of cans, buckets, wood planks, pipes as well as traditional instruments and energetic musicians. Hallie loves it feeling the beat as though it is coming from inside her chest. People are moving to the music, others are sitting around soaking in the sun, and kids are running and playing. The four of them sit on the grass enjoying the music for a while before moving further down the mall area.

They run across the Jack Tale Players, a group of traveling actors that bring mountain folk tales to life. Their bright red suspenders accent their checkered shirts. The foursome sit and listen to one of the tales about Jack's adventures before heading further down the mall passing a display of art work. Hallie and Becky admire the beautiful paintings, jewelry, quilts, wood carvings and pottery.

A barrel full of carved walking sticks catches Hallie's eye, and she wanders over to get a closer look. She lifts them up one by one appreciating the craftsmanship.

Liam steps next to her. "Nice." He lifts a stick from the barrel. It has a carving of an old man's face with a long beard that wraps around the cane towards it rubber tipped end.

"I know." Hallie admires a walking stick with an intricate carving of the moon and stars and a woman gazing up towards them. "I think Joan would like this. You know, for when she hikes."

"Now that," a man walks up to them, "is a fine choice. Made of willow—the tree that loves water the most and is sacred to the moon goddess who lays dew over the earth during the night bringing back moisture and life to the land."

Hallie looks up at the man in wonder. He stands very tall wearing a wide brimmed leather hat over a shaved head with a bandana tied around his forehead. His face, baring the stubble of at least three days growth, is pleasant.

He laughs and then shrugs off his comment as though it may have hung in the air too long.

"No," Hallie quickly jumps in. "You talk like my aunts do. They are…naturalists…herbalists, and they…well…they see the magic in things, too. I like it."

"Well, you know, there is so much to tell. There are all sorts of fanciful and magical connections to all the varieties of wood."

Liam stiffens a bit and steps aside looking down the mall.

Hallie glances at Liam and grasps her amulet bag for a moment finding comfort. She turns back to the man and smiles. "Well sir, I'll take this one."

He nods his head. "Very well young lady that'll be twenty dollars for the willow, sacred wood to not only the moon goddess, but to Hecate, Circe, Hera and Persephone as well. Good for healing, love spells…," he draws out the end of his sentence glancing meaningfully from Hallie towards Liam, "and, like most of the feminine persuasion, a strong will only enhances its power."

Hallie hands him the money. "Thank you for the beautiful stick and for sharing its story."

"The pleasure is mine, Miss."

Hallie says goodbye and walks over to Liam. "You okay?"

"Is it truly everywhere?"

She presses her lips together. "It was his reference to magic that upset you."

"You know, before I met you, I had no confusion about the subject. It fit into one category. Darkness. It elicited one emotion. Hatred." He purses his lips and makes an effort to swallow.

Hallie watches him hoping he will open up to her. *How unfair to want this. I can't even find the courage to tell him about Resmelda. About Beattie and Dot.* She clears her throat. "Before I made this trip magic was the roll of a wave, a beautiful sunrise, the dance of a camp fire during trips with my aunts, and so much more that is just part of everyday life. My Aunt Beattie always says magic is everywhere if you know where to look for it."

He smiles and reaches out sliding a loose strand of her hair behind her ear. "Yes, I have begun to see this reference as a description of the beautiful things around us."

"Yet you still…I don't know…develop this fierce edge."

"It is a hard habit to quit."

"Yes. Especially given how you have felt about it."

"Still feel about it." He squares his shoulders. "But, willing to see what it looks like through your eyes."

She raises her eyebrows and puffs out air from her nose. "If only I knew what I was seeing." *Now. Tell him now.* "My aunts. Well there is this story that Dot tells. I mean I have heard it a hundred times. And, well since I left home it…"

"Hey, Hallie." Becky comes up tugging David along with her. "Look at these great ear rings I got. Such a great jewelry artist on the other side of the mall."

"Oh, Becky they are really different and so pretty." Hallie flicks a smile at Liam and he takes her hand.

"What next?" Liam asks.

"There's a hot folk band playing at the end of the mall." Becky offers.

"Let's go then." Hallie says. She sighs. *Almost, but probably best Becky and David came along. I still think I will only look crazy, if I tell him about being swallowed by Dot's tragic love story and Resmelda.*

A melody with a fast beat is being accented by the tapping and stomping feet of people flatfooting on a make-shift dance floor made of plywood laid out over the grass. Hallie has never seen flatfooting before, and she takes a seat next to Becky clapping with the music.

The song ends, a petite young woman with a warm smile steps up to the microphone, and the band switches gears to a sweet mountain tune. People break off into couples to dance. It is a dream-like sight Hallie thinks as she watches couples getting up to dance in the middle of a summer day under the shade of trees. She starts to feel a little ill-at-ease as she watches the twinkling sunlight pattern playing off the couples dancing until the view is blocked by Liam. She realizes he is standing with a hand stretched out towards her.

"Dance?"

Her cheeks flush, but she does not look away reaching up to allow him to grasp her hands and help her stand. They step onto the plywood, and he embraces her tenderly yet confidently. He skillfully leads her across the dance floor until they are immersed in the music moving smoothly amongst the other couples. Hallie draws in her breath. *Where did he learn to do this?*

"*My Love Follows You Where You Go,*" Liam speaks to her.

She looks at him unsure of what to say although her heart forgets a beat.

"It is the name of the song." He devilishly grins at her. "I believe that Allison Kraus and Union Station recorded it, but this version is very nice."

Hallie is still at a loss for words, and she simply closes her eyes smiling as she listens to the song and moves slowly in partnership with Liam. It feels as though they are the only two there, and she leans her head against his chest enjoying the music. Towards the end of the tune she opens her eyes seeing Becky and David dancing not too far away. Becky gives her an enthusiastic thumbs up, and Hallie smiles at her. As Becky and David move across the dance floor Hallie looks off beyond the group dancing and catches site of a slender well-dressed man with an ivy cap. A petite ballerina-like woman is standing in proximity to him. *Oh my God. Joe and Hester. Here.* Her heart fires off a rat-tat-tat like a machine gun. Their backs are to the dance floor with their attention focused on something off in the distance. Hallie's throat tightens, and her pulse quickens.

"Liam," her voice cracks, and she clears her throat. "Liam, I think I'd like to leave."

The song comes to an end, and Liam looks down at her making an effort to bring himself back from some far off place. "Hallie, are you okay? You look pale."

She takes his hand as she moves him through the crowd away from the source of her anxiety. She spies Becky and David while she is on the move and motions them to follow as she picks up the walking stick and her bag from next to the dance floor.

"Is everything okay?" Becky asks with concern when she and David catch up to Liam and Hallie.

Hallie forces a casual tone into her voice. "Oh, yes. It's, uh, just getting late…, and I don't want Joan to worry. Are you ready to head back?" Hallie's nerves are sparking a jittery tap as she keeps the small group on the move away from the blue grass music, past the art display, theatrical troupe, and into the parking lot.

"Do you want to call her?" Becky asks hurrying to keep pace with Hallie. Liam glances over their heads towards David and shrugs.

Hallie stops short for a moment trying to think. "Um…yes, I'll give her a call on the way back. I'm so sorry…I lost track of the time, and it caught me a bit by surprise when I realized how late it is."

Becky's face relaxes. "Oh, well I can understand that." She smiles at Hallie and then Liam.

Hallie slows the pace relaxing a bit as they near David's vehicle.

Her heart hitches though when she spies a sleek black sports car like the one from the bridge-tunnel parked a little way beyond them. The sun glares off its back window making Hallie squint as she stares at it trying to convince herself that it's not really their car and not really them she just saw. She wipes her sweaty palms on her shorts and makes an effort to take slower, deeper breaths.

"Hallie, what is wrong?" Liam stops short and steps in front of her.

"Um, nothing. Really." She commands her nerves to lose their tic. "Just a…ghost," she blurts it out trying to find an explanation for her behavior. "Metaphorically speaking. It's silly—really." Again she issues a mandate to her unruly nervous system. She doesn't want to look like she is crazy even though that is exactly how she feels, so she displays a winning smile and reticent shrug of the shoulder.

Liam holds a hand up to David to wait a minute and walks Hallie over to a nearby tree. "Okay, what is wrong?"

Hallie glances over her shoulder towards the festival and then at the black shiny car. She closes her eyes and opens them to see Liam waiting. "It was this guy and his…his…I don't know what she is to him." She presses her lips together. "I saw them on my way here. Twice. Talked with them the second time, but it was creepy." *Tell him why.* "I…I…" *Can't.* "I don't know why he makes me feel this way. It's silly. Really. I think he reminds me of this guy back home who had done some really awful things." *A lie? Don't lie.* She clutches her amulet bag.

Liam glances down at her hand on the bag and nods. He runs a hand through his hair. "I see. Well, are you okay? Do I need to go and confront this man with you?"

"No! Ah, no. I think I just want to go."

He nods reluctantly.

Hallie tenses. *He thinks something is wrong with me.*

But he smiles, and with a warm caring voice he says, "I understand. Truly. Your eyes Hallie say there is more. They are beautiful *and* very revealing."

She opens her mouth to speak, but he gently places a finger over it. He traces her upper lip to the corner of her mouth and brings his hand to the back of her neck.

Hallie leans into it bringing her hand up to caress his wrist no longer needing the comfort of her amber heart inside the amulet bag.

"When you are ready. Then, we will see what sparks those hazel eyes to flash that mysterious green every so often. Okay?"

Hallie nods and he leans down giving her a gentle kiss.

The warmth of that moment stays with Hallie on the ride home. Despite the immense comfort she feels having Liam close, thoughts of Joe and Hester race through her mind. *Why are they here? Is it a coincidence, or is it something more?* Her silent questions go unanswered. She can't fathom any explanation for their presence and fights a feeling of being hunted. The conversation in Williamsburg, Dot's story—now coming to life, the dreams, the trance-inducing sparkling lights, and the intrusive chiming voice all crowd her mind. She spends the ride home quietly—desperately trying to make sense of it all.

Chapter 21, Tinder

Despite Hallie feeling on edge after seeing Joe and Hester, the next two weeks pass uneventfully. She and Becky spend their working hours at the snack bar. Hallie gets the routine down and manages to avoid any run-ins with Ivy and, best of all, Liam spends Hallie's lunch breaks with her. She senses Joan enjoys seeing them together, but often worries that she may begin to have concerns given they both live in the same home. Acacia is pretty much recovered spending her daytime hours grazing in the pasture near the stable while becoming a favorite with park visitors.

During this time Hallie struggles with the fear of Joe and Hester showing up at the park. The worry consumes her thoughts any day a park visitor remotely looks like one or the other. Her amber heart gets grasped many times, and it unfailingly washes her in comfort, but she eventually has to come to terms with her fears. *If they come they come. It is a crowed place. I won't be alone.* She straightens her back practicing what she feels brave looks like. Clear eyes. Set jaw. Square shoulders. She laughs out loud and quickly looks to be sure no one sees her. I won't have to tell my Resmelda story to be declared crazy, if someone sees me like this. Then she remembers Liam's willingness to confront Joe. Stand by her. The calm from that day washes over her, and she bites down on her lip determined to make a go of being a little less afraid. It works. Usually.

Joan and Rick finalize the plans for the park reunion. They are going all out with the 50's theme. They have a band, menu, and decorations all set. A local antique car club is going to have a car show highlighting cars from the era. It is going to be held at Fayerdale Hall, the community center, in the park. Invitations to employees and their families have been sent out. Everyone going is planning on wearing styles from the time. Joan helps Hallie get an outfit together finding her a beautiful vintage black dress with a blue floral print. It has a cinched waist with full pleated skirt and a bright blue crinoline slip with a hem just a bit longer than the sleeveless dress' hem. Hallie bought a pair of flat black shoes that set the whole thing off.

"So, you going to the shin dig this weekend with Liam?" Joan asks as she puts the final stitches in for the hem while she and Hallie sit out on her back porch.

"Yes, I am," Hallie replies knowing that Joan is already aware they were likely to go together. There isn't much that gets past her.

Joan smiles at her and goes back to finish sewing.

"Joan," Hallie starts hesitantly.

She looks back up waiting for Hallie to continue, but Hallie can't find her voice. "Hallie, are you okay?"

Hallie's mouth opens to talk just as an uncontrollable flutter high-jacks her stomach, and she knows the heat rising up her neck comes with a pink flush. She closes her mouth and feels a pounding in her chest reminiscent of the raw tribal beat the musicians at Ferrum College created.

She clears her throat and starts again. "I just…I wanted to explain my feelings for Liam, but I'm not sure I can. I can't express to you what the last few weeks have meant to me. I feel different. I feel at home and in unfamiliar territory at the same time. He is important to me—like no one before." She hesitates again, and Joan sits quietly giving her time to gather her thoughts. "Well, you know I had that crush on Lucas Gentry—I wrote you about it back in tenth grade but nothing else since. And even that was nothing to compare with this. I just want to be sure that it is okay with you. I mean with both Liam and me living here with you, but I guess dating. Is it okay?"

"Is there any reason that I should be concerned about you both living here feeling the way that you do for one another?" Joan asks with an authoritarian tone tempered with a gentle smile.

Hallie feels her cheeks flush hotter. "Oh, no….no of course not. Even though he has become so much more relaxed, he still has an old-fashioned reserve about him—you know?" Now that Hallie started the conversation, the words pour from her mouth. "Not that I haven't thought about…well, only *thought* about it. It's like he has found this hidden place in my heart, and I just want to stay in his arms. I have always been comfortable with who I am, but somehow I feel more complete with him." Hallie rolls her eyes. Joan sits and listens.

"It sounds so cliché. It's like I know exactly what it all means while, at the same time, I have no idea what it all means. I do know that I need to know you are okay with it. I have known and loved you nearly my whole life. I don't want to disappoint you. I haven't even talked to Beattie and Dot about it yet, but I think it is because—before right now—I haven't had the words. I am not sure I have the words for it even now. I feel like I am just babbling."

Joan sets the dress down and gets up to sit next to Hallie. She puts her arm around her and gives her a squeeze. "Don't you know Hallie? Don't you know that you are in love?"

Hallie stares off. "Love," she says it like she is trying it on for size. *Yes, that is it. I have never felt like this before, and Joan is right!* She hugs her arms around herself.

"Yes, Hal, yes—it is a wondrous and mysterious thing, and it is the most powerful magic there is. It is an awesome force whether it is a young girl's first crush, a summer time romance, or…more. But then only time can tell what kind of love you've got. They're all good when you're *in* love. The hard part is holding on to what the sensible part of your brain is telling you when you have that twitter-patted feeling in your heart trying to over-rule what is reasonable, but that is what love does." She pauses and strokes Hallie's hair.

"Enjoy it, Hallie. Embrace it. Cherish it. And get carried away. Just don't be careless…, but I have no fears for you in that regard."

Hallie feels a strong need for motherly advice. She needs some reassurance about a concern that has been intruding upon her thoughts. She looks directly at Joan. "Tell me, Joan. Why do I feel so different from before I met him? I know it's silly. I can't explain what I mean, but I just feel different. Is that what love does? I don't want to lose who I am."

Joan nods. "Well, I believe that we make an exchange of sorts with every being we meet forming some sort of connection.

We share a part of ourselves—an idea, a feeling, an emotion, anything. Every connection, no matter how insignificant it may seem, makes an impact and imparts some influence on us. And the important connections make an even bigger impact. It might be something in how we're made up. Perhaps it's our Creator's way to bring unity between living creatures—an ever-hopeful desire for us all to find peace. Some people see it as a mating of the souls. I don't know what best describes what it is. I do think that *all* 'that' can happen, and you can still be true to who you are. I think you are safe with this Hallie."

Hallie nods. *Safe? Yes, safe with Liam. But, not so safe with Joe and Hester.* Her visions have been non-existent the past couple weeks, and she has been wondering why. A sigh escapes her, and she gives Joan a hug as the rumble of the old truck sounds from the lane. Joan kisses Hallie on the forehead, and holds her out at arm's length taking stock of her and smiles approvingly.

Liam is up the stairs opening the screen door and walking towards the back door before he realizes that Joan and Hallie are on the porch. He stops short as the screened door sounds a bang when it shut. He worked today and there's a smudge of dirt that Hallie can see over his eyebrow. His slightly baggy work pants gather over a pair of heavy boots. "Oh, hello! Apologies, did I interrupt something?" He puts his hands in his pockets.

"Not at all." Joan gets up and picks up Hallie's dress.

Hallie takes a long, deep, savoring breath and glides her fingers below her chin.

"Hey, is that your dress for the dance tomorrow?" He asks Hallie.

"It," her voice pitches up. She clears her throat. "It is." She flushes.

"Very nice! I look forward to seeing you in it."

Joan gives a quick gasp. "Liam, I have spent so much time helping Hallie find something to wear. I never thought to see what you needed."

"Oh, it is not quite the same challenge for me. Pants, shirt, a can of pomade, and I am set. The hardest part is finding pomade that does not smell too badly." He shifts his weight.

Joan gathers up her sewing. "Okay, but if you need something, let me know. Here, sit and relax. I have lasagna cooking in the oven, but it will still be a while before dinner is ready."

"Yes ma'am, thank you. I think I will." He takes a seat next to Hallie, and she sits enjoying listening to him tell her about his day.

Chapter 22, Timber

Hallie leans over the top of her bureau to make a final check on her makeup pressing her lips together and wiping the corner of her mouth with her pinky. She combs her hair out one more time and takes a deep breath patting her waist. Her pouch with the amber heart and pressed penny is lying next to her hair brush. No pockets and no belt loops on her dress pose a problem for how to carry it with her. She squinches her face. "I can't wear it around my neck." She looks around and picks up the black clutch that Joan loaned her and puts the pouch inside before heading out of her room. She passes the bathroom where Joan is making some final touches to her hair.

"Hallie, you look amazing!" Joan stops what she is doing to check out Hallie's dress. "Very cute! I will be down in a few minutes. I think I just heard Liam come into the kitchen. Make sure y'all wait until I come down before you leave, so I can snap a picture, okay?"

"Sure," Hallie says and turns to head down stairs. She comes through the hallway into the kitchen where Liam is leaning against the counter waiting patiently.

"Oh, my God!" she exclaims. "You look so…so different! It's amazing what a little hair grease does! You look VERY 1950's! Kind of like Johnny Depp in that movie *Cry Baby*."

Liam's attractive features take on a classic bad-boy charm with his hair combed back away from his face—a couple thin strands of hair hang down towards his eyes. He has on a pale blue shirt that compliments the color of the flowers on Hallie's dress. The sleeves are rolled up to his elbows. The shirt tail is tucked neatly into a pair of belted black flat front slacks with a tapered leg.

He smiles almost shyly and reaches out to take Hallie's hand lifting it above her head and motioning her into a spin flaring her dress as she turns. "I would say that you are the one who looks good!" He stops her spin short so she is just inches in front of him, and he reaches behind his back bringing a clear plastic box around from behind him. It has a delicate wrist corsage inside. He lets go of Hallie's hand to open the box and take the corsage out slipping it over her wrist. "I believe, back in the day, it was traditional to give one's date flowers. I hope you like them."

Hallie looks at the corsage. *It's perfect.* She thanks him and gives him a tender kiss. His eyes are closed and his face serene when she comes down off her toes to stand flat. He opens his eyes to look at her, and Hallie feels herself tremble. His eyes divert from Hallie to look just behind her as Joan comes around the corner.

Joan is distracted shoving something into her purse and juggling her camera as she walks in. "Okay, ready finally. I'm heading over to Ida's house to pick her…." She looks up stopping short as she meets Liam's eyes. She falters a moment resting her hand on the back of a kitchen chair. Setting the purse and camera down, she pulls the chair out taking a seat composing herself as she fumbles trying to snap her purse closed.

Hallie rushes over to her taking her arm. "Joan, are you alright? You're pale. How about some water?"

Liam fills a glass and hands it to Hallie to give to Joan.

"Thank you." Joan takes a sip of the water. "I'm fine. Just too much rushing around. I'm running late, and I told Ida I'd be over to her place early to pick her up. I finally convinced her that cast on her leg wouldn't keep her from having a good time." The color returns to Joan's face, and Hallie relaxes a little looking over at Liam. He is studying his shoes before looking up at Hallie. He too looks unsettled, but she cannot read the expression on his face.

"Why don't we all ride together?" Hallie asks Joan. "We can go and pick up Missus Cox in your Jeep and Liam can drive. I'll call Becky and let her know. She and David can head over to the park and just meet us there."

"Oh, don't be silly. I'm fine, just fine. Let me snap that picture of you two." She gets up and turns on the camera checking the settings. Hallie stands next to Liam.

"Ok, say cheese!" She snaps the picture and sets the camera down then smooths her skirt out still looking a little distressed. She walks over towards the phone.

"You two go on and get going. I just need to give Ida a call and let her know that I am on my way." Joan motions them out with a wave of her hand avoiding looking directly at Liam. She turns picking up the phone receiver.

"Hm okay, if you're sure."

Joan flashes Hallie a smile and waves them on.

They step out to the porch just as Becky and David pull around the corner of the house, and Hallie stops short with her hand on the screen door. "Liam I will be right out. Can you wait for me with Becky and David? I just can't leave without knowing for sure Joan is alright."

"Yes, of course. I will wait at the car."

Hallie looks through the kitchen door window seeing Joan across the hall at the large barrister bookcase in the den. She slides open the door of its upper shelf pulling out a thick photo album. Hallie opens the kitchen door quietly stepping in. She walks across the hall and rests her hand on the door frame of the den. "Joan?"

She jumps grasping her chest, and an old piece of news print floats to the floor. Hallie steps forward picking it up. Hallie stares at the newspaper article with a picture of the back of a dark-haired man carrying a little girl. Her eyes stare back at the camera over his shoulder shell-shocked. Hallie reads the story, and her arms drop to the side.

July 4th Celebration Ends in Tragedy

The latest of attacks on young girls in Franklin and Patrick Counties results in the death of one sister while another is heroically rescued by a Ferrum resident. Joan Canaday is carried away to safety by her rescuer after some suspect she witnessed the brutal murder of her older sister, Priscilla. An interview with Sheriff Shively reveals that law enforcement is still baffled by

the case with no arrests and no new leads,
although the sheriff states they do have a person
of interest that is being investigated.

She starts to speak and has to restart. "I had no idea. I
didn't know that your sister died this way. And you…" Hallie's
eyes fill with tears, and she hugs Joan.

Joan sobs and snatches tissue from a box on top of the book
case handing one to Hallie. "It was years ago Hallie. I have been
able to put it all behind me until…"

Hallie looks back at the kitchen door, and finishes Joan's
sentence. "Until you saw Liam just now." Her brow furrows. "I
don't understand."

Joan stares down at a photograph of her sister and a pressed
daisy next to it. She runs her fingertips over the page. "I can't
believe I didn't realize it before." She walks over and sits on the
sofa. "It has to be why he touched my heart when I first met him."

"What, Joan?"

"He saved me. It had to have been him."

"Liam? But, when did this happen?"

Joan looks up at Hallie. "1958."

"That can't be Joan. That was sixty years ago."

Joan nods and gently takes the newspaper clipping from
Hallie setting it back in the album and closes it. "I know." She puts
the album away and slides the door closed. "Maybe a look alike
then."

"That makes sense." *But nothing has made sense recently.*
Hallie rubs a chill off her arms.

"Yes, that would make sense." Joan pats the side of her hair
and adjusts her dress collar. The phone rings startling them. She
hugs Hallie again. "You best be on your way Hal. Immersing
myself in the 1950's getting this shindig ready has just made me
nostalgic. Silliness really. You go now. I'm sure that's Ida on the
phone."

"But, are you sure you're okay?"

"Yes, I am very okay."

Chapter 23, Ensue

"Wow! They have really gone all out!" Becky exclaims taking a look around. The sound of laughter and 50's music is in the air. A table is set up with scrap books and photographs from the park's early years up through present day. Several pictures show highlights of previous dances and gatherings.

"Looks like the park was quite a social hot spot back in the day." Hallie turns the pages of one of the scrap books.

An elderly woman sitting in a lawn chair by the table looks at Hallie. "I remember coming here as a teenager for dinners and dancing. This is where I met my husband. Lots of good matches came from this here place. There's magic in these hills you know. When my daughter Lottie—she's right over there honey—told me about this I knew I had to come." She points to a cheerful woman chatting with one of the car owners just a short distance away. Hallie turns and gives a wave as Lottie looks over towards the elderly woman. "Looks like lots of folks felt the same way."

"Yes ma'am." Hallie smiles at the woman.

Lottie comes up and smiles at Hallie and then turns toward her mother. "Doing okay momma? How about we head on inside and see if any of that fried chicken is ready?"

"Oh, that sounds lovely." The woman grasps her daughter's arm and stands to leave. "You enjoy yourself young lady," she says to Hallie.

"Yes ma'am, you too." Hallie and Liam walk around the car show with Becky and David.

Ivy and her entourage are walking around. She is wearing a simple but elegant skirt and a pearl brooch on her sweater. Roxanne and Tessa are there as well. Ivy is rather subdued talking with her father near a beautiful vintage Corvette.

"Whoa." David comments as he and Becky walk up alongside Liam and Hallie. "A 1956 Corvette with a 265 V8 engine, 210 horsepower, tied up in that hot red finish, and awesome side door detailing. Chrome all the way around and white wall tires. Hot, very hot."

Becky, Hallie, and Liam stand for a moment watching David. He looks at them clueless to why they are shaking their heads laughing.

"Oh, come on. Liam tell me you don't appreciate that car sitting over there. Tell me you wouldn't—just once—want to take that for a spin."

"Oh, no it is definitely a nice car. And it is definitely a nice ride," Liam replies.

"*Is* a nice ride? You've driven that car?" David is incredulous.

"Not that one, but one like it," Liam says without elaborating.

David is on edge. "And…where, when, why were you driving it?"

"I used to work at a service station with a mechanic's garage. There were some definite perks to the job."

"Sweet!" David's look of a star-struck teenaged girl seeing a rock-star for the first time puts Becky over the edge.

She rolls her eyes. "David let your 'cargasm' go. Nice car, but jerk man owns it. And even worse, Ivy is standing next to it. Somehow the car gets cancelled out by that. Sorry, just not feeling it."

David gives Becky a squeeze and a kiss. "Thanks Beck, thanks for bringing me back down. I almost fell off the cliff. Thank you, thank you very much." He lowers his voice to do an Elvis impersonation.

Becky laughs leaning her forehead against his. "You are such a geek David. You're lucky I let you hang out with me."

"How about we head in?" Liam suggests. "That chicken smells pretty good even way out here."

They head towards the hall. Hallie looks up feeling eyes on her, and her heart jumps anticipating seeing Joe and Hester, but instead, she meets Ivy's eyes. The intensity of the stare, and the dislike that fuels it, bores through Hallie. She turns her head away able to shrug off Ivy, but the thought of Joe being nearby somewhere leaves a deeply frosted chill in her bones. She bites her lip and wills herself to let it go. It works. For now.

They walk through the door where a buffet line is going strong. People socializing and eating sit at tables bordering the room. The center of the room has been left open for dancing later in the evening. Streamers decorate the room, and a space is set up for the band with a big banner hanging up on the wall that reads "Fairy Stone State Park Employee Reunion".

The band is taking a break and people are at the buffet line getting food. Joan and Ida are already there, and Joan calls Hallie over.

Ida pulls Liam aside. "Liam, my boy, take a seat and chat with me for a while. I haven't seen you since this darn leg has had me laid up."

Liam complies and Hallie sits near Joan who points out different people in the room giving her their history and involvement with the park introducing her to a few. She is back to her old self, and Hallie feels less worried about her. Soon the band starts back up and Liam catches Hallie's eye. They excuse themselves and go to find Becky and David.

"Hey, where have you two been?" David asks. "Let's eat. I'm starving and this food smells so good!"

They make their way through the buffet line. It is loaded with southern fare including greens, chicken, potatoes and gravy, pinto beans, biscuits and corn bread. Cobblers, pies, and cakes of every variety fill the dessert table. Folks chit chat and comment on the decorations and outfits that are worn. A few of the younger women serving behind the buffet table blush fumbling a bit with serving spoons as Liam passes near. One nearly misses his plate dropping some of the greens onto the table.

Becky leans in to whisper to Hallie. "It's always like that. When he first moved here it was ridiculous! Sometimes I wonder if he even notices, and other times I think it's one of the reasons he keeps a distance from everyone. I don't think he is comfortable with the attention."

Hallie and Liam had not really been anywhere public since officially dating, and she glances at a woman near him noticing what Becky said is true. Hallie smiles as she catches his eye, and he smiles back at her as though she were the only person in the room.

"Of course," Becky goes on. "He has met his perfect match. He couldn't have been given a better gift." She looks at Hallie smiling sincerely.

They manage to find a table and Liam and David go to get drinks. There is a table set up with tall servers of tea, lemonade and coffee nearby. The room is bustling with activity and conversation as the band returns to play a soft tune while people eat.

The meal ends and, after things are cleaned up, more room is made by sliding tables further out towards the walls to expand the dancing area. The band kicks in with lively tunes, and soon the floor is full of people dancing and having a good time. There are some couples there from a local dance studio that are mingling and helping people learn, or remember, some of the dances that were popular from the 50's. Everyone is having a great time and Hallie, seeing Joan, gives her a big double thumbs up. Joan smiles and nods back in agreement.

The band switches gears and plays a slow tune, *Wicked Game*. The singer has a soulfully haunting voice when she sings it.

"Wicked Game?" Hallie looks at Liam. "This isn't a 1950's song. Is it?"

"No, it isn't. It could be though. It could be any decade really." Liam draws Hallie close, and they get lost in the swaying of the dance. The heat rises not just from within, but encroaches from the fringe as more couples get up to dance. It's sultry on that crowded dance floor, and when the song ends Hallie and Liam linger for a moment in their embrace.

"Would you like to take a walk outside for some fresh air?" he asks her after a moment and she nods. They step outside to walk down towards the beach area. Ivy and her minions are sitting on one of the picnic tables near the snack bar area taking turns sipping from a flask.

Hallie and Liam walk along the water's edge stopping to look across the lake. Frogs sing from the distant shoreline and the crisp twinkle of stars lights up the night sky.

"It's so hard to believe that a town used to be here and some of the remnants are just below the water and over those hills," Hallie says.

Liam nods and points towards the diving platform located about thirty yards off the beach. "When the water is clear you can see the railroad tracks at the bottom of the lake from over there. In the early years of the park, the house where summer employees lived was across the lake over that way. Most of the town of Fayerdale was through here and across the lake where we hiked."

They hear voices and look back. Randy and a few other guys are heading over to the boat house. "Hey Liam! Hey Hallie!" Randy greets them cheerfully. "Don't let us get in the way. We're going to head out for a bit on the lake—just don't tell anyone." He winks at Hallie.

He starts to walk away and then turns walking backwards and calls back. "Hey, this week a bunch of people are going to meet over at the Triple C Beach after the park closes to have a bon fire and party. I'll let you know the night once we figure that out. You should come."

"Sure," Liam answers. "Maybe we will."

"Well, see ya!" Randy runs to catch up to the others.

Liam turns to Hallie. "So, Joan seems to be doing fine now."

"Yes, she said it was just silliness, but I'm not so sure."

"What was it?"

"She said that seeing you dressed like you are triggered a memory of someone from a long time ago. A tragic time when her sister was murdered, and Joan was rescued from the same fate by this person. You."

"Me?" He coughs out a short laugh.

"Uh, huh. I think that she was so startled by it at first that she actually said that it was *you* that saved her."

He wets his lips. "She must have been pretty upset to think that."

"Yes, it had to have been horrible to go through that, but when I reminded her how long ago that was—back in the 50's sometime—she seemed to snap back to present day. I think it was just that you looked a lot like the person who saved her."

He nodded his head. "Yes, that makes sense. So, she is good now? I mean she looks fine and seems to be enjoying the evening."

"Oh, yes. She is good."

"And, how are you this evening?" He moves closer putting his arms around her waist.

"I'm pretty good." She slides her hands up his chest.

"Only pretty good?" He leans down and kisses her.

Hallie loses all sensation of the ground beneath her. The kiss is lingering and electrifying and delicious.

A loud cat-call whistle rings out from somewhere in the shadows. Liam pulls back from Hallie only a few inches, looks at her eyes, and kisses her with heightened passion. The thought of someone seeing them seems to be no concern to him. He reluctantly withdrawals from the kiss. "And, how are you now."

She smiles at him. "I'm really good."

"Yes, I am too." He hugs her. "I suppose we should go back up."

She sighs. "If we must."

They walk back up towards the hall finding Becky and David sitting at the edge of the dance floor. Becky is fanning herself.

"Hey! Wow, it's getting hot in here, but what a good time. Who would have thought this could be so fun? Hallie, you need to tell Joan they should do something like this every year."

Hallie starts to answer, but suddenly there is a scuffle at the drink table next to them between Ivy and her date. Ivy jerks away from him knocking into the iced tea container. It tips towards the table dumping the ice-cold drink all over Hallie.

"Whoa, that's cold!" She stands up to look around.

Ivy's mouth drops open, and she rushes forward to help until she sees that it is Hallie that took full force of the accident. She stops short pursing her lips and looks from Hallie to Liam and then walks away. Roxanne hesitates looking to be sure Hallie is okay. Tessa calls her to follow, and she sighs before yielding to the harsh command.

"Oh my gosh!" Becky exclaims. "That bit---"

"It's okay," Hallie cuts her off. "Even though she didn't seem to mind she drenched me, I don't think she did it on purpose.

That guy was harassing her, and it's only tea—not the end of the world, really."

David goes to get some towels and Liam checks to be sure Hallie is alright.

Joan comes up. "Hallie, you okay?"

"Oh yeah, I'm good. Joan do you think I could get a change of clothes from the gift shop? I can go by on Monday and pay for them."

"Sure, Hal. Come on with me, and we will get you all set. You can go into the ladies shower room and rinse off and change. You certainly got soaked!"

"I'll come with you." Becky says.

Hallie looks at her pitifully and then Liam. She just laughs. Liam's look of mortification softens into a smile. It wasn't in Hallie to hold a grudge or get upset over something like this. She heads out behind Joan while others from the dance move in to help clean up the mess.

Hallie turns back and sees the hard set of Liam's jaw just before he turns to leave.

"Where is Liam going?" she asks.

Becky's eyebrows arch and she jerks her head back. "My guess is to go find Ivy. You go Liam."

Hallie stops short. "Aw, I don't know Becky. Maybe we should…"

"Should what?" Becky curls her lip. "He is civilized. You just let him handle it, and let us get you fixed up."

Hallie bites her lower lip and nods.

Chapter 24, Seethe

Liam finds Ivy leaning against one of the buildings just below Fayerdale Hall. Tessa and Roxanne are standing next to her talking and laughing when Liam walks up glaring at the two sidekicks. Tessa tosses a cigarette onto the ground stepping on it with her shoe and eyes him before turning to Ivy who nods to her and Roxanne to leave.

Liam waits for them to get out of ear shot and turns to Ivy who looks at him with a pouty face.

"What was that all about Ivy?"

She puts a hand up to her throat and raises an eye brow, but doesn't answer.

He waits her out.

She twist her lips biting the inside of her cheek, and her eye lids draw two thin slits. "Oh, come on Liam. It was an accident. At least it wasn't the pot of hot coffee that spilled onto her. She survived unscathed!"

He places his arm on the wall beside her head and leans in closer to her. "Back off. Keep your distance. Leave her alone." His words are pointed and short.

Ivy scoffs, and her face reddens. "What—is—the—big *deal* with her? You all but swoon when she is around."

"It is none of your concern. Just leave her be." His words slide through gritted teeth.

"Liam White, are you in love with her?" Ivy huffs stopping short to study his face. "Oh my God. There is NO way. You are incapable of loving anyone. You barely like yourself."

"What do you know about me?" His eyes are fierce, but he pauses sizing Ivy up for a moment. His gaze drops to look at the brooch she is wearing. It has a pearl in the center with eight smaller pearls circling it and small diamonds bordering the pearls. The setting for the pearls is yellow gold while the diamonds are set in platinum with lacy loops enclosing the setting. It is a beautiful piece of vintage jewelry.

He is unsure of himself for a moment but pulls himself together stiffening slightly. He clears his throat and resolutely asks her. "Do you know who I am?"

She stares at him with a Cheshire-cat-grin. "Of course I know you. I have known you for what, just over a year now? I know you're hot-looking and, now, I know you're hot-tempered too. I've never seen your feathers ruffled." She challenges him.

He reaches down and takes the brooch on her sweater between his thumb and fingers looking at it. Ivy looks at it as well before both raise their heads to look at one another. Her breaths come in short bursts, and there is a quiver to her lower lip. She bites down on it.

"Well, I think you do know me. I think you know exactly who I am, and you will know what I mean when I say, 'Connie was right'. She was right." He stands up straight taking a step back letting go of his anger and averting his eyes from her. Inside his heart drops.

Ivy stands up straight too lifting her chin and glares at him until he meets her eye-to-eye. Her face reddens. "I…" She shakes her head. "*Connie* was a fool. It did not end well for her, and *this* will not end well for you. You know better." She hisses at him and inhales deeply through her nose—her tone softens only slightly. "I will steer clear, if that is what you want. And when it is done, I will let you find your own way back. You will trudge through regret and angst to what *our* reality is. It has not changed in nearly three hundred years, and it will not change now!" She looks at him as if waiting for submission, but it doesn't come. Seething, she walks away bumping his shoulder belligerently as she passes him.

He stands for a moment and looks up at the stars, his eyes moisten with emotion, and his hands tremble. He drops his head raising his hands to the back of his neck interlocking his fingers. Then, pulling himself together, he makes his way back to find Hallie and solace.

She is standing with Becky and David near her mustang. Liam takes her in. Her hair is damp and hanging loose, and she is wearing a t-shirt and shorts. Her corsage remains on her wrist.

"There you are!" She exclaims.

He is amazed at her good spirits despite what just happened, and he is even more amazed at his good fortune for having her in his life. "Wow, you look amazing! I like the new outfit." He teases. "What is up next?" He looks at his three companions.

"Well, we thought we would head over to Becky's for a while. Maybe do some gaming." Hallie says.

Liam comes over hugging her lifting her off her feet and spins around. "That sounds perfect!" He sets her down taking her face in his hands and kisses her gently. She looks up at him a bit surprised noticing a strange look in his eyes.

"Liam, are you okay?" She asks in a whisper.

He says nothing but gives a reassuring nod and walks her around the car opening her door. She looks at him a moment and gets in. She leans over to unlock his side of the car and helps Becky hold the front seat forward, so she and David can slide into the back seat.

Liam and Hallie arrive back at Joan's house around midnight after staying at Becky's for a few hours in a fierce Fortnite battle against the husks. Liam cuts the engine. He sits gripping the wheel of the car. Hallie presses a hand against the nervous flutter in her stomach. The time at Becky's was a great distraction, but the melancholy she had seen before they left the park is back.

He doesn't look at her when he speaks. His voice is husky with emotion. "Hallie, I…" he falters and clears his throat before turning to look at her and starts again. "I love you, I love you more than words can describe. Never…" again he loses his voice.

Hallie relaxes taking a breath in and reaches to touch his hand, but he moves it away before she makes contact. She stops short, withdrawing her hand but keeps her gaze fixed on him.

"Let me finish while I still possess my resolve to say what I need to say. I told you that day in the woods, the day we first kissed, that people who care about me get hurt. Your kiss saved me and gave me hope, but I have been forced tonight to consider that it may not be the same for you. A kiss of salvation for one may result in destruction for the other. A price I cannot let you pay."

"Liam, I am not sure…"

"Please," he starts a bit harshly, and stops grabbing his lips with his hand in order soften his words. "Please, just let me finish. I do not know how to get you to understand. I have been cursed. Cursed in a way beyond description or comprehension." He struggles to explain and reaches over pushing up the sleeve over his arm revealing the horrific scar. "This, this is the corporeal proof and, as gruesome as it looks, it is nothing compared to that portion of the curse that leaches into the mind and spirit—into my entire being. I fear that I have clung to the idea that the absolute novel attachment I have found with you could somehow mean there is a chance to break the curse, to move forward, and to find freedom. If I am wrong, however, and something were to happen to you, the consequence would be one that would torture my soul and threaten my sanity for all time. I will lose a fight that has preoccupied my existence for longer than I can remember."

Hallie sits for a moment. *What sort of demonic person could have abused him this way?* She turns to face him leaning over to kiss him. He withdraws slightly keeping a distance of millimeters from her lips holding his breath. She leans in kissing him slowly and deeply. She feels his passion flare, and it intensifies as he kisses her back with a desperate hunger. She forces herself to pull away holding onto the nape of his neck where his hair comes to his collar. The pomade feels slick on her hand while her blood slides through her veins with a pounding beat. She struggles to regulate her breathing. It is a battle that seems Liam too is attempting to conquer. He looks at her with wonder.

"That, Liam, is the primal physical proof of what we have between us. It is only a hint, an insinuation, of what permeates our spirits and minds. I know that I can speak for both of us because we have forged a bond. Something I feel deep and true, and something I am sure you feel just as much. I don't know what 'curse' you think has seized you and possibly threatens me, but whatever it is, it is too late for me. I am already there." She places her hand on his chest over his heart. "And you are already here." She takes his hand and places it over her heart. "I am truly sorry, but there is no turning back. I, however naïve as it sounds, believe that light always overcomes dark. Without the darkness we cannot see the stars, right? A single flame always wins out. If you have a demon to fight…well, we will have to take it on together."

He smiles sadly and barely shakes his head. "You have no idea, Hallie, no idea at all." He kisses her forehead, each cheek, and her lips where he lingers. He leans his forehead against hers and draws a breath in before speaking again. "Very well. Together."

Chapter 25, Calidity

The hour of departure has arrived and we go our separate ways; I to die, and you to live. Which is better? Only God knows.
Socrates (BC 469-BC 399) Greek philosopher of Athens

The day was a little busier than usual, but Hallie and Becky get the snack bar closed and cleaned up by seven thirty. They have a couple errands to run before returning to the park. The crew decided to do the beach party tonight. Hallie and Becky change in the shower room and head down towards the boat house to look for Liam and David. Neither are there yet, so the girls sit on the edge of the pier waiting for them. They see several groups of staff getting into canoes and heading out before Liam and David arrive carrying a cooler and their back packs.

"Sorry we are running late," Liam says as he sets the cooler down on the pier and stretches a hand towards Hallie to help her up. She starts to stand but gets tugged back down. Her leather amulet pouch is snagged on a split plank.

"Whoops!" She exclaims and loosens the leather strap setting herself free. She checks for damage, but the nylon surfer shorts she has on are strong and didn't tear.

"You might want to take that off, so you don't get stuck on anything else." Liam says as he turns to lift the cooler and carry it over to the canoe. David already has his and Becky's canoe loaded and comes over to help out.

Hallie fiddles with the pouch a bit adjusting the strap and tucks it into her waist band. "I don't really have a good place for it, and I don't want to leave it behind. This ought to do okay."

Liam helps her into the canoe, and they head out just behind Becky and David. It is just starting to get dark, but the moon is already brilliant lighting the evening with a soft glow. A trail of its glistening light stretches out before them on the water.

Hallie looks down into the water alongside the canoe as they paddle through it. The canoe cuts across the wet blackness, and she wonders about the secrets held below its depths.

They get across the lake to the beach without difficulty and run the canoes onto the shore. Someone has gotten a bonfire going and groups of people are sitting on blankets. Others are getting together to move the diving dock out into the water and anchor it.

Hallie notices Ivy sitting with her beau-of-the-moment several blankets away. She does not seem to be drinking tonight, and she seems rather subdued. She does not even muster the usual sneer that she typically greets Hallie with. Their eyes meet briefly, but Ivy turns her head over her shoulder to talk to Roxanne. Hallie turns to help Becky carry a cooler.

Liam and David pull the canoes up onto the beach, and they settle in. Becky pops the top on a can of soda and hands it to Hallie. "Here, I brought some chips too—help yourself."

"Thanks!" Hallie looks up at the moon and stars. "Wow, the night is so clear you can see the Milky Way."

The frogs are out in full force competing with the music for some air time.

"Ay-eeee!" Randy whoops and takes his traditional first jump into the water to start out the swimming. Several others jump in after him.

"Hallie, Becky come in! The water is great!" David yells from the dock signaling them over.

Becky and Hallie stand pulling off their t-shirts and walk out into the water making their way to the dock. The water erupts with splashes and waves as people dive into the water from the dock.

The cool water engulfs Hallie when she dives in after Liam, and she swims a distance away racing with Liam in the lead. He stops and treads water until Hallie catches up.

"Don't tell me, you were swim team captain in school," she asks as she approaches him.

"No, not at all." He laughs. "Just a lot of summers in the water. Come on, I will let you win this time."

She splashes him. "Don't do me any favors. The taste of victory would not be as sweet, but...I *will* take a head start on you." She turns and starts swimming. He waits a moment before following her catching up quickly.

He reaches out grabbing her ankle and pulls her back sputtering. He gives her a gentle splash and broad smile before moving forward to beat her back to the dock. He climbs up and waits for her at the edge. When she arrives he stretches his arm down to hoist her easily up.

"Foul play, Liam White!" she scolds, but is unable to even pretend to be angry with him.

He apologizes and gives her a kiss just before Randy and David tackle him into the water pulling him under.

Hallie looks over the side until she sees him surface just after Randy and David shoot up. She laughs watching them carry on for a moment and then walks over to the other side of the dock to sit next to Becky and dangle her feet into the water. They sit in silence enjoying the beautiful night.

Hallie looks from the sky out across the water watching a patch of the moon's reflecting light. It begins to swirl and shoot out in an excited pattern sinking below the water's surface. Her skin prickles. It seems like forever since the chaotic dance of lights has beckoned her. "Becky, do you see that?"

Becky looks over. She frowns squinting to get a better view. "Just looks like the moonlight to me."

"No." Hallie says. "Deeper, over there below the water's surface."

Becky looks again and shrugs. "I don't know, maybe it's something reflecting off the bole. You know, that old hollow tree trunk. It's over in that direction somewhere." The sputtering light does not hold the same fascination for Becky that it does for Hallie.

Hallie stands up.

"What are you doing?" Becky looks up at her.

"Just going to check it out. I'll be right back." She dives into the water swimming under the surface towards the light.

She can hear a muffled chiming. She hesitates for a moment, but the light beckons to her. It illuminates the hollow tree trunk and then suddenly darts into the trunk. Hallie surfaces to get a breath and dives back down towards the glow now emanating from the opening of the trunk near the floor of the lake. She looks up into the bole holding onto its edge before shooting up into its hollow center. She gets halfway up and the light moves away sputtering a little and suddenly flashes brightly startling Hallie. She hesitates and then can't move even when she tries. There is a tugging at her shorts.

The leather strap on her amulet pouch has caught on something inside the trunk. She tries to reach down to set herself free, but she is not able to move her arms downward. Her chest constricts with panic as she struggles to get free. The sparkling light dims and floats downward with its electric-looking sparks dancing before her eyes. The sing-song chiming voice emanates from the light.

There can be no beginning without an ending and one cannot reach the ending without first beginning. Angel song will take you there while fairy tears assure your passage and care be ever vigilant of the harmonizing ring.

Hallie is panic-stricken, and her chest burns as the oxygen in her lungs quickly disappears. She fights fiercely to pull herself free. It's getting dark but Hallie cannot tell if the sparkling light is fading, or if she is losing consciousness. Numbness spreads, and she forgets why she is struggling at all. Her struggle inside the bole cannot be seen or heard above the water. Her muscles give a final twitch and the struggle is over. She feels an airy weightlessness at first and then nothing.

"Hallie!" Becky's voice is at a fever pitch and drawing attention. Liam and David come up from behind her on the dock hoisting themselves up. Others swim over and more are standing along the water's edge on the beach.

"Becky!" Liam takes her by the shoulders to get her attention. Her face is fearful with tears rolling from her eyes. "Becky! Where is Hallie?"

"She saw something in the water near the bole. I don't know what it was, a sparkling light or something. She dove in to check it out. I saw her rise and dive back under, but that was a while ago—too long ago! She hasn't resurfaced!"

Liam lets her go and dives into the water.

"It's too dark! He isn't going to be able to see anything!" Becky cries.

David dives in behind Liam, and someone comes up to Becky putting an arm around her standing alongside her to wait. The music still plays from the beach, but no one makes a sound as they wait. Ivy walks up through the group on the beach, her arms folded across her chest as though she is cold, and she stands waiting with the others.

Liam shoots up from the top of the bole and David comes up just behind him. It is just the two of them. Liam dives back into the water. David looks back at the dock illuminated with the moonlight shaking his head at Becky. She covers her face with her hands and cries. Liam dives over and over again into the water until David gets him to swim back to the beach. Someone has already left in a canoe to get a ranger.

Liam reaches the shore catching Ivy's knowing stare. He turns away to sit in shock on the beach looking out into the water. Becky sits with David just behind Liam. No one approaches him. His overwhelming sorrow creates a barrier between him and those around him. He folds his arms over his knees and drops his head onto them. His shoulders ache with an immense weight.

Suddenly, he is jolted with a flashing image of pulling Hallie from the water. He looks up startled. The water before him remains still and dark. Another flash, and the sound of his panicked breathing dominates his senses. He feels the weight of her limp body in his arms, and he sees her pale skin and blue lips. Another flash, and he feels the grit of dirt and pebbles pressing into his flesh as he kneels over her body trying to push water from her chest. Then, he feels an electric shock as his lips make contact with hers attempting to blow life back into her lungs.

He looks behind, confused, seeing Becky with her face buried into David's chest and her shoulders shaking with sobs. He looks side to side and back towards the water. Nothing.

Flash. Hallie coughs and sputters. He feels a sense of relief that is not really there. His thoughts race. Closing his eyes he tries to focus on what he is seeing and feeling, but he is unsure where it is coming from. He feels his chest rising and falling with air rushing in and out. His heart pounds from the exertion, and then a final jolt sparks, and he catches his breath as recognition strikes.

It is a memory…she is *there…in my memory. What is happening?* The panic rises as his thoughts swirl. *How can this be?*

A spot light illuminates the beach, and two small motor boats steered by rangers approach. Liam runs his fingers through his hair, otherwise, he is incapable of moving. Hallie is alive and breathing somewhere in his past.

Chapter 26, Aglow

Memory always obeys the commands of the heart.
Antoine Rivarol 1753-1801

It's stifling as Hallie draws in air with some effort. She can tell she is laying down on a soft surface, but she can't open her eyes, and her limbs feel like lead. Her dream is vivid as flashes of a panicked suffocating feeling, an ineffective struggle to break free, and a feeling of weightlessness dance before her. There is another flash, and she feels herself being carried strongly and securely with a steady pace. Muffled voices drift through the air. There is another flash of Liam's face and Randy's then later Becky's. They look concerned and worried. Words of reassurance for her love and friends form in Hallie's mind, but she can't get them to her lips.

In a moment her eyes open. She looks around with bleary vision in a dimly lit room. She blinks several times and finds the use of her arms and legs returning. Several layers of quilts and blankets weigh her down, and she peals the layers back feeling her heavy arms working in slow motion. She hesitates as her head swirls when she sits up swinging her legs over the side of the bed. Welcomed cool air greets her bare legs. She scans the room.

Becky is curled up on the floor covered with a blanket sound asleep. Hallie rubs her eyes and tries to figure out where she is. A hurricane lamp glows softly from a table where Liam sits sleeping in a chair with his head bent slightly to the side. Hallie's eyes adjust to the light and her vision clears. The room is unfamiliar. There is the bed she is now sitting on with a small night stand beside it. A rack with hooks and some clothing hanging from them on the wall. Beyond Liam sits a small cast iron stove and various cooking pots and utensils stored on shelves and hooks. To her right is a dresser with a basin and pitcher, and a towel is neatly folded next to the basin.

Hallie stands having to pause over weak legs that threaten to give out on her. Collecting strength she walks over towards the basin suddenly realizing that she has on a long thin white dressing gown. She reaches the basin and pours some water into it rinsing her face and mouth. Looking into a small mirror that hangs above the dresser, she cringes. *Oh, my God! I look like death warmed over.*

She takes a moment leaning her hands on the dresser trying to remain steady. She forces herself to take a few slow deep breaths into what feels like scorched lungs in an effort to improve her air flow and reduce the discomfort. It works a little.

The last thing she remembers is diving into the lake. She can't remember why…why did she dive in? *The light! But this is not a colonial setting from what she can tell.* She remembers the twinkling light, the chiming voice, and the hollow tree log! *Oh, my God, my God!* A flash of panic and feeling trapped under the water hit her. She has bizarre images of a stark foreign place misty and gray. *This is not like the visions from the tragic love story. This is not the same craziness that has become my norm.* Her chest starts to constrict again and her heart takes on a flutter. She needs comfort, and she remembers her amulet pouch.

Reflexively she reaches towards her waist forgetting about the dressing gown. Frantically, she looks about the room relaxing when she sees the leather pouch lying on top of her folded surfer shorts and bathing suit top on the night stand by the bed. She turns back to the mirror and reaches to straighten her hair and pinch a little color into her cheeks. She stops what she is doing noticing shelves to the right of the dresser.

It's set with familiar objects. A selection of books, some trinkets, a basket of blue feathers with a delicate ribbon tied to each one, and the leather bound journal. It is just like the collection in Liam's room at Joan's. She looks around again feeling a little confused but, no, this is not any place she has been before. Liam stirs in his chair, and she looks at him.

His handsome face is evident even in the dim light. She looks at him more closely. The shiny shock of hair that forms his bangs hangs down towards his eyes, but the sides of his hair seem shorter than she recalls. He has on a pair of old denim bibs without a shirt. The knees of the bibs are torn and muddied. He looks as though he had been run though some sort of obstacle course challenge or something.

She steals a look back at the journal and reticently reaches to remove it from the shelf. The cover is soft and worn. It is tied with a single piece of cord. She looks at Liam and Becky—both are soundly asleep—as she pulls the tie on the journal opening it up.

The first page has "Book of Lineages" written across the top. She turns the pages glancing at them. It appears to be a ledger of some sort. Each section has a family name with a symbol drawn next to it. From there, names are written in and branch off in a family tree fashion, but only one line from each generation is traced. Occasionally, years are written in. The sir name from the original name at the top of the page changes through the generations that are being tracked, but the symbol remains constant, and only certain names on each listing carry the symbol in their dedicated box. Usually only one or two names per generation although one of the lines of generations consistently has several symbol-marked names. It looks like there are a total of six lines being followed. Two end without further notation at the year 1781. She turns the pages again to look more closely at one of the lineages. It ends at 1928 where the sir name is Pettigrew with boxes for a Madeline, Geoffrey, Luke, and Elijah. Madeline's and Elijah's names have the symbol for the lineage drawn in. Luke's name is written in blue, and she looks back through the line noticing that one male name in each generation is in blue. It is a little odd though because she notices that there isn't a true generational flow to the lineages. There are points where thirty years pass before any names are written in and sometimes only a few years have passed.

She starts to look at the other lines more closely when Liam sighs and starts to rustle a bit in his chair. Hallie jumps and closes the journal tying its cord before placing it back up on the shelf.

"You are awake," he says cheerfully. "You gave us all a bit of a scare. Quite frankly Miss, for the life of me, I cannot figure out what you were doing in that pond. Do you not know how dangerous it is? The timber company did not get all those logs in there cleared out when they shut down a few years ago." He gets up walking towards her bringing the blanket that was laying over the back of his chair. "Uh, let me cover you. I know it has been mighty warm weather, but nights are still cool, and Doc Hutchison said once the fever broke you might get chilled." He backs away once he covers her putting some distance between them.

"Thank you," Hallie says staring at him for a moment trying to figure out why it feels as though they have never met, as though they have not spent every day with each other for the last six weeks. She feels the burning in her lungs re-ignite and her mouth goes dry. *Why is he calling me Miss?*

He falters for a moment before stretching his hand out towards her. "I am sorry Miss. Billy White. I am pleased to meet you."

What? Hallie stands hesitating and then slowly extends her hand grasping his. He stops short looking down at their hands, and back up looking her directly in the eye, but saying nothing. Their hands slide apart lingering just seconds at the finger tips.

She breaks the silence. "Billy? *Billy* White?"

He nods once to confirm.

"You mean Liam White."

He frowns and raises eye brows. "No, I mean Billy White."

Hallie raises her head back looking at him from the end of her nose and gives a quick nod. Her head swims, and she grasps back onto the dresser to keep herself steady. *This has to be a dream. I know it isn't one of my visions, but it is not my reality either.* She clears her throat. "Well, nice to meet you…Billy. My name is Hallie O'Meara. Is it you I have to thank for pulling me out of the water?"

"Well, yes Miss…"

"Hallie."

"Yes, of course, Hallie. Actually, Jeb…uh, that would be Jeb Curry. He and I were over by the old holding pond when I saw you just below the water's surface. Bit of an unusual site with those colored skivvies and…," he hesitates before motioning across the top of his chest, "that top you had on." He breaks eye contact mistaking Hallie's look of shock for embarrassment about her swimming suit.

She is startled because 'Jeb Curry' is one of the names in the Book of Lineages. Her knees still will not cooperate, and she tries hard to hold it together. "I'm sorry if I have caused you any trouble or inconvenience. I want to thank you for saving me and helping me. Truth is I am not sure just exactly what happened. I am staying with a family friend, Joan Shively. Perhaps you know her?" Hallie feels a sense of uneasiness settling in with a prickle at her palms and back of her neck starting. She tries to stall it. *If this is a dream, how long before I wake up?*

He thinks for a moment tightening his lips and shakes his head thoughtfully. "No, cannot say that I do. There are some Shively's over Philpott way, but I do not know one that goes by the name Joan. Is she from here?"

The prickle wins, and Hallie's palms start to sweat. She loosens her grip on the dresser but is terrified to completely let go. She is distracted when she notices the silvery scar on his right arm that etches its way up from his inner wrist towards his elbow. It is not missed by Billy, and he moves his arm to conceal the scar much the same way that Liam did the first time she met *him*.

She battles her weak legs. *What were we talking about...?* She thinks, trying to hold it together and remembers the question. "Um, she is just over on Fayerdale Drive not too far from the lake...uh...here. I think." She can't remain standing much longer, and it must be obvious.

Billy takes her by the arm and walks her to a chair. He gets her a drink and takes some bread from a cabinet near the stove setting them down in front of her. "Here, try to eat and drink something. You have been out for over 24 hours and must be weak. If that does okay for you, I will make you something a little more substantial to eat."

Hallie just looks at him in wonder. He picks the cup of water up from the table handing it to her.

"Drink." He directs her with a kind but firm tone waiting for her to bring the cup to her mouth before he sits in the chair next to her at the table.

"Fayerdale *Drive* you say? Huh, I have lived here for a while now, and I do not know of any roads around these parts that anyone has ever bothered to give a name. You sure you are not talking about something over in Stuart or Danville?"

"These parts?" Hallie asks. "And where exactly would 'these parts' be then?" Her eyes narrow. She gives up on the thought of this being a dream and begins to picture a different scenario. *If this is some weird joke Liam, Randy, Becky and David concocted, it isn't funny anymore.* She didn't feel well at all.

He shifts in his chair. "I am sorry. Maybe you should lie down for a while. You do not look well."

"No. Tell me where 'these parts' are."

He chuckles, but cuts it short when she glares at him. He clears his throat. "Well, Fayerdale. Or what is left of it. Folks have been gradually moving away over the past three years since the ore and lumber company folded in twenty-five."

"Twenty-five what?" She slaps a hand down on the table. The lamp light plays off the walls, and she wonders if it is taunting her.

He grunts and furrows his brow. "*Nineteen*—twenty—five. You know, as in 'the year of our Lord'."

She purses her lips and stands, waits, and is satisfied her legs will cooperate now. She walks to the door pulling it open and steps out onto a wood-planked covered porch. An old blood hound is laying near the door and lazily looks up at her. The sky shows a faint amount of light filtering through the trees. Hallie can't tell if it is dawn or dusk. The cabin sits in a small clearing situated in the woods. She steps off the porch and looks around. Billy steps to the door but does not follow her outside.

Hallie walks around the cabin. A heavy dew on the sparse grass feels cool on her feet. There are no other houses to be seen and no vehicles. There is a pile of wood in the yard, and an ax leaning against a tree stump. An outhouse sits near the wood's edge. She is startled by a ruckus up in the tree branches, and looks up to see several flying squirrels jumping along branches taking daring leaps from branch to branch chattering and carrying on. The woods have the sound of awakening creatures instead of the quiet settling-in of the evening hours. The air is cool but has the feel of a summer day starting while a misty blanket of fog lays across the woodland floor. She envisions the gray wisps that she saw accenting blue peaks when she first arrived from the Eastern Shore. As a mourning dove croons its quiet lament, she wonders if she could still be in the same hills of the Blue Ridge that she has grown to love. Hallie walks in an arc along the periphery of the clearing and back towards the front of the cabin amazed by the beauty even in the dense woods where distant views are limited.

She looks back at the cabin to see the young man she has known to be Liam. He stands with an arm propped against the door jamb looking curiously across the clearing at her.

Chapter 27, Swelter

Hallie sits on the porch sorting over the last several days trying to make sense of it all. She is worried because she has not 'woken up' despite many efforts on her part to break the trance. She wonders what Joan is going through, and how Beattie and Dot are doing. And, she worries that Liam is blaming himself. *He was so worried about something happening to me, and I know he is freaking out.* She has been trying to figure out how to get back to her own time, so she can let them all know she is safe. When searching the nearby woods for a hidden door or passage back didn't pan out she tried simple pinching and willing herself to return home each time she laid down to sleep. She had even resorted to clicking her heels together three times and reciting 'There's no place like home', but to no avail the scenery remained the same.

She thinks about how the story of the beautiful witch turned from a childhood story, to a dream, to a feeling of being part of the story. She thinks about movies and novels where a character is pulled into a book living out some tale of heroism much like she has already been experiencing, but she is obviously not in colonial times, and there are no signs of Resmelda that she can see. This is definitely something different. *Could I be lying comatose in a hospital on life support experiencing this grand delusion?* She struggles between an intense desire for, and an even greater fear of, the plug being pulled at any moment.

The blood hound, who she learned is called Holmes, walks up beside her nudging until he situates himself in a prime spot for getting a nice long scratching of his head and back. She chuckles at him. "Used-To-Be-Becky" as she thinks of the young woman named Sadie is inside the cabin preparing something to eat for breakfast. Sadie apparently came to the cabin the night of Hallie's accident with Doc Hutchinson in order to assist him. It was decided by the doctor, Billy, and Sadie that Hallie staying in the cabin alone with Billy would be an impropriety in the small town of Fayerdale. Hallie has a hard time wrapping her head around this notion though because the doctor often carries tales during his daily visits of some new brawl or goings on in town related to the apparent growing business of moonshine making and bootlegging. She imagines a lawless, ruckus-filled place where no one would give a second thought to her staying here with Billy.

Today is to be an eventful day in that it has been deemed that Hallie is strong enough to walk to town with Sadie for the "rigor of exercise and improvement of her constitution," according to the doctor. Hallie made no arguments because she is anxious to see more of the area, and to figure out just how delusional she really is. Plus, she is very curious about what can be found "in town".

In many ways Sadie is a lot like Becky. Hallie enjoys being with her and finds comfort in her presence. Sadie, unlike Becky, has a shadow of sadness that lingers near her, but Hallie cannot figure out the source.

"Hallie, come on in. Breakfast is ready." Sadie calls through an open window.

Hallie pushes aside her pondering. "Come on, Holmes let's see what Sadie has for us." Holmes, probably smelling the rare treat of some bacon, is on her heels. Doc Hutchison said it is important for Hallie to have protein to recover, and Billy does his best to have meat every day for them to eat. He works various odd jobs to make a living, and he already left to work this morning at the last remaining general store in town, Pennymaker's Mercantile.

She steps inside the cabin taking a deep breath through her nose. "Oh, Bec...uh, Sadie." Hallie shakes her head still struggling with her new surroundings and companions' identities. "It smells so good in here!"

"Well, wait until you eat it before you give your praises. I can bake cakes but breakfast is a whole other story." She pauses for a minute and laughs. "I'm just messing with you...come on and eat. But that does remind me, today when we're in town we are going to get some things for making a cake, and I am going to show you how to use this oven. How does that sound?"

Hallie notices that Sadie speaks almost as though Becky would when it is just Billy or herself in the cabin, but when Doc Hutchison comes for visits she speaks with an accent and drawl that Hallie remembers hearing in older movies. Hallie pondered this at first. She isn't sure what she did to earn Sadie's trust or comfort, but she is grateful for it. She cannot stand feeling any more an outsider than she already does.

Hallie smiles at Sadie. "Sounds just fine. Thanks…," but then she notices a young man walking out of the woods from the back window of the cabin.

Sadie sees him too and turns to Hallie. "Hallie, you go on and start your breakfast. I will be right back." She sits Hallie's plate on the table so Hallie's back will be to the window and heads towards the cabin door.

Hallie takes a seat and starts to eat. Sadie glances back at her before stepping outside. *Is that anxiety on her face?*

Hallie waits a moment before standing just inside a shadow to look out the window. The young man's face lights up when he sees Sadie, and he embraces and kisses her taking her face in his hands lingering as though they have not seen each other in a while. Sadie is lost in the moment, but she quickly pulls herself together drawing away from him. Hallie cannot tell what is said, but is certain that Sadie gives him a warning of some sort. He glances over at the cabin, and Hallie instinctively steps back further into the shadow.

She gasps. "It's David." She says out loud in revelation.

"David who?" Billy asks.

Startling, she turns to look at him feeling like her hand is caught in the cookie jar.

"Oh! Li…uh, Billy you scared me." Hallie rubs her hands against her skirt as his eyes move passed her to look through the window.

"That would be Luke Pettigrew." He says to her very matter-of-factly. "He and Sadie are in love, but being he is white and she is colored it is not something they can openly share with others around here. It is illegal for them to be together, and some folks would not take too kindly to it. Occasionally, they meet here just to steal a moment together. He has been gone this past week, so he did not know you were here. It would be a good thing if you did not mention this to anyone." He moves over to the stove to get a plate of eggs.

"Oh…no…I…wouldn't…" Hallie falters recognizing Luke's name from the ledger.

Billy carries his plate and a cup of chicory coffee back to the table and sits down. "Sorry," he says. "I did not mean for that to sound so scolding. I can tell you do not see things that way, but I am not sure you have a good understanding about how things are around here. It is best you know, so you do not say anything that could put any of us in a dangerous situation."

Hallie sits down at the table and looks at him for a moment. She wonders just how much he does know about her. She wants to blurt everything out to him, but a nagging feeling inside her cautions her not to. This past week has been so hard for her to be around him. She is convinced this person in front of her is Liam, her Liam, but the wall around his heart she knocked down at Fairy Stone seems to be built higher and stronger here in Fayerdale. She is afraid to say anything to him about their other life.

She takes a bite of the eggs and looks back up at him. Her heart flutters being this close to him and alone. Sadie does not leave her alone with him usually. "I thought you were at the general store until later today."

"Mister Gravely at the livery stable asked Missus Pennymaker to let me work over there today. Jeb normally helps out at the livery, but he went with Luke's brother to work the railway." Billy nods his head towards the window. "Since Luke, as you now know, took the day off."

Hallie remembers that Jeb was with Billy the day of her accident and went to get Doc Hutchison while Billy brought her to the cabin. Jeb is 'Used-To-Be-Randy'.

"Anyway, I did not want to wear my good clothes—being I only have one set—over to the livery to work, and I came home to change. Breakfast smells too good to pass up, so Mister Gravely is going to have to do without me for about fifteen minutes more." He smiles his great smile and again Hallie's heart flutters.

"There are horses in town?"

"Only a few. Enough though for Mister Gravely. He is coming up on sixty some years, and he is starting to need help with keeping the place going."

They finish breakfast in silence. Billy reaches over and takes Hallie's plate.

"Oh, I can get it." She goes to reach for it and their hands come together. She feels her skin flush, and admonishes herself knowing he can see her reaction.

He holds onto the plate not moving his hand from hers gently saying, "It is fine, I have it."

She releases the plate.

He carries it over to a pot, and turns back to look at her. He clears his throat. "I will go fetch you some water to put to boil for the dishes before I change and head out." And he is out the door before Hallie could even respond.

Hallie gets a cloth to wipe off the table. During the time she has been here she has noticed that, although the cabin is small, it is organized and clean. The bed and night stand designate the sleeping area which now has a small pallet set up nearby for Sadie who insists Hallie sleep in the bed. Billy has taken to sleeping out on the porch on a hammock. Socializing is done in the kitchen area. They spend the evenings playing card games or listening to Billy play the guitar. Sadie often has some sewing to work on. Despite the circumstances Hallie finds it a very pleasant place to be.

Sadie noticed Hallie fumbling for a way to secure her amulet pouch to her skirt, so she sewed a loop to the waist. Hallie smiles with the thought as she finishes wiping the table. She is very thankful for the clothes and for Sadie's companionship.

Hallie looks up as the cabin door opens. It's Sadie. "Well, Billy told me you saw Luke, so he told you the truth about us. He was a bit worried I would be upset."

"Sadie...I'm sorry...I saw him...."

"Hey," Sadie interrupts quickly. "No sense you worrying yourself over any of that. Me and Luke have plans. We aren't going to be staying around this place for much longer. We've got plans to go to Mexico. We're gonna put this place far behind us. Just gotta get a few more dollars together."

Hallie nods and puts the cleaning cloth away. She thinks about the year—1928 and the potential hardships a couple like Sadie and Luke are likely to endure, if they remain in Southwest Virginia or just about any place in the United States. As a matter-of-fact, she recalls a relationship like theirs would remain illegal in Virginia until 1967. She decides that this burden of worry is what she sees in Sadie's eyes that is not in Becky's.

"Sadie, if you want to put off going to town so you and Luke can have some time together, we can go tomorrow."

Sadie puts her hand on her hip and gives Hallie a typical 'Becky' smirk. "Humph, that boy has gone and made plans with Billy to help him finish early at the livery, so they can go on over to Gobbletown Creek and fish!" She shakes her head.

Billy comes through the door with a bucket of water and hands it to Sadie and then pulls his shirt off.

"Fool!" Sadie fusses at him. "What *are* you doing? You've got ladies in here!"

He chuckles walking across the cabin to hang the shirt up and unbuckles his pants. "Well, *ladies*, please turn your backs because I need to change and there is just this one room. Sorry, but I gotta get going."

Sadie rolls her eyes and turns to pour water to boil. Hallie makes busy getting together a few other dishes that need to be washed. As she sets a plate of leftovers on the floor for Holmes she cannot help but glance Billy's way. He catches her, but she doesn't look away. His dark eyes penetrate hers, and she feels her traitorous skin flush. He gives her a crooked smile as he fastens the clips on his overalls before stealing a look towards Sadie who remains with her back towards him washing dishes.

"Okay," Billy says, mostly for Sadie's benefit, as he heads out the door. "Your virtues are safe again!"

"Um-mm, that boy is way too happy. Not that I have been around him nearly as much as I have this past week, but Little Miss Sunshine has done melted that heart of ice." She looks over at Hallie raising an eyebrow.

Hallie is floored that Sadie would think that she has any effect on Billy. *'Used-To-Be-Liam' has to be Liam.* She feels it in her heart, but she knows he isn't the same. She dismisses Sadie's insinuation and finishes the task of cleaning up. Her heart aches wanting to be back with Liam.

Sadie and Hallie finish up and head out to town with Holmes trailing behind one moment and running ahead the next when the scent of something interesting catches his nose. Sadie comments on different sites along the way. "Now remember, always stay on the trail." Sadie cautions. "Otherwise, you may stumble onto someone's still site. That may not work out too well for you."

"Got it." Hallie falls in step beside Sadie.

Chapter 28, Burned

Hallie and Sadie cross over Gobbletown Creek and Sadie steps up her tour guide duties. "That big house over that way is the hotel. Not too much goings on these days, but at one time it was a busy place. Down that way is the general store and postal station. The livery stable, where Billy is working, is just around the bend along the creek a ways."

Sadie is talking, but it is Liam's voice Hallie hears. She looks about familiar land with structures that had been only in her imagination's view before. The smell of a fire burning and the clanging of metal on metal rings out as they walk past the blacksmith's shop towards what was the company store but now stands empty. Two little girls sit on the steps of the building with kittens in their laps and no shoes on their feet.

It is a fading place within the rich beauty of the Blue Ridge where memories of happier times struggle to shine through. Clouds of dust kick up behind them as they walk along the dirt road bordering the creek, and Hallie's vision flashes to the lake at Fairy Stone. She can see the water's image superimposed over the dying town.

"Over there, where that burnt rubble is, the school house once stood."

Hallie blinks and pulls herself back to focus on Sadie. "Oh…, what a shame. What happened to it?"

"Lightening. The real kind. Not the white liquor kind. Although a gallon of that mess and a match would have had the same effect." Sadie shakes her head, and smacks her lips. "Miss Nichols, the teacher, holds classes in her home now. With folks leaving town after the closing of the iron works and later the timber company, there wasn't too much interest in rebuilding the school house. 'Course us colored kids have to go at a different time from the others."

Hallie frowns, but Sadie holds up her hand. "Just the way it is, and it didn't hurt me none when I was goin'. I still got the same only less distractions." She laughs. "Yep, my daddy taught me to read and about numbers, but Miss Nichols taught me about science and history."

Hallie looks back at the burnt timbers trying to picture a more prosperous time for the little town.

They walk past the train depot where an old man is sweeping dust through the doorway. "Hey do, Mister Elkins. This here is Hallie O'Meara. She's new to town."

Mister Elkins gives a nod and Hallie smiles offering a wave.

"Mister Elkins does a little bit of everything at the depot. He cleans, sells tickets, helps passengers board, and loads shipments. Since it isn't very busy these days he mostly socializes and works on carving walking sticks.

"Luke and his brother, Elijah, run the train from Fayerdale to Philpott. Sometimes Luke works the line going all the way to Danville, and that was what he did this past week. It's a good way for him to make extra money, and keeps him outta the trouble that seems to flourish around this place. He's gone for several days at a time when he makes that run."

Sadie stops with a look of satisfaction. "Well, here we are."

Hallie looks at the neatly white-washed building and then curiously at Sadie.

"Doc Hutchison's office." Sadie steps up and opens the door.

Hallie rolls her eyes. "Sadie, I'm…"

"Yes, I know. You're fine, but let's see what the doctor has to say about that." She raises her eyebrows and motions Hallie to step through the door.

"Well, young lady, you look mighty fine. Mighty fine to be sure." Doc Hutchinson is a pleasant sort. He walks with a limp and has a beautifully carved walking stick. Hallie thinks about the display back in Ferrum at the Blue Ridge Institute, and the story about that very stick.

"Yes, indeed, you are fit as a fiddle." He pats her shoulder.

Hallie appreciates his care, but can't help feeling that all the fuss is silly. None-the-less she sits patiently through the rest of his exam answering questions and nodding towards Sadie crediting her for the progress. Once Doc Hutchison is satisfied that she is well without a doubt they depart heading back outside.

A woman on the porch of the general store calls them over. Holmes had still been tagging along, but veers away from the general store heading towards Mister Elkins at the train depo for a quick rub of the head. Sadie stiffens a bit sucking in her breath.

"Sadie, is this the gal Doc Hutchinson told me about?" An air of authority peels from her words. Her thick-soled brown shoes hit the wood sharply as she moves across the porch closer to them, and her crisp starched presence is a contrast to the fading town around her.

"Yes 'um, Miz Pennymaker," Sadie replies avoiding direct eye contact.

"Well gal, you're looking well. I'm Maybelle Pennymaker. Can't say I've seen you before, and don't see any family resemblance in you from anyone around these parts. Where do you come from?"

Sadie interjects. "Her memory has bin a bit off since her accident Miz Pennymaker, ma'am."

Missus Pennymaker frowns impatiently and looks sharply at Sadie. "Did the accident affect her ability to speak, Sadie?"

"No, ma'am," Sadie briefly catches Hallie's eye.

Hallie takes this as a warning that it may be best not trying to explain about staying with Joan and who Joan Shively might be, so she goes along with Sadie's version of her situation. It's a white lie, but a necessary one. "It's nice to meet you Missus Pennymaker." Hallie looks her in the eye. "My name is Hallie O'Meara, and I am sorry to say that, although I have been working hard on it, I don't remember too much about why I was wandering in the woods, or how I ended up in the old timber holding pond ma'am."

Missus Pennymaker studies her for a moment with her arms folded. "Well, I'll get word out, and have my husband ask around when he is over in Stuart and Martinsville way to see if any folks are missing a gal your age."

"Yes ma'am. Thank you."

Missus Pennymaker turns her attention to Sadie again. "Sadie, you've been staying over at Billy's place, that right?"

"Yes 'um ma'am. We was thinkin' it be better givin' that he was there alone, and Doc said she needed to stay put."

"Hmm, yes I suppose that was a good way to arrange it at the time. Might be though that your momma needs you back home soon to help out with things. If that happens, you bring Hallie over here, and she will stay with me and Mister Pennymaker."

"Yes, ma'am. My Aunt Tessie be stayin' with us through the summer, so momma says she's okay for now."

"Yes well, if it changes, you do what I say. Billy is a good boy, but it just wouldn't be right."

This one voice likely holds the weight of the town, Hallie thinks, now understanding her living arrangements better.

Missus Pennymaker switches her authoritarian voice to a more casual tone. "If you stop by the livery, tell Billy I need to see him before he goes home." And just as quickly goes back to sternness. "You all mind yourselves over there. Ain't nothing more than a bunch of hooligans hanging around that place all the time."

"Yes ma'am," Sadie gives Hallie's sleeve a slight tug.

"It was nice meeting you Missus Pennymaker." Hallie says to her as she and Sadie turn to head over to the livery stable.

Sadie speaks in a low voice to Hallie as they walk away keeping her head forward so Missus Pennymaker doesn't notice. "Don't you worry. I've already talked to my momma. You are fine where you are, and when you aren't you can stay with us. Mister Pennymaker is thick with moonshiners and bootleggers, and you don't need to be around that. He may not be as ready to shelter a stranger from that sort, young woman or not, as much as he did his daughter before she died."

"Their daughter died." Hallie feels a bit of sympathy for the sergeant-like woman.

"Yeah, she was only eighteen. Sudden kind of thing. I might feel sad, if I liked any of them."

Jeb comes bounding out of the woods.

"Jeb! What are you doing here? You're supposed to be covering for Luke with the train run." Sadie scolds.

"There was trouble on the line." He answers her while fidgeting and looking to see who can see them talking.

"What kind of trouble?" She asks him not worrying who sees them.

Jeb hesitates.

"Jeb Curry you tell me what it was!"

"Daryl Lee," Jeb starts. "He and his brother, Jake, laid timber across the track and we stopped to pull 'em away thinking it was a tree that had fallen during the night. When we got out of the engine they busted out from the woods looking for Luke."

Sadie pales and hesitates before asking, "Did they say why they wanted him?"

"Nah, but Elijah cancelled the run and is backing the train up all the way here into town right now." He fidgets more anxious to get going. "Mister Pennymaker is going to be pis…uh, excuse me Miss." Jeb looks at Hallie. "He is going to be fit-to-be-tied. He has a shipment on board that he wants to go out today. I gotta go let him know."

Sadie looks worried, but she quickly pulls herself together and doesn't detain Jeb any longer. He heads over to the general store while Hallie and Sadie walk towards the livery.

"Sadie, is everything alright?"

"That fool, Daryl Lee." Sadie's fists clench, and her jaw tightens as she hisses out the words. "He works some with my daddy, but he is a no-account, two-faced, crook. Twenty-two years old, and got no ambition except wanting to grab hold of what he thinks my daddy has. Thinks I am the means to that end." Sadie stops short and turns to look at Hallie, she stands close to her and looks at her straight in the eye.

With a low voice she continues. "My daddy is a hard-working man. He has earned a good living for a black man in these parts. Hell." She lowers her voice even more. "He's managed a pretty good living for a white man in these parts. That Daryl Lee suspects something is going on between me and Luke. He is going to stir up trouble 'cause folks around here, including daddy, don't believe in no mixing. No mixing." With this she stops. Moisture rims her eyes, and Hallie wants so badly to reach out to hug her, but knows this is not the place.

Sadie turns on her heel walking towards the livery again.

"Sadie, how much longer before you and Luke can leave here?"

Sadie pulls her resolve back. "Not soon enough. If things get out around here about us there's gonna be plenty of trouble, and not just for me and Luke, but for our families and everyone connected to us."

They reach the livery and Sadie pauses before going in. "Don't mention none of this to Billy. I gotta talk to Luke first, alright?"

"Yes, of course."

They step into the cool stable. Holmes beat them there, and he is lying just inside where the shade starts but close enough to the door to see the comings and goings outside. They walk down the center aisle stopping to pet the velvet nose of a dark grey draft horse that has his head poking over the top of his stall door. Hallie can hear laughing and carrying on out in the back of the livery where a group of older boys and teens are gathered.

Billy makes his way around the loiterers and comes through the back aisle carrying two buckets of water. He gives Sadie and Hallie a nod and sets the buckets down by a stall door.

"You two might want to stay there for a minute until I get Detonator's water buckets changed out. He has been known to bolt through this door on a good day."

Hallie and Sadie oblige while Billy takes care of the stallion's water and moves some hay into the stall. He finishes up and walks over to them as he pulls out a bandana to wipe his brow.

Jeb strolls in drinking a Coca-Cola. He punches Billy in the arm, and makes his way through the livery to join the boys out back. There is a rise in the ruckus momentarily before slowly dying back down to its original decibel.

Billy turns his attention back to the girls. "So, the walk went well then?"

"Fine, just fine." Sadie looks out the front distractedly. "Billy, when is Luke supposed to meet you?"

"He is supposed to be coming by here anytime now. I ended up getting everything done, so we will be heading out just as soon as he gets here."

"Well, Missus Pennymaker is wanting you to go on over there before you leave outta here."

"Okay, then. I best wash up a bit. She will not take too kindly to me walking in the store smelling like a horse. Give me a minute, and I will walk on over there with you two."

Sadie fidgets.

"You okay? What can I do to help?" Hallie asks.

"I need to talk to Luke before he and Billy go fishing. I don't want him being caught off-guard if Daryl Lee and his idiot brother haven't given up on looking for him."

"Well, why don't we wait for him here while Billy goes to see what Missus Pennymaker needs?"

"No, we don't need to be staying here with that group of idiots out back. Even Jeb can act a fool when he gets around them boys. I'll leave him a note on the livery work board."

Hallie looks past Sadie towards the boys. They seem to be trying to coax Jeb into doing something. Several of them draw coins out of their pockets laying them down on a turned over barrel near the back door. One boy searches his pockets and ends up laying out a pouch of chaw. Jeb looks pretty confident walking into the livery taking a bridle off a hook on the wall as he walks over to Detonator's stall door. The boys follow him into the livery, but they hang back about ten or twelve feet laughing and carrying on. A few of the younger boys stand even further back with their hands stuck down in their pockets wearing worried looks on their faces.

"Uh-oh, this don't look too good." Sadie shakes her head looking around the aisle until she sees a couple square bales of hay stacked in front of one of the stalls. "Hallie, step up here on these bales with me and hold onto that bar." Hallie looks at her. "Trust me on this." Sadie climbs up onto the bales and takes Hallie's hand pulling her up too.

Jeb puts the bridle on the stallion and leads him out the front side of the livery. The ruckus continues, but at the safe distance already established.

Sadie and Hallie watch him climb up on a crate and mount the horse bareback then kick him in the sides coaxing him forward and into a lope quickly moving down the dirt lane with swirls of dust lingering behind.

"Come on," Sadie says shaking her head. "Let's see what that fool is up to."

The girls hop down from the bales of hay stepping outside. A few of the boys shift their position taking a brief look at Hallie curious about the new face, but too intrigued by Jeb's ride to keep their attention focused on her for too long.

"Dang!" The oldest-looking one in the group says. "He's going to get that spit-fire to ride clear to that creek bend and back, and we are all going to be out of our money."

"He ain't done it yet," another speaks up

"Yeah," chimes in a third. "Ain't no one stayed on that stud's back that long before he shows them what's for. You just wait and see."

Hallie feels someone walk up beside her and turns to see Billy. His attention is focused on Jeb and the stallion who is now galloping full speed down the dirt lane.

The horse is maintaining a steady gait and Jeb turns back with a cocky look on his face giving the group at the livery a raised fist full of confidence. The shift in weight must have triggered the horse's response. He makes an abrupt stop lowering his head and, with a powerful force, arches his back kicking outward in a manner that would have made the most seasoned bucking bronc proud. Jeb flies off the back of the horse hitting the dirt hard sliding on his tail end at least five feet with Detonator running full speed down the lane. The reins from the bridle swing back and forth as they hang from the horse's neck.

Billy shakes his head and the rest of the boys laugh slapping each other on their backs.

"Oh, my God!" Hallie says half to herself and half out loud in disbelief. Jeb's dungarees are flaming from his back pocket.

A few of the other boys notice as well pointing. The rolls of laughter grow.

One of them shouts out, "He musta had his strike 'em anywheres in his back pocket setting 'em off with that skid he done made!" The laughs rise to a new level.

Hallie looks curiously at Sadie.

"They mean matches." Sadie answers Hallie's unasked question.

Once Jeb realizes what is happening he tries unsuccessfully to pat himself out. Seeing the creek bend just a few feet away he runs jumping into the water.

The whoops and roars of laughter from the group at the livery are wild.

Within moments there is terrified yelling from the creek. Jeb's voice is panicked, "Help! Help! There's a rumba!"

Hallie gasps out loud, "My God, we have to help him. He's afraid of snakes."

Billy is already on his way to help, but hears Hallie and stops short for a moment turning to look at her before Jeb's pleading voice pulls him away. The laughing ceases abruptly, and the other boys follow Billy.

Jeb is sitting in the water resting back on his hands frozen. Just inches from him on the bank is a fallen log with a few snakes slithering and winding around it. One has its head up with its tail rattling off a warning to the uninvited visitor.

"Jeb, just stay still a minute," Billy cautions him. "It won't strike, if you keep still. There are too many of them for me to move them out of your way, so you need to calm yourself down."

Oh, my God. He is too frightened to even hear Liam...no...Billy. Hallie clutches at her skirt. She sees a long fairly straight stick and fetches it. She takes it to Billy. "Maybe you can use this."

"Right. Good idea Hallie. Jeb!" Billy's voice is stern. "Look at me. Not them."

Jeb's chin and lips are trembling. Hallie kneels down beside Liam to get closer to Jeb's eye level. "Jeb. We're here. Let me see you look up here on the bank." Jeb reluctantly complies.

"Yes, well done Hallie." Billy edges closer to the snakes with the stick at the ready. "Jeb, the water is shallow all along here. You just stay low and slowly back yourself away. I'll keep them focused on this stick."

Jeb darts a look at him.

The small group behind Billy is silent. Hallie sends soft comforting words to Jeb. "Take a moment and collect yourself Jeb. Find your strength. I know you can do this." She finds as many encouraging words she can think of that Beattie and Dot used whenever she had a challenge to overcome.

"Hallie is right. You listen to her. Go on now, Jeb. You can do this." Billy maintains a steady reassuring tone.

He moves slowly backward having to change his course a bit when he bumps into a rock jutting up from the creek bed, and he loses focus. Water splashes. The snake reflexively coils tight and springs towards Jeb. Billy swings the stick down catching the snake as it lunges forward hitting it down the creek away from Jeb. The other snakes slither in agitation, but do not poise themselves to strike. Jeb stumbles back, recovers, and runs awkwardly up the creek climbing back onto the embankment upstream.

Hallie rushes up the bank and meets him offering her hand to help him up. He nods an acknowledgement and sits down not able to speak. Hallie stays beside him, and Sadie walks up as well to offer comfort.

Everyone had been quiet until Jeb is safe, and then they return to their same level of harassment and laughing. Billy doesn't join in, and most of the group doesn't speak to him directly, but comment amongst themselves on how he foiled the snake's strike, and how that new girl had some gumption. A couple of the older teens nod Billy's way, and greet Hallie as they each give Jeb a pat on the shoulder. Billy tosses the stick off to the side. He looks over at Hallie. She fidgets with discomfort feeling as though he is taking stock of her. She wonders what he is thinking. One of the older boys gets a hold of Detonator and leads him back towards the livery.

Jeb finds his voice. "Thank you Hallie. Billy. I think I best get to work now and make sure Detonator is stalled properly." He stands brushing off his clothes and slowly walks back to the livery.

Sadie's previous state of impatience returns. "Billy, you going to get on over and see what Missus Pennymaker is wanting, so we can go find Luke?"

"Sadie, I told you that Luke is coming to get *me*. And yes, I will go see Missus Pennymaker now." He looks at her to see if she has any other words for him.

Hallie suddenly feels the prickle of her nerves in the aftermath of Jeb's near-death experience, and she is once again reminded that she is so very far from home, her time, her life. *What will it take to get back?* She crosses her arms and rubs them trying prevent herself from shaking and giving away her emotions. She hears Billy and Sadie's banter continue.

"Nothing else then?" He mocks Sadie teasingly, and she cuts her eyes at him walking off towards the general store. Hallie catches up to her while Billy follows with a slower pace.

Missus Pennymaker is behind the counter and looks up when the doorbell clangs as they come in. She smiles at the girls and goes back to her work making entries into a ledger. Hallie walks down an aisle of the small store looking at items on the shelves when the doorbell rings out again announcing Billy's arrival. Missus Pennymaker waves him over.

Sadie comes up to Hallie and hands her a sassafras candy stick. "My treat."

"Thank you."

They walk up to the counter and Missus Pennymaker looks up at them. Sadie lifts her candy stick up and holds up two fingers then a penny. Missus Pennymaker distractedly nods motioning her to put the penny on the counter, and continues her discussion with Billy.

Hallie puts the candy in her mouth and turns to lean against the counter. She glances sideways at the wall beyond where Billy is standing and sees a picture of a young girl sitting on a shelf with a small vase of flowers. She walks over taking it off the shelf to get a better view realizing that it is Ivy. Or, at least it looks like her. It has to be a 'Used-To-Be-Ivy' given that seems to be the way things are right now. She feels her stomach drop and a wave of nausea hits, as she is reminded once more that she is seriously out of place here and has no idea how to get back home. Every turn of events spirals her further into a disarray of emotions, and she fears losing the battle of staying in control.

She starts to set the picture back up on the shelf just as the office door next to where she is standing pulls open startling her. She misjudges the shelf knocking the edge of the frame into the flower vase causing it to wobble. She reaches to steady the vase dropping her sassafras candy stick on the floor shattering it into pieces. Her throat squeezes tight, but she manages a sigh of relief grateful it's not the picture frame or vase shattered on the floor.

She looks up seeing that Billy, Sadie, and Missus Pennymaker are looking at her and she shrugs apologetically. Billy has the same look on his face that he had at the livery. His glance shifts slightly beyond her, and a glint of anger lights his eye. Again, alarm tenses Hallie back up thinking she has done something to make him mad, but swiftly realizes that he is looking past her at the two men stepping out of the office.

One is dressed in a pair of brown trousers with suspenders over a starched white shirt. He appears middle-aged with a pleasant-looking but stern face. The other man looks out of place in the small country store, and he barely takes notice of her as he passes. He raises a slender pale hand to adjust his smoked-lens glasses higher onto his nose, and she sees a familiar gold ring with simple green stone adorning one of his spindly fingers. It feels as though some cosmic force has swirled away all the air around her triggering a vertigo that threatens both the previously saved vase and framed picture to the same fate as her sassafras stick. She falters on a set of weak knees. *Joe. Is. Here.*

Missus Pennymaker comes from around the counter putting her hand gently on Hallie's arm reaching for the framed picture. She mistakes Hallie's distress for concern about her blunder. Missus Pennymaker looks at the picture longingly, and reverently replaces it on the shelf and then adjusts the vase of flowers. Gazing at the picture for a moment she says, "That's a picture of my Roberta Mae. She was taken from us way before her time. Beautiful girl, wasn't she?"

Hallie swallows hard trying to will the dizziness away, and keep her eyes on Missus Pennymaker not allowing them to follow the two men as they move towards the front of the store. "Um….yes, yes ma'am. I am so sorry for your loss. I am so sorry that I disturbed her picture and the beautiful flowers. I…uh….I thought she looked familiar to me. I have been trying to get back my memory, but…I was mistaken."

Missus Pennymaker adjusts the frame's position talking under her breath to the picture enshrined within its boundaries. Hallie wonders if she even heard her apology. Hallie glances at Billy. He seems upset and his knuckles whiten with the grip he has on the ledger. His face is tense, and his jaw tight. He keeps his eyes fixed on Hallie, and she sees him bristle as Joe brushes against him ever-so-slightly as he walks past. Sadie is standing next to Billy, but she is no longer focused on Hallie. Hallie follows her gaze to see Luke standing a few isles over looking at Sadie willing her to come across the store to him. He must have come in while Hallie was distracted because she does not remember hearing the ringing bell at the front door. Sadie walks almost hypnotically away from the counter across the store towards Luke.

Hallie feels as though time suddenly stalls and each person in the store is moving in slow motion until the door bursts open and the bell rings out harshly in protest. There is a rush towards Luke.

Sadie yells out in a shrill voice, "Daryl Lee! What are you doing? Let go of him!"

Billy races across the store in an instant lunging past Luke pushing Daryl Lee away.

The man with suspenders pulls Daryl Lee out of Billy's reach. "What is wrong with you Daryl Lee?" He asks as he holds onto him. Daryl Lee resists until he sees who is holding him.

"I'm sorry, Mista Pennymaker, Sar. I don't mean to cause no problems here."

"Well, Daryl Lee what your intentions are, and what is actually happening are two different things. Now, you collect your things—it seems your hat is lying on the floor—then you walk out that door. You keep yourself out of here for the next week. After that, we'll talk. Ya hear me?"

Daryl Lee agrees and Mister Pennymaker releases him. Billy stands next to Luke who is twitching with anger. Daryl Lee leans down to pick up his hat. He straightens meeting Luke's eyes whispering, "She's gonna be my woman. You keep clear or *you* gonna be dead."

Luke lunges forward but Billy pushes passed him standing chest-to-chest with the threat. Daryl Lee smiles putting his hat on his head meeting eyes with Billy and then turns to the door. He walks past Joe who tilts his head down to look over his spectacles

223

at Daryl Lee. Daryl Lee hesitates a moment before stepping out. Joe surveys the general store and follows him out.

Hallie forces her legs to move her forward towards Sadie, and she has to force the air in and out of her lungs as well. It is as though she is drowning all over again. *Joe is here. Joe is HERE.* She tries to recollect what had just happened and what it could all mean. She barely saw the scuffle between Luke and Daryl Lee because she could not take her eyes off of Joe. She realizes that, just like everyone else here from her previous life, he does not seem to know who she is. It is just like she is living in a reversed amnesia. No one remembers her and, in this case, she is grateful.

She realizes she is about to bump into Billy who is walking back to the counter, and she stops, hearing him say to Missus Pennymaker. "Yes ma'am, I will keep an eye out for the order when I am here tomorrow. I hope you and Mister Pennymaker have a good trip. You do not need to worry about the store."

Missus Pennymaker smiles at him and closes the ledger walking back to the office to put it away.

He looks over at Hallie. "We need to go. We need to get Sadie and Luke out of town for a while." She just looks at him and nods. He walks passed her towards Luke, and she finds herself wishing he would take her in his arms and offer her comfort. She misses Liam so so much. Sadie is standing near the front door while Mister Pennymaker is talking with Luke. He gives Luke a solid pat on the back and turns to walk to his office.

"Are you alright Luke?" Billy asks as Hallie walks up to Sadie.

"Yeah. I need to go on over to the depot and let Elijah know that Mister Pennymaker is not too happy about his shipment not going out today. He wants me and Elijah to drive the load out tonight."

Sadie tenses and looks disbelieving at Luke before she turns to leave in a huff. Hallie follows her outside.

Daryl Lee is just stepping off of the porch. He rubs the back of his neck and turns his head back to look at Joe who is leaning against a post with one foot resting on an old half keg barrel. Daryl Lee has a strange look on his face and a chill climbs up Hallie's spine. Joe is pre-occupied with inspecting his cuticles not looking up to acknowledge the girls' arrival or Daryl Lee's departure. They step onto the path in the woods leading out of town and back to Billy's cabin. Holmes comes running up behind them when they pass the depot to follow along. Except for Holmes' occasional woof and turning up the ground cover to see what may be underneath, it is a quiet walk back to the cabin.

Chapter 29, Luminous

"I know Mister Pennymaker is punishing Luke for not being on that train and making sure his load was delivered." Sadie's voice quivers with emotion. "All that fighting amongst them shiners that's been goin' on too. A month ago a bootlegger for the Wilson clan was killed when his truck crashed and went ablaze burning that poor soul to death. The Wilson's suspected the Mitchell clan done something to the truck, and it was a suspicious crash, but no evidence was found to prove anything more than an accident occurring. Who knows about that though? The folks supposed to put an end to the illegal whiskey making are just as crooked, so it's hard to know where the truth truly lies. And now Luke is who knows where, and it is all my fault."

"Sadie, maybe the load had nothing to do with moonshining. Maybe it was something from the Pennymaker's farm." Hallie sits watching Sadie pacing back and forth.

Sadie purses her lips and tilts her head towards Hallie blowing out a harrumph.

"Ok, say you're right. But, if Luke was on that train today, he may have been hurt badly. Or, even killed. Sadie, I think if anything you saved his life."

Sadie stops pacing. "You think so?" Her face relaxes for the first time.

"I do." Hallie walks over putting her arm around Sadie's shoulder and guides her to bed. "Why don't you try to sleep awhile?"

Sadie nods and gives Hallie a warm and grateful hug before climbing into her bed. She falls asleep within minutes.

Once she falls asleep Hallie is alone with her thoughts. She decides to come out onto the porch to clear her head, but it has done no good. The hours pass slowly in contrast to her racing thoughts.

"You are up late."

Her heart jolts and her breath catches as Billy steps onto the porch.

"Um, yes." She adjusts her seat unable to read his face. Her heart disobeys any command to pace more slowly. "So, I'm guessing you made the liquor run for Mister Pennymaker to keep Luke and his brother off the road."

"I did," he starts to say something else, but pauses for a moment and then sits across from her on the porch leaning his back against a post. Holmes lifts his head to look at Billy, but lays it back down again opting to stay near Hallie.

Billy looks at Holmes shaking his head good naturedly then looks up at Hallie's face which is fully illuminated by the moonlight. His smile fades, and he sits for a moment longer studying the wood planks of the porch before looking back at her. He clears his throat. "Who are you?"

Hallie blinks unsure what he means. She feels the pluck of a skipped beat in her chest.

He only gives her a moment before firing at her, "I-*said*-who-are-you?" His words are pointed piercing her now racing heart.

"I've told you who I am. What are you talking about? *You* found me!" She wants to be firm, but he startled her with his harshness, and her voice waivers.

His lip twitches, and he shakes his head minutely. His words come through gritted teeth. "I saw you…," he looks pained. "You know things that you should not know. You recognize people who I know you do not know. You know things about who they are that you should not know." He pauses and studies her.

She looks back at him but makes no comment. *How can I explain this and still appear sane?*

"And," he continues, "I saw the look on your face in the general store when you saw the revenuer with Mister Pennymaker. He scares you—you know him somehow. So, tell-me-who-you-are."

Hallie swallows, her heart is pounding, and her mouth feels desert dry. *What does he know about Joe?* She feels confusion in the mix of the fear he caused. She takes a deep breath surrendering. "I am Hallie O'Meara just like I told you." She pauses willing her heart to slow. "I was born in the year 2000." She expects him to interrupt her at this point, but he doesn't flinch. Her palms prickle with sweat. "I met you in the summer of 2018 when I came to work here. Only the 'here' from *now* no longer exists. All this has become a state park, a big part is under water from where they built a dam to fill the valley and make a lake—a place for recreation." She begins to feel antsy with his silence. *Why is he not swearing me to be crazy?*

"How do you know the revenuer?"

Really? That's his first question? "Who says I know him?"

He instantly angers and moves across the porch putting his face inches from hers startling both Hallie and Holmes who looks up in alarm seemingly confused about who to protect.

"Do NOT toy with me. *I* say you know him. I saw the look on your face. You know him. Now, tell me how."

Hallie's breathing catches. She forces herself to hold it together. She feels the sharp pull as her heart tears apart. Tears moisten her eyes, but she refuses to let the first one fall. "I…I don't know…he walked up to me when I stopped in Williamsburg. I…I was driving to come here…to Fairy Stone State Park from my home on Burton's Shore. He told me a story—one I thought I already knew, but I guess not. He frightened me. I saw him only one other time after that, but I left before he saw me." She feels herself pressing her back against the cabin. Her eyes still burn with the sting of his words.

"So, you met him sometime in the *future*? Who else knew about him?"

Again, she thinks this question is odd. She grows hesitant to answer him, as confusion and fear churn into anger and suspicion, but he motions her impatiently to give him the answer.

"No…no one. I never mentioned him to anyone."

"Why? If he frightened you why would you not mention it to someone? Are you sure you do not know him in some other way? Are you…traveling with him?"

"What? No! I felt that my fear was irrational. Something other people would shrug off, and think I was crazy." Her anger starts warming her blood. She finds her resolve, and she stands up skirting around him to walk away.

He stands too grasping her arm. "How do I know you are telling me the truth, and you have not been sent here by him?"

She turns to look at him. Confusion and anger battle inside her for precedence. *How does he know who Joe is?* She has no idea what this means. She looks down at her arm where he is holding onto her and then back up at his eyes. "Are you for real? Who is he to you? Why would you think I am connected with him?"

He looks at her blankly, and she doesn't give him a chance to answer. "I'm just wondering because I have been trying…trying to figure out how to wake myself up from this nightmare. I tell you I am from the future. You did hear that part of what I said, right?"

He gives a half nod.

She is exasperated. "I just don't know what to say." She throws her hands up breaking free from him and steps off the porch. The weight of her amulet pouch bumps against her hip, and she looks down at it. An idea glimmers through her murky frustration. She anxiously loosens her pouch from the loop Sadie had sewn for her and spills out its contents, the amber and pressed penny, onto the palm of her hand. She lifts the penny into the moonlight. "This is a souvenir from the Chesapeake Bay Bridge Tunnel, and I scratched in the year 2018 on it with my initials. I got it the day I first drove here from my home on the Eastern Shore. That was the day I met the man you ask about."

He steps off the porch to stand next to her studying her steadfast until she feels a twinge of discomfort. He hesitates, and then takes the penny holding it up between his finger and thumb moving it slightly to catch the detail in the moonlight. "What is this bridge tunnel?" He asks turning his attention full force back to her.

His eyes are beautiful in the moonlight. Hallie's fear and agitation are being overrun by a feeling of intoxication. Her heart pushes a turbulent flow of heat that rushes up her neck catching her by surprise. She self-consciously takes a step back from him to allow herself space to think. He seems to be aware of what she is feeling, but she can tell he does not release his suspicion of her. The tendons in his neck stand taunt, and he flexes his fingers.

Her ire rekindles. "It...It's an extraordinarily long tunnel and bridge connecting the shore lines at the Chesapeake Bay. It does not exist yet—at least not for you. It won't be open for use until 1964."

He sets the pressed penny back onto her palm sliding his fingers over her skin to pick up the amber amulet and holds it up in the moonlight as well. The moonlight hits it kindling a golden brown glow. The edges that Billy touches fire brighter. "And this? Where did you get this?"

Hallie snatches it from him. "It was a gift from my aunts."

"Your aunts? Is that so?"

She eyes him. *Is he accusing me of lying about the amulet now?* "I told you, my aunts gave it to me!" Her eyes narrow. The anger inside her has definitely won out. "You tell me why this crazy story about me 'being from the future' is not flipping you out? And, tell me why you are accusing me of being involved with that man...the revenuer. How do you know him?"

He ignores her questions. "Who is Liam?"

Her mouth drops, she tries to speak, but stutters, then stops, forcing herself to respond. "Why?"

"You called for him several times that first night. You were very restless and agitated. You cried and apologized for leaving him to deal with your disappearance."

She hesitates, the anger has stalled again, and she takes a long melancholy look at him with the ache of her heart showing in her eyes, "Liam...is you."

He looks at her, and understanding comes to his eyes just before they hardened again. "No, I would never. That is *not* possible. People who care for me end up getting hurt. I don't let anyone get that close."

"Yes, you said that almost word-for-word to me. Right after we kissed the very first time." She looks around. "Somewhere in these woods actually." She strangely feels vindicated knowing he is now the one off-balance.

"No. Why would I do that? Why would I put another soul in so much danger?" He begins to walk away with agitation and stops short turning to her taking a step closer.

She stiffens a little unsure of what to expect.

He bites his lip. His voice is throaty. "I feel it right now. I felt it the day I pulled you out of that water and put my mouth over yours trying to bring life back into your body. I have felt it *every* day since you have been here. It has been so incredibly difficult. *Anything* I felt then, or will feel in the future…about you can be no stronger than it is right now. And right now, I would not act on it. I would not put you in that kind of danger. What is going to be different? Why?"

Hallie is so confused. She feels weak and sits back on the edge of the porch with her feet on the step below it. The pendulum like swing of her emotions has overwhelmed her senses, and she crosses her arms over her legs and lays her forehead down on them. Her head throbs, she is feeling exhausted, and yet she has to figure out what is going on. She lifts her head looking at him. "I have no idea what was, or what is going to be different for you. None. But there is obviously a connection between us. I know it. You knew it then, and you know it now. You can't ignore it. Whether you're willing to act upon it or not. It's stuck there inside your head and your heart. You need to be honest with me about what is going on. I have told you what you've asked. Tell me why you are so angry with me. Please."

He looks down at her leaning his arm against the porch. He bites the inside of his cheek and rubs a hand through his hair. "It is not safe for you to know everything. But, I *am* telling you to stay away from the revenuer. He is not what you think he is. He is dangerous." Billy reflexively rubs his scarred arm and Hallie notices.

"He's the man who did that to you isn't he? You told me about living a cursed existence and, at the time, I thought you were being metaphorical. I know how he makes me feel—on edge and fearful. Can it be that he has something to do with all this? All those weeks in 2018 I thought he was after me, but it is you he is seeking out. Isn't it? I see why he is dangerous to you, but why to me?"

He looks at her incredulously. "My, God! Who am I in 2018? Why would I have told you about any of that?"

"You didn't reveal any dark secret! You told me the scar came from a run in with a vile man. That was all. He fits the description." She tries to control her emotions, her nerves tremble until she looks back up into his eyes, and again the intoxication washes over her. She finds strength in those eyes, her breathing regulates, and her heart rate slows. "You're eighteen years old. You live with a woman named Joan Shively. She is a friend of my aunts, and I came to stay with her for the summer.

"That is how you and I met. We...I don't know...felt a connection and grew close. You work at Fairy Stone State Park, and so do I. You are kind of a loner, but you have friends who I know you care about and who care about you. Jeb, Sadie, and Luke are there—even Roberta Mae, and...you have me. We love each other. You tried to deny it, but you weren't able to. And you were happy once you surrendered to it—happier than people who knew you had seen you before. I don't know what it all means. We were good together I guess. And no matter how complex the situation, that kind of emotion, that kind of love makes the impossible possible. Maybe, the person you were...*are* going to be knows that...*feels* that, and nothing else matters. I don't know. It was simpler then—before I ended up here." She flushes feeling suddenly vulnerable.

"Yes." He looks at her a moment and sits on the step beside her. "I do see that. I *feel* that. All of it. Look, I am sorry. I am sorry if I was...or will be...reckless with your emotions...with your heart. We have to figure out how to fix this for you. I cannot have you in danger. If I am eighteen when we first meet, what month is it?"

"We met in early May, but it was near the end of June when I...I guess I drowned." She feels worried again. "Do you think I died?"

"I do not know. Obviously, you are here, so if I had to guess I would say you are still alive. I do not know how, but you are real, and you are here. Tell me what you remember."

Hallie gives him an account of the night at the Triple C Beach, the sparkling light, the hollow tree log, getting snagged, and the chiming voice."

"A light and chiming voice?"

"Um—hmm"

"What did it say?"

She shrugged a shoulder. "Well, it talked about no beginning without an ending and not reaching the ending without first beginning. It said angel song would take me there and fairy tears would assure my passage and care with a harmonizing ring."

He nods, almost like a mad scientist would. "Okay, so there is a chance we can keep you safe. I am not sure what it means about passage…unless it is a way we can get you back to your own time. You sure it said angel song?"

"Um—hmm"

"The revenuer. When you saw him did he have a companion?"

Her mouth opens and her eyes widen. "Yes, a young woman. She was petite. Beautiful and…angelic."

"Yes, indeed so. Have you heard a chiming voice at any other time?"

"Yes. A few times." Hallie feels chills go up her arms startled that he knows about all this. "But the voice in the song does not sound like Joe's companion's voice. It has a different quality. At least I think. I have only heard Joe's companion speak one time, and it…it was under unusual circumstances."

He pauses. "Yes, well she is not the only one."

"Not the only angel here?" *This is getting very weird. Maybe. My fall back in time falls into the world of the weird too.* She shakes her head.

Billy forges on. "Not necessarily here, but just not the only one."

"Huh, so it is all real. No one is going to cart me off with claims of insanity."

He smiles. "Never." He leans in closer. "Okay, so you said this place becomes some sort of park named after the fairy stones. Is that correct?"

"Yes."

"It would seem that you are going to have to wait until the angel song comes to you again from what you've said. Have you ever been able to call out for the angel?"

She shakes her head.

He nods. "Fairy tears are legend to be fairy stones, so that has to be why you are here. I do not know though. They can be found all throughout the woods, but they have to be here in the future too. Are they?"

"Um, yes. Joan found one when we were walking on a trail."

"We have to figure out why here and why now. I just hope that there is enough time. He tilts his head to look her in the eye.

"Enough time?"

"Yes, Hallie. Each life ends, and this one is drawing to a close. Soon I fear."

She can no longer maintain control and a tear rolls over her lashes.

He reaches out wiping it away. "Remember, there can be no beginning without an ending. We can get through this."

She lifts her chin. "Yes. Together." But, she quickly looks away towards her hands in her lap.

"What? What is the matter?"

"You are not going to be reckless with my heart."

His face goes blank and he averts his gaze, but quickly forces himself to look back at her. "I am sorry, but you being here is proof that I am."

Hallie's eyes sting with a new well of tears.

He hesitates clearing his throat. "Here, there is something else. Let me see your amber piece again." She hands him the heart, and it shimmers once again.

"Hallie, what do you know about this heart?"

"It belonged to my aunts for as long as I can remember. I always admired it, and they gave it to me as a gift when I turned eighteen."

He looks at her waiting. "What else do you know about it?"

She presses her cheek towards her shoulder. "It brings me comfort. I like to keep it with me."

He twist his lips. He motions asking permission to take her hand and she nods intrigued. He grasps her hand with the amber piece between them closing his hand tightly. A glowing light escapes from within their hands illuminating their fingers shining out brightly. It forms an arc of light around the two of them. Hallie looks up and around them, and then at Billy. He loosens his grip on the heart and her hand. The light fades around them but lingers within the heart.

It takes Hallie back to the sick room of Harry White momentarily. She blinks and looks at Billy waiting for him to explain.

He holds the heart up for her to see. "This," he says. "Is blood from the Tree of Life. Amber. Have you ever noticed the small wisp of a feather trapped inside it where the loop of the heart is?"

Hallie shakes her head. But, the bit of feather inside the amber is evident now with the glow Billy induced.

"It belongs to an angel. Did you know it has not always looked like this?"

She nods her head. "Yes, I had a vision. There was a man—he was horribly ill—and a beautiful…woman…"

"Witch. She was a dark witch." He cuts her off.

Hallie flinches remembering Liam's hatred of witchcraft, and her fear about telling him the whole truth. But, the idea of someone thinking she is crazy for believing the story no longer exists. *He already knows.* She takes a deep breath. "…Yes, Resmelda. She healed the man with a ritual, but he was not fully responding. The amber gave him energy to heal completely. It changed into this heart-shaped amulet after she laid it on his chest and covered it with her hand."

"She and the man were…friends." He hesitates.

Hallie looks at him with amazement. "Yes…Harry *William White*…she loved him." She looks at Billy with a realization that she can't believe this hadn't connected for her before now. Her fear of Joe, her new job, the insights not just about Joan's involvement with witchcraft, but Beattie and Dot's too, and mostly her fall into love all crowded her mind at the time. But, opening up to Billy and sharing what she knows has given room for more.

"Yes…if she was capable of love, but the truth is his heart was already taken."

"By Sarah, his wife who died in childbirth…, but she died long before he and Resmelda met."

"Yes." He nods to her searching her eyes., and Hallie knows that he is wondering how she knows all this. She knows how he feels because, before she made the connection to who he is related to, she too wondered how he could know the details of her childhood story.

Before he can press her Hallie muses, "He could have found happiness with Resmelda too though."

He shrugs and frowns.

"She could have chosen another path."

"But, that is not what happened. Instead she laid out a curse that has condemned me to a life of servitude along with the unfortunate souls bound to me. It has been over two-hundred years."

Two-hundred years? Hallie's head begins throbbing again with this unexpected declaration, and she knows she is putting him on edge as well, but she decides to push forward in hopes of finding out more about what is going on. "I don't understand what you are saying. This was only a story when I was growing up— something my aunts told me to provide entertainment. It has only been recently that the tale has begun to become something else. I know from the story that Harry's *son* is cursed. What do you mean that *you* are cursed?"

"It is not a story. You have to understand that. You are here…in a time before you were even born…as incredibly unreal as it seems here you are. And I think you can accept that the story you have come to know for 'entertainment' is really the foundation of my reality. It also has become, or maybe it always has been, your reality as well. I do not know how or why, but it has." He moves closer to her, and Hallie feels a desperation in his mood. "The amber piece… it has the ability to energize life and to preserve it. I have seen the piece once before, a long time ago. Your aunts *have* to be connected to all this somehow as well." He hands the amulet back to her and waits holding his breath. Its glow fades. She looks at it in her hand and feels it start to warm. She squeezes it as Billy had done. It grows warmer but does not glow. She looks at him and searches his eyes.

"What do you feel?"

"It is getting warm, and it is making me feel at peace. It…it always has. It is a bit of security. A bit of home."

237

A shaky laugh escaped him. "Yes, I could feel this too when we held it in our hands together. It is okay. It glows with my blood line and warms with yours. When the two forces within us come together the intensity is increased and more evident." He runs a hand through his hair and lets out a long burdened breath. "I know now that you and the revenuer have nothing to do with one another."

Her eyes narrow. "I already told you that. What, was this some sort of test?" She squares her shoulders and straightens her back.

"Hallie, listen to me." His voice cracks. " I had to know. I had to know for sure."

She cocks her head and smacks her lip looking at him. She raises her eyebrows. "Go on."

He closes his eyes and breaths in through his nose. He opens his eyes searching her eyes.

Why is he doing that thing where I can feel him so deep within me? You're angry, Hallie, don't cave.

He blurts it out. "Harry William White was my father. The amber glows when it touches my skin because it glowed when it touched my father's skin. It warms to your touch because I believe that it warmed to the touch of someone you are related to—someone in your blood line, but I cannot say for sure. It has something to do with how we are made—how the Tree of Life recognizes those connected to it."

"What? Your father?" She looks up to the moon and shakes her head, and then she looks back at him. "Billy…I…don't understand. How can you be the *son* of Harry White? I was thinking you are a descendent who inherited the curse. Maybe some kind of reincarnate enduring the tortures every life. How…how can this be?" She draws in her lower lip, and says mostly to herself, "Over two hundred years."

"Yes. Just like you, I am from a different time. I was born in 1700. I was cursed. I alluded to this information to you previously, or I will in the future. I am not just a descendent of Harry White. I am his son. The revenuer…the man you met…"

"Joe."

He pauses, "Joe," saying it like it leaves a bad taste in his mouth. "He is not what you think he is. He is a demon from the underworld who, as a result of Resmelda's curse, holds my humanity captive in order to use it over and over again to gain access to the mundane world—our world. Demons must possess or have an accord with a human to cross otherworldly boundaries. But, he is not only any demon, he is the Demon King. He determines passage through otherworlds after judgement has been passed on the dead. He uses this power to preserve my humanity, my flesh, and my servitude. All but my free will is his. That is God-given, and no creature can take it unless we, as humans, bargain it away. You need to stay away from him. Your instincts about him are right. Do not let him near you. Do not let him touch you. We need to figure out how to get you back to where you came from before something happens to you."

"Now I have a demon to worry about in addition to everything else?" Hallie's head swims as she tries to make sense of everything. "And what about *my* blood line?"

"I do not know for sure. The last time I saw the amber it was in the possession of two little girls. Hallie…their names were Beattie and Dot."

She looks at him. "You…you knew my aunts? When? How?"

"I did not really know them, I only had a brief encounter with them. At least I think it was them, but I am just not sure. The amber's power is strong, and if it has been in their possession, they very well could be your aunts. Although I do not remember much from the night I got this scar, I know it was the amber that healed my arm. It preserves life."

Hallie looks at him, shrugging and raising her eyebrows for him to continue.

"Hallie…it was in 1720."

Hallie feels sick. "You know…I know this is crazy… but I can't not believe in the possibility of it all given what I—we have experienced. Can I? I mean…I guess…could they be the same people? Yes, yes they have to be. It makes sense. All the vintage things in our home. The old old things in our home. Their youthfulness." She brightens with understanding. "But, the amber does not completely preserve life though because they have grown up. It must just rejuvenate and prolong life."

"Yes, and heal. Do not forget about my arm."

Hallie closes her eyes wrapping her arms about her waist. *My whole life—is something I could never imagine in my wildest dreams.* Her eyes glisten and she looks at Billy. "I think I have reached my limit. I'm overwhelmed…I want to know more…I do…I'm really sorry, but I think I need to get some sleep. I can't think about this anymore—not right now."

"Right. Yes, of course. That is probably a good decision. Sleep will help." Billy stands up and holds a hand out to help Hallie up. She looks at him briefly before accepting his assistance. There is an awkward moment where she is lost in his eyes. She forces herself to look away and let go of his hand. He walks with her to the cabin door holding it open with his arm outstretched.

Hallie looks at him—a flash of Liam holding Joan's back door open for her that very first night comes to mind. Her chest feels heavy. She walks passed him crossing the threshold, and turns to say good night before stepping inside the cabin. He shuts the door behind her and she walks over to her bed laying down not even bothering to undress. The moonlight filters through the window, and she wishes she could walk up on its glow like the goddess Iris' rainbows carrying souls to heaven. Hallie only wants to go back to her time. Surely there has to be a way.

Chapter 30, Ignited

Hallie wakes and looks over at Sadie's pallet finding it empty. She washes up with the fresh water that Sadie left for her in the pitcher and gets dressed. The sweet smell of corn cakes lure her to the stove, and she picks one up and goes outside.

Billy is sitting on one of the chairs on the porch, Holmes is by his side. "Hello."

"Morning." She walks over and sits on the hammock finishing the corn cake. Holmes gets up and walks over to her. She smiles at him and rubs his head.

"I am sorry," Billy says.

She looks over at him. She is caught up in some bizarre dream, yet what worries her more is the aching of her heart. She can deal with anything, if he would stand by her side, but he seems to remain distant and unavailable. She can't answer him.

He looks across the clearing towards the woods. "I am going to take you to Sadie's place this morning. She's gone ahead to let her mother know about it."

"I see…Sure."

"Look…"

"No, you look! Tell me Li…" She shakes her head. "Billy…does anyone else know about what we talked about last night? I mean who else do you have that can help you figure it out except me? And you're sending me away!"

"I am not sending you away. I am trying to keep you safe. If the revenuer thinks you and I are connected in any way you will be doomed to my fate. There is nothing to figure out. It is only a matter of time before he finishes harvesting souls. It has already started with Roberta Mae. I do not know how to make you understand what that means. I told you I was cursed. I relive my life over and over. Not like a reincarnation. I just show up in the mundane plane. My life is already in progress, and I have to find a way to catch up." Pain accents his words. "And each life has to end. Usually within a few years, although, it can be longer. It ends in order for the demon to have another beginning later. In between it is hell—literally. It will not be long before the harvest is over, and we are back in the underworld. There are others connected to the curse, and you could become one of them. You are in danger, if you stay here with me."

His pain pierces her core, and she walks over kneeling in front of his chair. "Listen I…I think I am already dead. I mean I am gone from the world I know. And this…this doesn't even exist anymore. Not really. No matter how real it feels right now. Let me help you. Together we can break the curse."

He just looks at her. He gently strokes the side of her face.

"You know I would walk into the darkness with you and not think twice about it," she says reaching up taking his hand and gently kissing it.

He turns her hand and entwines his fingers with hers. "I believe you. I am sorry that I thought you were bonded to the demon. I should have known better, but he is very skilled in deception, and I had to be sure."

"I understand, really, I do."

He looks down and nods. "Thank you. It means a lot that you understand my feelings, but Hallie you have no idea what 'walking into the darkness with me' means. I never live long enough to truly accomplish anything of value. I struggle to survive and, even though I am looking out for the other souls tethered to me, there are times when things go wrong. We are a Circle of Souls. We are bound together somehow. But even with them, it is still a solitary existence. I always return to the mundane world, and I always try again to keep the souls safe while trying to defeat the demon, but it is never any different. He always wins in the end. Before a new life on Earth starts we endure what feels like an eternity of torment in the underworld. My failure to defeat the demon pulls the souls of those tethered to me into the underworld. Time does not pass there as it does here. It does not matter if the time between our lives is only a few years or fifty years. It feels like an eternity there. That is what hell is Hallie. I do not want you to ever know what it is like." He shudders.

Hallie is lost at what to say. She doesn't doubt any of the agony he describes, and yet she is willing to risk it to be with him. She can't help but feel optimism that if they fight together things can be different. She remains quiet and lets him talk.

"You would become part of the Circle of Souls. I have to keep each of their lineages intact during our time on earth, or they are destined to remain in the underworld forever—or maybe even worse—I just do not know." He rubs the back of his neck.

"They are people who I knew in my original life. There were six in the beginning, and two of them have since been lost. I carry that responsibility with me forever. The thought of them being lost is torture. The same could happen to you. I do not know what caused them to be tethered to me in the beginning, and I cannot take any chance that the demon will take an interest in your soul as well. Do you understand why we cannot be together?"

"You think my soul will be…tethered to yours, and be cursed?"

"Yes, and you will lose your memory of me. You will not know me during our time here on earth. Only rarely does one carry the memory of past lives into a new life. There is a ceremony at the Mesu—it is a great tree that has portals to other realms. Some call it the Axis Mundi. During the ceremony the Demon King forces the souls to drink from the river Lethe. It abolishes memories. Its effects are not lasting, but long enough usually. Sometimes the effects wear off more quickly. I am the only one who does not drink. It makes his game more fun for him. Knowing I am alone and struggling." He closes his eyes for a moment and presses his lips together.

"That is not possible. We are not tethered by a curse, but destined by something pure. He would not have any power over our love."

"How can that be? If there had been no curse, I would have lived in the 1700's and you three hundred years later. We would have never met. We would have never known each other."

"Well, maybe the curse is part of a destiny intended for us to meet. How is it that my family knows the story you have lived? You met my aunts, and they have been living miraculous lives for nearly three hundred years! It is all truly fantastical. It is not likely coincidental. I have no idea how or why, but maybe we have been meant to be together all along."

"I think what you are speculating is a manipulation of the facts to make them paint the picture you want to see."

"I don't think I'm manipulating it. Why can't you consider a different version of the story—a different outcome for your reality? This summer I have seen different versions of the story. Maybe there is a version that we just haven't discovered. Why have I been pulled back through time to meet you again? I know I am right. There is more to be sure, but I am right about us." Hallie's heart feels a little lighter. Hopeful.

He laughs. "You are incredibly optimistic. I wish I could say I feel the same way, but I do not think that the world will stop if we disagree."

"True. I'm not trying to win an argument. I'm just saying that I don't know how it was meant to be with your original life in the 1700's and mine in the future, but we found each other and we just fit. I feel it, and I know you do too even if there is some supernatural influence responsible. Maybe *that* is what we need to focus on—the magic of the connection. My aunts always say there is magic everywhere, and love is the most powerful magic there is. Perhaps, if we work together, the curse *can* be defeated. We could break the darkness."

"That is speculation on your part, and I know you will understand, if I prefer to keep any thoughts of magic far far away. I am not willing to risk your safety or your soul based on magic or speculation. Come now, it is time to go to Sadie's." He stands and helps Hallie up.

She nods knowing it is impossible to convince him to let her stay. "So, what are you going to do? How long has Joe been in town?"

He looks over at her with a crooked smile and tilts his head. "Just so you make no mistake, he goes by Mister Steele here. Do not call him Joe. If he were to hear, it might tip him off that you know him in some other realm. Joe Tasker is a name that he uses often but so is Max Steele. *Here,* he is a corrupt revenuer who turns a blind eye to illegal whiskey-making activities for a price. I am not justifying the making of moonshine, but some families in these parts would starve without the income it generates. Most cannot afford to buy him off, and he terrorizes them. Not directly, but through influence of others. Others with weak souls. He is likely the source of the recent feuding between the Wilson's and the Mitchell's.

"His specialty is manipulating the weaknesses of men. He plants seeds like jealousy, greed, hatred, and then he waits for them to grow. It is what he does in order to make bargains and to collect souls and trinkets from those who succumb to temptation and his false promises. Some are tricked into it while others find the pathway on their own. He feeds on all. He came into town several weeks ago harvesting Roberta Mae first."

"She is one of the tethered souls then?"

He looks at her nodding. They make their way across the clearing towards the path to Sadie's house. "I thought I saw recognition in your face when you saw her picture. You know her?"

"In the future her name is Ivy. She is…" Hallie squinches her nose. "A piece of work."

He looks at her and furrows his brow giving a shrug.

"You know, hard to be around, manipulative, self-centered."

"Well then, yes, you do know her. We had a rocky start to our relationship in our original lives but became friends eventually. Like the others, I do not know why she was tethered to me. It was after the curse that our relationship became strained. I made a mistake, a horrible mistake, and she rightfully hates me for it, but I wonder about her loyalty to the remaining circle. It has never been a challenge to keep her lineage going, and it makes me wonder if she has some sort of agreement with the Demon King. Or he may just know that she irritates me, and it amuses him to keep her lineage going." He sniffs as though something foul is the air and then smiles wryly. "I am not sure that I would make a huge effort, if her lineage was in danger anyway."

"You don't mean that." Hallie playfully slaps his arm. "How does the lineage work?"

"That first day, after you woke from your fever, I saw you look at my ledger."

She looks at him feeling bad about going through his things.

She starts to apologize, but he cuts her off. "It is alright. Each soul in the circle has a family member each lifetime who has the power to leave a pathway for their return. This is the anchor relative, and he or she is marked with the lineage symbol—like a birth mark. It is usually on their neck behind an ear. Each line is represented by a different symbol. The symbol is in the book by each lineage. The pathway must be protected. It is the demon's way of keeping me occupied while he pillages. He has this fascination with all things human. Not just our souls, but our material possessions. He collects them like he collects souls."

"Can he be stopped?"

He shrugs "I hope to find a way to defeat him, and set the Circle of Souls free one day."

"Even the lost souls?"

"I do not know. I worry that they have been lost forever. It is called a death of death. A person who dies a death of death is lost to all realms."

"All realms?"

"Yes, Hallie there are more than can be imagined. It is why I have never truly learned about the lost souls, and it weighs heavy on me. One was my cousin and the other a childhood friend. Their lineages were disrupted when their anchor kin had been murdered."

"Oh, Billy, I am so sorry. I cannot imagine the heartbreak you must feel. But, in your ledger some generations had more than one person with a symbol by their name."

"Sometimes that happens, it always happens for Roberta Mae's, or Ivy's, lineage. Usually though there is just one. There was only one each for my cousin and our friend."

"What about the person in your Circle of Souls? Can his or her life be spared ever?"

"Occasionally someone will live beyond me and that is a success. It keeps them out of the underworld for a while longer. They do not always live during my time on earth either. Most of the time though we are all together. When the circle is full we have the best chance to defeat the curse, however, amnesia of their true identities does not help. And, a full circle means I have to assure the continuation of the lineages for all of them—make sure nothing lethal happens to their anchor kin. When the souls are not alive during my time on earth the demon has vowed that he will not threaten their lineage. He is obligated to keep his word, and he is skillful enough not to give it very often."

"It's all very complicated, isn't it?"

"Yes, yes it is. I don't start my new life with my memories because there is some confusion just traveling through the Mesu's passages, but they eventually come. Sooner or later, those in the circle for that life come together. We have some sort of attraction that draws us together. We all maintain our original appearance, so it is not hard for me to recognize them." He reaches up to hold a branch out of Hallie's way as they walk and talk.

"Do they ever know? Do they ever know who they are or who you are?"

"Always when we are in the underworld, rarely when we are on Earth. When it does happen there is always a feeling of distrust, it is instilled by the Demon King. So, I do not always know if someone has vision into our circumstances. Occasionally, I can figure it out."

"What about now?"

"I am not certain, but I think perhaps Jeb."

"Really?"

"Yes, he does not have a very high self-esteem, so he likely thinks his memories are imaginary—you know, not things he would be capable of achieving. His past endeavors were quite extraordinary. He has become a bit reckless with this life, and that is usually how it is when the realization about our circumstances hits. He or she feels like there is no reason to achieve more in life, and there is anger and then helplessness due to uncertainty about how to conquer the problem. Jeb has gotten worse since Roberta Mae died. We are a full circle during this lifetime, and the pattern has been that once one death occurs others soon follow. Jeb must know, or at least sense this, but he has not given me any sign for me to come out and ask him."

"What about the snakes yesterday? He certainly did not want to take them on."

"No, he did not. He has acquired a fear of snakes over the course of time. It was not always that way. I cannot explain it, but it seems the curse has a different effect on Jeb than it has on the rest of us. He loses a bit of himself every life."

"I am truly sorry to hear that. He is a good guy which is all the more reason for us to find a way to stop the curse. Quickly, since Mister Steele has started reclaiming souls.

"Yes, and I am afraid Luke is next. I believe it was intended to happen last night, but I took the shipment for Mister Pennymaker and sent Luke home convincing him that Sadie would be safer, if he stayed in town. His brother, Elijah, is the pathway for his lineage, so I have to keep him safe as well."

"What about Sadie?"

"Her Aunt Tessie has two girls that are pathway anchors. She should be okay."

"But, what about *Sadie*?"

"Hallie, I do not know. Right now my experience makes me feel that she is okay."

Hallie nods. Some of the climb is steep, and she feels a little tired. They stop for a rest sitting at the base of an old sycamore tree. Holmes is still energetic and runs off to explore a scent that he picks up.

Hallie looks around. She loves the woods, its voice, and its pungent spice that induces a calm matching the feeling her amber amulet gives her. She lays her head against the large tree and looks up towards the sky and then over at Billy. He is also sitting relaxing against the tree and seems to have the same appreciation for their surroundings. Sitting beside him feels like a gift, and she closes her eyes enjoying the moment.

After a while she asks, "How much longer?"

"Their place is a little further over that ridge. I guess we should get going. It is getting late, and I need to relieve Jeb at the Pennymaker's." He stands up.

Hallie looks up at him disappointed that they have to leave this beautiful spot and soon be separated. She is distracted by this thought when she starts to stand. The pebbled ground shifts and her shoe slides downward. Loosing balance she starts slipping down the steep ridge alongside the path. Billy is quick and grabs her arm pulling her away from the danger of falling.

She stares at the ravine below and draws in a shaky breath feeling clumsy as she looks up at Billy. The heat of embarrassment rises up her neck. He has not let her go and pulls her close.

"Thank you," she whispers quietly.

He nods still holding onto her looking at her intensely. Hallie is aware of his breathing as it quickens. He leans down kissing her catching Hallie off-guard, but she responds eagerly. She feels the warmth of the kiss spread through her. Their lips part, but he doesn't move away from her. Holding her, he searches her eyes and seems torn with indecision.

Billy then kisses her again, slowly, lingering over her mouth to explore it. Her pulse quickens, and she moves her hands up behind his neck. He groans and kisses her more deeply. She willingly returns his kisses as she feels him draw her closer. Time vanishes. The intensity rises, and his skin feels hot against hers. His hands move down to the small of her back. She shivers as desire overpowers any ability for reasonable thought.

He sinks back down to sit at the base of the tree bringing Hallie with him, over him. Her skirt slides back exposing her thighs, and his hands move smoothly up the outside of her legs as he grasps ahold and pulls her closer. She looks at him, his face is flushed as his mouth finds hers kissing her again escalating the heat.

His lips move down her neck, and she arches back surrendering to the moment. She reaches down to pull his shirt out of the waist of his dungarees. She is trembling overwhelmed by the feeling of the unknown. He comes back up to kiss her mouth, gently, slowly, deeply and then he unwillingly interrupts the kiss leaning his forehead against hers. She is acutely aware of his hands at the small of her back enmeshed in the tangles of her skirt and the heat that they create.

His voice is breathless, "I don't want to stop."

She kisses him. "It's okay because I don't want you to stop." She kisses him again. He brings his hands up her back. She fumbles with the buttons of his shirt. Her hands are shaking and ineffective. She feels Billy tense slightly as he draws back from her. He takes ahold of her hands kissing each, and he brings them close to his chest until they steady.

He struggles to regulate his breathing looking into her eyes.

"Hallie, did we…did we ever make love before you came here?"

She shakes her head. "No, no we didn't."

He sighs and holds onto her hands. "Then, we cannot now. We should not—not now."

She looks at him. She feels like she has crossed a line that she shouldn't have even been close to. Her ears ring with a resonate hum of mortification. "I'm sorry, I'm so sorry. I didn't mean for this to happen. I just…"

"No." He gently puts a finger over her mouth and kisses her bringing her heart rate immediately back up.

"No, that is not it. You must understand," he searches for an explanation. "The demon does not see people like you and I do. He sees our souls. He knows that mine has been altered—enhanced, if you will. He saw it in the store yesterday and brushed against me trying to see more. Just me knowing you and being close to you was all it took. But now, us taking what I only thought about…longed for…well, we *almost* took it." He smiles at her and she smiles back. "If we make it any more intimate, I will not ever be the same. What has passed between us has intensified what was already a significant change in the aura of my soul just me knowing and loving you. He will know. He will see the difference. We can only hope that he will not recognize that it is you that has made the change and come for you.

"I am thinking that your soul has already been unified with mine up to *this* point—in 2018—and your soul will not look different to him since he saw you yesterday, so he may not recognize your connection to me, if he sees you again. But if we were to take this any further, further than we have been before, the aura of your soul too will change. He will know.

"All our connections to people, nature, experiences we have leave an impression on our soul. It is not always obvious to people, but it is very much so to a demon or a soul seer. You will not be safe. We cannot go further, not now."

"Are you sure? I don't think he paid me any attention yesterday."

"Yes, very sure. He surveys all souls. He is always looking for the weaknesses in mankind trying to find something to be preyed on. You likely did not emanate any weakness that would attract his attention. If, however, he sees a change in your soul, one that links you to me, he will pull you in."

"When then? Back in my own time?"

"When it is safe. I do not know when, but I promise. I believe now, like you, that we can find a different path, but we cannot afford to be careless. Our time will come but it is not now. I am so sorry for…for losing control."

"Well I think I am guilty too, and I'm sorry. I'm sorry that it has to end even if just for now. I love you." She smiles sadly at him.

"I love you too." He sighs but holds onto his strength to resist and gives her a rueful smile.

Her smile brightens understanding now how he feels, and she reluctantly shifts her weight to stand up.

Billy stands up with her, and draws her close embracing her in a warm hug kissing her tenderly. He sighs. "I promise we will find a way."

She nods, a chill moves up her arms as she hears the twinkling sound of chimes from the distance. She cocks her head to listen then looks at him. Her eyes sparkle with the sunlight filtering through the trees, and he looks at her expectantly.

"The last time we were together in these woods, in 2018, I heard the angel song. It called to me and said, 'The threat draws near, beware! Cleave its course by clinging to the hope that whispers near the edge of darkness, at the borders of new lovers' hearts. Allow hope to gently stir memories from forgotten lives. Hold onto lost keys unlocking the path meant to entwine two lives forever setting free more than the pair. It is a course interrupted by a fate endured beyond unimaginable time.'" She pauses and laughs, "I can't believe that I remembered that. It seems like a lifetime ago when I heard it."

He looks at her. "You are certain there is no other way?"

251

She shrugs her shoulders. "I admit this song has more meaning to me now, and when the songs come they have seemed to give some insight to what is ahead."

"Danger is entwined throughout its message, but the song sings about lost keys unlocking a path just like your message in the lake."

She nods her head. "Yes, I thought about that too."

"The song you heard in the lake talked about the fairy tears—the fairy stones—helping you to find your way."

She twists her lips and closes her eyes and moves her head up and down slowly.

"So, maybe an angel has literally left keys behind, in a time lock for some reason, and has sent you back to collect them."

"Yes that is what I think too, but *with* you, not alone. Maybe our joining forces will help accomplish whatever I have traveled back to do, and help you accomplish whatever you have been moving forward to do. No matter what your identity is for each life because each life is the same you."

His mouth opens and then closes. His eyes show a realized hope, a chance for victory, and humbled gratitude.

Hallie just smiles looking up at him and gently kisses him just under his chin and then up towards the corner of his mouth. She brushes her lips across his to kiss the other corner of his mouth. He brings his hands up to cup her face in them and kisses her.

He holds her close, her head resting against his chest, and she can hear his heart keeping pace with hers.

They stand that way for a while until he breaks the silence. "Okay," he struggles to focus. "You still need to stay with Sadie, especially now. We—*I* cannot risk your safety. We will try to find the keys, protect the remaining Circle of Souls, their lineage, and keep the demon at bay."

"Piece of cake." Her heart feels truly joyful despite the dangers that lay ahead.

"Perhaps. I am not convinced, however, it can be done within just one lifetime."

Chapter 31, Sparked

They top the ridge and come to the clearing where Sadie's house is. "They're beautiful!" Hallie exclaims looking up in wonder at an eclectic collection of metal works fashioned into pipes, strips, and spirals singing out harmoniously.

She looks past the musical wonder into the clearing ahead. "Oh, my God!" She runs down the remainder of the trail and stops short. "Incredible!"

"What?" Billy comes up behind her.

"This is where you live in 2018. Only the house has been converted to a storage building and studio. Over by that small grove of trees is where Joan's house is going to be built. That willow tree in the back grows huge, and its branches create a sheltered area for the stone next to it. I play on it when I am little, and Joan sits by the stone and sends out her morning spell, or requests, I guess. I can't believe it!"

He stops short. "Wait. Joan, the woman I am living with, casts spells…as in witchcraft?"

Hallie doesn't understand at first because she is overwhelmed by the site before her, and then it hits her. "Oh, uh…not Resmelda witchcraft…not dark magic. It is more like an honoring of nature and creation. No manipulation of the balance of life. I'm sorry I forgot that it was the Liam-you and not the Billy-you who knew about this."

He scuffs his foot. "I am not sure about this outlandish idea, it contradicts everything I know related to spell casting and witchcraft." He starts to ask Hallie more, but she gasps stepping back into the shelter of the woods a bit further.

"Billy, what is Daryl Lee doing here?"

Daryl Lee is carrying a long copper tube. He walks from the back of the house towards a path just beyond the willow tree.

"It is alright. He works for Mister Hairston. Remember? That is to make a coil for a moonshine still. They must be trying to get a new still up. Mister Hairston is a metal smith. He is very talented as you can see from the beautiful wind works above us. Moonshine still parts are some of the things he fabricates. They are a little more marketable than his artistic pieces."

"Oh," Hallie pauses for a moment. "Billy, Daryl Lee is dangerous. There's something more to his anger than his jealousy of Luke. He looked so wild-eyed yesterday, and I think he was talking to Mister Steele after the fight."

Billy watches Daryl Lee carrying the copper tubing across the clearing. A pistol is tucked into the back of his pants. He stops and takes a suspicious look around before he disappears into the woods. Billy nods thoughtfully. "That would explain Daryl Lee's volatile mood lately. He would not normally be so confrontational, especially in public, and never in the Pennymaker's store." Billy starts to step out into the clearing to walk towards the house.

Hallie reaches out to take his hand. "Billy, would you kiss me one more time before we go to the house and you leave?"

He doesn't hesitate leaning in gently cupping Hallie's cheek kissing her. He takes her hand, and they step out into the clearing towards the house. Holmes comes running out from another part of the woods stopping short when he sees Billy and Hallie and walks over between them.

Two little girls are sitting on the ground and Hallie notices they are playing what looks like a game of jacks in the compact dirt. They look up at Hallie with hesitant looks on their faces, but then they cheerfully call out in unison, "Billy!" Holmes runs over to them, and they laugh in delight.

"Hey, Zephyr and Olivia! Playing a game of knucklebones I see. Who is winning?"

The older of the two speaks up, "Olivia—believe it or not!"

"So the student is surpassing the teacher, then?"

Olivia beams. "Yes, I am!"

Zephyr rolls her eyes and goes back to her next move. Hallie watches wondering if knucklebones is different from jacks, but she sees that it is pretty much the same except they use stones. The stone that is tossed upward is called a jack, and they attempt to pick up a combination of stones that have been tossed on the ground. Currently, they are up to four at a time before the jack lands back onto the ground.

Billy waits for them to finish a round and asks, "Is Sadie inside?"

"Uh, huh. Is that the girl she was telling Aunt Myrlie about?"

"Probably," he answers. "This is Hallie—a friend," turning to Hallie he adds, "and *this* is Zephyr and Olivia, Sadie's cousins."

Hallie smiles. "Hello, it's nice to meet you."

"Hello!" They answer in unison and immediately go back to their game.

Hallie and Billy walk up to the door and knock. The house is neatly white-washed with flowers blooming in tidy-kept beds. Two wooden chairs sit in front of the house with a small table between them. It is simple and cheerful.

Sadie comes to the door. "Hello!" She is much happier than she had been last night.

"Hello Sadie," Billy says. "I hate to not spend time. I have not seen your mother or father for a while, but I need to get into town and wait for a delivery Missus Pennymaker is expecting, and…" He glances at Hallie, "I am running behind."

"It's no problem. Momma's getting ready to leave anyway. She is going to help out over at Miz MiMi's to set things up for the picnic day after tomorrow. You gonna come there for a while? I have to go and help out and figured Hallie would come along too."

"Sure, I will definitely try to come over. Well, I better get going." He pauses a moment looking uncharacteristically awkward and looks at Hallie. "I will see you both on Sunday then."

Hallie's cheeks color. "I'll see you then."

Sadie looks from Hallie to Billy. He turns and leaves. Sadie looks back at Hallie and raises her eyebrows. They step into the house.

"What did you do to him?"

Hallie gives a shy smile and shrugs. "We had a moment."

"Explain 'moment'."

Hallie only offers another shrug and takes a look around. The front room is a large kitchen area with a table flanked by two benches and a chair at one end. There is a mason jar with wild flowers sitting on the center of the table with a lace doily underneath it. A cook stove is to the left and two wide windows are across the room with a breeze billowing in the curtains. Brightly colored flowers are embroidered along the lower hem. Hallie decides that the windows must have been converted to a doorway with an addition off that side of the building because Joan's studio seems much larger than the room is now.

Hallie's reverie is interrupted when a slender woman with her hair pulled back in a tight bun comes into the kitchen. She has on a pale blue cotton dress with an apron tied over it at the waist, and stands tall with a pleasant, but tired look on her face.

"Momma, this is Hallie O'Meara. Hallie, this is my momma, Myrlie Hairston."

"How do you do, ma'am?"

Myrlie looks over at Sadie and Hallie. "I am just fine, child. You may do better just calling me Myrlie. It's nice to finally meet you. I have heard so much about you since Sadie has been home."

"It's nice to meet you too."

"Now, Sadie go on and take Hallie up to your room. Show her around then y'all come on back here. I need you to mix up a short cake for dinner tonight. Your Aunt Tessie is going to fix a stew. I gotta get on over to Miz Mimi's, but I will be home before supper."

"Okay, momma."

The girls head out of the kitchen into a small side room with simple furnishings and stacks of books piled on the floor and lined against the walls. There is a table with a small collection of arrowheads and rocks. There is molded iron works, some decorative, some functional, and a few unusual pieces made of copper including a hat hanging on a hook on the wall. Hallie stops to take it all in.

"My daddy's people come from a long-line of educated and gifted men, even during the slave days. Most came out of Williamsburg over this way, and they worked on the Hairston's plantation and iron works. The Hairstons were the original settling family in these parts. My daddy's kin just took on the slave-owners last name like most folks did back then. Daddy's a proud man and always says that no one can take your education from you, so you best get as much of it as you can, and he did. Just a shame ain't much for an educated black man to do in these parts." A shadow of sadness crosses momentarily over her face as she follows Hallie's gaze at the marvelous creations that crowd the walls and corners of the room. "Come on, let me show you the rest."

Sadie's parent's room is just beyond the middle room. It is the same space where Liam is set up in Joan's outbuilding. Hallie looks at the high set windows lining the back wall and she can almost see the top of Liam's head going by.

"You coming?" Sadie looks back at her.

"Sorry! Right behind you."

Sadie is already halfway up a narrow set of stairs that lead to the loft of the house. Her room has a sloping ceiling and small window. There is a rack with hooks and three cotton dresses hanging up. Sadie has a small bed, and Hallie sees a padded area set up on the floor across from the bed. The room is decorated with the same embroidered linen that is in the kitchen.

"Sadie, this is so nice! Thank you for sharing your loft with me. I am sorry if it's an inconvenience for you."

"Don't be silly. I like you, Hallie, and it will be fun to have you here. I don't have any sisters and my two brothers died long ago."

"I'm sorry."

"It was a long time ago, but thank you. So, anyway, I got my bed all set up for you, and I am gonna sleep over there."

"Oh, no…no. I'll sleep on the floor. You have been sleeping on that pallet over at Billy's. Really, I'll sleep on the floor."

"Are you kidding? My momma would skin me alive, if I let you do that. Just hush, that's how it is going to be. Now, come on. I still got to show you where the outhouse is."

Hallie turns to leave and a picture on Sadie's dresser of a distinguished young woman catches her eye. "Sadie, who is this?"

"She is Sadie Tanne Mossell Alexander, and she is my friend." Sadie opens the top drawer of her dresser and brings out a cigar box that she covered in fabric with a delicate flower pattern. She opens it to reveal letters addressed to her.

"When I was ten years old I got to take a trip to Washington D.C. to visit my Aunt Tessie. Her husband, Gerard, works as a maintenance man at the great Howard University. Me and Aunt Tessie went to work with him one day when they had a big goings on. They needed some extra help. It was a graduation day, and there wasn't just colored men graduating that day, but colored women too. I had never before that day thought someone like me could accomplish something like that."

Sadie looks through the letters in the box. "They had a reception after the graduation ceremony, and I was serving at it while Aunt Tessie worked in the kitchen. I tripped and dropped my tray making a mess, and one of the regular servers there was scolding me when Miss Sadie came over to see what happened. She was Sadie Tanne Mossell then. She hadn't gotten married yet.

"She bent down and helped me. I was so embarrassed with tears rolling down my face, but she took me by the hand and walked me off to the side until I calmed down. She asked me my name, and when I told her she said, 'Well, how about that! You and I have the same name!' She dried my tears, and told me she was a very clumsy person and probably had dropped more trays, books, dishes—you name it—then I ever would. She told me that she was there that day because she had earned her PhD in economics! Not the same as Doc Hutchinson, but a doctor in economics. She was so kind explaining to me what it meant.

"Well, she must have got my address from my Aunt Tessie because not even two weeks after I got home a letter came for me in the post. It was from Miss Sadie. She has kept in touch with me ever since by writing me a few times every year, and I write her back too.

"When she got married, her husband is Raymond Pace Alexander, I sent her two tea towels that momma made, and that I embroidered with my favorite flower pattern. She wrote me saying they were her favorite wedding gift. That was in 1923. In 1927, just last year, she sent me this official announcement." Sadie pulls out white parchment with embossed writing giving the particulars of Sadie T. M. Alexander's graduation from the University of Pennsylvania Law School.

"She and her husband are partners in their own law firm, and they fight for the rights of colored people in Philadelphia." Sadie closes the box and carefully places it back in her dresser drawer.

"She sounds amazing," Hallie says realizing how much potential Sadie has for the same sort of accomplishments. She and Billy have to find the keys and set them all free.

"Come on now. Momma is going to have a fit, if I don't get that cake done in time for supper tonight."

Chapter 32, Sultry

Hallie gets to know the rest of Sadie's family later that night. Sadie's father, mother and Aunt Tessie are very welcoming. She gets to know Zephyr and Olivia much better and has never laughed so much in her life with their antics. Mister Hairston is a kind man who pretends to be in great pain being surrounded by so many strong-willed women, but Hallie can tell he would have it no other way.

After dinner, they go out onto the large screened porch where Aunt Tessie and the girls have been sleeping during their stay. They sit in comfortable chairs and pillows on the floor listening as Mister Hairston reads to them from one of his books. He has his wire-framed glasses down low on his nose, and changes his voice as he reads the different character's lines. The piece he reads is about two men who struggle with the oppression of their race by society in general. One character is centered in negativity and victimization while the other believes that people can rise above their past. Mister Hairston's voice booms then whispers, and his facial expressions have a way of bringing it to life. Everyone on the porch is so engrossed in the story that they are startled when a man walks up to the porch door knocking on the wood frame.

"Otis, you in there?"

"Yes sar, Mista Mitchell. Let me come on out."

Sadie's aunt and mother exchange looks and get up taking the little girls inside.

Sadie's father comes back up on the porch a few minutes later. "Sadie, let your momma know I got to go over and help the Mitchells. Tell her it might be tomorrow afternoon before I get back home—maybe Sunday."

"Yes sir, daddy."

He grabs his hat and the book slipping it into a back pocket of his trousers.

Sadie waits until her father and Mister Mitchell disappear into the surrounding woods. "Moonshining! There's not a family around these parts that's not involved some way or another including mine." Her mouth twists into a grimace. "My daddy needs the money though. Even so, momma hates it."

"Sadie, isn't it the Mitchells who are feuding with the Wilsons?"

She rolls her eyes. "Yeah, well that's the most recent fighting that's been going on. It will be some other families at each other's throats in a week or two."

They walk inside, Sadie's mother and aunt are sitting at the kitchen table. Her cousins are on the kitchen floor renewing their game of knucklebones.

"So, child," Aunt Tessie says to Hallie. "Where are your people from?"

Hallie isn't sure why she doesn't go along with the amnesia story. Instead, she tells her the truth. "I came this way a while ago from the Eastern Shore, a place called Burton's Shore. I live there with my aunts, Beattie and Dot, but I came out this way earlier in the summer to work. Right now things are a little hazy, and I can't say how I actually ended up in Fayerdale."

Tessie looks at her. She is smoking a thin cigar and takes a long drag on it blowing out a purple hazy cloud above their heads. "Your aunts got funny names for white women. They short for something?"

"Well, yes ma'am. Beatrice and Dominica."

Tessie looks across the table at her sister and takes another long drag off the cigar squinting her eyes as she inhales. She sends the smoke up towards the ceiling. "Zephyr, Olivia—time for bed. Y'all give everyone a good night hug and head on out to the porch."

"Yes, momma." They obediently pick up their game and give hugs all the way around, even to Hallie. She hugs each one warmly.

The two older women and the two younger women sit and talk about the plans for Sunday, and what Sadie's mother prepared today. She complains about Miz Mimi who apparently is a fretful sort of person insisting things being done her own particular way whether it takes more time, makes no sense, and worries a poor working woman like Myrlie to death. They laugh and carry on until Tessie's cigar smoke has a cloudy haze hanging over their heads that lingers long after she stubs the cigar out saving what is left of it. Hallie feels light-headed just from being in the same room with it.

Myrlie stands up all of a sudden saying she is going to bed. She looks over at Sadie. "You look worn out Sadie. Why don't you go on up to bed? Hallie can sit a spell longer with your aunt until Tessie is ready to go to bed."

"Momma…"

"Go on now. I said you're looking tired."

Sadie looks confused but stands telling Hallie and Aunt Tessie good night and walks out of the kitchen with her mother.

Tessie gets up and pours herself and Hallie a cup of water from a pitcher near the sink than covers it with a piece of cheese cloth to keep insects out. She sets the tin cups down with a clink onto the wood table.

"Thank you," Hallie says. She shifts in her seat with a twinge of awkwardness from being left alone with Tessie.

"So, your people are from over on the Eastern Shore."

"Yes, ma'am."

"Uh, you best make that Tessie—white girl like you round these parts will do better with that when you talking to colored folk."

"Yes, ma—Miss Tessie."

Tessie smirks and looks at Hallie as though she is looking over the rim of a pair of glasses.

"Sorry—Tessie."

Tessie turns sideways draping an arm over the back of her chair. She is a tall slender woman like her sister with dark brown skin that is beautifully smooth. Her dress is long and straight, sleeveless and airy. "Me and Myrlie got kin from way back that hailed from over your way. I'm thinking it was one of those islands on the bay. Not Tangier, but that one that's done washed nearly out now."

"Watt's Island."

"That's the one. Way back towards slavery times when everything was English colonies. We don't know a whole lot about them, only what stories have been passed down through the generations. Lots of mystery and all. Some folks talked about the family line back then being involved in voodoo, witchy kind of stuff, you know."

Hallie starts to feel that she and Tessie being left alone was premeditated.

"You got any of that silliness in your family?" Tessie looks her directly in the eyes like she can see deep down inside Hallie, and then her face relaxes breaking into a broad smile waving a hand at Hallie. "Don't' mind me. I just think it makes for interesting conversation."

Hallie shifts in her seat again unsure how to answer. A couple months ago she would have thought not. No 'witchy' stuff going on around her, but now she is in the thick of it. Still, she opts to go with the two-months-ago version of her life. "Uh, no," her tone jumps a few notes upward, "nothing that I am aware of."

Tessie takes a drink from her cup and clinks it on the table studying Hallie. Her lips twist sideways as a change in strategy takes hold "What kind of living can your two aunts do to keep your household going? Do you have any men folk around?"

"No, ma—Tessie. They grow herbs for medicinal remedies and other things."

Tessie looks as if she hit the bull's eye. "Herbs, now they are a powerful gift from the Lord above, the great Creator. Funny how some folks just have a natural knowledge about how to release the power of them and how some folks don't. I've heard of gatherings of them gifted people who would get together during different times of the year and share their knowledge, some with herbs, and some with other things. Your aunts got one of them groups?"

It isn't quite an interrogation, but pretty close. Hallie shifts in her chair again. "Um, well I remember when I was younger I would travel with them out this way a few times a year…"

"All that distance—that often?" Tessie's eyebrows perk with surprise. Hallie forgot about the more difficult travel expenses and arrangements that have to be made for them to cross the bay in the 1920's, but it's already said, and she can't go back now.

"Uh, yes. They…had a friend…that owned a shipping company who offered passage in exchange for some of their medicinal remedies. We would come and meet with a group of women friends and visit for a while. We stayed with Joan Shively. You know her?" Hallie tries to see if this gets her any information, and maybe sway the conversation to a less intense feeling.

Tessie thinks a moment lifting an eye brow and pursing her lips in thought. "No, can't say I do." Hallie's strategy isn't successful, and Tessie clicks her tongue refocusing on the original conversation. "Course, understanding the power in herbs and plants is only one kind of talent. Some folks are good at reading signs, you know like rainbows, shooting stars, or what it might mean if you see an owl during the day—that sort of thing. Some folks call 'em omens. Other folks don't need to see a sign. They are tuned-in and have visions or premonitions by feeling the energy around them. Heck, some folks can even *see* the energy that is around them or other folks."

Hallie sits and listens. It suddenly feels dreamlike sitting in this kitchen with Aunt Tessie relighting her cigar and the purple haze re-accumulating above. Her long pulls on the cigar ignite its tip to glow brightly through the haze reminding Hallie of the lighthouse near home on a foggy night.

Tessie leans forward towards Hallie stretching out the arm that is draped over the back of the chair while her hand casually holds the smoldering cigar. "I likes to think I've got a bit of that kind of magic—the premonition kind I mean. Thing about that sort of magic though is that sometimes we come looking for an answer expecting to find it like a key that can be grasped and pushed into a lock revealing what is behind a door. But, I've learned that it's best if you just let the answer come to you. Thing is being patient and smart enough to know when it's there. Don't rush it or hold expectations for it. Sometimes you can use cards or runes to help figure it out, but most the time you gotta wait it out." She pauses to lean back and take another drag on the cigar while studying Hallie.

Aunt Tessie's long dangling earrings sway twinkling in the lantern light. Her hair is wrapped in a headscarf Creole-style, and Hallie realizes how much of a contrast she really is to her sister,

Myrlie. Hallie's thoughts are drifting and time clicks by imperceptibly. She struggles to clear her mind realizing that a message is being conveyed to her. She meets Tessie's eyes which are fixed directly on her.

Tessie keeps talking, "Some folks look to the stars to help guide the seeing they do. You know anything about the constellations?" Tessie takes a pull on the cigar.

"I know the ones from the zodiac and some of the other ones like the big dipper, little dipper, and Orion." Hallie clears her throat.

"That's pretty good! You ever heard of Ophiuchus?"

Hallie shakes her head.

"Oh now, child, that one is a good constellation. Some folks look at stars and find science while others look at them and find magic. Plus, there's always a bit of folklore in the mix. The secret is to understand the science without losing the magic and to pay attention to the folklore 'cause sometimes there's some truth in the stories."

Tessie's eyes sparkle and her voice takes on a rich timbre. "Ophiuchus, you know, means serpent-barer, and its story is about a man punished by one of them ancient gods. I think he was called Zeus. Ole Zeus was mad because this man found the way to immortality so to speak. He brought the art of medicine to mankind, and his name was Asclepius. Zeus felt only gods should have the power to heal and prolong life, so he struck down Asclepius and put him up into the constellation. It shows Asclepius holding tight onto that serpent, and the serpent holding just as tight onto him." Another drag on the cigar fuels Tessie's banter.

"What Asclepius was here on Earth back in those days is what Doc Hutchison is here in Fayerdale right now, a physician. Asclepius helped to cure people of illnesses that may have otherwise killed them. He is an interesting part of the constellation to be sure. He even holds some of the science part in the stars that make him up, but that is another story. The part of the constellation that I likes the best is the snake." She pauses and takes a drink of water and another pull on her cigar exhaling the smoke.

Hallie watches as the smoke rises to join the rest of the haze circling the room.

"The snake, Tessie? Why?" Hallie's eyes burn a little, and she drinks her water trying to soothe the parched rub in the back of her throat.

"The snake inspired Asclepius when he saw one serpent bring healing herbs to another. Snakes renew themselves you know. They shed their skin and start anew. They have all kinds of symbolism hiding in their simple form. Take a snake that swallows its own tail for example. By doing that it makes itself the ending *and* the beginning. The image of a never ending circle, symbolism of the alpha and the omega, just like it's written in the good book. There is no ending without a beginning and no beginning without an ending." Tessie pauses pursing her lips in thought before going on.

Hallie's haze clears for a moment, and she perks up.

"Some folks might get lost in that, but I think a few—a few that are smart and have a different view of what's around to be seen might understand it." She takes a last draw on her shrinking cigar and stubs it out patting the end once again before setting the bit of stogy aside.

Hallie stares off still listening intently while Tessie uses familiar words to paint a new image in Hallie's mind.

"You ever see that walking stick Doc Hutchison's got?"

Hallie breaks away from her thoughts and looks over at Tessie. "Yes, he said it was a gift from one of his patients."

"That it was. You ever take a close look at it?"

"Um, it is carved, but I haven't looked at it in detail." She shrugs almost apologetically and the room wobbles a bit. She shifts in her seat yet again finding her balance guessing it is the cigar smoke that is affecting her.

"It has a snake spiraling up it. Old Isaac Elkins, the train depo man, carved it for him. A snake is a healer's symbol because they inspired Asclepius. Doc's walking stick is just like the official symbol of doctor's everywhere. He is a part of something bigger, yet here he is in this little hole of a town. You might recognize something by the big meaning of it, but it's all the little meanings up there underneath it that really give it definition."

"So, are we really just talking about stars and snakes and healers? Or is there something more?" Hallie asks as she supports her head on bent elbow.

"Ummm, child I'm just sitting here passing the time. A little story telling helps it go a little quicker."

Hallie catches the transition from mystic to ordinary. She is used to it because it is Dot's favorite way to tell a story. She takes the cue musing out loud, "I never thought about snakes like that. Most people are so afraid of them. Jeb was terrified yesterday when he came up on some rattle snakes."

"A healthy fear of that which can kill you ain't a bad thing. Too much fear though can keep you from discovering the vigor you can get from pushin' on and figuring things out. I think sometimes those in positions of power use this kind of fear to control people. Either to keep the people away from something new, or keep them afraid to leave something old." Tessie drinks the last of her water and stands up motioning to Hallie to see if she is done with her cup.

Hallie nods and Tessie picks it up carrying it over to the sink with her own cup. She pours some water into each and adds a little soap powder to wash them.

Hallie watches as the purple haze of smoke swirls when Tessie walks away from the table, and as it settles back into its lazy rotation above. The sluggish wobble from earlier hits her brain, and she doesn't realize that Tessie has sat back down and is looking at her once again. Hallie blinks slowly feeling the weight of her eye lids as they struggle to remain open.

"Here child, you go on and sleep in my hammock tonight. I don't think you can make it up to Sadie's room as worn out as you look. I still got some things to do tonight, but I'll be back by morning."

Hallie looks at Tessie and nods sleepily. She rises from her chair and walks to the screened porch gratefully climbing into the empty hammock. Zephyr and Olivia are curled up comfortably on mats and snuggled under light sheets while a warm gentle breeze blows across the porch. The chimes from the nearby trees rock gently releasing their song into the air, and Hallie tilts her head back to look beyond the screen. She can see the night sky with the twinkling of stars above. She is exhausted with Tessie's face settling in her thoughts, but eventually the haze of cigar smoke obscures the view. When it clears Hallie can see Billy from now and Liam from the future, and then as he was from the night of the 50's themed reunion at Fairy Stone State Park—yet another version of the man she is entranced by. These are her last thoughts before drifting off to sleep.

Chapter 33, Smolder

Hallie and Sadie get up early and help Myrlie before going outside to sit and enjoy the morning sun as it filters through the branches of the weeping willow.

"Hm-mm, well that didn't take long," Sadie says with a smile in her voice.

Hallie is lying on the flat rock near the willow feeling a little tired from the late night. She turns her head towards Sadie with her arm draped over her forehead. "What didn't take long?"

Sadie points towards the woods casually with the hand she has propped on her knee. Hallie follows her point and sees Holmes bounding across the yard. Just behind him is Billy. She sits up smoothing out her dress.

Sadie smiles at her. "You look just fine. I'm gonna go inside and see if momma needs any help with that bread she's making for the picnic tomorrow."

Hallie nods at her. Holmes greets Sadie and then runs to Hallie.

"Hey Holmes! What are you doing big guy? What a good boy!" She rumples his head and ears.

Billy comes up. He has on a pair of dungarees and a light blue shirt. Holmes nudges him, and he pats the old blood hound affectionately.

"So, you missed me." Hallie looks up at him. "It's okay, you can admit it."

Billy smiles at the ground and gives her a sideways nods taking a seat on the rock next to her. "I came to be sure you were okay. And, to see if you wanted to come into town with me for a while. There's something there I want to show you."

Hallie smiles, but she ponders unsuccessfully the meaning of the look on his face before answering. "Okay, sure. Let me just go tell Sadie." Holmes whines when Hallie disappears, but he bounds towards her with a renewed greeting when she returns.

"The path towards town is over this way," Billy indicates and they walk towards the same path they saw Daryl Lee step onto yesterday.

There isn't too much conversation between them as they make their way through the woods towards town, but they walk hand-in-hand. Hallie startles when a flying squirrel misses its branch falling a little lower then intended. It loudly protests as it scurries to regain its original altitude catching up with its comrades. Shortly after the squirrel's mishap Hallie smells smoldering wood and a sour yeasty smell. She turns to say something to Billy.

He just looks at her with a finger up over his mouth and leans in whispering into her ear, "Moonshine still." Taking her hand he leads her off the path. They cut up and over and back to the trail further up on the hill crossing over the ridge.

Billy waits until they are on the other side of the peak before speaking. "The Mitchells usually keep a still going near here, but they are always so careful only running the heat at night."

"Why just at night?"

"Harder for revenuers and anybody else they do not want knowing where they are set up to see the smoke from the smoldering coals needed to distill the whiskey. They must be getting up a big shipment to risk running into the morning hours. It is pretty daring with Mister Steele lingering nearby so much. Maybe they know something, and he is not in town today." He moves forward at a slightly faster pace, and Hallie hurries to keep up.

"Well, that would be a good thing, if he weren't in town today. Right?"

"Yes," says Billy pushing on, "but then what is he up to? The other side of it could be just that he is on their payroll, but I doubt that. The Mitchells are not that well off."

They near the edge of town and Billy stops turning to Hallie. "Meet me over at the livery?"

"Sure." Hallie watches a moment as he turns to leave.

He walks towards Doc Hutchison's office calling Holmes to follow.

She steps into the cool stable appreciating its peaceful cloak. Horses are in their stalls eating hay or standing with their heads low and eyes closed. She sees Detonator looking over his stall door, and she walks cautiously up to him reaching up to pat his neck. He turns his head nudging her gently making her laugh.

"You better be careful. Someone might think you like me, and you wouldn't want to be accused of getting soft now would you?" She picks up a brush and opens the door carefully stepping into the stall. The stallion eyes her fidgeting a little, but she croons to him brushing his neck gently. He relaxes and nibbles at his hay.

"You sure you should be in there with him?" Billy is by the stall door.

Hallie looks up and smiles. "He seems to have pretty good ground manners. I'm not sure I would want to saddle him up and ride him, but I think he'll behave himself if I keep to this."

"Well, I am glad you are getting along with him." Billy steps into the stall holding a wooden box. "This is what I needed to show you, and I am going to put it here behind this loose plank in Detonator's stall wall. People do not tend to linger in here more than they need to and it will be safe here."

"What's in it?"

"The Book of Lineages for the Circle of Souls, a few items that I have held onto over time, and a couple of new tokens. It helps when the memories start coming back in a new life to have something concrete assuring me it was all real. At least that is how it is in the beginning. Eventually, the reality is undeniable."

Hallie looks at him feeling the sting of panic pierce her chest. "Why are you bringing it here?"

"When the time comes I need you to take it and bury it for me. There is a tree near the lower mine entrance on this side of the ridge to the south. It is a maple with a triple trunk. You will not have to dig a hole. Put this blue jay feather on the box and wrap the box in this piece of cabretta. If you lay it on the ground, it will slowly sink below the surface. Wait just long enough for it to be covered, and then a minute to see if the blue jay feather rises back above the surface assuring my return. Do not stay any longer than that."

"I don't understand," Hallie says. "What happened? I thought that we were going to look for the key and break the curse?"

"Hallie, I need you to know about this. It is important." His tone is urgent and Hallie's alarm is laced with curiosity, but doesn't ask anything else. She only nods.

He puts everything between the wood planks in the wall and stands up turning to Hallie.

"All will be well, Hallie. I do not want you to worry. I just have to be sure that ledger moves forward. You understand—just in case."

"Sure, yes of course. I promise I'll take care of it if it comes to that, but it won't Billy. It's going to be different this time." In spite of knowing something has changed she clings desperately to optimism.

"I hope so too, Hallie." Even with his words he sounds defeated.

Hallie stands for a moment and closes her eyes forcing herself not to tense with fear. She then looks into his eyes, "So, why not go out today and see what we can discover? Did you find out where Mister Steele is?"

"Uh, yes. Doc Hutchison said that he saw him late last night with the Pennymakers and talked to them before they left. They went to Stuart."

"Good, then where should we look first?"

Billy looks at her apologetically. "Hallie, I do not have the first idea of where to look. I am not even sure we *can* look. I think it is something that has to find you. What about the angel song? Have you heard anything yet?"

"No, no I haven't, but Aunt Tessie and I had a strange conversation last night. It was like she knew who I am. She went on about stars and signs and messages. It was strange, really strange. I went to bed, but I think she left the house for a while."

Billy unlatches the stall door and they leave Detonator to finish his hay. "What did she have to say?"

"She talked about reading symbols mostly. She talked about a serpent constellation, the symbolism of snakes, and knowing when you see a sign that has meaning what the meaning is. It was so strange. I was exhausted, so I'm not sure that I heard everything she had to say."

"She told you about Ophiuchus?"

"Yes! That was the constellation."

They walk along the dirt lane over to the train depot, and Billy starts to say something else just as Jeb nearly runs into them. "Oh, Hi Hallie, Billy. You aren't going to believe what just happened!"

"What is it Jeb?" Billy asks.

"I was coming past the Wilson's place. Jedidiah Mitchell had just pulled up and backed that old Ford of his nearly to the Wilson's porch. The truck was filled with parts of a still in back. I'm thinking it was from the Wilson's set up over by the old holding pond. Anyway, Jedidiah popped down the tail gate, pushed the still out in front of the house, and took to bashing it up with an axe. Right in front of the house! It was crazy.

"It was just the women folk and young Hiram Wilson home, so Jedidiah just gave 'em all this hard look, got back in the truck, and spun his tires out when he left. Old man Wilson is going to be pis…uh, sorry Hallie, fit-to-be-tied!"

Billy shakes his head. "I suppose this has something to do with the Mitchell's still that was broken up."

"Yeah, I heard about that. Heard Daryl Lee was stirring up trouble telling the Mitchells one of the Wilsons reported their still to the revenuer. I don't think Jedidiah and Newell paid him no mind until they found their still all tore up. I hear they just got it back up and going, and they been working it overtime to get an order out." Little beads of froth form at the corners of Jeb's mouth as he speaks. The turn of events is exciting even in a town used to bickering and fighting over such things.

He wipes his mouth with his sleeve and goes on, "Looks like the Mitchells decided for sure it must have been the Wilsons that had done it. I reckon Jedidiah decided to get even. Whew. He certainly made a statement. Yes sir! Man, when Hiram finds Polk Wilson and tells him what happened there's going to be trouble to be sure."

"Yes, I know," Billy answers looking over at Hallie.

"Well, I told Mister Gravely I'd get some of the stalls cleaned out today, so I best be getting to it."

"I guess things are going to get pretty heated around here."

"Most likely." Billy runs his fingers through his hair.

"You know, Mister Mitchell came and got Sadie's father last night. Sadie commented that she thought he was going to work one of their stills."

"Do you know which Mitchell came to get him?"

Hallie just shakes her head with a shrug of the shoulder.

"Well, he should be alright. I doubt the Wilson's will try to go after one of the Mitchell's stills so soon. They are probably going to go directly after Jedidiah and Newell."

The train is in at the depot. Hallie sees Luke and a slightly younger boy sitting on the platform eating lunch. She and Billy walk over to see them.

"Hi," Luke says. "Hallie, this is my brother Elijah. Elijah, this is Hallie."

"Nice to meetcha, Hallie." Elijah pauses from whittling a piece of wood with a broad-handled pocket knife. He folds it and puts it in his shirt pocket extending his hand to Hallie.

She takes his hand, and he gives her an enthusiastic shake.

"You hear about Jedidiah Mitchell's stunt over at the Wilson's just a little while ago?" Luke asks just before he finishes his sandwich in one big bite.

"Yes, Jeb told us about it." Billy surveys the station and cargo waiting to be loaded onto the train.

"Ought to make for some interesting fireworks sometime soon. I just hope I'm not anywhere around when the sparks fly!" Elijah says.

"You think it could be bad?" Hallie asks.

Elijah shrugs. "It's hard to say for sure. But yeah, it could get pretty bad."

"Yep, pretty bad," Luke says as he wipes his hands with a bandana and tucks it into a back pocket of his overalls.

Mister Elkins walks up with his broom in hand and bends down towards Luke speaking in a low voice. "I just heard that Hiram already found Polk Wilson, and Polk has driven up to Stuart to get the sheriff to issue a warrant against Jedidiah and Newell Mitchell."

"You're kidding," Elijah says. "Wonder how that is going to work out? Old Sheriff Mitkey ain't one to get involved with feuding shiners." He shakes his head, and says good-bye to everyone to go load the train for the next run.

Mister Elkins goes back to sweeping. Hallie smiles at him noticing that his broom handle is beautifully carved. He moves across the platform and Hallie turns her attention back to the conversation.

"What do you think Billy?" Luke asks.

"It is hard to say. It is unusual for them to want to bring the law into town. I am not sure what is going on, but we are going to have to be careful for a while." Billy changes the subject. "Anything else from Daryl Lee?"

"No," Luke says. "I haven't even seen him."

"Luke!" Elijah calls him from the loading platform. "Give me a hand with this." There are wood crates stacked high. A few passengers are sitting inside the train with the windows open fanning themselves waiting for the train to pull out.

"Well, I've got to go. You coming to Miz Mimi's tomorrow? It's starting to look like most the town folk are going to be there."

"Uh, yes," Billy answers. "I may be a little late, but I am going to try to come for a while. Sadie's mother is cooking, and I do not want to miss out on that." He smiles at his friend, and looks to Hallie to see if she is ready to head out.

"See you tomorrow, Luke," She says.

"See you tomorrow. Let Sadie know I'm coming, will you?"

"I sure will."

Billy whistles for Holmes who is sitting by Mister Elkins. The old dog stands and stretches lazily before making his way over to Hallie and Billy. As they start to leave Luke calls Billy over to give him and Elijah a hand with some of the larger crates.

Hallie walks over to Mister Elkins to wait with Holmes on her heel. She nods a greeting to the old man who is shriveled with skin like dark leather. His brown eyes have a smoky blue circle along the outer edge, and the warmth of his smile could melt ice.

"I couldn't help notice your beautiful broom handle." Hallie says as she sits down on the bench next to him. Holmes steps up laying his head on the old man's lap.

Mister Elkins gives Holmes a rub. He looks at the handle of his broom and then looks beyond it towards Hallie. "I create what the wood calls out to me. You know every tree has a spirit within it, some call it the dryad. Some say the tree withdrawals its spirit from a limb it senses is about to be cut away, but when the tree gives the branch freely the spirit remains. This piece of mountain ash was laid across my path some years ago when I was walking in the timber. A gift from the tree itself. It is a powerful wood."

He looks up at Hallie. She sits spellbound next to him. It is the second time a wood carver spun an entrancing tale for her.

He continues. "It protects against lightening, black magic, and evil of all sorts." His voice trails off as his gaze shifts towards the roadway in front of the depot.

Hallie turns to look seeing a dark green Cadillac Phaeton cruise by the depot. Mister Pennymaker is driving with Mister Steele in the front passenger seat. Hallie feels a chill run up her spine. Neither man seems to notice them as the car passes stirring up dust onto the platform.

Mister Elkins gives Hallie a nod and stands walking to the edge of the platform to sweep the dust from the wood planks as it settles onto the surface. Billy comes around from the back of the building extending his hand to Hallie. She takes it and stands to leave bidding Mister Elkins goodbye. He pauses to give her a wave before continuing his task.

They step off the platform walking across the road and into the woods leaving the dust and demon behind. She looks over her shoulder catching a view of the back of the Cadillac wondering if Mister Pennymaker's soul is in the Demon King's pocket. The same frosty chill she felt so long ago on the bridge-tunnel runs up her spine. She wonders how many lives Liam has endured in the shadow of the Demon King, and feels admiration for his ability to not only survive it all, but to keep his sanity and soul intact.

Billy breaks her reverie to finish their conversation from earlier. "Last night I was not able to sleep, so I went into the middle of the clearing where my cabin is and laid down to look up at the stars." He looks over at Hallie for a moment and shrugs. "It just helps to clear my thoughts."

She smiles encouraging him to go on.

"It turned strange."

"In what way?"

"It was a clear, beautiful night. There was a warm breeze blowing—it was nice. I was not gazing at anything in particular. Mostly, I was trying to sort through everything, you know?"

She nods.

"Anyway, the breeze stopped all of a sudden and this thin haze of fog, or something, swirled into the clearing. It was very strange. It hung low near the level of the tree branches."

A deer runs across the path just fifteen feet in front of them. Billy pauses and holds his arm out to keep Hallie from moving forward. Two more, bucks this time, shoot across the trail in the same spot.

Their speed sends a thrill through Hallie's chest, and she looks over at Billy. His brow is furrowed, and she knows his mind is not on the deer. "What about the fog, Billy?"

They continue down the path, and he recounts what happened. "It swirled around the clearing getting thicker except for this one section near the middle. All the stars had been covered except one constellation."

Hallie waits for him to continue, but she knows what he is going to say.

"Ophiuchus," they say it together.

"It has to mean something Hallie, but what? It has nothing to do with either of the angel songs you have told me about so far. Is there any other times you have heard the song that it mentioned a snake or anything about a constellation?"

"No. The only thing has been the strange conversation with Aunt Tessie last night. She talked about the symbolism of the serpent, how it renews itself and how a snake that swallows its tail forms a circle representing the beginning and the ending. *That* is the same as the message in the angel song, but I would not have thought about it without Tessie's conversation last night."

"I do not know, Hallie. It just seems like a whole lot of puzzle pieces—some fit and others do not. Perhaps there is more to the angel songs than just the words within them."

They reach the ridge by the Hairston's home. The house is barely visible from the trail, but Hallie can hear laughter coming up the hillside from Zephyr and Olivia.

She nods. "I know, but we will figure it out." She looks down the trail, the wind chimes are gently ringing out. "I'm okay from here." Billy nods and she turns to leave. He reaches out to grasp her arm gently, and she turns back to see what is wrong. He leans towards her and kisses her tenderly on the mouth.

"I am glad you came. I am glad you came *here*, to Fayerdale, I mean. We *will* figure it out and get you home. I promise."

She kisses him knowing his promise does not include defeating Joe. She paints her mournful thoughts with a smile and turns to head down the path towards the clearing. She looks back seeing him watching her. She lifts a hand as she nears the bend in the trail and he returns the gesture. She knows that he is thinking the end is near, and her heart weighs heavy.

Chapter 34, Dusk

A hustle and bustle dictates the rhythm at the Hairston's on Sunday morning as final preparations are being made for the picnic. The heat from the cook stove burning on an already hot morning is almost overwhelming for Hallie, and she wonders how Myrlie does it without fainting. But, of all the minor inconvenience Hallie has experienced in 1928, the worse has been the outhouse. She looks around the interior from her perch seeing sunshine stream in from between the wood planks, the bucket of newsprint and corn cobs still make her shudder, and someone's sense of humor represented by a small sign hanging on the door that reads "enjoy your stay" does bring a smile to her face. She gratefully steps outside the outhouse taking a full breath of fresh air. Sadie and the girls are waiting for her.

Myrlie and Tessie have shooed all of them from the kitchen, so gratefully Hallie and Sadie head over to Miz Mimi's by foot with Zephyr and Olivia tagging along. Aunt Tessie and Myrlie plan to ride in a car sent over by Missus Pennymaker, who happens to be Miz Mimi's sister, to bring all the baked goods to the picnic.

Miz Mimi's place is a big white two story house with a large wrap-around porch. Tables are set up in the yard with white table cloths and wood folding chairs scattered about. A few cars are parked off to the side, but most people walk up carrying a dish for the meal. There are groups of men and women talking and laughing. Kids are running around, and the crack of the screen doors sound regularly as people move in and out. The aroma of fried chicken and a variety of other delectable food wafts through the air riding the breeze towards the girls as they approach.

"Sadie, can we go play?" Zephyr and Olivia are bouncing with excitement.

"Sure!"

And they are off like two bees sprung from the hive.

"Hey, Sadie. Hallie" Luke walks up with Elijah.

"Hi, Luke." Sadie greets him flashing a smile before she excuses herself to go out back and help her mother.

"Sadie, I'll go with you." Hallie calls to her trying to catch-up.

"Oh, no you go on and stay with Luke and Elijah. Get to know some of the folks in town." Sadie turns and heads to the back of the house.

"Um, okay." Hallie stops and looks at Luke and Elijah turning to walk back to them.

Elijah brings Hallie a glass of lemonade, and they mill around.

"Well, I am happy to see you have recovered so well young lady." Doc Hutchison gives a cheerful greeting. He has his walking stick, and Hallie now notices the incredible craftsmanship that Mister Elkins put into the snake carving.

"Yes, sir. Thank you so much for taking such good care of me."

"Well, that's what I'm here for." Before he can say more someone walks up to him to ask about a sore elbow.

"Hey Hallie," Jeb says as he approaches them. "Luke, Elijah."

Luke and Elijah nod at Jeb.

"Hello, Jeb!" Hallie looks him over. "You are looking very handsome today!"

Jeb blushes and adjusts the stiff color of his Sunday bests. He looks over at Luke and Elijah who are fake primping and laughing. Hallie cuts them a look bringing them to a halt quicker than Luke could have pulled brakes on the train.

"Uh, thanks Hallie. Uh, Billy wanted me to let you know that he is on his way. Mister Pennymaker had him come over to his farm to help with something this morning, but Billy said he won't be too long."

"Okay, thanks Jeb."

A young girl with blonde hair in a pale blue dress waves at Elijah, and he excuses himself to go across the yard to see her. Luke excuses himself as well saying he wants to go into the kitchen to see how much longer before the food will be ready.

Hallie stands and sips on her lemonade. Jeb fidgets and tugs at his collar again and then straightens his suspenders.

"Jeb, you don't have to stay with me, if you have something else you want to do. I'm fine, really."

"Uh, no, I'm okay. Besides Billy wants me to stay with you until he gets here."

"Oh, alright then. It will be nice to spend some time with you." Hallie wonders if Billy has talked to Jeb about *everything*, and if Jeb knows who she really is. Suddenly, she has a panicked feeling wondering if Mister Steele is at the picnic. She surveys the yard just in case he came.

"He isn't here." Jeb says. He sticks his hands in his pockets, and he shifts his weight from foot to foot studying his shoes and the dust they kick up.

"Who?"

"Mister Steele. I saw the look of panic on your face."

She studies him for a minute. "Jeb, do you...do you know about me?"

He continues staring at his shoes and the dust. "Yes-um, I do. Billy and I spoke this morning about...the past...and he told me about you." He looks up at her, and she sees the black discs of his dilated pupils vacillate. "It's dangerous for you. You...uh...you don't want to be drawn into any of it. Once the harvest of the Circle of Souls starts, no matter what you might think, the Demon King cannot be beat. We are trapped in a bargain not of our making."

Hallie studies Jeb. Both he and He-As-Randy remain mostly on the periphery, from what she can tell, while being very unassuming and accommodating as well. Hallie feels there is much more to him than he lets on, and she likes him. Concern for him plucks at her heart. "Jeb, I know it seems that way—like it is hopeless."

"It *is* that way, and you are about to find out. It's getting close. I can feel it."

She looks at him unsure what to say. He remains unwavering. She brushes her finger tips along her thumb trying to rid them of a sudden prickling.

"Your lemonade is empty," he reaches for her glass. "You stay here and let me get you another one. Don't move. I will be right back."

"Okay." She smiles and watches as he disappears behind the house. She sees a girl with shiny black hair, a bit unusually dressed, almost gypsy-like, watch as Jeb walks past. She raises her hand in a quiet greeting. He turns his head smiling and returns the greeting while his face paints itself a shade of pink. Hallie watches the girl seeing the flush of her cheeks, and her lingering look towards Jeb until he disappears around the back corner of the house. A sudden sadness for those in the Circle of Souls and the lives they never get to finish fills her heart.

Standing like a wall flower, Hallie fidgets self-consciously. A shock of recognition hits her as she looks at the house and activities around it. It is one of the photographs on Liam's shelf. She looks towards the yard and sees someone taking the picture. *Hm, if I ever get back home to 2018, I will have to look at that picture again to see if I am in it.*

She looks past the photographer and sees that Missus Pennymaker is sitting in the shade of a tree briskly fanning herself while chatting with a few other women. Then suddenly, like a team of synchronized swimmers, the women's eyes widen, their heads turn in the same direction, and their mouths drop open to gawk at something just beyond Hallie.

Hallie hears the rumble of an engine and the skid of tires. From the corner of her eye she sees a dark blur slide up into the yard just to her right. She turns seeing two men climbing out of a weathered gray sedan. Neither man bothers to shut his door. One has a pistol drawn, and the other holds a shot gun in hand with a pistol tucked into his belt. Hallie's throat twists closed, and her muscles seize refusing any command to take action forcing her to stand and watch them walk into the house. When she is able to move her legs are sluggish. She looks at the others in the yard.

Two men get up from their chairs and move towards the house. One of them calls out, "That be Polk Wilson and that skinny cousin of his. Damn, what is going on?"

Hallie advances towards the front of the house, but feels like she is trying to run through a waist-high swamp. She jumps hearing several shots followed by screams and then two more shots. Silence. Everyone stops in their tracks. The two men from the sedan come out of the house looking around. The one with the shot gun holds it towards the picnickers assuring no one tries to stop them. No one does. The skinny man is holding his left arm. Blood pours from under his hand staining the sleeve of his plaid shirt. Hallie's heart is racing, and she is breathing as though she just finished a 5K. The two shooters get into their car and leave hap-hazardly.

For a moment, no one moves, and then there is a mad dash to the house. Hallie is unaware how she gets to the front porch. She hesitates at the steps and someone bumps her shoulder as he runs past her into the house. Someone from inside calls for Doc Hutchison in a panicked voice. A woman comes out the front door in tears holding two children by the hand leading them across the porch and out into the yard. The little girl has blood splattered across the front of her dress and blank wide eyes staring at nothing. Hallie reaches for the screen door.

Jeb comes running around from the side of the house towards her. He drops her lemonade. "Hallie, stop! Don't go in there!"

She turns her head to look at him. "But Sadie and her mother...her Aunt Tessie...they're in there. I have to go in!"

"Well then," he says. "Not alone."

He steps up on the porch, and they walk through the front door together. They have to step over a body to get into the front room. Jeb looks down. "That be Newell Mitchell. Looks like he took one right at his head."

Hallie looks down and sees a blood-smeared paper with 'warrant' written on it lying on the floor next to the body. She looks around the room. It is bathed in crimson. The sick turns in her stomach as she looks to the left seeing Luke. His shirt is dark with a sticky-looking stain of dark red. He isn't moving. His brother, Elijah, is several feet away. His head is bent to the side propped against a wall. The girl in the light blue dress, who was with Elijah, is sitting next to him sobbing splattered in blood.

She looks up at Jeb. "Mister Wilson...he...he said he had a warrant for the Mitchells...and, and...Mister Mitchell pulled out a gun and shot that skinny fella….there were more shots, shots and blood…and…" She drops her head sobbing.

Hallie feels an acidy lurch towards her throat and puts her hand to her mouth. Jeb puts his arm around her to steady her.

Elijah stirs moving his hand up to his chest near his left breast pocket letting out a groan. He opens his eyes reaching into the torn shirt pocket removing his pocket knife, the broad handle is dented. He sits and stares at it with a look of amazement.

"Oh, my God Jeb." Hallie exhales holding her stomach. "The knife saved him just like the story in the exhibit at The Blueridge Institute in Ferrum."

"Uh, huh." Jeb looks at her furrowing his brow. "The what in Ferrum?"

"Oh, sorry. It's a future thing."

Jeb rubs his neck with his hand and nods his head. "Well, I don't know anything about that, but I do know it's a good thing to be sure."

Elijah reverently puts the knife back in his pocket. He smiles at the girl in the blue dresses starting to reach over to her when he looks beyond her seeing Luke. "Oh, God…No!" He crawls over to his brother pulling him up to his chest. Luke is limp and unresponsive.

Sadie comes running into the room from the kitchen stopping short when she sees the blood on the walls and the body by the door. She looks up and meets Hallie's eye and then turns to see Luke and the pool of blood on the floor next to him, more of his blood is on his brother Elijah who continues to hold him rocking and sobbing. Sadie's knees buckle just as Aunt Tessie comes up from behind taking her into her arms and walks her out through the back of the house.

Hallie starts to follow, but Billy comes running through the door taking survey of the scene. "Where is Sadie?"

"Her Aunt Tessie just got her out." Hallie feels a quivering release of tension with the sound of Billy's voice. It is like a blanket of comfort.

"Well then, be quick. We have got to get out of here before Mister Steele comes to make a claim. We will go to my cabin for now." he whispers to them nudging Jeb once more. "Jeb! Be quick about it!"

Jeb blinks and looks at Billy and nods somberly. They each take hold of one of Hallie's arms and walk out of the house. Doc Hutchison makes a quick survey of them as they pass, and then he urgently moves on towards the house. Hallie stumbles and feels the nausea churn again, but Billy and Jeb steady her keeping their momentum going. They step into the woods just as the green Phaeton pulls up to the house.

"Wait!" Hallie jerks her arms free. Billy and Jeb stop. Billy's eyes are full of angst. "David...uh, Luke is back there. Dead! We can't just leave him! What about Elijah?"

Billy takes Hallie by the shoulders looking her in the eye. "Mister Steele will claim Luke, but not now—none of the other tethered souls are there with him. Besides, Luke has family, and it was a witnessed death. The demon is going to have to wait until no one will realize Luke's body is gone. He takes body and soul when he makes a harvest. He will not touch Elijah. Luke will have an anchor to return for a future life." He speaks kindly and reassuringly to Hallie. "We *have* to leave. Mister Steele can claim anyone from the circle who lingers near a conquered soul. It is just another way he torments us...no time to grieve one another. Please, right now he cannot link you to us—let us keep it that way for as long as we can. We need to go."

"But...Sadie..."

"She will be safe for now. Tessie has taken her home. We are going there later." He looks at Hallie and waits.

She nods and follows behind Jeb not paying attention to the trail stumbling a few times. Billy reaches his hand to her, and she grasps it gratefully.

They wait out the afternoon at Billy's and arrive at Sadie's as the sun drops below the mountain ridge. Tessie, Myrlie and the girls are busily gathering clothing and a few necessities into luggage.

Hallie looks around confused. "Tessie, where's Sadie?"

Tessie stops what she is doing and looks at Hallie and then Billy and Jeb. Her face softens, and she walks over to Hallie. "There you are child. I'm glad to see you. We are getting Sadie out of here. Daryl Lee is the reason for all the goings on. We found out from Missus Pennymaker's hired man that Daryl Lee has been going between the Wilson's and the Mitchell's stirring up trouble. He is probably even the one that done sabotaged that still in the woods that started all the trouble."

"Tessie," says Jeb. "Why is that a problem for Sadie?"

"First off, it's a problem because everyone knows Daryl Lee works for Otis, Sadie's daddy. It won't be too long 'fore them dead men's kin folk start looking for revenge, and they ain't going to stop to ask too many questions to find out what's true and what ain't." She walks back over to the sack of food she was putting together and adds a loaf of bread to it before tying it closed. "But that probably wouldn't be as much the problem. 'Cept yesterday morning, after Jedidiah Mitchell went and tore up that still at the Wilson's, Daryl Lee went over there stirring up more trouble saying that Luke Pettigrew was in cahoots with the revenuer and bringing the law in to find them other stills. I'm guessing Daryl Lee thought getting Luke out of the way would clear the path to Sadie and what her daddy has, but that fool done gone and run his mouth about Sadie and Luke too. He was drunk with the shine that the Wilson's gave him for the information that he provided them. It is a mess! We got to get Sadie outta here—I'm taking her and her momma to my place."

"Where's Mister Hairston?" Hallie asks.

"He went up to the still site looking for Daryl Lee. We couldn't stop him. He insisted we get Sadie out of here, and he is meeting up with us in Danville. From there we are going to my place. They won't be able to come back here. Fayerdale is turning into a ghost town anyways. Myrlie is sick about leaving him here, but she's gotta do what's best for her girl right now."

"So, what? You are going to walk, at night, to where? And then what?" Billy asks.

"Billy, it's gonna be alright."

"No, no it is not. You are right to get Sadie out of town, but you are not going to get it done your way." He turns to Jeb, "Listen, go into town and ask Doc Hutchison to borrow his car. You can get the Hairstons and Tessie and her girls to Danville where they can pick up the train in the morning."

He turns to Hallie. "I have to go and get Mister Hairston. He should not be alone with Daryl Lee, especially if what you suspect about Daryl Lee is true. Okay?"

It isn't okay. Hallie doesn't want to be separated from him right now, but she agrees.

He pulls her close and kisses her. "I am going to see you again," he promises her.

With tears in her eyes, she nods.

"Jeb, go and get the car and, listen, if I am not back with Mister Hairston by the time you get the car here you take Hallie, and the rest, and leave."

"What?" Hallie grasps Jeb's arm. "You will not do that."

Billy reaches over and takes Hallie's hand. "Listen. I am going to try my best to get back here, but you need to understand that may not happen."

She starts to object. He slightly nods his head and moistens his lips. "Hallie. I understand. I do, but we have to think about Sadie and Jeb. Right?"

She looks at him with glistening eyes, glances over at Jeb and Aunt Tessie, then back to Billy. "Yes. I understand."

He kisses her and turns to Jeb giving him a nod to go.

Jeb turns running back towards town.

Billy takes the path near the willow.

Desperation is in the air, and Hallie breath s it in daring her very fiber to succumb to it. She searches the house for Sadie finding her on the screened porch. She looks like the fragile shell of an egg, hallow, and alabaster pale skin with a pearly glistening of sweat. Her eyes are dry because their dark wells are empty. Hallie sits wrapping her in the warmth of her arms and love. They sit that way until Jeb pulls up with Doc Hutchison's car blowing the horn.

Hallie walks Sadie out of the house to the car helping her into the back seat. Olivia and Zephyr solemnly climb in next to Sadie while Myrlie gets into the front passenger seat, and Tessie gets a few more items from the house.

"Hallie, once Billy and Mister Hairston get here we'll all get on out." Jeb tells her as he packs the car trunk. Hallie just nods.

Tessie walks out of the house and steps next to Hallie lighting a cigar. "Yes, child you have travel ahead of you, but first a task needs to be completed. I saw it in the runes last night."

Jeb looks over at Tessie and Hallie senses disapproval.

Tessie squares up her shoulders and looks hard at Jeb. "Boy, you of all people should see beyond what is and isn't disdainful to the Creator. You define your journey your way, and I will do mine my way."

He starts to speak, but Hallie interrupts. "Oh, my God! Jeb, Billy's box. I promised him I would take care of it…if things look bad. I'm thinking that things are looking pretty bad. I've got to go to the livery!"

"Hallie, what are you talking about? He didn't tell me anything about a box. Whatever it is, it's not happening tonight. He was very clear that I was to get you out of here. We are waiting a little longer, but if he isn't back we are leaving." Jeb's voice takes an unfamiliar edge.

Before Hallie can reply a gunshot rings out from further up the mountain. She flinches. Myrlie looks out of the car to Tessie while Sadie sits in the back seat without reaction.

"That would be 'bout the general location of the Mitchell still." Tessie squints as she blows out a cloud of purple smoke.

Hallie grabs a lantern from the small table by the house and starts to go towards the direction where the shot was fired.

Jeb catches her by the arm. "What are you doing?"

"Billy and Mister Hairston are out there!" She starts towards the path in the woods.

"I can't let her go alone. Wait here for me. I'll be back soon as I can."

Tessie takes a long draw on her cigar blowing the smoke straight up. She looks over at her sister. "Myrlie, I know your Otis is out there in them woods, but ain't a one of them coming back here. We gotta get Sadie outta here. Now."

Myrlie's eyes glisten wet as she nods to her sister. Tessie stubs her cigar out on the bottom of her shoe then tucks it in a pocket before she walks around the car to climb into the driver's seat. She pauses a moment to look at the layout of the dash and turns the key bringing the engine to life. The transmission moans as she puts the car into gear pulling away from the house but bringing all the sorrow surrounding it with them.

Chapter 35, Douse

Jeb catches up to Hallie. They come to the point of the trail where Hallie and Billy were yesterday. The same sour smell is in the air. She starts to step off the trail in the direction of where she believes the still site is, but Jeb touches her arm.

He whispers, "We need to leave the lantern here. I know the way in. The lantern will help you...us find the way back. Just stay right behind me."

Hallie nods and sets the lantern down. Within moments they come up to the still site. A lantern is burning nearby, and a low-burning fire is glowing underneath the still. There is a large odd-shaped tree at the edge of the clearing growing into the mountainside with a cascade of roots spilling down the slope near the still helping to conceal it. Hallie looks from the tree to behind her, and she is amazed by how close to the trail they are. Skillful camouflage keeps the setup well-hidden. Jeb puts an arm out to signal Hallie to stop and sit low. They crouch behind a tree with a trunk wide enough to conceal them both.

Hallie leans cautiously around the tree to take a look, and her heart drops. Mister Hairston is lying face down unmoving. Daryl Lee stands with a pistol pointed at Billy moving back and forth with agitation. She can hear rustling in the woods across from her and Jeb. Someone is approaching and does not care that his progress towards the still is heard. Suddenly Mister Steele steps into the lantern light. He has on a pair of black pressed slacks with a white shirt and a brightly colored striped vest. A pocket watch chain is draped across the front of the vest glinting in the lamp light. Despite the lack of sunshine, he has on the smoky-lensed glasses. Mister Steele brushes Billy's arm as he walks by him.

Billy's face is set. He remains focused on Daryl Lee refusing to acknowledge the demon.

Daryl Lee's agitation is now shrouded in fear. "Mista Steele, uh…"

The demon moves inches away from Daryl Lee in an instant. Daryl Lee lowers his gun wielding arm looking nauseated.

"Hmmmm," The sound slides over his tongue. "You've added murder to the mayhem you created young Mister Hobbs, how delightful." His words are measured and pointed as he walks a circle around Daryl Lee. "Who knew you had it in you? I obviously underestimated the potential of your petty and pitiful jealously of Luke Pettigrew. What a lovely surprise." He completes his circle standing in front of Daryl Lee. Mister Steele leans back inhaling deeply as though he smells the aroma of a well-cooked meal.

"Mist…Mista Steele, I did it like you sss…said and it www…worked jjj…just like you sss…said."

Mister Steele smirks with annoyance waving a hand in front of Daryl Lee's face. Daryl Lee blinks and slowly finishes speaking without the stutter. "The Wilsons took care of Luke when they went after the Mitchells. It was just like you said."

Hallie's stomach churns, and she moves her hand up over her mouth. Jeb reaches out touching her arm gently.

"Yes that was convenient that they were so obligingly predictable." The demon reaches up and grasps his glasses by the side frame moving them up his nose a bit.

Hallie notices that Billy's eyes flit towards her and Jeb's direction. She wonders if he is aware of their presence. His face remains unreadable. Jeb must have noticed too, and he leans in towards Hallie to whisper at her ear. "You need to remain behind this tree. The demon will not see your soul if you stay behind the tree. The forces of nature are strong in this clearing and will give some protection to the innocent. He knows I'm here already. He is familiar with my aura and, when he calls me out, do not linger. You must leave. It won't take him long to see your soul once he has made his harvest. The tree will only be able to shield you while he is distracted by the rest of us."

Hallie looks at him, and tears well. "Harvest. Now. There's nothing we can do?"

He gives her a firm look until she closes her eyes pulling her strength together and gives him a single nod. She looks at

Billy. He stands tall waiting for the demon to finish toying with his prey.

Mister Steele turns from Daryl Lee walking over to Mister Hairston who remains motionless on the ground. He stands arrogantly over the body and glances at Billy and then back to Daryl Lee. "And, this...how did you manage to shoot him?"

"It was an accident."

"Yes, well accidents do happen. Unfortunately, this one is no benefit to me. He is to cross over towards the side of the light. At least both heaven and hell will be satisfied tonight." He looks directly at Billy. "Keeping balance is important after all."

Mister Steele turns back to Daryl Lee, and a thin smile curls up looking out of place on his face. He walks towards the trembling man again. Leaning his head downward he reaches up to lower his glasses on his nose. Hallie sees his eyes glow red. He speaks matter-of-factly. "Daryl Lee I am going to need my scorpion back, and then I would like for you to die."

A glistening sweat shines on Daryl Lee's skin, and he mechanically raises his hand palm up. Daryl Lee's skin behind his ear on the same side ripples. He trembles in pain. The ripple moves below the collar and sleeve of his shirt and down his arm towards his wrist where the skin tears and a black wiry scorpion emerges crawling across his hand. Mister Steele extends his hand, and the scorpion moves from Daryl Lee to the demon and marches up the demon's arm to his neck. It creeps across the side of his neck and settles into the skin melding into the back of the demon's neck forming a tribal tattoo in scorpion form. The demon lifts his chin and stiffly cocks his head adjusting the vertebrae of his neck.

He turns taking a few steps from Daryl Lee. The red glow of the demon's eyes is unmistakable now. He pauses sighing in bored disgust and turns towards Daryl Lee. "Now, Mister Hobbs, if you don't mind. I have quite a bit to do tonight."

Daryl Lee still has a grip on the pistol, and his arm slowly rises bringing the barrel of the gun into his mouth. He squeezes the trigger, and it misfires. He twitches removing the gun from his mouth. He looks at the gun and his muscles relax. The demon rolls his eyes in disgust and, in an impatient manner, grabs the gun and shoots it point blank. Daryl Lee shutters and falls to the ground. The demon tosses the gun aside carelessly and stands over the body. He waves his hand as though swatting a fly, and Daryl Lee slowly sinks into the ground disappearing from site. A prickly vine swirls up from the earth twisting back on itself coming to rest in a tangled mess where Daryl Lee once stood. It explodes with long spikey thorns that peak sharp and dangerous just before crumbling into a pile of dust.

Mister Steele sniffs and turns to face Billy. "So, Mister White, should we invite Mister Curry to join us?"

Billy stiffens but keeps his face unrevealing.

"Come, come now. It's not as though you don't know he's there. Always so willing to do *this* alone. I'd say you gave it a good go this time around. Just about a record time on Earth for you, and you have the consolation that the one named Sadie seems to have escaped. Assuming you come with me tonight. You can hold onto that thought when I plummet you back to the underworld. It will give you something to sustain you while you serve the protectorate and cling to your soul." Mister Steele's voice is smooth and cool. Shifting his attention away from Billy, he looks upward in disgust. "Mister Curry! Anytime please!" His impatience sets a brighter glow to his eyes.

Jeb gives Hallie a final look. A single tear rolls down her cheek. He gives her a brave smile and points back towards the trail before he stands and walks into the circle of lantern light towards Mister Steele who turns to face him. A poisonous smile appears on the demon's face as he looks at Jeb.

"Welcome, Mister Curry!"

Jeb glances down at Mister Hairston's body and then looks at Billy. They each stand on opposite sides of Mister Steele, but he shows no concern about being flanked. Once the harvest begins submission is their only option.

Hallie cannot make herself leave. Her minds races still trying to find a way to stop all of this. She remains behind the tree leaning just far enough to the edge to see them. She desperately tries to will Billy to see her and assure her that he is going to win this confrontation. He does not divert his eyes from the demon. The demon turns his back to Billy and focuses on Jeb, and a hissing sound fills the air as he speaks to Jeb, but what he says is lost to her.

A bright single light comes into view from the woods behind Billy advancing towards Hallie reaching her within a matter of seconds. No one but Hallie seems aware of its presence. It advances to within inches of her face and falls onto the ground shattering into several shards of light that spin and waver in a repetitive pattern. The familiar chiming voice whispers into her ear.

> *When their life-force is extinguished yours will be unshielded—you must walk away now. This is not the time to confront the demon. This is the time to find strength, leave behind what waits for you ahead. Complete the task agreed upon, and the key will reveal itself to you. Look for one who symbolizes the ending and the beginning. Go quickly, another opportunity will not present itself.*

The pieces of light swirl into a single bright spot on the ground and disappears. Hallie wipes the tears from her face, her throat tightens, and her chest struggles to contain her pounding heart. She looks up from the ground towards the trio in the lantern light. She averts her eyes when Jeb is struck down. He is tortured, and his agony shatters Hallie's heart. She bites hard on her lip holding her hands over her ears, but it does not deafen the awfulness. She grasps her amulet pouch and looks back up to Billy.

An instant before the demon turns to face him, Billy looks pleadingly in Hallie's direction holding a hand up towards her. He mouths the words, "Go...for now." Hallie holds her hand up as though she can touch Billy's. It is all they have before the demon turns, and faces him moving closer.

Hallie cannot hear the conversation over the roaring in her ears. Billy seems to be stalling. She knows he is buying time for her to leave, and she won't prolong his suffering. She clings to the hope that the angel song's words are true, and that he will be waiting for her in the future. She forces herself to stand, turn away, and not look back.

She stands for a moment trying to slow her breathing and stop her shaking hands. Hallie wipes her hands on the sides of her skirt. She picks up the lantern holding it out in front of her, and forces herself to make the first step up the trail moving through the night towards town and the livery. A fine mist is in the air slowly becoming a drizzling rain that finds companionship with her tears.

Chapter 36, Torch

The wooden box is more awkward to hold than heavy, but Hallie cradles it in her arm while holding the lantern in front of her. The light glows meagerly, and her heart's racing pace is fed by an urgency to get to her destination. She has been there only once before but knows exactly how to find it. This part of Fayerdale was not covered by the waters of Fairy Stone's lake the last time she walked this path. She thinks back on that day with Liam, and how he described the layout of the land and the town of Fayerdale. He knew it like the back of his own hand, and she never thought twice about it then. *How many other towns does he know?*

The dark mouth of the abandoned mine entrance looms ahead of her. No bars cover its entrance this time. She turns her back to it holding her lantern high trying to find the triple-trunk tree. She stumbles a few times and stops abruptly listening to the sounds in the darkness beyond her lantern light. She thinks she can hear someone or something approaching and forces herself to focus managing to keep her fear at bay while she searches for the tree.

A slow and steady rain falls. Her arms ache. Fear tugs at her nerves and broken heart while her legs object to going another step further. Feeling discouraged, she sits against a tree setting the lantern and box down. The rain taps gently on the leaves of the underbrush. Emotion overcomes her, and she cannot hold back the guttural wale that escapes as the grief pours out. When she is spent she rests her head against the tree. She has no idea how long she has sat there, but the rain is gone, and the lantern light is fading shrinking the circle of illumination it casts. Reaching up Hallie wipes her face with her hands leaving streaks of dirt that accentuate the trail of her tears.

She strains to see beyond the periphery of wavering light and catches site of something wafting in the breeze. She picks up the box and lantern moving closer. It is ghostly how the image floats in the air. It looks like crepe paper at first. Reaching out to see what it is, she instinctively recoils realizing it is the skin of a snake. But then she stops and sets the box and lantern down taking hold of the snake skin. It is rippled with the cast of the snake's scales. A branch of mountain laurel has it snagged, and the head is entangled with the tail forming a circle.

"No beginning without an ending...the renewal of life," she says to herself and hastily bends down to pick up the lantern lifting it high. Behind the mountain laurel is a maple tree branching up with three conjoined trunks. Hallie takes Billy's box and kneels at the base of the tree. She pushes aside the ground cover at the tree roots. The cool damp soil clings to her hands, and she brushes them clean. Sitting the box on her lap she reaches for her amulet bag untying it from the hand-sewn loop on her skirt. It makes her think of Sadie renewing the flow of tears. She prays for her safety, and then shakes her head forcing herself to focus.

Hallie opens the pouch and takes the pressed penny out. When she opens the wood box a small collection of items and the Book of Lineages are revealed. She lightly runs her hand over them and opens the book cover laying the penny inside She closes it and wraps the leather strap around it. Shutting the lid of the box, she takes the blue jay feather and sets it on top of the box before wrapping it all in the soft sheep skin. Holding her breath she puts the box on the moist forest soil and waits.

Hallie gasps as it sinks slowly below the surface of the dirt disappearing from site. She waits. In a few seconds the earth trickles away at the center, and a bit of white and then blue pokes up from the soil as a flower would do in the early spring. It rises straight up revealing itself. She smiles through her sadness at the feather and reaches down to pick the promise for return from the ground holding it up staring at it with wonder.

At the periphery of her vision, in the fading lamp light, she sees a sparkling glint on the ground. It sits within a shallow pool of water. The shards of light remind her of the bright colorful lights that appear before an angel song, and she cocks her head anticipating the chiming voice, but it doesn't come.

She waivers a moment as her shaking hand reaches into the water laying ahold of the red sparkle examining it by the remaining lamplight. It is an uncut fairy stone, a Maltese cross, with a brilliant garnet at its center. Her fingers bump over its irregular edge. Despite being uncut, the cross is incredibly distinct within the stone with the garnet glowing from its center. Its warmth courses across her hand, and she knows this is the key from the angel song.

The moment is interrupted by an ice-cold trickle tingling up her spine when she again senses a presence in the woods that seems to be getting closer. Sitting silently, she strains to hear any motion, but there is none. There is only the wary feeling that someone is approaching, so she urgently puts the stone and the feather into her pouch pulling the cord tight and re-securing it to the loop.

Is that a whisper of a voice floating in the air? Her heart takes a flip as the last bit of lantern light flickers out. Hallie sits for a moment focusing on breathing and her breath's harsh echoes in her ears. She remembers Billy's warning not to linger once the box has been buried. She stands, feeling crowded by the darkness, and swats away the prickle at the back of her neck. Only the sound of crickets and frogs are in the air, but she knows there is something else. There is no rustling or snapping of tree branches, but she knows someone or something is there. Near. Looming.

She turns and moves away from where it seems the approaching predator is advancing. She walks as quietly as she can, but it is hard to see without the lantern. The rain clouds are moving out quickly though, and she has some moonlight to help her see. She stumbles as she quickens her pace. Her knees wobble, and panic overwhelms coaxing her to run and not worry about being quiet. Her shoes slide over gravel slick from the rainfall, and she hesitates before she realizes the mine opening is near. Refuge. The presence rushes up towards her becoming terrifyingly close, and the shadow of a voice beyond comprehension whispers. She picks up her speed to get to the mine misjudging her location. She stumbles falling into the mine striking her head on a piece of rock that juts out from the side wall. The pain is sudden and brief as she slips into near unconsciousness. She lays back touching her head and feels the warmth of blood leaking from her wound.

Through bleary eyes she sees a swirl of wind picking up at the mound of discarded scrape iron just outside the mine. Leaves from the vines growing over the mound shudder with the disturbance and then suddenly everything stills. The sound of heavy breathing is in the air next to the mound. Hallie pushes herself closer to the mine wall holding her breath and waits.

"Azure, hold up that lamp. Somethin's happened. I can't hear 'er anymore."

Azure complies with a knobby hand grasping the lamp handle. A smaller hand waves over the lamp, and the light brightens glowing around the two shadowy intruders and outward.

Hallie squints to clear her vision and a sharp jab of pain punishes her for the effort. Azure stands tall and slender while his female companion is petite. They have similar features, pitch black hair, and icy blue eyes. The woman is dressed in black textured layers save an amethyst-colored sash that she has tied around her waist. Her leggings are of the same purple color and can be seen from the top on her ankle-high boots to the hem of her skirt which hangs low. She has long dangling earrings and an arm full of bangles and bracelets.

Azure wears a simple shirt, and his plain trousers' hem hangs slightly too short over his long legs.

It is as if a portal has been opened outside the mine. She sees the two intruders outside the mine opening, but it appears that they are in a cabin. Their lantern's glow gives a circular view into their surroundings. The pain in Hallie's head hammers steadily, and she rubs her eyes trying to keep focus, but the view is narrowing, darkening, and gone. Her head falls back unconscious.

"Odina, can you see her?"

"Hold the lamp up higher." Odina leans forward and Azure stretches his neck out to extend his view holding the lamp just above and in front of his sister.

"Careful!" Odina scolds. "Do not break tha circle!"

He adjusts the lantern position and, at the edge of the ring of light, they can see Hallie lying on the ground just inside the mine entrance. They look at each other smiling.

"It worked! Odina we have found her!"

"Aye Azure, now bring tha pages from tha grimoire ta me and hold them for me ta see, so I can summon tha angel."

Chapter 37, Hope

Hester looks at the girl lying on the ground in front of her and around the mine to survey her surroundings. The pull of the summoning was one she has not felt since the time Resmelda called her forth from the underworld. She turns to look behind seeing the glow of a lamp light filtering through the misty haze. Looking closer she sees an odd pair of humans staring back at her. One tall and lanky making her think of the Angel Sandalphon's amazing height. She smiles sadly, missing her mentor. Hester pulls herself away from the memory, and drops her gaze to meet eyes with a woman who stands much shorter.

You summoned me here. Tell me why, and then tell me...how. Hester speaks to the woman directly, silently, testing the odd human's third eye.

Odina answers her with a humbled tone. "Hester, fallen angel of heaven's seventh realm below Raphael, I am but a humble servant of tha craft. I have summoned you ta guide tha child of tha Traveler forward ta my time—ta help her wings of time spread and take hold. Your summoning was a task accomplished with a page from tha grimoire of tha great but dark witch Resmelda, and tha magical blood of my ancestors allowing me ta see tha Enochian text calling you forth asking for your presence ta be with tha girl."

Hester takes stock of this rather unassuming-looking gypsy-mountain woman and her companion with a sense of astonishment. The task described is extremely complex magic. Magic that strong requires one to know herself well. With such conjuring the risk of losing one's will is great. The woman must be not only skilled but of great strength and character. Hester studies her, a feeling of familiarity wraps around her like a warm winter scarf, but what it means escapes the angel. She turns looking at Hallie, and kneels down near her gently moving blood-matted hair away from her face. Hester holds up her hand, and a cloth soaked with a soothing elixir appears in it. She cleans Hallie's face and is amazed by the resemblance to her mother.

You are descended from the Rom? She asks Odina.

"Aye." Odina's chest swells with pride at the angel's acknowledgement of her Romany heritage.

Why is she here?

"That we don't know. Tha signs foretold of her coming but very little else. There was a message from tha oracle, Tessie, late last night ta let us know that her arrival was eminent, but tha prophesied time of remuneration has not bin revealed."

Hester stands to face Odina. A*nd, how did you know who she was and where to look for her?*

"Tha oracle's message gave an indication. I have a crystal of great power that I used to find her within tha hills. She has an amulet that's akin ta it"

This girl is in great danger, if the Demon King…uh, Paimon, finds her and realizes who she is. Let us hope that he remains in the dark about her identity.

"Have you not bin guidin' her? The writing says that she will be led by tha song of an angel."

Hester blinks for a moment, starts to speak, and hesitates starting again. *No. It is not by my song. I…I…do not sing out loud anymore.* She fights a chill and looks through the mist at Odina. *I…I had hoped for the girl's survival, but had no confirmation of it. I would not have known where to summon her from. It seems she has been well-hidden by the sisters.*

"Well," replies Odina with a straightforward tone after some thought. "We need ta move 'er on forward. It is in tha writin' that she has a task ta complete here. 'Tis time for your stolen keys ta be returned. We were of tha thinkin' that she was ta come here first. It was only a chance reading of tha signs that said otherwise, so we have remained vigilant until Azure received tha message last night. Her genetics allow for tha travel, but she has no knowledge—no control—of it yet. She needs a guide since the sacred union has not yet occurred. We need you ta help her."

Hester looks at Odina incredulously. *You ask no small task! She must cross through Tartarus in order to travel. Her genetics will give some protection, but Tartarus holds many dangers for a flesh-barer. She will need to cross its territory to get to the Mesu and its passageways. There is no other way, and it is not safe.*

"But *this* time—for tha moment—is tha safest it will be."

Hester looks around the mine shaft once more. *Is this the place of the iron and fairy stones?*

"Aye, before tha filling of tha valley, and at tha beginning of tha harvest of tethered souls during the Fayerdale lives."

Beginning?

"One soul has escaped an one remains. Tha demon waits for tha time his claim can be made ta take tha body of tha one that remains. Tha others were taken just a short time ago. We have been watching from within our protective circle since late last night."

Hester nods. She looks back at Hallie who is starting to stir. *Alright, I will try. There are no guarantees even with the Demon King out of Tartarus. If he calls out to me, resistance is futile.*

"Thank you." Odina bows slightly.

You don't have much time. Hester starts with a directive tone. *What may take me quite some time will transpire for you within minutes. You may need to break your circle in order to gather what is needed. Do it quickly, and then close the circle again. You need to gather Aloe, pepper, musk, vervain, and saffron. Grind and mix it. Then light it with a white candle, and place it on the floor in the center of your circle. It will serve as a beacon for the girl when she crosses over to your time.*

"It will be done," Odina replies.

The image of Odina and Azure fade and the mine darkens again. Hester lifts her hand upward and a single orb of light illuminates the mine. She looks at Hallie and tries to speak silently coaxing her back to alertness.

Can you hear me?

Hallie brings a hand up to her head and winces. She blinks trying to sharpen her vision looking up and over at the jagged rock walls. She turns looking up into Hester's face squinting her eyes and blinking several times. Her vision sharpens. "Hester?" Her voice squeaks as fear tightens its grip, and she looks around attempting to move away unable to gain any ground with the rocky floor. *Oh, God the Demon King has found me.*

Calm down! He is not here!

Hallie is too distraught to be able to hear Hester's silent voice.

Hester looks upward, closes her eyes, and opens her mouth. "Calm down!" It rings out causing a tremor and dirt falls from above. Hester steps back and exhales a puff of air from her nose. "Sorry about that. It has been centuries since I have spoken out loud, and the volume escaped me."

Hallie stops and looks at Hester. She manages to stand and searches with her eyes trying to find the Demon King, but her head is throbbing, and she holds her hand up over her wound.

"He-is-not-here. Calm yourself." Hester breathes heavily with the effort of speaking out loud. "You know, I have broken a vow of silence for you." She looks about in expectation. "But, it seems there is to be no upheaval of earth or sky. Perhaps I have been forgiven." She grasps her vest as she pulls in a deep breath exhaling it almost joyfully before returning her focus back on Hallie. Their eyes meet.

Hallie nods, maintaining a wary expression. The adrenaline has her blood coursing through her veins in a torrent making the throb in her head skull-splitting. She forces herself to stand firm. Hester is still as china-doll-like as Hallie remembers. She has on an ivory shirt with lace edged sleeves, a silver gray vest over a black layered skirt with boots. There is a Celtic cross hanging from a chain around her neck that reminds Hallie of the Maltese cross stone now in her amulet pouch. Hester's cross is made of a deep brown wood. The bottom portion of the cross is broken diagonally. Hallie keeps her eyes fixed on the cross as she reaches for her pouch seeking reassurance and comfort. It is not missed by Hester.

"I am not going to harm you." She notices Hallie's regard for her necklace and lifts the cross up towards her. "It is made of katalox."

Hallie hesitantly pulls her eyes away to look up at Hester's face. She struggles to regain control of her breathing.

Hester speaks to her as though addressing a cornered feral cat she is trying to sooth. "Katalox is a wood of balance— especially the balance between light and dark. Many of us struggle with this challenge, but I assure you it is the light I seek to regain. I am here to help you cross over." Hester hesitates a moment before asking, "How do you know me? Furthermore, who I travel with? Only one…being induces the fear I see in your eyes. And, as I said, he is not here."

Hallie cannot help but notice the slight chiming quality to Hester's voice. It is similar to the song she has been hearing, but Hester's words carry an exotic sound as her lips move almost hypnotically. Struggling with the pain in her head, Hallie looks up from Hester's lips to her eyes. "Yes, yes I see that you mean no harm. I never truly feared you. Just him. We uh met, or I guess meet, in the future. Uh…it's kind of a long story. My name is Hallie by the way." She replies with a raspy voice.

Hester's eyes glance towards the pouch and back to Hallie's face. "Very well then Hallie, I am to be your guide. I can help you get to where you need to be, but we must leave now, if we want to improve our chances for success. The passage is dangerous. Will you trust me and come with me?"

Hallie swallows with effort and nods once to express her assent. She has no idea what she is really consenting to, or what choice she has. Luke is dead, Jeb died before her eyes, and she knows that Billy has met the same fate. She doesn't even ponder where she will be 'crossing over' to. She doesn't care.

Hester looks down again at Hallie's amulet pouch. She lowers her tone as though someone may hear. "Did the key reveal itself to you?"

Hallie follows Hester's gaze towards the pouch, and looks back to Hester to answer her. "It did."

A look of relief briefly passes over Hester's face. "We should get started then. You MUST stay close to me at all times."

Hallie looks at her and nods hesitantly.

"Hallie, this is important. We will be traveling in very dangerous territory. I will be able to cloak your presence, but only if you remain close."

"Where are we traveling to?"

"I am taking you ahead in time, but first we must pass through Tartarus. It…it is part of the underworld. All who are passing through realms must do it by way of Tartarus. For most, unless he or she is dead or a traveler, the voyage requires a guide."

Hallie nods. Exhaustion has stolen any curious thoughts.

Hester turns to walk deeper into the mine. The walls expand within the narrow passage to allow them to walk through. The orb of light floats just ahead of her leading the way. She pauses to turn back to Hallie looking deeply into Hallie's eyes. "I will transform as we move away from the boundaries of this realm. Do not let this frighten you. I am still the same—in here." Hester points towards the center of her chest where the cross rests.

Hallie looks at Hester and gives a languid, "Okay."

They turn and resume walking into the depth of the mine. The darkness engulfs them while the tiny orb struggles to push it away. Hallie feels the ground below her change to a smooth surface with its coldness seeping through her shoes. She notices that Hester's clothing is slowly looking tattered and torn, the ivory shirt is gone with only a bodice and tunic remaining. Patches of her skin are visible through the gaps in her clothing. From between her shoulder blades a set of black wings with leathery flesh, similar in appearance to the tattered clothing she now has, evolve. Her boots are a series of straps wrapping up towards her knees and her hands are covered with gloves of the same design extending up towards her elbows. Hester holds out her right hand and a sword appears in her grasp.

Hallie maintains her pace behind Hester watching the transformation. She wonders if she may still actually be lying unconscious on the mine floor dreaming all of this, but she knows that nowhere in the depths of her imagination could she design what is appearing before her. Maintaining her pace she feels another transition into a deeper darkness. It presses in harder, and just expanding her lungs is an effort.

The ground escapes from below Hallie as the path shifts into a steep downhill slope. The first step takes her by surprise, but she quickly finds her footing. The darkness is unrelenting, and time no longer holds any importance to her. Hester stops and turns toward Hallie. The orb stops as well bobbing gently in the air regaining some of its strength, and Hallie can see the tortuous path looming before them. She looks at Hester and is taken aback by her beauty and…fierceness. The porcelain doll appearance is gone, and Hallie wonders if it was ever really there.

"We have passed through the first two layers of darkness, and you have done well. The first layer brings fear and the second oppression. I have been able to shelter you through both. The third is much stronger and brings grief and loss. You are going to have to have physical contact with me in order for you to survive this layer. Are you okay with holding my hand?"

"Yes," Hallie replies and holds her hand out to Hester. Hester grasps ahold and Hallie feels a cooling sensation rise up her arm bringing calm to her tense muscles and relief to her pain. It is the same calm feeling she has with the warmth of the amber amulet and with Liam.

Hester looks at their joined hands and back up at Hallie. She raises their hands giving a single thrust forward towards Hallie and a nod of the head to signal approval and unity. Hester turns and begins the descent into the final layer of darkness. The orb leads the way with its renewed energy.

They have only gone what seems like several feet when Hallie feels like she is being crowded and confined. She sees a flash of Billy in the clearing at the still site only he quickly becomes Liam—longer hair, more modern dress. She sees him turn to look at her and mouth the words "*My Love Follows You Where You Go.*" He holds his hand up towards her as though he can touch her. Another flash, and she sees his face right in front of her spangled in filtered sunlight with his hair lightly fluttering in a gentle breeze, as he leads her rhythmically across a dance floor to a sweet melody. She can see it all in her mind's eye and feel the warmth it inspires until a final flash cracks, and the demon's hand grabs him by the throat pulling him away from her. Liam is struggling to free himself. He reaches his hand up to grasp onto the demon's arm and immediately lets out an agonizing roar of pain. Dozens of mechanical-like scorpions march down the demon's arm plunging themselves into Liam's flesh. Hallie stops short, her breath is pulsing involuntarily with a staccato pace, and her heart sears as though it is being pulled apart. The image churns and dissipates like smoke.

Hester stops and looks at Hallie whose eyes are filling with tears as her lower lip trembles.

"Your grief from everything that has happened is fresh. There is bound to be some contact from the darkness despite my cloaking. I know it is hard, but you need to keep moving and hold onto my hand tightly. It is too dangerous to linger here long. Can you do this?"

Hallie wipes the tears from her eyes and nods her head. She feels like a little girl who is lost and searching for home.

They move forward. The resonating ache in Hallie's chest remains. She longs to get through this darkest layer of night not caring what lays beyond it. The walk seems endless as the path becomes a vortex spiraling down into the abyss of the final layer before Hallie suddenly feels as though she has walked through a sheer curtain. The blackness turns to gray. Hester stops and Hallie looks ahead through a murky mist hanging thick in the air. Within the mist a rocky wall appears. She looks up seeing that its height is never-ending. Hester releases Hallie's hand and moves towards the wall walking its border searching for something.

"Can I help you find something?" Hallie asks.

Hester continues searching. "A gravel ghost."

Hallie looks at her still not sure what they are looking for, but Hester points her sword downward at a rock on the ground near the wall. Hallie moves forward looking at the rock and then notices a small flower with white petals and a yellow and red center floating on a wispy stem. "That tiny flower?"

"Tiny, but powerful."

It is growing from a crack in the ground near the rock, and it amazingly is the same type of flower that had occupied the vase on her table at the Gull Island Café so long ago.

Hester holds her sword pointing its tip towards the flower, and she blows an icy mist gently down the blade causing the flower to bend. A bronze-colored sap drips from its petals flowing towards the wall. At first there is nothing, but slowly, a crack forms in the wall starting near the ground expanding upward. The wall rips and pops first softly then loudly as it pulls further apart creating a crevice in the ominous barrier. As the wall opens wider, bronze ooze spills outward along the ground like blood from a wound. It ebbs away from the flower, but otherwise soaks the ground pushing forward. Hester steps back with her arm outstretched towards Hallie guiding her away as well.

"We must enter the wall. We cannot stop for even a moment or the bronze blood will consume us, and we will become part of the Wall of Sorrows. Once the crack finishes opening we must move quickly. Be sure to stay right behind me but not too close, and try not to touch anything." Hester watches the crack widen and expand upward beyond their view.

Hallie gasps, now noticing that the irregularities of the rock formation are actually bronze-coated parts of what was once living creatures. Some are human form, some animal, some with large wings like Hester's, and others that are not recognizable to Hallie. An involuntary shudder shakes through her bringing a feeling to her stomach akin to the one she experiences during the dive on a roller coaster.

One last booming pop occurs and then silence. "Now!" Hester yells, and she moves forward into the wall. Hallie shakes off the queasiness and runs in behind her. The bronze ooze is thick as it bleeds onto the ground from crevices in the walls of the newly created cavern, and Hallie feels as though she is running through a shallow stream of tacky glue. Her lower legs are splashed with the glossy liquid, and it grabs into her skin hardening. They run into momentary darkness and then a gray light appears ahead of them.

Hester cries out in pain. A creature from the wall has reached out and grabbed her wings. Hester drops her sword. She arches back, head butting, kicking, and elbowing the creature, but it draws her closer.

Hallie rushes forward and picks up the sword. It's heavy, and she has to use her other hand to lift it. She can once again hear the bone-cracking sounds of the wall, and she realizes that it is starting to seal up behind them. She widens her stance and lets out a growl as she lifts the sword. There is only a narrow margin between Hester and the creature. Hallie takes a breath, holds it, and then brings the sword down with all her might.

The creature gurgles a high-pitched scream through the bronze ooze as its hand flops down on the ground. Its fingers scurry it toward the wall opening until a large forked tongue curls out from the wall pulling it back in.

Hallie hands the sword back to Hester just as the sound of the closing wall is nearly at her back. She runs out at Hester's heels into the damp murky mist that continues on the other side of the wall. She stops and catches her breath while looking back to see the wall sealing. With a final hissing sound the finest hint of a crack seals itself, and a shiny line of bronze siphons back into the wall leaving no trace of the opening.

"Thank you for that, Hallie."

"You're welcome, Hester." Hallie leans her hands on her knees breathless as she stares disbelievingly at the wall. The side of a face frozen in an agonized expression stares back at her with its single bronzed eye moving about until it too becomes paralyzed by the hardening bronze. Hallie straightens stepping further away from the wall. The ooze of bronze that had coated her shoes and splashed her legs turns to a fine powder and floats to ground where she stands. She brushes away what remnants cling to her skin and turns to look out into the mist.

There are a few barren trees looming just beyond them. There is movement in the upper branches, and she squints trying to see more clearly. Hallie realizes that it is large vultures moving about, or at least something like vultures sitting atop the tree branches which hang low with the heaviness of misery and gloom.

Hallie looks further out seeing a brilliant orange glow coming off the horizon silhouetting the dismal trees and their inhabitants. She sees Hester holding her sword in a defensive stance looking about and moving forward between the trees towards the orange horizon. As Hallie follows, an intense heat swallows her and sizzles away the damp mist. Ahead of them is a flowing river of burning water with waves of flames lapping at the singed shore line.

Hallie startles when a large flat barge made of thick charred-black wood slowly moves around a bend in the river and into view. It floats by creaking as though it is under a great strain. Its hull is scorched, and the wood hisses as it slices through the tributary, but it does not burn. She can see a wispy image of hundreds of people sitting listlessly on board and totally unaware of her. The extremely crowded barge makes its passage without benefit of a crew. It floats by them, and Hallie cannot look away despite the horror it inspires. She gasps as the barge jostles and one of the people on the back of it falls limply to one side hanging precariously over the edge with no resistance before he plunges into the burning water. He bobs a moment turning charcoal black and disappears below the sizzling liquid's surface.

Hallie looks to Hester who is now standing near the bank of the flaming waters looking further upstream. She appears rippled through the heated air rising from the river with her hair and clothing fluttering behind her. Hallie is speechless from all she has seen, and now astounded by the image of the forlorn, but beautiful angel before her.

Hester looks back at Hallie. "They are Shades," she says this matter-of-factly with no sympathy for their lot.

Hallie looks at her blankly extremely aware of the heat from the river with the vapors blowing dryly at her skin as she walks closer to Hester. She hesitates keeping her distance from the shore line.

Hester moves towards Hallie relaxing her defensive posture lowering her sword to her side. "Shades." She nods at Hallie thinking her silence is because she did not hear her expecting understanding to come. She pauses in contemplation when it doesn't. "Shades are the shadows of what is left when the soul leaves the body of one who is not granted passage to heaven or anywhere else. The body decays eventually, and the soul is lost. There is no regeneration. The Shade maintains the image of what it once was, but not much else. It has no strength, and no action. A being from the other side—heaven, underworld, or even here in Tartarus—can conjure remnants of life and lure it into the Shade in order to use it for a variety of purposes, but the shade never regains its free will nor its own soul. Until they are needed, or finally fade away, they ride this endless river in Tartarus, the Phlegethon, on storage vessels like the one that just passed."

Hallie looks at Hester wearily feeling her lips chap and a sandpaper grit rub her eyes when she blinks. She looks down river as the barge disappears in the distance feeling sadness for its inhabitants. She turns back to Hester who is studying her.

"And…" Hallie's voice croaks. She stops, licks her lips with her dry tongue, and starts again. "And, what is Tartarus?"

Hester takes a look up and down the river. Two barges are approaching from opposite directions. They would have narrow passage as they meet each other. "I will explain later. We must cross now! I am going to hold you and make the leaps. The river cannot be crossed any other way. The danger of being consumed by its heat is too great. Even flying is not an option as no one can fly high enough for the whole crossing to avoid incineration."

Hallie looks at Hester fearfully, but Hester gives her a reassuring look. "Hallie, now! It may take longer than we are able to wait for two barges to cross here again!"

Hallie steps to the edge of the river next to Hester. Hester grasps her at the waist as the barge nearest them approaches, and they leap onto it making their way across the deck stepping between countless shades knocking several over but pushing on desperately to get to the other side before the second barge gets out of reach. She holds Hallie by the hand pulling her along. Hallie feels sick as they move across the barge and through the Shades. They sit in rows with blank looks on their faces—some with features still discernible others have faded to nearly nothing. The whole barge has an overwhelming feeling of desolation and it reeks. Hallie's nose burns with the sulfurous stench of brimstone. Even worse, Hallie feels like something is clinging to her legs trying to hold her back like the bronze blood from the Wall of Sorrows.

She slips losing her grip on Hester's hand falling forward between the rows of shades. She catches her breath and tries to get back up when she notices a cracked floor board with a hole in it. An eye stares up at her through the crack. It is the face of a human man! It's smudged with dirt and sweat but unmistakably human. He has a thin scar splitting his eye brow in two. Hallie sees the desperate look in his eyes. But before she can say or do anything, Hester grabs her arm and pulls her up.

Hallie resists trying to explain about the man, but Hester pulls her forward not hearing. She is focused on getting them safely to the other side of the river. The oncoming barge nearly passes before they reach it. Grasping Hallie by the waist, Hester leaps the ten foot span between the two barges. She slips on the edge but Hallie stretches out and grabs ahold of the side of the barge. She pulls them closer while Hester flaps her wings helping to bring them in the rest of the way. Her wing tips are scorched and smoking.

"That's twice now."

"You're welcome." She glances over her shoulder seeing the barge starting to pass the narrow passage of land, she turns racing to the other side. *No way am I getting stuck on this thing any longer than I have to be.* She jumps onto the edge and raises her arms as Hester makes a final leap grasping her waist and soaring to land solidly on the opposite side of the river.

"You are a quick study."

Hallie puffs air from her nose. "Not much choice around this place. She looks back at the barge where she saw the man. It is moving towards the bend in the river and, as it makes the turn floating out of sight, she sees that the back of the barge juts outward with a scorched carving of a woman stretching her arms and torso out over the river as though she is desperately trying to grasp for something lost. Hallie shudders.

They walk away from the river back into cool gray mist. There are no trees on this side. As they move further inland, Hallie feels a chill over her burnt and dry skin.

"There is someone else on that barge," she says.

Hester looks at her. "That is not possible. You are mistaken. So much has happened and confusion is to be expected. There are many tricks played in this place to try and keep one stuck within each of its tormented existences."

"I don't think so...I..." She rubs the sides of her arms doubting herself. "No, I don't think so." Her head throbs. "Well, perhaps...the wall, and even the barge, something was there like it was tugging me back...trying to slow me down. I just don't know. You may be right." She runs a hand through her hair. "Hester, may I rest a moment?" The place has siphoned her energy, and she cannot muster the strength to argue with the angel or walk another step.

Hester surveys a small perimeter before walking back. "Sit for a moment, Hallie."

She complies gratefully while Hester stands near. "Hester, what is this place and how…how does that happen?" She points down river towards a barge.

"Tartarus is the place below the underworld. It is the place of demon wars and the place of transition, and one can become entrapped here if not careful. You have already seen that, but it can happen anywhere once you step across the wall's boundary. All must pass through here before moving onto their next realm. It can be any of the realms beyond or, as in your case, another time within the mundane plane. The dead enter one way. The living, if they remain living, another—the way we have come; although, not many 'living' human beings ever pass through here. You are a rarity."

"I don't understand. I didn't go through this when I passed from 2018 to 1928."

"You did, you just do not recall it. You died and you…were pulled back through time where you were revived. It is not the same when you make the passage as a conscious flesh-barer, a living soul—at least not most of the time. It can be different depending on…one's genetics." Hester offers no further explanation.

Hallie isn't sure she understands, but nods her head anyway. "And the Shades? How does that happen?"

"Indifference." Hester says it with repugnance as though there is something distasteful in her mouth. She goes on, "They lived indifferent to their world and fellow beings. Their judgment and placement, therefore, is deferred indefinitely, and they exist as the shade of what was. Neither eternal suffering nor eternal joy is theirs. It is truly a fate worse than the most tortuous existence in the underworld."

"Are they aware?"

"Yes, aware and trapped."

Hallie looks back at the river, and at another barge as it moves morosely through the flaming waters. She thinks about the man staring up at her through the cracked floor plank. It had to have been a Tartarian trick to trap her. No one on that barge could be alive. She turns away looking in the opposite direction through the mist pulling herself together despite the weight of sadness that presses down on her. The thought of Liam and the hope of returning home to him gives her strength. "Where do we go from here?"

"The river Styx lies parallel to the Phlegethon in that direction. We need to follow it to the Axis Mundi where the head waters of the five rivers flow from the roots of the great Mesu. From there you can find a pathway to cross over."

Hallie looks at her for a moment having no clearer idea of their destination than she did before Hester answered her question. "We can't just cross the Styx for passage over?"

"It's not quite that simple. The Styx is a netherworld boundary. And crossing the Styx is not for passage into the mundane plain. It's a one-way route that not even all the dead are able to cross. They wait on the banks of the river until their destination is determined. They are then granted an obolus to pay Charon, the ferryman, who takes them across."

"You mean the ferryman like in Greek Mythology?"

"Yes of course. Legends and Myths are not merely figments of men's imagination. They have been embellished some through the generations, but there is much in universal lore that comes from a foundation of truth. It is evident in the similarity of the stories shared across civilizations by people of every culture. It is mankind that chooses to dissect what parts they wish to accept and not accept."

"Well, then what about the coins put in the mouth of the dead by their surviving relatives before burial, or the pyre, or whatever to pay Charon? Why can't one just pay with that?"

"Do you think an earthly coin would suffice? It may bring comfort to those left behind who practice the tradition, but the truth is that each must 'pay' for passage to the next destination based on how he or she lived life. The obolus is granted based on that judgment alone."

She does essentially understand what Hester is saying this time, yet it gives her no clarity on her situation, or the direction she needs to travel to find home. She decides that further inquiry will not tell her what she needs to know. A heavy sigh escapes her, "How about I just follow you?"

Hester actually smiles at Hallie. "Of course. I told you I was your guide. From here on out, however, it is imperative that you remain close, so that I may cloak your presence. It is hard to say who or what we may encounter until we find the roots of the great Mesu."

Hallie stands and brushes herself off. She is still very thirsty and dry, but regains some of her energy from the brief rest. "Thank you Hester. I will be like your shadow, and I *am* grateful that I have you here with me—truly."

Hester swallows with effort. "It is a pleasure Hallie. Being with you reminds me of pleasanter times." She nods cordially to Hallie unable to give any more acknowledgement for the sentiment than that. Turning, she leads the way across the dismal land.

Hallie has no idea how much time has passed. The walk seems endless, and they have not crossed paths with a single being that she is aware of, yet Hester remains vigilant. Her sword is sheathed but readily available should it be needed. Trees once again come into view. They too are barren, but their branches are wispy like the weeping willow by the flat rock. Despite their sharp contrast to the green beauty of the willow, the trees make Hallie think of lying on the rock looking up through the tree branches while feeling the warmth of the sun on her skin. It renews her hope to be able to return to it soon.

They come into the grove of trees, and Hallie can hear rushing water. The mist is still everywhere, but it thins enough that she can see further out. Along the horizon there are small rises in the ground. Hester draws her sword looking back briefly to assure Hallie is close. Hallie is not aware of any imminent danger but doesn't question Hester. They approach the hilly area and the flowing river beyond.

Hallie looks around. She stops short as the landscape comes into clearer focus. The hills are collections of bodies lying along the ground, naked, bruised, cut and contorted in some cases. Several are lying over others giving the illusion of small hills. She sees the ground start to shift and rise breaking apart, and the body of a woman rises up through the opening. Hallie grabs ahold of Hester's arm.

Hester speaks without stopping. "This is the collecting area of the Asphodel Fields. Most of the dead arrive here and remain until one from the legion of furies sorts through and brings them to the place of judgment and passage to their destination. It usually takes three days' time, but when the Demon King—the same demon you know—is absent, it becomes a slower process, and they accumulate here."

Hallie looks as they continue to walk holding tight to Hester's arm. They are now so close to the river bank that they pass near several bodies, and Hallie can see them more clearly. She realizes that not all are beaten or bruised, some look very peaceful as though they are lying in the meadow fast asleep. Beyond the bodies she can see the swift and powerful river flowing. Its width is too vast for her to see the opposite shore. The terrain is lusher near the water with thick grass and the star-shaped flowers the field is named for growing in clusters on tall stems.

They progress along the river's edge, and Hallie looks ahead stopping. Hester turns to look at her. Hallie's face contorts with a retching blaze of sorrow. Several yards ahead of them lay Daryl Lee Hobbs. He is lying prone, but his head is turned towards them, and she recognizes him. A few feet from him is Jeb and just beyond Jeb is Billy. He is lying on his back, his neck bruised with cuts on his face, and the scar on his arm is an angry red. She covers her mouth and, without thinking, releases Hester's arm to run to his side dropping to her knees. She reaches out to touch his face.

"Hallie! Do *not* touch him!" Hester shouts to her. "You have broken through the cloak and are now visible. You cannot help him. He must be left to complete his transformation and serve the Demon King until he is released to return to Earth."

Hallie looks up at Hester with tears spilling from her eyes. A sharp constriction in her chest cuts deeply into her sorrow, and she struggles to breathe.

Hester's face softens, and she holds out her hand. A silk cloth appears pouring onto the ground near Billy. Hallie reaches for the edge pulling it across his lower torso to cover him. She goes to reach for his hand.

"Do not touch him I said!" Hester warns sternly. "He maintains his flesh and soul here, but in order to survive he will transform to…to…something more like me. Something demon-like that will afford him some protection. He…he has some lethal attributes that may cause you harm."

Hallie looks up at her with eyes brimming and a quiver of her lip. Hester simply points the tip of her sword towards his scarred arm. The scar is bright red with three of the larger tentacles slithering along his arm snake-like. Hallie looks up at his face to see if he is aware but there is no response. She can see wounds healing and a silvery tattoo-like mark etching onto his left upper chest that she has never seen before. It forms three interlocking spirals that are spiraling outward from their centers until the intricate marks join to form a triskele.

"The mark on his chest is a protective mark. You can see it is silver and unlike the others starting to form which are black. Those dark ones are demon marks," Hester says softening her voice. "More will come as the transformation continues. The one on his arm, of course, is from the original curse, and he carries that with him always. The triskele on his chest is actually a gift from me to protect him in battle. It represents balance. I am glad to see it still is with him."

Hallie looks at her and back at Billy; although, he looks more like Liam with his hair hanging longer than she has seen it before. It definitely is closer in appearance to Liam's style than Billy's. Somehow his connection to Hester brings her comfort, and Hallie turns to ask her a question when a horrible shriek comes at them from nowhere.

"It is one of the furies," Hester says raising her sword. "She can see you now that you have broken the parameters of my cloak. Stay right there." Hester leaps forward hissing and cat-like to come between Hallie and the demon girl.

"What is she doing near the flesh-bearers?" The fury snarls.

Hallie looks at the fury legionnaire. She has long blonde hair and dark violet-blue eyes encircled with thick heavy lashes. The skin on the outer corners of her eyes extending towards her upper cheeks and temples is red giving the impression that blood is flowing from her eyes. She is fierce with dark wings, and a sword that she crashes down upon Hester's weapon.

Hester's petite build is no hindrance and, with a powerful assault, she pushes her opponent away advancing towards her in order to create distance from Hallie.

Billy stirs and Hallie turns her attention back to him. His wrists are now bound with leather bands as are his feet up towards his calves. The silk cloth is to the side and he has leather pants in its place. He is still unconscious. Hallie looks at him intently and then down at her amulet bag. She opens it removing the blue jay feather holding it up giving it a gentle twirl between her fingers. She looks down at the hand of his scarred arm. The three tentacles are now three red and black striped snakes bound by their tails at his wrist and writhing along his arm with their heads weaving back and forth at his elbow. They seem oblivious to Hallie. She feels no fear as she reaches down to place the feather in his hand.

His fingers curl enclosing her hand and the feather. The snakes move more restlessly along his arm raising their heads to now look at her intently. His arm lifts maintaining his grasp on her, and she watches in amazement as the flesh of her hand and lower arm glow intensely. She feels heat as a halo of flames ignite around his hand and fingers and the snakes weave around both their wrists binding them gently together. Hallie feels serenity, and the incredible warmth at her hand moves up her arm towards her heart. She looks back down at his face, and his eyes are open. She smiles sadly at him.

"Have I crossed to the Elysian plain of heaven?" he asks her.

"No, you are in Tartarus."

He nods, still a little groggy. "And, do I know you?"

Hallie pauses. "You did."

He looks at her and at their joined hands. "I am not sure that is safe for you, but I do not want to let go."

"It's okay, I don't want you to."

She watches as another demon mark comes to life carving a dark line of intricate patterns from the corner of his left eye along his cheek and towards his jaw. He seems unaware of everything except for Hallie. She gazes at him and is entranced by his beautiful dark eyes. They remain constant.

Hallie notices it has become silent and glances towards Hester and the fury legionnaire. They are standing mesmerized staring back at her and Billy.

Hallie turns to Billy. "I'm sorry. I have to go. I don't want to but, just for now, I have to go."

He gives a single nod of his head and looks at their joined hands. He loosens his grip. The three snakes unwrap themselves. Their tongues flicker in and out as they watch Hallie. The flame goes out, and the glow of her flesh dims. He lets go of her. The feather remains in his hand, and he looks at it curiously. Hallie looks at the feather and notices behind it, on the palm of his hand, there is a tiny hand print—silvery like the triskele on his chest.

Hallie reaches up with her fingers gently stroking the mark. It glows faintly under her touch. She moves her finger away and the glow subsides. Smiling, she turns to look at him. The serpents on his arm sway continuing to watch her intently. Hallie gently closes his fingers around the feather. She leans down and kisses him. One of her tears falls onto his cheek leaving a glistening path as it rolls down and out of view.

Hester blinks with her mouth agape. She looks back at the fury, and balls her fist striking the demon girl full force in the middle of her face knocking her out. Hallie catches it from the corner of her eye and turns towards Hester looking shocked for a moment. She shakes her head grateful Hester is on her side. The fury is flat on her back unmoving. Hallie turns to look back at Billy. He is once again unconscious, and the snakes continue writhing along his arm no longer paying attention to Hallie. She smiles and kisses her fingers and then presses them gently to his lips.

Hester walks up to her softly resting her hand on Hallie's shoulder. "You should not be alive right now. Those snakes are lethal."

"And, what would happen if someone died here in Tartarus?" Hallie keeps her eyes fixed on Billy.

"It is thought to be a death of death. There is no existence beyond that. None of any kind."

Hallie nods and looks away from Billy. She stands facing Hester. "I know he is safe until his life in 2018. After that none of us know. He cannot come back here after that." Determination echoes in her words.

Hester draws her lower lip in. Her eyes glisten, and she starts to say something, but Hallie walks past her resolutely refusing to acknowledge the solicitude offered to her. "I'm ready to go."

As Hallie approaches the fury she recognizes her. "Ivy," she says out loud. Hester looks at her curiously. "She's a frien…someone that I know. She is someone that Billy and Liam know."

"Yes," Hester says as she walks up next to Hallie. "She is one of the tethered souls in the Circle of Souls." She grasps Ivy by the wrist and begins walking away dragging the fury behind her. Hallie steps up next to Hester and looks questioningly at her.

"I do not think she will betray the boy to the demon, but I am not sure. At this point in time she does not know who you are, but she knows now that there is a connection between the two of you. This would be valuable information to the demon. He has an insatiable hunger for such things, and it would give him the upper hand where the boy is concerned."

"What are you going to do with her?"

"We are going to where the five rivers are born. I am going to force waters from the river Lethe down her throat." Her fierceness is tempered with a devilish grin that almost looks out of place on her angelic face.

"You're going to drown her?"

"No, simply make her drink. The waters of the Lethe induce amnesia. She will forget about you, and about what she has seen here. I will have to measure carefully what I give her. I don't want to obviate all her memories. There is still purpose there."

They walk for a while in the mist not encountering any threats. The air begins to cradle a spicy sweet smell that Hallie is not familiar with, but it makes her think of the woods in the spring as new foliage comes to life.

Just ahead she is able to discern a network of huge twisting cords. They are hanging down from above with a fleshy appearance. Many are embedded into the ground and when she looks up at their abundant expanse the flesh takes on more of a woody appearance, and she sees they are roots from a tree. *We must be at the Mesu.* Her heart leaps, and her step lightens with the thought of being near to home and Liam. They have been traversing the expanse of the Asphodel Meadows just far enough away from the bank of the Styx to not see any of the waiting dead but close enough to hear its flowing waters. Now, however, Hallie can hear the harmonic flowing, churning, and bubbling from more than just the Styx. They have come upon the head waters of the five rivers. The network of cords and roots become more dense and larger in diameter as they climb a gentle slope. They eventually come to a spring of flowing turbulent water.

"This is the beginning of the Styx, and over there," Hester points to a spring where the roots and cords are entwined around the opening of what looks like a cave. The water swirling from it moves slowly and listlessly making its way from the cavern within the roots and down a steep drop, "is the mouth of the Lethe. It flows from the Cavern Hypnos."

Hester lets go of Ivy's wrist and steps across the churning waters of the Styx towards the Lethe. She raises her hand up and a glass bottle appears. She uncorks it and dips it into the water filling it before returning to Hallie and Ivy.

Hallie looks all about them. The mist above them prevents her from seeing the full extent of the root system. Further away from them the Phlegethon erupts from the ground near a huge tangle of roots that are scorched and black. She steps through the cords next to her and looks down at a glassy still pool of the clearest water she has ever seen. There is a small canal where the water stands extending away from them beyond her view. She looks over at Hester who is working, actually quite gently, on getting the water into Ivy's mouth. She looks over at Hallie and the pool of water.

"That is the Acheron. Some say it is the river of pain, but it is actually the river of purification. It cleanses the soul. For most, it is a painful process—it depends on the life that has been led how painful the purging of past transgressions is."

Hallie looks back to the water. It looks as though it is glass instead of flowing water. She drops a flower petal into the water creating ripples with hundreds of tiny waves that persist picking up the intensity. Hallie panics looking over to Hester.

The angel enjoys Hallie's predicament, and lets it simmer before she reassures her. "You have not broken the river, Hallie. It is just that the waters do not know what to do with a pure spirit."

Hallie looks at her quizzically.

"All of God's creations have a spirit—even a flower's petal."

Hallie nods and relaxes when she sees the petal start to float downstream taking its wake of ripples with it. "I see four rivers. I thought there were five."

Hester finishes her task reserving a single drop of water in the bottle and corks it. She sets Ivy's head down before turning to Hallie. "Over there beyond that larger root." She uses her head to indicate the direction. "The river Cocytus flows from there. It is the river of lamentation, and it eventually merges with the river Acheron further down into Tartarus."

Hallie nods and walks back to Hester and Ivy. "Will she be okay?"

Hester picks up her sword. "Yes, I will come back for her once I get you through the Mesu." Stepping over a root, she walks through the network of the tree's entwined footing.

Hallie follows behind as they climb upward. Occasionally, she has to hang onto the thinner free-hanging roots to help with her ascent as the path steepens, and she is surprised by their warmth and the pulsing sensation they make. Her pupils dilate and she is intoxicated with the strange and wondrous beauty that surrounds them.

"Hester, is this the Tree of Life?"

"No, it is the Mesu, the place of the Axis Mundi, or center of the earth. It forms the connection between the otherworlds and your world. It is but a sapling of the Tree of Life. Mankind was closely connected to both in the beginning, but the Tree of Life and her daughter have been neglected over the generations. Even their ethereal presence has withered and died in the world above; however, their essence exists deep inside each person waiting to be nourished and given the ability to grow. There is always hope their gifts will be discovered once again. So many great prophets, men and women, over the course of time have tried to enlighten people. Sadly, it has yet to have a universal impact."

Hallie runs her hands along the cords and roots as they rise higher through the weave. They move into a channel surrounded on all sides by the tree. A muted glow filters around them, and Hallie can now hear the gentle pulsing as they move deeper into the tree. Thin cords still hang from above, there are pools of clear liquid in crevices within the walls from which the cords drink, and tiny brightly colored flowers grow near the crystalline pools. Hallie hears the bubbling sound of water flowing and walks over finding a small fountain with sparkling water bubbling up and flowing over the rim of a dish-like impression where it seems to disappear. She pokes her finger into it, and there is no ripple, and she wiggles her finger and still nothing. Withdrawing her finger she looks at it, and it's wet. Hallie bends down looking curiously at the water trying to see where it goes once it spills over the rim. Its champagne-like water reflects her weary and bruised face back at her. She gingerly touches her forehead.

"It is the sixth river of Tartarus, a secret underground waterway that is not known to many beings any longer. The water spills over the rim into a cavern forming the hidden river below. It is the Mnemosyne river, and the water from it, if drank, will give one complete memory of their past experiences. It gives the potential to attain omniscience. The ancients tried to use it in the past in an attempt to defeat the powers of the underworld. The Demon King conquered them ruthlessly, and he now forbids its waters to be consumed because he wants to be in charge of what is remembered and what is not. It is not even permitted to acknowledge its existence." Hester walks away moving further up the passage.

Hallie lingers a moment longer thinking she can see images floating up towards her, but before they come into focus she feels the shocking surge of panic when she realizes Hester is nearly out-of-sight. Hallie rushes to catch up. Darkened off shoots occasionally come into view as they walk along. Hallie's skin tingles with fascination as she passes Hester who has stopped to scoop refreshment from a crevice with a white shell that has appeared in her hand.

Hallie stops when the path in front of her darkens and an off shoot of the tunnel emits a faint glow. She looks curiously back at Hester.

"This is as far as I go Hallie. I have been honored to share this time with you."

Hallie turns taking the few steps back towards Hester. "Thank you Hester. I am so grateful to have had you with me. You know, we will meet again."

"No doubt, and when we do listen for my silent voice. For all intents and purposes I am technically in a two hundred year vow-of-silence." Reminds Hester with a twist of her lip. "Here, you must be parched, and this will sustain you for the last leg of your journey."

Hallie gratefully takes the shell and pauses. "Do I have long to go?"

Hester shakes her head.

Hallie raises the shell to her lips and drinks. Her thirst vanishes with a refreshing cool sensation taking its place as she finishes the last bit of the Mesu's nectar.

Hester takes the shell and points. "Walk down the path. You may have a strange sensation as you cross over. Do not turn back. It is a one way passage only."

Hallie starts tentatively down the pathway. She bids farewell to Hester whose image fades as the glow behind her dims. Hallie continues down the path feeling very light. Her heart flutters and her throat tightens with panic rising from her chest towards her neck but, before she can react, the ground beneath her disappears, and she drops swiftly into nothing.

§

Odina and Azure are startled when Hallie appears on the floor in the center of their circle. Azure had just finished closing the circle as Odina ignited the ingredients Hester had told them to gather. Odina looks through the smoke that wafts up from the stone mortar and sets the pestle aside onto the floor seeing Hester through the smoky haze.

"Has she arrived?" Hester's voice chimes through the swirling smoke.

"Aye, she is here and seems ta be in one piece. She is unconscious."

"I gave her a drop of water from the Lethe. She needs some time to heal before she has to think about what she has seen here. It shouldn't affect her memory for very long, but she may be a little confused and disoriented for a while. The bump on her head is a good explanation to give to her for the condition."

"We will take care of her."

"Do you know if he is there?"

"We think that he is but cannot be sure. Much time has passed since I last saw him, and he was of a different sort at tha time."

Hester nods. "They have a connection that I cannot explain. If he is there, they will find each other. You must allow the choices that lay ahead be known, but how to act upon them up to Hallie and him. Do not interfere—no matter the difficulty you may feel with this."

"As you wish Hester. Ta be sure it will be done."

The smoke begins to dissipate as Hester's image fades.

Odina looks at Azure, and they bend down to attend to Hallie.

Hester steps out of the Mesu walking back down the network of roots to the head waters of the Lethe. She looks around. The blond fury is gone. There is a muddle of foot prints where she had left her. Hester circles the area raising her sword defensively while her nerves twitch with anticipation. She looks more carefully following the footsteps back up the network of roots towards the channel of the Mesu tree. They are too large to be the fury's. Hester sighs and turns to start back towards the Styx when another set of tracks catches her attention. She follows them with her eyes seeing that they meet up with the first set of tracks closer to the Mesu. There does not seem to have been a struggle. The second must have come up later following the first. Both sets of tracks eventually disappear within the tree's channel.

She ponders the meaning of this realizing that the fury must have been carried into the Mesu and then followed by another. Hester gathers that at least one, and perhaps two beings from the underworld, have used the fury's humanity to cross over to the mundane world. This is not good, and she feels a shudder of dread. She should not have left the fury unattended, but it's beyond her power to rectify. She hates her role in all of this cursing the day that she stole the keys and leapt from the heavens. She allows the shudder to pass, and sheaths her sword before beginning the journey back to await the demon's inescapable call.

The story continues with Secrets of Time…
First two chapters

Chapter 1—Tartarus

The chain binding the demon conquests rattles with Jeb tugging to urge them forward. Blood melds with rust as the cuffs twist with each conquest's step and swing of the iron links. Billy glances over at the group they are escorting and imagines seeing their souls cascade into the dismal mist of Tartarus creating a hiss from cold indifference meeting fiery retribution.

He feels a jolt as though a cold hand has grabbed him. "Missus Pennymaker," he whispers her name. She brings up the end of the line of conquests, and she turns her hollow eyes towards him but says nothing. *What bargain could have snatched her soul?* He runs his hand through his hair and takes a step back.

The judged souls follow the conquests. Some twitchy like caged birds, others with mouths agape as though caught in a Ripley's Believe It or Not side show, and a few bold souls don masks of self-righteousness. Billy clears his throat and sadly shakes his head. It won't be long before the waxy sanctimonious expressions melt as they near the blazing pits throughout the underworld.

"Charon, what has you disgruntled today?" Billy's thoughts are distracted as Jeb teases the ferryman.

Luke flashes a quick grin Billy's way.

"Ach, you three back again. That in itself is enough to sour my mood." Charon grabs their coins jerking his head to signal for them to move to the front of the ferry. Luke and Billy take seats by Jeb resting their arms atop the hilts of their swords. Billy's three serpent companions twist around his arm and dose.

The chained souls start to sit on the deck and are quickly yanked to attention by Jeb. "You will be standing for the crossing. Move in closer to make room for the rest."

The iron cuffs glisten crimson and Billy's eye gives a quick twitch. He turns his head with furrowed brow catching Jeb's eye.

Jeb's throat coughs up an imaginary insect. "They all make me sick. Especially that murdering Daryl Lee. Best to let them get used to what lays ahead of them with eternal repayment for whatever deals they made with the Demon King."

Thinking of Daryl Lee's brutal act towards Mister Hairston, Billy raises an eyebrow shrugging. "As if standing on this excuse of a boat is anything like what lays ahead for them."

Faces fall and then a few of the chained passengers actually fall over as Charon burst through knocking into them. He stops short by Billy. "You. What name would you be goin' by this time 'round?"

He sees the crotchety old demon through the hair hanging over his face. Now that he is finally sitting, it is as if he had never done so before, and to have to move even a bit is torment. Aside from this aching fatigue, he is plagued with frustration to find himself back in Tartarus once again. And, this journey is haunted by the image of a beautiful young woman who he feels he knows but just cannot remember how.

"I asked a question flesh-barer." Spittle sprays from between sharp black teeth.

"Billy." He responds with a thickened voice.

"Well, you watch what you say 'bout my ship Billy." More spittle. "She has served to carry yar sorry excuse for an existence 'nough times asn't she?"

"Yes, Charon. What was I thinking? It is a fine craft. Very fine."

Charon's chest puffs out a bit. He gives a you-betacha nod of the head and stomps off mumbling under his breath sending more demon conquests brutally flat onto the deck.

Billy shakes his head before resting it on his arm. This will be his last opportunity for peace, and he chooses not to have it disrupted by arguing with the cantankerous Charon. His companions chuckle, and he looks up at them in disdain. "Jeb, Luke do not aggravate the old demon. He has a miserable existence as ferryman considering he once ruled Tartarus."

"Yes, we know you are right about this. Right Jeb?" Luke amiably agrees.

Jeb just snickers and reluctantly nods his agreement before shouting at the fallen conquests to stand back up while jerking on the chain.

Billy pulls a small blue feather from his waist strap spinning it between his fingers. He found it after awakening along the shore of the Styx. Although the memories of his lives on Earth are always somewhat cloudy after a transition, the blue jay feather is a memorable symbol of pending departure with the hope of return that he clearly recalls. Never has one presented itself to him in the underworld. Why would one? It is a plain feather though—unlike the ones on Earth that have a delicate ribbon tied to them. Laying it against the hilt of his sword he secures the feather with leather cording. He spies Luke watching him. A flush of heat brings color to his cheeks, and he quickly diverts his eyes.

Suddenly, raucous screeching from above cuts through the air as dark creatures start veering towards them. The three humans look at one another without alarm, but the remaining occupants squirm with apprehension. Luke and Jeb casually look down the rows of the judged souls laying lots against who is to be taken.

The creatures drop down, and each grab the shoulders of a judged soul violently flapping its wings tugging viciously. Those near the victims cower like frightened children leaning as far away as they possibly can. The birds shake their chosen targets until an iridescent image of the person is torn away trapped by the lethal talons screaming and kicking. The beasts fly away with their prizes filling the air with victorious caws. Remaining behind is a shaded view of the person who was taken—blank-faced with terror reflecting in the eyes.

The remaining passengers are reluctant to return to their former positions warily looking up towards the murky sky.

Charon, who has been leaning casually against the tiller, suddenly stands straight taking on a look of demon authority mixed with cruise ship cordiality. "Aye, thar now. Thems just the gargoyles of Tartarus laying claim on tha Shades. A tasty treat for thar young. Twern't no random act, and tha rest of you lot 'ave nothing else to fear while aboard my ship. Take yer seats and settle down. Tha trip be near done now." Charon settles back to steering the ferry and the boat's occupants reluctantly reclaim their original positions.

An exchange of arm punches occur between Jeb and Luke. Billy cannot help but reveal a thin smile. Such is the way of existence in Tartarus. He looks ahead seeing the ferry has reached the opposite shore. The chained passengers are led off the vessel by Jeb into the mist that hangs heavy throughout the land. All of the judged souls follow and make their way to the shoreline where they meet with their guides and slowly disappear from view. The newly formed shades remain sitting listless in their seats, and will be transferred to barges on the Phlegethon.

Charon moves to close the ferry's ramp as the last of the passengers step off. Billy rises preparing to leave as well. He is holding his sword over his shoulder while the three asps on his arm awaken and sway with their tongues twitching in and out.

"Ahoy thar, scab." Charon growls at him.

Billy stops to look at the old demon.

"Until the next time then?"

Billy nods and starts to move off the ferry.

"You know." Charon reaches up and rubs the back of his scaly neck turning it to noisily release a kink.

Billy stops again to look at Charon.

"Before I was thwarted from my throne I lived up on that hill where you be headed."

"Yes, I have been told this. You were a most formidable lord they say."

A prideful nostalgia lights the demon's face. "That I was, and yet this is what I 'ave been reduced to. Memory can be both curse and blessing."

Billy nods in agreement.

"I have found within tha monotony of my current existence a certain advantage transporting both tha doomed and blessed to their next destination. I 'ave more knowledge of tha souls who pass by me now than I ever did as lord and master. Paimon, our current demon king," his voice snarls with this acknowledgement, "is too busy finding new conquests and adding to his collection of human trinkets to take interest in the humdrum crossings of judged souls. Only I have full understanding of the general make up of Tartarus' inhabitants."

"Yes, Charon, I can see the advantage with your situation." Billy maintains a stiff cordiality unsure why Charon has now spoken more words to him than in any other time they have crossed paths.

"In all yar crossings, flesh-barer, no despondency has ever emanated from your soul. Thar has been a change to all that with this crossing. You are dragging it behind yerself to be sure, an it needs to be dealt with before tha Demon King becomes aware and uses it to his benefit. I canna have that." Charon rubs his chin with a crooked finger eyeing Billy.

Yes, it would seem this conversation is leading to something. But, what? Billy keeps his cards close.

"I remember up thar on tha hill, behind tha dwelling of tha Demon King, thar grows a pomegranate tree."

Billy looks at him curiously, and nods knowing the tree he speaks of.

"It be Persephone's tree. It be said that tha seeded fruit of that tree—when eaten—creates a passage back to tha great Mesu and realms beyond."

Billy looks at him comprehending fully what is being said. The Tartarian mist slowly swirls around them as though understanding the conspirators' conversation and, sympathizing with them somehow, draws near affording them a shroud of protection from prying eyes and ears.

"No debt payment, no demon wars to battle, no sacrifice of self and blood to the whims of the lustful sirens and thirsty lamia." Charon steps closer to Billy. The asps raise their heads poised to strike. The ferryman glances their way before peering into Billy's eyes.

Yes indeed, I want this. Do not let it show, Billy begs of himself. No demon can be trusted.

"Of course," Charon slides into his finale. "If one were to return to Tartarus after such treachery the suffering would be great. Perhaps so great that not even the blessin' of a fallen angel, not bathin' in the waters of the mighty Styx, and not a band of tethered comrades would prevent a death of death."

"What payment Charon?" *Keep your emotions in check.*

"Perhaps something later. For now, just enjoyment for me. Enjoyment watching tha Demon King lose his bridge to Earth." A sharp-tooth grin spreads wide on his face. "One way or another. For any amount of time. Brief or permanent."

Billy gives a curt nod before stepping off the ferry into the water. He stops turning back, but the misty shroud has wrapped around the ferry and demon pulling them away from the shore and Billy's view. He makes his traditional dive beneath the surface of the Styx still hopeful of some protection from mortal harm before making his way across the rocky terrain to catch up to Luke. His walk is distracted by Charon's words.

"What is on your mind?" Luke is waiting for Billy while Jeb has moved on to get the conquests to the Demon King's dwelling.

He tells Luke what Charon said. "If this is something I decide to risk, I want you and Jeb to consider it as well. If we left of our own accord, we would not be forced to drink the water from the Lethe. If we cross on our own accord, our memories will not be tampered with. We will have strength in unity during the next life and perhaps find a way to break the curse."

"Yes, that is a possibility." Luke speaks slowly and almost as though asking a question. He takes a deep breath and exhales slowly. "But I cannot leave here until Sadie returns. She was able to escape this place for the moment. I want her to have her life on Earth. She deserves it. I do not want to go back without her though. What if we beat him, break the curse, and it is our final life to live? To live completely? We do not know if the other tethered souls will be freed and, if they are, we will not know if we can ever find them. We all need to be together before taking the risk of conquering him. I do not want that without her."

"You are right of course. I was not thinking clearly about your situation. We will stay until Sadie returns and then give it consideration."

"No, you misunderstand me. *I* cannot leave but *you* certainly can. I think you should. There has been a change in you. I can see it, and I think there is something else you are meant to do. Not here—on Earth. If you return to Tartarus after that, we will deal with the Demon King's wrath as we always have in the past."

"If I were to go now, I will have to return later and bring together the remaining circle before we can make a final stand. There will be significant consequences, if I defy the Demon King in such a way—perhaps even a death of death." He pauses forcing himself to suppress a shudder. "I have much to consider."

"Perhaps," Luke says tentatively. "However, I sense the decision is made."

"Perhaps."

They remain silent until they reach the crest of the hill where their destination lays before them. They see Jeb leading the conquests to an entrance at the bowels of the abode while Luke and Billy walk around to a side entrance. The sentry is a pair of monkey-like creatures who are separate beings but who function as one.

"Cercopes, what a pleasure to see you again." Luke bends forward in mock reverence.

There is no verbal response, but Cercopes on the left tilts the handle of its spear ever-so-slightly tripping Luke as he passes. The pair briskly return to a statue-like stance with set faces.

Luke shoots them a threatening look.

Billy closes his eyes and shakes his head walking past the sentry without a word.

They step into an entryway that is gleaming in torch light. The walls are white and the floor a brilliant red. In the center is a gold inlayed black lacquer table with a lit candelabrum and bowls of fresh fruit, nuts, and other refreshments. Luke and Billy know from previous experience that the food is unobtainable. One can reach for, and even grasp the desired item, but once it is lifted from the platter it becomes vaporous and disappears. They stand by the doorway waiting while ignoring the table and its elusive treasure.

A rectangle of wall opens inward, and a conquest in an ill-fitting butler suit lumbers into the entryway holding his head at a strange forward-tilted angle. He motions for Luke and Billy. They sheath their swords, and step through the passageway into a large room. The space is exquisitely decorated from the 1920's era with several collectibles and furniture tastefully arranged.

The boundaries of the curse allow Paimon free passage to Earth only during Billy's life times. Since Paimon's lust for mortal collectibles can only be satisfied periodically by the bridge Billy's humanity creates, he wastes no time in updating his home with décor obtained through trickery, thievery, and the occasional bargain.

Billy looks around the room. A demon with blue-black skin is lounging on a settee. She appears nearly human except for the unusual color of her skin and two small horns protruding from her upper forehead. She wears a slinky flapper-style evening dress and is lazily fanning herself. She eyes Billy and Luke as they walk across the room towards a lavish desk. Behind the desk is a huge window that spans from ceiling to floor and the entire length of the wall. Paimon is sitting at the desk talking with a lamia who still has blood at the corner of her mouth from her last meal. Desire's twitch flicks at her lips when Billy and Luke approach, but she follows Paimon's suit and does not overtly acknowledge the two humans. A strange bird-like creature sitting on a perch near the desk, however, shows great interest in the pair staring at them while bobbing its head back and forth. It croons coarsely as it moves, and Billy cannot help but feel they are being sized up for a meal.

He looks beyond the desk and demons through the glass wall to the garden outside. It is the only place in Tartarus that hints of sunshine. The ground gently slopes away from the dwelling, and at its center grows Persephone's pomegranate tree burdened with fruit. Billy stares at it, his jaw set, as he waits to be called up to the desk.

The lamia eventually bows and backs away from Paimon for several feet before turning and disappearing from the room. He sorts through some items on the desk, and reaches for a cup holding it up several seconds before looking up and bellowing, "Smyth!"

The awkward butler moves forward from the back of the room bumping into a pedestal nearly knocking a statue off of it. Recovering the piece, he places it gingerly back on its perch. Paimon rolls his eyes and waits impatiently for him to approach. Smyth stands dull-eyed shifting his weight from foot to foot until Paimon waves the cup emphatically.

"It's empty, Smyth. Why am I waiting?" He snarls like a rabid dog.

Smyth reaches for the cup and a thick black substance begins soaking into the collar of his shirt.

"Damned cursed wounds. They never heal. Blood everywhere." Paimon jumps up from his desk looking over it at the floor.

Billy glances down seeing a few dark drops on the elaborate rug. He quickly moves his eyes up as Paimon walks out of the room in search of a conquest to take his fury out on. Smyth gropes at his throat and sulks his way back to his corner of the room.

The pomegranate tree seems to have a spot light on it drawing Billy's attention once more. Charon's words echo in his mind. There is a flash of the young woman's face that he had woken up thinking about in the Asphodel Meadow, hazel eyes, a soft curl to her auburn hair, and a sad smile. He even catches a light scent of warm vanilla. Then there are several different flashes in rapid succession of her, and he realizes that he knows her outside of Tartarus, and that she is someone important. His pulse explodes against his neck, and a swirl of heat steals his breathe away.

He looks around. Sweat rolls down the side of his face. Eurynomus, the blue-black demon, remains reclining and now studying her nails. The bird creature is sleeping. Luke is standing next to him, and the drops of Smyth's black blood remain on the carpet. Billy's nerves take on a twitch matching the slow ticking of a clock on the wall that doesn't keep meaningful time since time in the underworld is irrelevant.

He blinks focusing on the memory of the girl and remembers her name is Hallie, and he loves her. There is a flash of a kiss, lingering, sweet, and powerful. He feels an inferno that is ignited even with just the memory of her. Finally, he also remembers she was there at the edge of darkness when the Paimon came to Fayerdale to complete the harvest. Billy's throat suddenly constricts, and the next memory is of incredible pain and then nothing. He has no idea what happened to her, but he is certain that she was in Tartarus before he crossed the Styx. He draws his sword holding it up and stares at the blue jay feather he fixed to the hilt. His red and black serpent companions weave their heads also studying the feather.

He remembers Hallie has a journey to make, but he can't remember where. He does know that if she passed through Tartarus, she would have had to go to the great Mesu to leave the underworld. The Mesu is the only way one can pass to the mundane plain. How could she have known how to get into Tartarus as a living soul and traverse its territory safely?

Luke looks over at Billy. "How long is he going to have us stand here?"

Billy doesn't reply. Instead he studies the tree in the garden a moment longer.

Luke follows his gaze through the glass wall out into the garden and releases a deep and heavy sigh before speaking again. "I'm sure it will not be too much longer. He is trying to make a point by making us stand here before telling us what our task for this stay is. Wouldn't you imagine?"

Billy still doesn't reply. He walks around the desk, past the sleeping bird creature, and up to the glass wall. He taps it with a fingertip.

Luke watches him closely pulling his sword from its sheath obviously anticipating what is coming next. "Of course," he says drawly, as he surveys the room. None of its inhabitants are giving either human any consideration. "Someone could get his attention somehow and shorten our wait." His muscles tense as he continues to watch Billy. He adjusts his grip on his sword.

Billy sees all his friend's preparation from the corner of his eye, but he says nothing. For a moment, Luke's grip relaxes. Billy looks back and flashes a penitent smile to his friend. "I have to go, Luke."

"I know."

"Will you explain to Jeb? Apologize for me?"

"Yes, of course. He will understand. Hell, he will probably find a way to make it entertaining. Do not worry about us. Go."

Billy gives a quick nod and turns to the glass wall drawing back his sword swinging forcefully like a baseball bat. The glass wall quivers before a network of cracks form from the point of impact shattering glass onto the floor and out into the garden in thousands of shards. They rain down over Billy who is completely oblivious of the nicks in his skin. The bird creature squawks and flies to another part of the room.

"Damn, Billy that made a mess." Luke's voice slides with thick sarcasm.

Eurynomus runs from the room and collides into a conquest from the scullery that just arrived carrying Paimon's full glass on a tray. The tray and glass crash to the floor, and the conquest stands trembling with eyes bulging.

"Billy you need to go now. I will cover you. It will only be moments before he returns."

They run through the fractured glass wall with swords at the ready and race to the tree.

Paimon steps through the broken glass wall into the garden moments later and lets out a tremendous roar. Demons of all sorts begin spilling over the garden wall.

"Billy get a piece of the fruit. Be quick about it," Luke yells out as they reach the tree.

Billy swings the sword upward cutting fruit from the tree and catches one in his hand. The first swarm of demons is quickly approaching. "Luke, come with me," he shouts over the bedlam of demon war cries.

"No, open it and eat the seeds." Luke strikes down the first demon to reach them. "Do it now!"

Billy tears open the fruit and pulls a cluster of red seeds from it pushing them into his mouth. They burst with a bitter sweetness as he bites down. He sees Luke turn taking down two more demons easily. Billy raises his sword fatally striking a keres demon and turns to take down another just as he starts to dissipate. There is a melting sensation and then a brutal yank upward. His thoughts spin and then suddenly it all stops, and he is standing at the roots of the Mesu.

His chest sears with pain and panicked concern for Luke's safety. *What have I done?* He paces haphazardly over the roots berating himself for leaving Luke behind. He catches site of the feather on his sword and stops short. He pinches his lip and forces slower more purposeful breaths reminding himself how extremely capable Luke is and, if all else fails, he knows his friend will signal a surrender. He finds the three asps swaying and studying him intently as though asking, "Are you quite done now? Then let's get on with it."

He nods without thinking and starts the trek over the twisting roots ducking to avoid the fleshy cords hanging down from above. He surveys the area feeling satisfied he is alone, and begins looking for the head waters of the five rivers. The glassy Acheron comes into view, and he strips down kneeling by its edge. He dips his hands in to cleanse himself. Although he has not been in Tartarus long, he feels a need to purge himself of its evil residue before entering the sacred Mesu.

The water remains motionless when his hands dip through the surface. He splashes his face quivering for a moment as the sharp pain of remorse courses through his body. His breath hitches as he forces himself to plunge his head into the waters allowing the purge to cleanse his soul. He pulls his head up and back flinging the water against the surrounding roots. The droplets quiver a straight path back to the river. The water from his skin and hair do the same taking his tribulations with it. He is dry and his heart is light for the moment.

He dresses and walks towards the tree's entrance where a soft glow welcomes him as he steps inside. The gentle pulsing of the Mesu's heart matches the wax and wane of the glowing light. He walks through the tree's core where nectar collects in crevices and small delicate flowers grow along the path. A portal to his right illuminates with a golden glow, and he steps into it. As he walks, the asps on his arm calm and lay against his flesh turning back into wiry scar tissue. The demon marks fade as do the protective marks.

His leather gear transforms into jeans and a white t-shirt and pair of black boots. His hair shortens slightly and is brushed back away from his face with pomade. Only couple strands hanging over his brow. A flutter captures his heart and a sudden weightlessness strikes when the ground drops from under him. There is a rushing plunge downward and then nothing.

Chapter 2—Ferrum

Rubbing the back of his stiff neck the newcomer steps off the train looking back and forth unsure of which direction to go until a large red metal box with "Coca-Cola" written on the front catches his eye. It is sitting next to a service station, and his curiosity pushes him to venture across the road to check it out. He remembers, in Fayerdale, the Pennymaker's used to keep bottled Coca-Cola in an icebox at their store, and suddenly thirst grasps ahold as he stares at the shiny nemesis before him trying to figure out how it works. Vending machines had not found their way to Fayerdale in 1928. Besides, yesterday's memories are now decades away.

"Hello there young man. Can I help you with something?" A middle-aged man wiping grease from his hands with a shop rag walks up.

"Yes sir. I was interested in getting a drink."

The man looks at him for a moment, and then his brows jump upward, and his face lights up seeming to realize that the young man doesn't understand the workings of the Vendo V-81 standing before them. He clears his throat. "Well son, you put a dime into that slot right there, the door releases, you open it, and take a bottle out."

The newcomer fumbles at the pockets of his blue jeans finding a wallet in his back pocket, but no coins. He opens the wallet staring down at the edge of a driver's license and slides it up reading: H.

William White, brown hair, brown eyes, 6' 0"", and 165 lbs. He slides it back in place and looks into the billfold finding a five dollar bill minted 1958, but not a single dime. Shifting his weight, he starts to ask about getting change when the man withdraws a dime from his own pocket and drops it into the slot retrieving an icy cold bottle of Coke. He pops the top off with the bottle opener on the door and hands it to the stranger.

"Thank you sir." He takes a long pull off the bottle drinking it about half empty letting the cool refreshment revive him. He holds the bottle out admiring it for the simple pleasure it holds.

"You new in town then?"

"Yes sir." He stretches out his hand. "Will White. It is a pleasure to meet you."

The man shakes his hand firmly. "Cleo Adkins. Welcome to Ferrum, Virginia son."

Will thinks back on that day realizing that the Coca-Cola machine was a beacon. Cleo Adkins' amusement with his befuddlement sparked conversation, and he took a liking to Will immediately. He offered both employment and a place to stay in a small studio apartment located off the back of the garage that very day. The job seems to suit Will's needs fine, and the apartment is the right price, no-charge.

Eventually, his   memories came back triggered by small incidences during the day—laughter between friends, hushed discussion about a nearby still operation, the smell of fresh-baked bread, or a gentle breeze with the spicy scent of the woods. All reminding him of past lives. The time he spent in the underworld of Tartarus have needed no gentle reminders. Those memories invade his sleep in the form of nightmares often waking him drenched in sweat.

He looks over at his bed where his Book of Lineages lays. He retrieved it some weeks after arriving along with his other things near the old iron mine even though the town of Fayerdale, where he lived in 1928, no longer exists. When he learned the land was turned into a recreational area called Fairy Stone State Park he lost his appetite, but not his focus. He hitched a ride to the park, and dug through the dirt with his bare hands. His stomach maintained a tight knot until his first glimpse of the sheepskin covering the box with the Book of Lineages. He resurrected it from its grave rifling through the pages to see the status of the Circle of Souls.

A lump in his throat was hard to swallow when he saw Sadie's unbroken line up through 1958. She escaped their previous harvest, and is still alive today. It won't be too much longer before their paths will cross. No one survives him twice. She most likely went to Washington, D. C. with her Aunt Tessie as this was the plan that last night in Fayerdale. He was shocked to see Maybelle's line had also moved forward with a new life as Connie Sealy starting in 1954. Until he retrieved the Book of Lineages, he thought it was just him and Sadie in this life. How had Maybelle crossed over from the underworld? After all, his own departure was in defiance of Paimon and without the required ceremony at the Mesu.

It was a few weeks after finding the book that their paths crossed.

"Well, hello there." She greeted him cheerfully when he walked into the Snip 'n Style salon gracelessly bumping into the manicure tray toppling bottles of polish over.

"Oh, I apologize." He set down the box he had and began picking the bottles up off the floor.

She paused from rolling pink plastic curlers onto the head of a freckled-face girl named Beezie who blushed candy apple red at his appearance in the shop. The women under the hair dryers smiled discretely enjoying his uneasiness with the situation.

The last of the polish was returned to the tray. "Uh, Mister Adkins sent me over with this package. He said to tell you it was left at the garage by accident." He lifted the box up for her to see.

"Well, that's where my hair supplies have been." She secured the final curler to Beezie's head and walked over to take the box from him. She looked to be in her mid-twenties. He hasn't known her to be this much older than him since their original lives. She had on a pair of black capris and a pink sweater with a pearl pin worn over her heart.

He searched her eyes for a moment but saw no recognition in them. It would have made no difference. She would not be an ally anyway. She barely has tolerated him ever since the loss of two souls from the circle—one being his cousin, the man she loved.

She looked at him a moment waiting for him to say something and laughed a little. "I can take that hon. Unless it's heavy, and then you can just set it over there in the back corner."

He snapped back from his thoughts. "I have it."

He set the box down and cleared his throat before making his way back to the front. Every eye in the salon followed him, and the tingling sensation that swept across his face was foreign, He didn't like it.

"Well, thanks." She said delaying his escape. "Say, what's your name any way?"

"Will. It is William White, but you can call me Will."

"Gotcha. Nice to meet you Will. I'm Connie Sealy. You tell Cleo I said thanks for sending that on over now."

"Yes, Miss I will." He reached for the door opening it to a pair of girls heading into the shop that were startled by him. There was a shuffling of positions as he cleared the way for them, and then he gratefully won his freedom from the shop. It was reminiscent of passing through one of the many gates of hell into a new realm.

There was a burst of giggles coming from inside, and a couple women fanned themselves in a mocked fervor generated by his presence. The door shut with a clang silencing the shop banter and he promised, "I must remember never to cross that threshold again during business hours."

Connie's presence in town was not the only surprise there was for Will. He also found a pressed copper piece, a refashioned penny, one night inside the Book of Lineages with the image of a structure and its name, the Chesapeake Bay Bridge-Tunnel, embossed onto the surface. With some research at the Ferrum College library, he learned the structure was non-existent, but plans were in place to build it in order to replace the ferry system being used to bring vehicles across the Chesapeake Bay at Virginia's Eastern Shore. On the flip side "HSO" and "2018" were etched into the copper.

Although he doesn't recall seeing the piece before, it is strangely familiar to him. His memories upon return to Earth can be muddled for quite some time even without the waters from the Lethe, and he tries to be patient hoping all will return. Will's mind shuffles through these events from the past several months like a juke box selecting the next 45 record to play while he finishes dressing.

He puts the pressed penny in his pocket, as he has done every day since finding it, and leaves his apartment. It is a work day, but not too many in town are going to work this morning. There is a funeral to attend. Pauline McCaffrey is dead. She was a pillar in town—known, respected, and liked by all. Will only knew her a short time, but he quickly realized that there are not many people he has come across like her. He knew her through the garage. Although her son, Dillon, usually brought her vehicles in for service there was occasion when Missus McCaffrey came into the shop herself. She was somewhere in her fifties and had survived her husband and then a daughter who died as a teenager. Dillon was her youngest child and in his twenties. He worshiped the ground his mother walked on, and Will wonders how he is holding up.

After the church and grave-side service there is to be a picnic at the McCaffrey home. The First Baptist Women's Auxiliary organized it all, and it promises to be worthy of Missus McCaffrey's memory. Nearly all the merchants, including Adkins Garage, decided to close for the morning to honor the memory of this highly-respected woman.

Will has on a pair of black trousers with a short-sleeved shirt. He doesn't own a tie, and these are his best clothes, so they will have to do. He smooths the front of his shirt while walking over to the '77 Restaurant to get some breakfast before heading to Mister Adkins' house where he is going to get a ride to First Baptist.

He steps into the bustling restaurant taking a seat at the counter. There are several customers sitting at booths and more at the counter. A few look up and give him a greeting or nod of the head.

The waitress, Sally, comes over and sets a glass of milk in front of him. "Well, morning sugar. You gonna have your usual?" Her voice is as sweet as the maple syrup they serve for pancakes.

"Yes ma'am, thank you." Will takes a long drink of the ice-cold milk. Sally puts his order in at the kitchen and comes back with the milk pitcher to refill his glass. He thanks her again and reaches over to get a section of newspaper that was left by a previous customer.

There is a picture of a young girl from Patrick County that has been missing for the past few weeks. Her body was recently found and there is a brief account of the circumstances surrounding her disappearance with limited detail concerning the murder. There are no suspects, but there is speculation that it was done by a serial killer. There was another young girl of similar appearance that was killed in a similar manner not too long ago. A single pearl was found at each crime scene. Will studies the picture of the pretty blonde girl. She had been sixteen years old.

The front door of the restaurant opens and closes and one of the customers in a nearby booth hops up from his seat hurrying towards the door. "Azure, I'm glad you came in hera. I'm needing ta talk to you about my cow. That sista 'o yourn done swore a spell on my Bessie and threatened ta dry up her milk. I dinna think nothin' ov it, but then yesterday we got barely half a what she's normally bin producin'. I need you ta do somethin' bout it dag gonnit." He swipes away a bit of spittle that has gathered at the corner of his mouth.

Will watches with interest. Azure Ridge and his sister, Odina, are rumored to practice witchcraft, and there is a lot of concern and superstition generated by this general thinking. Will doesn't know Odina too well. She tends to keep to herself only coming into town when there is a need; however, he has done some odd jobs for Azure around their farm and knows him fairly well. Will can hear Azure's deep velvety voice provide reassurance to the man that he will see what he can do, but it is a difficult task, and will require a dozen brown eggs to reverse a hex that seems to have taken effect so quickly. Will smiles to himself and starts to go back to his newspaper when he notices that Azure is not alone.

A girl about Will's age is standing next to him. She is slender with a fair complexion and auburn hair gently curling to her shoulders. She must feel his eyes on her, and she looks directly at Will. Her hazel eyes are surrounded by thick lashes and hold him captive. His heart forgets to move for a moment, he releases the paper to the counter, and turns on his stool to face her straight on. He sees a bruise on her forehead, and his brow furrows wondering what happened.

 She offers him a quick smile before walking with Azure to the back dining area, and it feels as though the room has inhaled stealing Will's breath while poking his pulse into over-drive, and he suddenly realizes where the pressed penny came from. Sally sets his breakfast of eggs, bacon, grits and biscuits on the counter startling him from his reverie.

"You okay sugar?"

"Oh, yes ma'am thank you." He tries to force his focus on his breakfast, but flashes of the girl are bombarding him. He knows who she is, her name, and where she is from. The HSO on the pressed penny is her, and she was with him in Fayerdale after traveling from the year 2018. She was supposed to go back. What could have gone wrong? He runs his fingers through his hair. She obviously traveled forward…just not far enough…another flash of memory, but the image is blurred. He knows that it is from the underworld though. How could that be? She was living and human, yet not a part of the Circle of Souls. He knows now that she is the reason he defied the Demon King and returned to Earth.

"Will, honey, you sure you're alright? You haven't touched your breakfast."

Will blinks and pulls Sally into focus. "Oh, yes ma'am just a little distracted this morning is all." He takes a bite of his eggs, gives her a smile, and nods showing her he likes them. He works on the rest of the food on his plate and drinks the milk. Sally seems satisfied and goes off to check on other customers. He finishes up and sits for a moment studying the empty plate and a small crack that runs along its edge. Will looks at the clock on the wall. *Still a bit more time before I need to meet Mister and Missus Adkins. Let's see what can be discovered.* He walks to the back dining area.

Azure and Hallie are sitting at a table near the far corner of the room. Both look up as Will approaches. Again, his heart revs up and his leg muscles falter with weakness. He commands well-practiced control, and it barely shows. He hopes.

"Will, good morning," Azure says.

For some reason, Will always thinks of Abraham Lincoln when he looks at Azure. Although Azure's features have a Gypsy influence not found in the president's, the resemblance remains.

Will puts out his hand, and Azure grasps it to give him a friendly shake.

"Good morning Mister Ridge. I am sorry to interrupt." He glances over at Hallie.

"Oh no, no problem young man. Will this here is Hallie. Hallie this is Will." He gestures a hand towards each as he speaks their names, and then reaches for his mug of coffee.

Will extends his hand to Hallie surveying her face for any sign of recognition. She takes his hand pausing for a moment looking at their joined hands and then up to his face. He waits. Nothing.

"It's nice to meet you, Will." That mesmerizing smile flashes again.

"As it is you, Hallie." Their hands reluctantly let go. A spark of warmth moves from his palm up his arm through his scar. He flexes his fingers and straightens them as if the gesture will allow him to grasp a bit more of the splendid feeling.

He reluctantly looks back to Azure. "Mister Ridge I heard over at the garage that you have been having trouble with that John Deer tractor you have, and I was wondering if you could use some help with it." Will had been planning a trip to the Ridge's place for this purpose, but now it will give him a chance to find out more about Hallie's situation. He glances over at her again, but she is focused on her oatmeal.

"Well, yes Will that would be mighty helpful."

"Good," Will reigns in what sounds to him like over-enthusiasm by clearing his throat. "Uh, fine." He shifts his weight pulling himself together yet again.

"How about you come by Saturday morning, and we will take a look at 'er. I'm sure Odina will make you some breakfast. I'm going to be picking up a dozen eggs from Abram Mayhew after we're done here."

Will glances down at his feet to hide the flash of a smile. "Yes sir, I will be there." He turns to Hallie. "It was nice to meet you, Hallie."

The sunlight catches the green flecks in her eyes giving them a sparkle. "It was nice meeting you too, Will."

ABOUT THE AUTHOR

Suzanne Barron lives in the foot hills of the Blue Ridge Mountains in Virginia with her family, including a feisty dog, grumpy cat, and two geriatric horses. Creative endeavors energize her, and Wings of Time was set to paper (or computer screen as it was) during a challenging time. The character conversations that helped develop the story were and continue to create a wonderful commotion in her life. She is awed by the beauty and raw splendor of nature, and spends as much time in its midst as possible. She deeply appreciates a good story that consumes her waking moments, and hopes to give a similar experience to her readers.

Made in the USA
Columbia, SC
14 October 2018